THE ICE

Published By Eric Gaeta

Formatting & Cover Design : Mayhem Cover Creations

ISBN: 978-0-692-23633-8

DEDICATION

For EJ,

May your dreams be as big as your smile. May your dreams be as grand as your laughter. May your dreams be as close to you as your heart. Keep reaching for and grabbing those stars. To you, my wonderful and precious gift, I dedicate one of my dreams to you.

TABLE OF CONTENTS

ACKNOWLEDGMENTS

To my beautiful wife Cynthia,
Thank you for always believing in me and your never ending support. This has been a long journey, but definitely not the end of the adventure. I love you very much!

CHAPTER ONE

GULFSIDE CITY (2017)

The City. She holds the lives of everyone within her. She watches over her people as they are born. She says goodbye when they pass away. She welcomes strangers who are looking for a place of comfort and someone to nurture them. She bids a kind farewell to those seeking answers elsewhere. She smiles proudly when her symbionts achieve great accomplishments. She weeps when they misbehave. The citizens of the City are connected by the tender bond formed by their energetic host. They live their lives and dreams with her looking on with watchful eyes. The spirit of the City lives as the people live, all growing, hoping, and praying for a better tomorrow. As the City grows and becomes congested, crammed, and crowded more are drawn to her. Why is that? Is it for the desire to belong to a community or the fear of being alone? Or is it to subtly seek solitude among the blanket of the many? For whatever the reason, The City is here...waiting!

Gulfside City was voted as "The Place to Live" by several social organizations. "Gulfside City has something for everyone," stated one magazine. "Gulfside City is love at first sight," stated another. Warm and sunny climate, proximity to the water, and extremely low violent crime rates make this locale an attractive choice for families wanting to relocate or citizens to stay for a lifetime. Access to a local seaport, an airport, and the recent addition of a train depot connected to the new multi-state high-speed rail system provides bountiful business opportunities. Sure Gulfside City has its issues and flaws; property crime rates that are slightly higher than the national average, overcrowding, and traffic congestion. However, longtime residents agree this is a small price to pay for paradise. They view this as a sign of the times and are confident these challenges will eventually be overcome. Many community associations have formed to graciously assist with these and other concerns, and to promote camaraderie throughout the city. Cooperation and understanding has been essential to Gulfside City's success. These groups are broken down into several generic and specific classifications to provide assistance, such as counseling, career training, mitigation of disputes out of court, and community events and entertainment. The associations hold regular meetings with citizens, not only as a way for everyone to get to know one another, but for everyone to trade ideas and build trust.

For more than a week, Gulfside City had an unusual abundance of rain. Most organized and planned outdoor activities were either cancelled or postponed, including the start of the annual Founder's Festival. This event was always a huge deal for the citizens. Set at the city's fairgrounds located on the outskirts of town and styled similar to a carnival, the festival was very good business for the local restaurants and merchants who participate. It was a great venue for local clubs to showcase their groups' talents and it was excellent for families looking for a relatively inexpensive and safe outing. The festival's core entertainment, rides and games, were provided free of charge to all attendees thanks to the community groups' fundraising strength and plethora of volunteers. This was one of the many perks enjoyed in Gulfside City. This event usually drew scores of crowds from nearby towns and states. The Founder's Festival always started with the mayor addressing the people with a state-of-the-city speech. This year, it was expected the mayor would be giving another glowing review of Gulfside City.

The start of the festival was re-scheduled for today and so far so good. Sunshine. Blue skies. Chirping birds. *What a beautiful day,* thought Jonathon, as he motored to work. *Still trees and calm waters, this would be a day to enjoy.* Jonathon was not much for spontaneity, but the perfect weather was very tempting. Even though he would enjoy himself, he would undoubtedly feel guilty for shifting the burden of his job to someone else just for his own wanton pleasure. While he contemplated his dilemma, he heard over his radio that a car was stalled in the middle of traffic.

"Vehicle is a white, small, 2012 sedan with a single driver, female, stopped on north bound Washington at 3rd."

Washington and 3rd was about a quarter of a mile from him.

Well I guess that takes care of that, he thought.

With his right hand reaching to the left side of his body just around his shoulder, he pushed the button on his CB receiver.

"Dispatch this is Lieutenant Scott, I will be responding to the stranded motorist on Washington."

"10-4 lieutenant."

He knew this was for the best and the reward for helping someone else was far greater. Reaching down to his car's console, he activated his siren and emergency lights.

CHAPTER TWO

TROUBLE?

After helping the distressed elderly woman around the corner and off the road, traffic returned to a steady flow.

"Thank you so much," said the woman, facing Jonathon. "I don't know what I would have done without your help."

"No problem, Mrs. Whitmore. I was in the area."

"I hope I can get this car resolved before the opening of the festival tonight. Are you attending?"

"Absolutely! I'm going with my family. My daughter and son have been talking about it non-stop. It's all I've heard out of them."

"Oh, that's wonderful. My granddaughter has been the same way. It's nice to see children still get excited about such things."

Sliding her hand into her over-the-shoulder red purse, she retrieved a black cellular telephone. Frantically, she started to scroll through a menu, "Oh where's that number. I know it's...ah here it is." Pushing the call button to dial the number, she set the phone up to her ear. Every now and then she would take the phone away from her ear to see the keypad and she would select certain numbers.

He surmised she was calling a tow service.

She shook her head. "Oh great, I'm on hold again."

"Again?" he uttered.

"Alas, I have been through this before."

As long as there were no pressing calls, Jonathon decided to wait with her until the wrecker arrived. "I'm going stay with you for as long as I can. Hopefully, they won't be too long."

"Thank you so much officer, I greatly appreciate it."

Strolling back to his cruiser, Jonathon paused for a moment to bask in the generous warm sunshine. It had been dark and gloomy all this week up to today. The sun's rays surrounded him like a cozy blanket, and he hoped the weather would stay like this. He thought of the festival and the nice outdoor evening he would have with his wife and kids.

Reminiscing when he was a junior in high school, at that year's festival he met an outrageous girl who was also a junior, but from a rival school across town. They were waiting in line for one of the events and started talking, eventually trading insults back and forth about each other's schools. At times the discussions got heated. At one point, Jonathon simply thought the girl was just plain crazy.

After entering the forum to be seated, Jonathon made every attempt to sit away from her.

"Oh no you don't ram boy, you're not getting away that easy," she said to him.

His school mascot was a ram. After sitting down, she obstinately claimed the seat next to him. Trying to pay attention to anything else, he simply could not ignore her…she was just staring at him with those grayish/blue eyes of hers. Jonathon looked her over and became more concerned, as she was now grinning at him.

She initiated another round of banter. "Okay, I know I bruised your ego a little bit there ram boy, but I can see you're not as rowdy like the rest of your school folk. I'm sorry."

"Don't worry about it," he said.

"I'm Dana, by the way," she said, holding her hand out and waiting for Jonathon to reciprocate. Jonathon stalled, hoping she would just go away.

After a few moments, with no such luck, he said "I'm Jonathon."

Reluctantly reaching over, he shook her hand. Quickly retracting his hand, he placed it on his lap away from her.

"See. I don't bite," she replied. "So, Jonny, how long have you lived here?"

"Uh, it's Jonathon."

"I like Jonny."

Rolling his eyes, Jonathon shook his head with disgust. He decided to answer her previous query with the aim of quelling the encounter. "Well, I have lived here all my life."

"Just so you know…my parents moved here when I was one, so that's kind of like my whole life," said Dana, obviously wanting to keep the conversation rolling.

"Yeah, that's the same I guess," Jonathon said, with clear sarcasm.

"Do you have any brothers or sisters?" she asked.

Jonathon thought, *What is this, twenty questions?*

"No, I'm an only child," he replied.

"Oh, no way, me too. I always wanted to have a sister, but I guess it's cool being by myself. I have friends with sisters and brothers and they're always at each other's throats."

"Yeah, one of my friends has a younger brother who plays that annoying copy game. You know the one where they say and do everything you do."

Dana nodded.

"I don't know though, even though his little brother gets on my friend's nerves a lot, he idolizes his older brother," Jonathon said.

"Yeah, I can see where that would be neat." Dana changed the subject. "So Jonny, you just came here all by yourself. That's pretty sad."

"Well if you must know, I was meeting someone here. But, I guess she changed her mind."

"She? Wow, that is pathetic," she said, with sarcasm.

"Whatever Dana. Wait a minute, aren't you here by yourself?"

"Well, no. Not really. I'm here with you."

"What?" Jonathon replied with a puzzled expression. Realizing she answered his question literally, he rephrased his question. "Did you come here by yourself?"

"Yeah. I just needed to get out of the house for a while and none of my friends were available. So, I hopped in the car to go for a drive and I happened to go by the festival here."

Jonathon decided to tease her and return the joshing. "Wait a second, you have friends?"

Dana stuck her tongue out at him and then smiled.

Still trying to figure her out, he nervously smiled back. Shaking his head, he thought, *What is her deal? She seems to be a nice person. Quirky, yet nice. But I have been fooled before. Yet, though, something appears to be bothering her. I'm going to regret this.*

"I don't know if it's okay to ask, but why did you need to get out of the house?" Jonathon asked with a sympathetic tone.

"Oh it's okay to ask. I don't mind. It's no big deal I guess. Just one of those things I'm going to have to face sooner or later. I had a fight with my parents about my future and how I need to get serious about it. They keep telling me to pick a direction in school and in life, but I just don't know what interests me. Of course, I do like talking."

Really? he thought.

Dana continued. "I guess they feel I have squandered my freshman and sophomore years, and I'm now wasting my junior year.

I just didn't like what I heard, I guess. I don't know. How about you ram boy, what do you want to be when you grow up?"

Jonathon respected the fact she just opened up to a complete stranger, but was not going to tell her he would probably agree with her parents, while also understanding everyone has their own pace and way of handling life. His own family was a good example.

"Well, my grandfather was a police officer here in Gulfside City," he said.

"Was? I'm so sorry."

"Oh no. He's still alive, just retired."

"Oh, cool."

"He's probably the most remarkable guy I know. I look up to him a lot."

"What about your father?"

"He's never around. He is like a big kid who never really grew up. So, with that said, my parents are divorced."

"Oh that sucks."

"When I was younger, I thought it sucked too. But, I don't think I would have gotten to know my grandfather as well as I have. You see, my mother works a lot, so he basically raised me. He always makes time for me and has always been there. He was a shift supervisor for the patrol division for many years. When I got older, he turned in his badge and took a civilian desk job so he could spend more time with me. He loved being out on the road, but chose me instead. Swimming, baseball, guitar, and, of course, poker are some of the things he taught me."

Jonathon shook his head. "My mother really isn't thrilled about the poker."

She chuckled.

"For me he has been a magician, clown, mime, Santa Claus, and once the Easter Bunny," Jonathon continued.

Dana giggled some more. "He sounds like a funny guy."

"He is always full of laughs. He has also been my mentor and most important, a father. So after high school, I'm enrolling into the academy to follow in his footsteps. Plus, I want to make some sort of difference in the world. While, I'm at the department, I'm also planning to go to college as well."

"Wow, that sounds like a nice…well thought out and busy plan."

I cannot believe I just told her all of this…this girl I just met and did not like a few minutes ago, he thought. Studying her facial expressions, he could see, she was gracious to him for sharing with her.

He continued. "Yeah, it's probably a bit busy and somewhat

lofty, but that's just me. My grandfather is like that, too. My father, I think, couldn't cope with being an adult. My mother, from what my grandfather has told me, was immature like my father. When she had me, she changed her viewpoints about life. She knew she had to grow up for her new baby, but got wrapped up in her career…I'm sorry this is so heavy."

Jonathon leaned back in his seat and pressed his hands into the top of his legs.

Dana briefly grazed one of his hands with hers. "No, please go on. This is good stuff."

"I guess what I'm trying to say, Dana, is that everyone finds themselves eventually. My father is a bad example, but I hope you know where I'm going with this."

"I do and you know what, I feel a lot better. I will try harder. Jonny, I know this is going to sound corny, but I am having a great time with you."

"Yeah, I guess you're not so bad yourself," he said with a grin.

She playfully slapped Jonathon's hand. "You guess, huh? I'm fun to be with. Oh, I think the show is about to begin."

"I hear this comedian is supposed to be really good," Jonathon said.

The surrounding lights dimmed.

The performance let out and both Dana and Jonathon walked out laughing.

"You were right, he was good," She said.

Walking over to the staggered midway, they perused at all of the games and rides, choosing what they were going to do next. They rode the bumper cars and bumper boats. Dana took every chance she got to ram her car into his. On the bumper boats, she managed to splash him a little bit. They went into the hall of mirrors and haunted house. She took every opportunity to scare him.

"Dana…you were the scariest thing in there."

"Jonny!" She playfully smacked Jonathon's arm.

Then, there was the water balloon toss game. She "accidentally" lost control of one. It hit and burst on Jonathon.

"Oops, I didn't mean it," she said, smiling.

"No…that was no oops. You did that on purpose." He smiled. "Oh boy, I can tell…you're going to be trouble aren't you?"

She batted her eyes innocently at him. "Who me?"

Jonathon picked up Dana's last balloon and dropped it on her head. It broke, drenching her in water.

"Oops," he said as they both laughed.

They played more games. He won her a stuffed animal and they got powdered sugar all over themselves after sharing an elephant ear. It was now getting late and the festival was starting to close down for the night. They made their way over to the exit. It was an elaborate white-painted wood structure with a decorative arched trellis on top and a small enclosed ticket cubicle in the middle of the concrete access walkways. A white lattice-like fence extended out from the outer sides of the admission vestibule, surrounding the property of the fairgrounds.

"Well, I guess tonight has to end," Dana said with a big grin. "It started out on the wrong foot, but it turned out to be so cool. I'm so glad I stopped here. It has been a long time since I've laughed as hard as we did and had this much fun."

"Me too," he said.

Dana reached inside her purse and fumbled around, obviously and frantically trying to find something. Pulling out a small piece of paper she said, "Do you have a pen Jonny? Oh, wait." Reaching in again, she fumbled around some more. Pulling out a lipstick, she ran over to a nearby table, uncapped it, and used it to write something on the paper. When she was done, she recapped the lipstick and tossed it back in her purse.

Dana sashayed back to Jonathon. "Here's my number ram boy. Don't lose it or you will be sorry."

"Sorry?"

"Yeah, if you don't call me, I will have to come to your school and do something embarrassing. Probably going to be awkward for the both us. That's a promise. So just call."

Folding the piece of paper carefully, he removed his wallet from his pocket and placed her phone number in a very safe spot. He did not want her to follow through with her promise. He returned the wallet to his pocket.

"Uh, okay. I will call. I have a feeling you're going to be trouble," he said.

"Yeah, but it will be fun. See you later Jonny."

Throwing her arms around him, she gave him a quick hug. Releasing him, she turned and walked toward, then through, the exit gate.

Jonathon, feeling chivalrous, thought maybe he should escort her out to her car. Second guessing himself, he thought, *She may think it is too forward.* He threw caution to the wind and called out to her. "Dana, do you want me to walk you to your car?"

She paused and turned slightly toward Jonathon. With the palm of her hand, she quickly pressed it on her lips, then blew Jonathon a kiss. He caught it, of course. She smiled at him and waved. He waved back. She turned and resumed going out to the lot. Watching her for as long as he could, she eventually slipped out of sight.

What happened? he wondered, standing there completely dumbfounded about what transpired this entire evening.

One of the best nights of my life. Jonathon's mind back on the present, noticed the tow service had arrived. Mrs. Whitmore gave her keys to the tow driver and the man got right to work prepping the car to be hauled.

Mrs. Whitmore walked over to Jonathon. "Thank you so much for waiting with me."

"No problem, Mrs. Whitmore. It was my pleasure."

"I hope you have a great time tonight."

"I know I will. I hope you'll be able to attend."

"Yes, me too. Good day, officer."

"Good day, Mrs. Whitmore."

She turned away, slowly marching over to the front of the tow truck to wait for the driver to finish putting her car on the flatbed. Jonathon opened the driver's door to his cruiser, and observed a large van moving at a high rate of speed across the street. He caught a glimpse of the colorful logo on its side: "Prompt Plumbing."

"Yeah, that is prompt service," he sarcastically mumbled to himself. He settled into his car and was about to pursue when he observed the van pull into a parking lot directly ahead for the new Washington Boulevard Art and History Museum. He closed his door, carefully entered the roadway, and maneuvered to the other side. Fortunately there was no cross traffic at the moment, so he kept his speed low. Driving up to the entrance of the museum driveway, he pulled in, navigating to where the van was parked. Two men were removing equipment from the rear of the van, and were completely unaware of Jonathon.

Jonathon radioed in. "Dispatch, this is Lieutenant Scott…I'm at the museum on Washington and 3rd, checking out a vehicle…I will advise if I have any info."

He opened his door and exited his vehicle, approaching the men and identifying himself. He examined the men. The one closest to him was about his height with a medium build. The second was about a half foot taller with a very muscular build. Both were wearing "Prompt Plumbing" overalls with names stitched on the front. "Max" who was the closer of the two, stood and turned to him while

"Frankie" continued to move about.

"What seems to be the emergency here?" Jonathon queried.

"The toilets in the museum backed up and we are here to fix them," Max replied. At this point, Frankie finished unloading the van and closed the rear doors. Jonathon quickly focused his attention to the equipment, which was all in what appeared to be closed duffel bags and there were a lot of them. Jonathon did not know much about plumbing, but felt it was odd that all of this was necessary to fix some toilets. Plus, what added to the mystery was the fact that all of the equipment needed was small enough to be concealed in bags.

"Why so many bags?" Jonathon asked.

"We just find it easier to take everything with us. This way we don't have to keep running back to the van," replied Max.

Jonathon had no right to search them and the plumbers were not acting suspicious otherwise. Jonathon figured he could not draw any conclusions based on the lack of knowledge he had about their profession.

"All right, but next time slow it down a bit," Jonathon said. "I watched you fly down the road here. There is no need to endanger everyone on the street. Right?"

Frankie glared at Max.

"We are sorry officer, we will pay better attention next time," Max replied.

"Thank you. You men have a good day!"

Jonathon turned away and began to walk back to his car, constantly taking brief glances at the two. Max and Frankie picked up their eight duffel bags and hiked towards the entrance. Jonathon shook his head and sat back into his car. Feeling uneasy, it crossed his mind to wait a few minutes and then go into to the museum to check on them.

"Attention, all downtown units. Be advised of a flight pursuit in progress on 3rd street. Any available units in the downtown area are directed to assist. Vehicle is a tan, late model coupe heading east."

"I guess that takes care of that," Jonathon said to himself.

Closing the door, he proceeded to drive out of the lot. "Dispatch this is Lieutenant Scott. I'm in route."

CHAPTER THREE

THE MUSEUM

As Jonathon drove, he could not shake off the museum. *Something is not right. I can't put my finger on it,* he thought. Jonathon took his nine year old daughter to the museum's opening last month and it had only one public restroom. *Does the job necessitate that many bags?* he wondered. *Is it because all the equipment was in bags? Maybe they are just neat and organized. Maybe the bags are used to keep the equipment from getting dirty. Of course they won't keep them from getting wet. The bags were some sort of cloth. However, the bags could have been lined. But then, they are working with water.* His thoughts did not sit well with him, but he had nothing else to go on. He kept going round and round in his mind.

"All downtown units, be advised, suspect is in custody. Resume normal activities if not in the engagement area."

"I guess that is that," Jonathon said to himself.

Nearing a stopped intersection, he pulled up behind a car that appeared to have an expired tag. Both vehicles stopped at the red signaled light and Jonathon started to type the tag number into his computer.

"Yes!" he said. "The museum is funded mostly by the city and is maintained by the city. The city has its own maintenance staff, including plumbers."

The traffic indicator turned green, and he readied to maneuver himself to turn around.

Arriving back at the museum, the Prompt Plumbing van was still there. He drove up behind it, wanting to get a closer view of the license tag. He typed the digits into his computer and the result came back: "Registered to the Prompt Plumbing and Pipe Company." He scrolled through the information on his screen. *Hmm…there are no issues or problems,* he thought. *Nonetheless, I want to check this out a little further.*

He radioed in. "Dispatch…Scott…I'm at the Washington museum again, following up on a suspicious vehicle."

"10-4 lieutenant."

Jonathon exited his cruiser and approached the van, which had no rear windows whatsoever. Strolling to the closed driver side window, he peeked in. Nothing worth noting was in the front, so he angled himself to look in the back. There was just enough light to see numerous plumbing tools scattered about. Scanning around the exterior of the van, he checked the tires, the roof, the undercarriage… nothing. Back to its rear, he stood, staring. His focus shifted back to the license plate. *This tag is from Desoto County,* he thought. *Desoto is about an hour away. If the museum had hired outside help, wouldn't they have found someone a little closer? Granted cost may have been a factor, but an hour away?* He then proceeded to the entrance.

The entrance was on a slight angle from the rest of the museum. Once inside, he flowed to the left, entering the main foyer. Glancing about, he did not see the plumbers. This was a local museum, which had only three large main wings all accessible from the main lobby. Other than an elementary school field trip, there were not many people present. The field trip group, led by a guide, was entering into a wing.

Jonathon slowly inched inward. *I may as well go to the restroom,* he thought. Located directly across from the main entrance, the men and women's restrooms were side by side. From the entrance, the men's room was on the left. Stepping up to the men's room door, pushing it inward. The door swiveled open and he entered. Once in, he was standing by the sinks. Proceeding further in, he walked past the open partition with the standing urinals, and crossed into the stall area. At first glance, Jonathon could not see any signs of a plumbing problem or any signs that there ever was one. The floors were very dry and clean. The stalls appeared to be spotless, as did the urinals when he passed. *No sign of the men,* he thought. *I need another pair of eyes.*

Touching his CB receiver Jonathon said, "Dispatch, this is Lieutenant Scott. Send another officer to the Washington museum. Something is a little odd here."

"10-4 lieutenant."

Exiting the restroom, he pivoted to the ladies' restroom door. He knocked on it. There was no response.

Pushing the door open, Jonathon poked his head in. “Hello!”

Silence. It had the same basic setup as the men’s, minus the urinals of course, but angled opposite. He walked in, passing the sink area to the stall area. Snooping around, he opened some stall doors and looked under others. Everything was clean, dry, and tidy. Reversing his course, he stomped out of the restroom.

He emerged back into the lobby, scanning around to see if he could find an attendant. Nobody was at the nearby front office. He remembered there was a docent station just inside the wing nearest him. Walking with a fast pace, he entered the annex and located the desk. It was vacant. *That’s right, she is probably with the field trip group.* Probing further in, he spotted a young couple gazing at some of Gulfside City’s early artifacts.

“Excuse me,” he said, marching up to them. “Sorry to interrupt you. Have either of you seen anyone who works here?”

“Yes officer,” the female answered. “I’ve only seen one person and I think she is showing some school children around.”

“Thank You.” Jonathon turned around and made his way out of the wing. As he went back out into the main foyer, he noticed someone who looked like an employee entering the men’s restroom. Jonathon quickly moved, following him in.

“May I help you officer?” asked the startled man, composing himself.

“Are you an employee here?”

“Yes sir. My name Christopher. Is something wrong?”

“I just wanted to know if you had any plumbing problems today?”

“No. Not to my knowledge.”

“Have you seen anybody who looks like plumbers anywhere inside the museum?”

“Well I did see…”

All of a sudden, the two of them heard multiple screams emanating from outside the restroom.

Lowering the volume on his radio Jonathon said, “Chris, stay put and be quiet.” The man nodded. Jonathon lightly made his way to the restroom door and cracked it open just enough to see what was going on without someone outside being able to see him. The men’s room was on an angle to where he could see the main entrance and two of the wings.

“What the…” Jonathon muttered.

Both Max and Frankie were rounding everyone up and corralling them in the main foyer in a corner between the two visible wings. The two were now wearing very bulky clothing and what seemed to be protective helmets. Jonathon closed the door.

"Officer, what's going on?" Chris asked.

"The museum is being held up, please be quiet."

Jonathon faintly heard, "Shit! Bailey! The cops are here!

Damn it. They must have seen me, Jonathon thought.

Jonathon whispered to Christopher. "Go to one of the back stalls and close the door."

Christopher complied and moved into the last stall. Jonathon drew his sidearm and pointed it at the restroom door.

"Only one guy is going to come in giving the other time to shoot hostages before I can get out there," Jonathon mumbled to himself.

He waited for someone to storm in, but nothing happened. Lowering his weapon, he upped the volume on his radio to a level low enough that he could hear it, but not carry outside.

"...at the Washington Street Museum, repeating there is a hostage state in progress at the Washington Street Museum. All north end units are to respond and converge at the location. Lieutenant Scott is already on scene inside the location, but his status is unknown."

Jonathon realized he was not the focus of their attention.

"It must have been my earlier call for help," he quietly said to himself. "They probably don't know I'm in here." Moving to the back where Christopher was, he clasped his radio receiver, softly speaking into it. "This is Lieutenant Scott. I am inside the restroom. We have about forty hostages, most of whom are children. They are being moved to the rear of the main foyer opposite and away from the line of sight of the main entrance."

"Lieutenant, Officer Wellman was the first to arrive after your previous transmission."

"10-4."

Jonathon turned his radio down, scurried back to the door, and cracked it open again. This time he witnessed all the hostages in the foyer sitting on the ground. Max was standing by the main entrance yelling at the officers who had arrived.

"Don't enter or we will be forced to punish our victims!" he said. Frankie carried one of the duffel bags and unloaded what appeared to be detonation equipment.

"They're not going to let anyone go," Jonathon quietly grumbled to himself. Gently closing the door, he dashed back towards Christopher, raising the volume up on his radio.

"Dispatch, perpetrators are unloading a vast amount of explosives. In my judgment, we don't have much time. Have Officer Wellman keep the one at the door distracted. I am about to go after the one he can't see. I will go in two minutes. After that, have

Wellman and anyone else here move in. Do you copy?"

"10-4."

Lowering the volume back down, Jonathon gently knocked on the stall door next to him. Christopher opened it.

"Officer what is happening?" he asked.

"Chris, whatever happens, keep very still and very quiet. Stay in here. You should be safe." *Hopefully,* Jonathon thought.

Christopher nodded and shut the door. Jonathon, while waiting for his mark, briefly imagined himself with his family tonight at the festival. Shaking his head, he refocused back on the crisis, inching up to the restroom entrance. Checking his wristwatch, he waited, playing out possible scenarios in his head. In some he was successful and some, not so much. His heart pounded in his chest and sweat started to run down his face. Twelve years with the department and he had never fired his gun while on duty. Today was going to be the first day. This was why he trained constantly. It was about time to go. With his gun still in hand, he slightly opened the door to further assess the situation. Max was still at the door and Frankie was nowhere in sight.

"Shit!" he whispered.

All of sudden he heard. "I told you assholes to get back!"

"We want to talk…let's work this out." Shouted someone from outside.

"We will talk when we are damn well ready, not when your…"

Jonathon rushed out of the bathroom and heard multiple gunshots ring into the lobby. Fortunately, where the hostages were sitting, they were not in the line of fire. Out of the corner of his eye, he could see Max taking on gunfire, but he was not going down. However, Jonathon's main concern was finding Frankie and protecting the hostages.

Facing the frightened individuals Jonathon yelled, "Lie flat on the ground now!" Jonathon ran toward the captives, remembering there was the wing behind him. Jonathon turned around and spotted Frankie running up behind him holding a handgun. Frankie stopped, raised the gun, and pointed it in the direction of the children.

Jonathon bolted in front of the children and Frankie discharged his weapon. Jonathon blocked them in time, and the round hit him in his chest. The impact forced Jonathon to the floor. Losing grip, his gun slid away from him across the floor. The other officers, finally making it past Max, advanced on Frankie. However, they were reluctant to fire their guns with the hostages now in direct sight. Three officers rushed Frankie. Frankie turned to them and began to fire on the approaching officers, immediately striking one in the chest. Another one was hit, twice in the right leg. The third officer was shot in the left arm. All three of the courageous officers fell to the ground.

As this was going on, the detainees began to get up and scatter seeking shelter in the nearby wings. Jonathon woke from his daze and realized he was not dead. His trusty bulletproof vest saved his life. Coming to his senses, he caught a glimpse of the third officer going down. Reaching for his back-up revolver just above his right ankle, he pulled it from the holster, quickly aiming and firing before Frankie could react. The round hit Frankie in his right arm just below his shoulder. Unfortunately, the shot did very little damage. The bulky clothing was apparently some sort of fabricated body armor. Frankie turned to face Jonathon to shoot at him again, and Jonathon fired a second shot, this time striking Frankie's right hand thrusting the gun from his hold. Scampering to get up, Jonathon lunged at Frankie, tackling him in a vain attempt to subdue him. Jonathon was only able to bring him down, only part way. At the moment, Jonathon thought this was a good idea, but because of Frankie's size, this action proved to be ineffective. Frankie forced Jonathon off, stood up and kicked him several times while he was on the ground. Finally, Jonathon was able to get a kick off, pushing Frankie back. While laying here, he realized there was a small opening right under Frankie's helmet, exposing a portion of his bare neck. Still holding his pistol, Jonathon lifted it, quickly aimed and fired. The round flew into Frankie's neck, and he fell face down on the floor. Jonathon stood up, incredibly sure the shot killed Frankie.

Hobbling over to his fellow officers, he could see all three were still very much alive. Officer Wellman, the one shot in the chest, was also wearing a vest. The other two, also, did not have life-threatening wounds. Other officers rushed in with the scene now clear and motioned for medical services to enter. The trauma personnel entered to tend the injured officers as other officers raced into the exhibit wings to search for the former hostages. Jonathon fell to his knees in exhaustion and placed his hands on the ground to level himself. One of the late-arriving officers ran up to Jonathon,

"Lieutenant, are you all right?" the officer asked.

"Yes… were there any casualties with the hostages?"

"We're not sure sir."

"I think there might be some patrons hiding in the wings."

"We're taking care of it sir."

Jonathon nodded. "Okay." He glanced around and noticed the scared and frightened people being escorted out of the wings toward the exit. "Thank goodness," he sighed. Then he collapsed.

Chapter Four

Homeward Bound

"Jonny have I ever thanked you?"

"Thanked me? For what, Dana?"

"For believing in me and keeping me on track this year. Last year before I met you, I wasn't sure if I was going to graduate this year."

Dana and Jonny were waiting in line for an event, as they did at last year's festival.

"I know it has been hard for you, but you are going to do exactly that...graduate," Jonathon said.

"Yeah, it's so cool," Dana said with a big smile. "I still don't know what I'm going to do after graduation..."

"That's okay. Worry about graduation now. Once we get past that, then you can sit down and fully listen to yourself. Only you can figure your future out. Whatever you decide, make sure you feel happy with your choice. You are the one who has to live with your decision or decisions for the rest of your life. I of course, will stand by you every step of the way."

Dana wrapped her arms around Jonathon and rested her head on his chest.

"I know you will."

"...and the future could be yours with ChronoSleep. Do you want to see your grand or even great grandchildren all grown up? Do you want to invest money in the market and have it grow without having to watch the ups and downs? Or do you simply want to wake up and go for a drive over the countryside? ChronoSleep: the next best thing to time travel!"

"What is going on?" Jonathon asked, sitting up in a panic. Scanning around, he realized he was in a hospital room. He had a wire, connected to a monitor, affixed to his left hand and a bandage on his right arm where it seemed as if someone had drawn some blood. Glancing up, he spotted a television set harnessed to the wall behind it. The dancing glow from the set provided the primary lighting for the room. The volume was low enough to not be a nuisance, but high enough for him to hear. Wrestling to get out of bed, a female nurse entered the room.

"Sir, you need to take it easy," she said as she neared him to assist.

"Where am I?" he asked, still struggling and with a raspy voice.

"You are at Gulfside City Memorial Hospital. Please be careful. Don't over exert yourself."

Jonathon carefully sat up and swung his legs over the side of his bed, readjusting his white hospital gown. "How long have I been here?"

The nurse positioned herself in front of him. "For several hours. You were brought here simply for observation."

"Observation? Why?"

"You were among the group who was brought in from the museum shootings."

"The museum? That's right. Am I okay?"

"Like I said, you were brought here for observation." Striding to the TV, she turned it off. "I will let the doctor know you are awake. Is there anything you need?"

He anxiously looked around. "No… no thank you."

"I'll check back with you in a little bit, meanwhile I believe there are visitors here for you." The nurse walked back to the front of the room. "Would you like more light in here?"

"Yes. Please."

She flipped a switch near the door. She opened the door and exited.

Still foggy, *Visitors? Who would…* Perking up, his heart started to race as he felt a wave of warmth and happiness. The door opened…

"JONNY!"

Jonathon experienced complete euphoria as she walked in.

"DANA!" he yelled with excitement.

Dana rushed in, ran up to the bed, and embraced her husband with the warmest of hugs. Jonathon's chest was very sore from the bullet impact, but he happily and graciously returned the love.

"Jonny, thank goodness you are okay! I just …"

"I know. I know."

Releasing him from her hold, she stood up, staring into her husband's eyes for a moment. Jonathon could feel nothing else, but the love she felt for him. She was so beautiful with her warm eyes and kind smile.

Playfully smacking his hand she said, "Don't scare me like that again. Okay?"

"But Dana…"

"Don't you BUT me mister…" The door flew open again and his two children rushed through, followed by his best friend Adam Stance in uniform. Adam and Jonathon met at the academy and had been inseparable ever since.

"DADDY, DADDY!" both kids screamed as they ran up, hugging and squeezing on to him.

"I'm okay you guys. How are you doing?"

"We're fine," said rosy-cheeked Kim.

"Daddy are you coming home?" asked seven year old JR. JR was a nickname for Jonathon Russell Jr.

"I believe I am, trooper," Jonathon answered.

Jonathon looked up at Dana. "Am I?"

"I spoke with the physician and she said she was waiting for you to wake up. She wants to have one more quick look at you and then we can go."

"Great!"

"I will go find her and let her know you're ready. I don't know how long it will be though. They seem pretty busy tonight." Dana gently laid both her hands on the children. "Come on, kids. Let's go find daddy's doctor."

Kim and JR freed Jonathon of their grips and slowly left the room with Dana. Kim quickly reentered, smiled, waved, and exited again.

Adam inched closer to Jonathon. "So how are you doing?"

"With the exception of soreness in my chest, I feel fine. Physically, anyway. I still cannot believe what happened. I guess this means administrative leave for me now."

"More than likely, it's department policy. You know that."

"How are the others?"

"Wellman left an hour ago. He asked about you. Murphy will be on crutches for roughly six weeks and Thompson will not be writing any tickets for awhile. It figures, our only left-handed officer was shot in his writing arm."

"Adam, I can't begin to tell you, I mean thank goodness everyone came out of this okay."

"Someone was definitely watching out for you all."

"It goes to show that anything can happen at any moment. Dana, the kids, and I were supposed to be at the festival tonight, but here we are. Again, thank goodness. I might not have been here at all."

"Jonny, we do have a little information on what happened," Adam said, with hesitation. "That is, if you are up to hearing it."

Even though it had only been hours since everything happened, Jonathon knew, at least professionally, he was going to have to hear and deal with this sooner or later.

"Go ahead and tell me, I just want to try and leave the emotional part of this here when I get discharged."

"If you're sure?"

Jonathon nodded. "I'm sure."

"Okay. I spoke with the crew assigned to investigating this mess. They are still sorting out many details. However, they have some information, although not that promising I'm afraid."

"Lay it on me."

"The guys we put down today were heavily into sordid dealings, but this was their first foray into our area. As for a motive or reason… we're still sorting out the details. By the amount and yield of the explosives, there definitely was enough to completely destroy the building. A detailed map, blueprints of the museum, and layout of the block and surrounding buildings were found on one of the men. We did ascertain, before they were going to detonate the charges, they were going to leave from an access tunnel connected under the building."

"Under the building?"

"Yeah. No one at the museum knew the thing was there. These guys were very prepared and were obviously ready for any complications with their plan. The men were going to raze the museum and leave undetected, but with you there they were stopped before anyone could be killed."

"Why didn't they enter through the tunnel and take everyone by surprise that way?"

"A good question, one of the first ones I had. Apparently, the hatch leading into the museum cannot be opened from inside the tunnel, at least not anymore."

Jonathon shook his head. "That doesn't make sense."

"Well going back through the city's records it somewhat does. The tunnel leads to a heavily fortified bunker that was to be used as a bomb shelter for city officials back in the 1950s."

"This was connected to the museum?" Jonathon asked, a little confused. "That does not make much sense either."

"Remember Jonny, back in that time, the museum was city

hall."

Jonathon nodded his head. "That's right. Now, how did our villains plan to get out if the hatch works only one way? I guess there has to be another opening somewhere else?"

"Yes, there is. The bunker itself is a half a mile northwest. This was included on their diagram and was confirmed with the city engineer. A second tunnel heading northward for about another half mile, leads to a door, or doors rather, which open up on the property of the water treatment plant. These are located outside and look like they are part of a very secure maintenance shed. These doors still do work both ways and because that portion of the tunnel inclines up to the surface, the bunker is currently being used by the city as a storage facility for equipment not used on a regular basis. For that reason, this is why the hatch under the museum was sealed from the inside… to prevent a possible security breach."

"Due to what happened today, it appears that was a good idea."

"Yes it would seem. As an interesting note, in the early 1980s, city engineers ascertained the bunker was so poorly designed, no one would have lasted very long if it had been used as intended."

Jonathon shook his head. "Did we get any information from these thugs?"

"The one you shot died immediately and the one blasted at the door died on the way here. From what we are being told, they had been planning this for at least a year. Informants say there is a bigger problem going on here, but they don't know for sure what it is. Apparently, these informants have been telling us tidbits here and there, but we never put the pieces together… at least until today."

Jonathon sighed with relief. "At least, this part of it, the bad guys are dead and the good guys came out relatively unharmed."

Adam stood there with a horrified look, "Not all of the good guys made it."

"Who didn't make it?"

"We did more research on the plumbing company and the van. This then lead Investigations to contact the Sheriff's Office in Desoto County. Prompt Plumbing is a small legitimate company. They killed the two plumbers today in Desoto used their identities."

"This would explain why everything checked out in the computer. Damn monsters," replied Jonathon.

The door swung open and a physician entered, wearing a white lab coat over blue hospital scrubs. "Jonathon, I am Doctor Joanne Wallace."

"Hello doctor."

"Jonathon, I just want to make sure everything is okay before you leave." Scooping up Jonathon's medical chart from a nearby stand, she perused through it while inching toward him. Adam stepped back a few paces to give the doctor more room to examine Jonathon. Paraphrasing from the chart she said, "The blood tests we ran came back fine. Your blood pressure and pulse rate, as shown here on the monitor, are normal. The report says here you were shot in the chest, but you were wearing a vest. Very good. After you came in here, I did perform a physical examination on you and could not detect any areas of concern. Still, I did order an MRI. Let's see…" Flipping up a couple of pages she said, "That report shows no permanent damage. The soreness you are probably feeling in your chest should go away in a few days. You may also experience some discoloring in the skin, but nothing to worry about. Nothing permanent."

Returning the chart to the stand, she then grabbed one of her instruments out of her coat pocket and moved in towards Jonathon. The tool was like a small metallic chrome hammer with a cone shape in the front.

Standing in front of him she said, "Please keep your eyelids open if you can." Shining a light in both of his eyes, she tested his responses. "Good," she said. "Good." Walking over to the wall behind Jonathon, she removed a small black funnel-shaped cone from a sterile dispenser, which housed several like it. She fitted the plastic piece over the front of her instrument and proceeded to check his ear by inserting the front of the cone into it. Looking in through the back of the device, she nodded her head. Circling around him, she repeated the process with his other ear. While still looking in his second ear she asked, "Do you have any ringing in yours ears?"

"Yes, a little bit more than usual."

Removing the tool, she discarded the plastic piece, placing the medical apparatus back in her pocket. "I don't think it's anything permanent. However, when you follow up with your physician and if it has not subsided, please mention it."

"Of course."

"I see no reason to keep you here any longer. Go home and get some rest. I've written a prescription for your pain, if you need it. Your wife, I believe, is obtaining that from our pharmacy here. If there is nothing else, I will leave your discharge papers at the check out station for you to sign before you leave."

"Thank you doctor." Doctor Wallace dashed for the door, proceeding out.

Adam stepped back up to Jonathon's side. "Well, everything sounds good. Oh, Dana brought you some clothes. They're in a bag on the chair over there. I will leave so you can change. I'll find Dana and let her know you are on your way out."

"Thank you," Jonathon said, nodding.

"Sure." Adam strolled out the door.

Jonathon, staring into nothing, reflected on the day's events, trying to grasp what happened. *If I wasn't sitting here, I probably would think this was some bad dream…or maybe this is the dream and I will wake up soon. I guess until then…* Rising to his feet, he carefully stumbled over to the aforementioned chair. Opening the sport bag, he found his change of clothes. Disrobing his gown, he felt the chill of the cold hospital air against his bare body. He began to shiver, but the sensation coursing through his body, was not a result of the cold. *What am I feeling?* he wondered. *Strange. I never felt like this before. What is it…loneliness…emptiness… sadness?* Shaking his head, "Let me get out of here. Let me surround myself with happier things."

Finally dressed, he placed the gown on the bed. Picking his bag up from the chair, he also situated it on the bed. Underneath the bag's former position was his vest and uniform, amongst his other possessions. Lifting up the vest, he spotted the indentation where the bullet had struck.

Teary eyed, he muttered, "What a lifesaver."

Composing himself, he quickly rounded up the rest of his belongings. Slipping the bag onto his shoulder, he carefully marched to the door.

Now in the bustling hallway beyond the quiet of his room, he was out in an area near the nurses' station. Staggering toward a pair of double doors and to what he hoped was the exit out, Dana; Adam; and the kids coincidently emerged through them. Dana, rushing up, threw her arms around his torso.

He returned the embrace. "It's going to be okay, Dana. I am so thankful I'm still here."

"Me to, Jonny."

Dana released her husband, took hold of the bag strap, slid it from his shoulder and placed it over hers.

Adam pointed to the vest. "Let me take that from you.

Jonathon lifted it up and Adam relieved him of it, firmly grasping the damaged article. With his hand free, Jonathon clasped onto Dana's arm.

"Lets go home," he said.

All five of them now facing the doors continued through them, out to the checkout window.

CHAPTER FIVE

HOME AT LAST

Dana guided Jonathon into his reclining chair along the rear wall in the television room just inside of the front door.

"Are you in okay?" she asked.

"I think so."

Adam, who at this point, had both the bag and vest laid them on the floor near the front door. "I'm going to leave now and let you guys get some sleep."

Jonathon somewhat sat up. "Thank you for helping. Dana and I both appreciate it."

Adam moved to Jonathon's chair and Jonathon raised his right hand. Adam leaned in a little with his right hand, and shook Jonathon's. Adam leaned in further and gave him a quick comforting hug. It took Jonathon by surprise, but he knew Adam was just glad to still have his buddy.

Adam stood and walked slowly to the door. "I'll see you soon. Everyone have a good night."

"Good night and thank you so much for your help," Dana replied.

Opening the door, Adam exited into the night, closing the door behind him.

Kim, quick to her feet off the couch, "Daddy, do you want a glass of water?"

"Yes, please sweetie."

Kim rushed toward the kitchen.

"Jonny, do you want to move into the other room?" Dana asked.

"No, I'm okay here."

Dana walked over to the door and locked the deadbolt. Reaching down, she picked up the vest and noticed the indentation. She instantly began tearing up. Turning herself in a way so no one could see her face, she went about picking up the rest of Jonathon's belongings. Jonathon knew what Dana was hiding.

JR, seated on the couch, stood up, ran over to one side of his father and gave him a great big hug. Laying his head on Jonathon's chest, Jonathon was careful not to let on to the fact this was where he was sore. He was so grateful to still be here for his children, he didn't care about the pain. This hug was the best gift of all. He never takes for granted, this affection, especially today.

"I am going to go put these in our bedroom for you," Dana said, composing herself. Freeing a hand she wiped away her tears as she walked away from the front door exiting to and through the dining room.

Kim emerged back into the room with a glass of water.

"Here you go, Daddy," she said.

"Thank you so much, sweetie." Jonathon gripped the glass, gulping a fair amount of the water. As soon as he finished, he set the glass down on the table next to him.

"Do you want anything else, Daddy?" Kim asked.

"No, but thank you for the kind offer. You have been a big help."

Kim inched up to the other side of Jonathon, not occupied by JR, and wrapped herself around her father.

"Ah, that makes the night so much better, you two," said Jonathon.

Both looked up at him and smiled. JR laid his head back on Jonathon's chest as Kim let go of her father.

Standing in front of him she said, "Look what I learned today at school."

Kim was enrolled in an after-school ballet program. She was showing him an abbreviated portion of a new dance routine. She loved to dance so much that she expressed to her parents last month that she wanted to be a ballerina when she grows up. Kim, jumping, twirling, and spinning, finished with a curtsy.

"That was wonderful, sweetie. You are going to be the star of the show next week at your recital."

"Thank you, Daddy. I love you." Kim smiled then darted through the dining room to, what sounded like, her room.

"Were you scared?" asked JR.

Jonathon hoped neither one of his children were going to ask him any questions about today, but understood this was not realistic. Children are naturally very curious, especially his. In addition,

Jonathon was amenable to the fact that children are more aware of what's going on around them then adults give them credit for. This did not make his task any easier though. He had to answer carefully. He did not want JR to be scared of the world, but did not want to him to be naïve, either.

"Well, that is a good question, trooper. I was in a situation, requiring a quick answer. Basically, I did not have time to be scared. I needed to figure out a way to come home safe and allow a lot of other people to go home safe too. I'm sorry if that does not make any sense."

"I don't care, I'm just happy you are here."

"JR it is time to go to bed!" Dana said from across the room.

JR, unfolding his arms from his father, "Okay, Mom." He stood, but paused his departure from the room.

"Do you think I will have to do something like that someday?" he asked Jonathon.

"I do what I do, so you will never have to."

"I love you, Daddy. Goodnight."

"I love you, trooper. Goodnight."

JR resumed his march to bed, leaving through the dining room. Jonathon struggled out of his chair and staggered toward the front door. The soreness in his chest made it difficult for him to move at this point. Upon reaching the entryway, he unlocked the door, then opened it. He wanted to feel the cool night breeze. His neighborhood was across a bay of water on the edge of downtown. Stepping down from his front door threshold, onto the welcome mat, he carefully wobbled onto the concrete walkway, bracing himself with his hand against the lining outer wall of his otherwise opened and covered porch area. The pathway continued to curve to the right to the driveway, but he stopped at the front edge of the porch. Jonathon was content to only go this far. From here, past the open lots across the street, he could watch over most of downtown Gulfside City in the distance.

As he stood there, staring off into nowhere with the cool breeze brushing against his face, he began to think of the violence of today. Not necessarily the specifics surrounding him, but in general. In a nearby downtown neighborhood, a police siren echoed through the air. *What kind of world are my children going to live in?* he wondered. *Will they be safe? Will they live in fear?* He was somewhat comforted with the fact the world has two fewer bad guys to worry about.

"Goodnight Gulfside. Behave yourself. See you in the morning." Having his fill of outside, he wobbled back to the door. Once inside, he relocked the door. He then switched the lights off in the television room. Following the walkway into the dining room, Jonathon carefully navigated forward. The dining room itself was more of a nook rather than a dedicated room, but this was where the family ate dinner. Standing along the far side of the nook, was a tall wood china hutch. It was about a foot taller than Jonathon. This was a piece of furniture given to Dana and Jonathon as a wedding gift by Dana's parents. However, it was more than that, a family heirloom dating back to Dana's great grandmother. Dana kept the family's fine dish and glassware in the hutch, displayed proudly though the glass windows.

Walking up to a light switch panel on the wall to the side of the entryway into the kitchen, he turned the kitchen and dining room lights off. The main living room was just beyond the nook and kitchen. Dana, Jonathon and the kids spent their family time together there, without the distraction of TV. The rear wall consisted of two large-framed windows equidistant from the sides and a double sliding glass door in the middle, which led out to the back yard.

This area was large enough for them to play games, piece puzzles together, or work on school projects. A hefty wooden flat desk faced the dining room which housed the family computer. On the kitchen side of the room was a simple table aligned against the inner intersecting wall connected at the rear. The table's surface was lined with photo frames.

The kids' rooms were accessible on the kitchen side of this room, while the master bedroom's entrance was on the opposite end. Staggering further into the dark main living room, he glanced over toward the children's side, noticing a light still emanating from Kim's bedroom. Walking over to see what was going on, he realized he never said "goodnight" to her. From the living room, facing the kids' side, straight ahead was the guest/kid's bathroom. On the right was Kim's room and on the left was JR's. Veering to the right, he traipsed down the short hallway, up to Kim's open door.

Kim's room was what you would expect from a little girl. Pink, pink, and more pink sparkled with hints of red and white here and there. She had shelves filled with dance trophies, dolls, and pictures of her beloved family.

By this time, Kim had changed into her pink princess pajamas. Jonathon noticed she was just sitting in the middle of her bed. She was facing somewhat near the door, but with her head down and cross-legged.

"Are you okay, sweetie?" Jonathon asked.

Looking up at him, he could see she was upset and was trying to hold back.

"I've never seen Mommy so upset before."

Jonathon thought for a second and speculated that Kim was

probably right. He had no idea how Dana reacted when she got the news. Dana had always been able to keep it together. She, as long as he has known her, always had a relaxed, laid back, outgoing, and positive attitude. If something did bother her, she usually hid it very well. Today probably rattled her. Again, Jonathon knew he had to answer carefully.

Kim unfolded her legs and scooted herself to the edge of the mattress to allow her legs to dangle off the side of the bed. Lowering her head back down a bit, she faced the floor. Jonathon entered her room and sat down next to her, still contemplating on the right words to express.

Angling his head to face her he said, "Well sweetie…you know when you cry, you usually feel a little better and little stronger afterwards."

"I guess?"

"Mommy is just like you, she needed to let her feelings out like that today. She also needed to be strong for you and JR. Adults, every now and then, do this so they can be a better person to themselves and for others." Kim didn't respond. Jonathon sat there wondering what was going through her mind. This was really not parenting at his best, but he wanted to try and alleviate Kim's concern.

Kim still had an uneasy demeanor about her. "I guess, I understand."

"I know mommy is not like this often, but today was a hard day for her and for all of us. It is like that with you and your schoolwork. On some days you come home with what you consider easy homework, other days you really have to work at it. Today was one of those days we really had to work at it."

She turned her head and looked up at her father.

"Math is always hard," she said, with a slight smile.

"I know," Jonathon said, chuckling.

She turned her head away and resumed staring at the floor. "I'm glad you're home. I was so scared."

Kim was old enough to comprehend that his line of work could be dangerous at times. This was perhaps what was really bothering her the most. She caught a glimpse into a possible future where Daddy may not come home. He stood up, turned to face her and knelt down in front of her.

He gently took hold of her hands. "I am home, sweetie, this is the important part."

She started to cry. "I was so scared that you were going to die. I don't know what I would do without you, Mommy, or even JR."

Releasing her hands, he shifted himself up onto his feet, but still crouched down. Leaning in, he swathed her in a hug. "It's okay, I'm here."

Unfolding his arms from her, he balanced himself back down onto his knees, staring at her. "Sweetie, I know this is very upsetting, but let's focus on the positive. Okay? Mommy's here, JR is here, you're here, and I'm here. Even though it was a horrible day, it still has a happy ending."

She raised her head to face her father, wiping away her tears. "Thank you, Daddy. You're right, I do feel a little better."

"I'm glad."

She hopped down and engulfed him in her arms. "I love you, Daddy."

"I love you, too."

She released him and stood up straight.

"All right, let's try and get some sleep, sweetie," Jonathon said, struggling to his feet. "We can talk more tomorrow if you would like."

"Okay."

Leaning past her, he pulled the covers partway down for her. Finishing the task, she leapt into bed. Placing the covers over her and up to her neck, he bent over, kissing her forehead, "Goodnight, sweet dreams, and I love you."

"Good night, Daddy. I love you, too."

Walking to the doorway, he turned off her light. Twisting back slightly, he checked to see if her little night light was on. It automatically lit up when the main lighting was turned off. She liked having this alert guard. It kept the monsters away. He walked out, closing her door only partway.

I should probably check on JR and make sure he is all right, he thought. Jonathon lightly treaded across the short hallway to JR's open door. He had a night light as well. Jonathon silently peeked into his son's room and found JR sound asleep.

"What a little trooper," Jonathon softly said to himself. Reversing his direction, he moved himself back out into the dark living room. A light peered from underneath the closed door of his bedroom, but wasn't bright enough to where he could see everything. Jonathon took two paces in and stopped. Pausing for a moment in the middle of the dark room, he noticed the absence of sound. For this brief time, he felt a wave of loneliness and emptiness. No Dana. No children. Only quiet. It was quite a strange sensation for him. There were some days things got so hectic with work, school, dance recitals, carpools, bake sales, science fairs, parent/teacher conferences, tree houses, and doctor's appointments. Sometimes he would wish for some peace and quiet. No more. This odd occurrence of solitude reaffirmed he should never take any of this for granted. Jonathon knew to cherish every moment, but a personal reminder every now and then was healthy. The thought of being, or an existence, without his family, even for a second, was very unsettling. His family was what gave him purpose in this world and everyone in this family was what gave them purpose. They were all very much apart of each other. One cannot function without the other. The longer he stood here, the more sad he became just thinking about it. It was concerning, however. This was the second time today he had these intense feelings. *I just need to get some sleep and put this day behind me.*

Carefully following the light to his bedroom, Jonathon opened the door and entered the room. Squinting his eyes, he gently closed the door behind him. His eyes adjusted as he staggered around to his side of the bed. Sitting down on the edge of the bed, he started staring at the floor, deciding if he was ready to sleep yet. Dana emerged from the attached master bathroom.

"Kim and JR are in bed," she said.

"I know. I just tucked Kim in and checked on JR."

"Are you ready for bed?"

"I'm not sure. My body is tired, but my mind isn't."

Dana sat down on her side and twisted toward Jonathon. "Would you like to talk about it?"

With his head still down, he answered, "I don't know."

"Adam was able to fill me in on some of the details. It's okay to feel whatever you are feeling."

"I don't know what I'm feeling."

"If you want help sorting out your thoughts, you know I'm here."

"I know." Jonathon picked his head up and shifted around on the bed as far as he could to see Dana's expressions.

"You have been focusing on me, how about you? How are you dealing with this?"

Dana turned away and did not reply. Jonathon sprung up, walked over to her, and sat beside her.

Placing his arm around her, he craned his head to see her. "You know the same thing goes for you. I'm here for you, too. I have a hunch when you heard what happened, you had a lot of disturbing things going through your head."

Dana started to tear again. "When I heard you were shot, I lost all feeling. I went numb. I just shut down. All the while, I had to some how keep it together for Kimmie and JR. Of course, when they told me it hit your vest and you were okay, I was so relieved. But, what if it didn't turn out that way? I hate to think like this."

"Dana let's be thankful it turned out the way it did."

"But what if didn't?" Shaking her head she added, "Maybe its time for you to…"

Jonathon removed his arm from Dana. "Let's not start that again."

"Kim and JR are getting older…the world is losing its mind. I don't think I can go through this again."

"This job is all I know. Besides, like I have stated before, I haven't had any close call incidents."

"Other than today. You can't make that claim anymore."

"Yes. Other than today."

"Don't get me wrong, Jonny, I'm so proud of you. You know that. I always have been."

"I know. You have always been my biggest cheerleader."

"However, we are still in a position to make some changes. Please think about it."

Jonathon nodded. "I go out everyday knowing that my loving family is here and that I must come home everyday. I was still able to do that today. I am glad you're here and I am glad to be here."

Dana, wiping away her tears, turned and hugged Jonathon tightly. "I'm never going to let you go, mister."

"Neither will I," said Jonathon, returning the embrace.

CHAPTER SIX

JR'S GIFT

Jonathon opened his eyes and woke to see Dana hovering over him. She was dressed in one of her professional outfits.

"Did you hear me, honey?" she asked.

"No," he said, shaking his head.

"The kids and I are almost late to school."

Dana was a fifth-grade teacher at The Lakes District School. The kids were enrolled there as well.

"Okay," Jonathon said in a raspy voice.

Dana left the room and he could hear her stomping across the room outside, presumably to round up Kim and JR.

"Okay you two, we need to finish up please," she said.

The single footsteps now proceeded to what he assumed was the garage. The muffled sound of the outer garage door opening reverberated into the bedroom and supported his assumption.

Jonathon slowly rose up and swung himself out of bed. Noticing he still had on the clothes he wore home from the hospital he thought, *I obviously did not change. I don't remember when I fell asleep.* Staggering around the bed, he went through the door and out to the family room. He heard a lot of rustling coming from the bedrooms across the way. Heading toward them to see what all the commotion was, both Kim and JR rushed out of their respective rooms.

The school had a uniform policy, so the kids were in their matching gear. Kim had on her backpack, while JR was carrying his. Both ran up to Jonathon and gave him a hug.

"We can't be late!" Dana said in the distance.

Letting go of him, they darted through the dining room and around the table to get to the garage through the now open inner door. Calm returned as the door slammed and the lighting from outside was subdued. Jonathon chuckled and headed the kitchen to see if there was any coffee. The aroma filled the air, so the prospect was encouraging.

Suddenly the light of outside filled the dining nook as the door whisked open. JR sped back into the house and raced around the table to Jonathon.

"Dad! Dad! I want you to have this." JR placed a small object in his father's open hand. JR was smiling ear to ear with so much pride. Dana, entering back into the dining area, followed JR's path.

"It was Adam's idea," she said. "JR, a couple of weeks ago, mentioned to him that he wanted to give something to his Daddy, something that would keep you safe. He was going to give it to you on Father's Day, but this morning he insisted on giving it to you right away."

Jonathon glimpsed down at the pointed silver object in his hand, then back up to Dana with a concerned and perplexed look. "Uh, Dana…?"

"Adam placed a rubber stop on the rear to prevent anything from happening and made sure it was safe to handle. JR never handled your gift prior to this morning." JR had given his father a bullet that was inserted and fastened to some sort of setting that could attached be to his key chain.

"This way you have an extra, in case you run out of bullets," JR said with a very excited tone. All Jonathon could think of is what a dangerous item for JR to be handling. But then he did appreciate the idea his son wanted him safe.

"JR this is a wonderful gift!" he said with a smile. "Thank You."

"Okay, young man, we need to go," Dana said.

"Yes, Mommy, Bye, Daddy!" He hurried back around the table, maneuvered around Dana, and then went back into the garage. Jonathon sat his gift on the dining room table and peered at Dana with a stern look.

"I would have never approved, but Adam says it is very safe," Dana said, nervously smiling. "Adam says it was deemed a dud. He packed the setting so that it was very cushioned. However, the setting is still a little loose…Adam will take care of it."

"I think…I will take care of Adam."

"Jonny!"

"I'm just kidding."

"Plus, I gave Kim and JR another lecture not to touch any of Daddy's police things and made sure everything dangerous remained hidden and locked up, including this. Okay. We've got to go. I love you, Jonny."

"I love you too, honey."

Dana, clopping up to Jonathon in her noisy shoes, hugged him and gave him a long kiss. She let go and with a big smile said, "You're going to make us late with all of your shenanigans." With haste she ran back into the garage, closing the door behind her.

Shaking his head, he walked into the kitchen to check on the coffee situation. Looking at the coffee pot, it was just as he had hoped, there was enough for one cup.

Oh yeah, that smells good, he thought. Opening and reaching into the cabinet overhead, he selected his "Greatest Dad" mug and placed it on the counter. As he poured his fragrant liquid, Jonathon could hear the garage door closing outside. He returned the carafe to the maker. Picking up the mug, he took a sip. Feeling it was just the right temperature, he slid back a bigger gulp. He then set the mug back on the counter. *That hit the spot!* he thought.

Walking back into the dining room and up to the table, he picked up his gift, examining it. Shaking his head and chuckling, he then maneuvered over to the key rack by the garage doorway. This is where Jonathon kept his spare set of keys to his personal car. He rarely used this set, moreover, he didn't drive his car that much, either. He figured he would just keep this set at the station for now. Removing the key ring from the rack, he attached the bullet's setting to the chain. *I guess I will go and face the music,* he thought. Deciding to take a shower and get ready for work, he placed his keys back on the rack and headed for his bedroom.

CHAPTER SEVEN

PREPARATION

Jonathon finished getting ready for his day and was dressed in his uniform. He cruised over to Dana's mirror to inspect himself and to make sure he did not forget anything. The one item he did not forget was his spare bulletproof vest. He picked up his impaired vest where Dana had set it, deciding he was going to keep it. Since there were no bad guys to put on trial and it would not be needed as evidence, he believed there would be no problem with him keeping it not as a reminder of the horrific day itself, but as memento of what could have been much worse. Tomorrow is never promised, but he was here this day. He was going to cherish his time with his family, not that he did not before.

He set the battered article just inside the closet and made his way to the bedroom door out. Jonathon left the bedroom and maneuvered to the key holder to get his car keys, realizing his police cruiser was not here. *I guess I will be driving my own car*. Selecting his spare set of keys from the rack, he briefly moved about the immediate areas of the house, inspecting certain appliances and fixtures to make sure everything was at a state they should be at. "Coffee pot off, kitchen light off, dining room light on, front and back door locked." Satisfied with his findings, he headed to the garage.

Depressing a small button on the wall next to the key rack, the sound of the outer door raising resonated into the room. Opening the door leading into the garage, the outside light slowly filled the space. He closed the door as he stepped down onto the concrete floor.

Staring at his dust covered car, he wondered if it was going to start. The vehicle was a mid sized four door gasoline/electric hybrid sedan that he bought new last year. Every time he looked at his car, he wonders why he paid so much for something he rarely drives. If he went anywhere, off duty, it was usually with the whole family or with the one or both of the kids in Dana's minivan. The van had all of the kids' creature comforts which made their driving experience more pleasant, including his. Walking over to the driver's door, he swung it open. A whiff of new car smell, still present, traveled through Jonathon's senses.

Maneuvering himself in, he sat down onto the seat, shifting his legs in making that distinctive noise indistinguishable from another noise a child thinks is funny. Inserting the key in the ignition and with one try, the car fired right up. Gliding his hand across the console to his side, he shifted the car into reverse utilizing the automatic transmission lever. He drove out of the garage.

CHAPTER EIGHT

THE STATION

Arriving at the station, he parked the car and switched it off. He rested his head against the rear of the seat for a moment. *I know I'm going to be relieved of duty for a couple weeks, but I just don't want to hear it,* he thought. Opening the car door, he still hesitated to get out. *I did nothing wrong. Being relieved is department procedure and not a reflection of any wrong doing.* His record was spotless. This action was not going to be a negative blemish on his exemplary service history. Still, the whole process was simply disheartening.

Locking the car with his wireless remote, he marched to the front of the station with his shoulders back and head held high. This was Gulfside City's main headquarters, governing four smaller precincts. The building itself was three stories and next door to the new courthouse, with a wide private service roadway separating the two properties. The county sheriff's office and jail were across the street. The jail was directly across from the station, with the sheriff's main departmental building to the right of it. The main office was roughly the same size as the city department. The jail, on the other hand, was far more slender with six stories.

The police department finished a major renovation last year, inside and out. It was like a new stationhouse, almost. The rear entrance door, not included in the original overhaul, had been having some issues as of late. The repair job on it was supposed to last a few days, but here it was, a month later.

Entering into the main lobby from the sidewalk and passing through the automatic sliding doors, Jonathon glanced around the sizeable reception area. The public help desk was straight across from the entrance, manned by dedicated reps serving the few citizens who were here with queries, concerns, or to pay a parking ticket. The area behind the customer representatives was an open administrative section, which could only be accessed from inside this section. These reps were dressed in matching uniforms.

From the front entrance, slightly off to the right and on a display wall above the desk, were framed pictures of the past chiefs of police all in sepia tones. The last picture, on the end of the line, was the photo of the department's current chief, in full color. All the past chiefs' pictures had a silver nameplate under their respective portrait. The current chief had a gold one. Slightly off to the left, on the same display wall, were several assorted pictures of art crafted from various local artists. The stairs and elevator to the other floors were located in a hallway accessible through a door by the help desk. The second and third floors were all of the officer's sections. The second floor was largely open and mainly had kiosks and workstations. The department's phone unit was located there. The only office on the second floor was home to the Investigation's Division. The third floor housed all of the offices, including the chief's. Every time Jonathon came here he always had a high sense of pride and dignity.

Jonathon veered to access the door to get to the elevator, took his access card out from his pocket, then swiped it through the adjacent electronic reader on the connecting wall. He opened the door, entering the hallway and returning the card to his pocket. The door closed behind him as he approached the elevator doors at the end of the corridor. Reaching the double sliders of the elevator, he pushed the up arrow button on the call pad. The doors quietly and smoothly open, revealing a pristine interior. A horizontal waist level handrail lined the interior of the car. Stepping inside, he quickly turned to face the front. With his index finger extended he paused at the No. 3 button on the floor selection pad. He was thinking about what was going to be said. Jonathon knew in his heart that everything he had done during the crisis was the right thing. However, he was still nervous. He had been part of other incidents from years past, but nothing this serious. This was the first time his direct actions were going to be questioned. Sighing heavily, Jonathon pushed the third floor button. The doors slid closed and up he went.

CHAPTER NINE

THE CHIEF

Jonathon exited the elevator and swerved to his left out into the main room. This section was organized with a massive open space surrounded by clear glass offices, which housed the supervisory staff, their support and administrative crew, and the chief at the head of the room. The area to the right of the elevator was a closed storage area, mainly the seized property room and evidence locker. The open area had several plain desks and workstations for officers to gather their thoughts, write reports, organize for roll call, and hold meetings.

Jonathon walked toward his office, which was relatively close to the elevator. Fortunately not many people seemed to be around, so he made it into his workspace without anyone noticing him. He missed the shift change role call, so most everyone was out in the field. This was just as well. He did not feel like having to tell his story over and over.

Switching on the desk light from a switch near the door, he sat down in his chair and turned on his computer to check the daily log to see what was happening. The computers here were tuned to load quickly, so his login screen popped up instantly. Entering his password, his main menu appeared. Utilizing the mouse, he clicked on the email program, checking his inbox. There was nothing spine tingling. Mousing over to another program, he accessed the daily reporting log, finding a small footnote about yesterday and that Lieutenant Olsen had been assigned to cover Jonathon's district. *Okay. I guess that settles that.* Jonathon knew this was going to happen, but nonetheless he was still taken back. Checking a few more reports, he concentrated on those concerning his colleagues who were injured in yesterday's event. The details about them were vague at this point, but the little amount of information did indicate all of them were expected to fully recover. Adam had stated they would be fine, but having it on the official record gave him a huge sigh of relief. As he closed those reports, he received an instant message from the chief, noting he was ready to see him. *Hmm, I guess he saw me.* Then he realized that the chief gets an alert on his computer every time someone logs on to the network. *Well, it's time to face the music.*

Jonathon logged out of the system, then turned his computer off. Standing up from his chair, he stepped to the door, turning the light off as he exited the office. Walking toward the chief's office, he kept his head high. As Jonathon approached his superior's door, one of the chief's assistants popped in front of him. She was a woman in her late twenties, wearing the same matching uniform as those on the front desk.

"Hey Jonny, how are you doing?" she asked.

"I'm okay Suzie, considering."

"That's good. Everybody around here is pulling for you and we're very proud."

"Thank you. That means a lot."

"I believe he is ready to see you."

"Yeah, I got the summons on my computer. I guess I will see you in a couple of weeks."

"Hang in there. Oh, please say hi to Dana."

"I will."

Suzie sat down at her adjacent desk and Jonathon continued into the chief's office. A cold shiver reverberated through his body as he entered. The chief who was standing behind his desk, walked from behind it and positioned himself behind the two chairs at the face of the desk. The chief stopped Jonathon, extending his right hand. Jonathon hesitated at first, but then raised his right hand. The chief clasped Jonathon's and shook it.

"Nice job, Jonny!" he said with a grin. Releasing Jonathon, he returned to his side of the desk, and sat down. Jonathon, very relieved, sighed quietly. His boss was not known for giving out compliments. "Close the door and have a seat, lieutenant."

"Yes sir." Jonathon complied as ordered and closed the door. Moving further in, he sat down in one of the chairs, making sure his back stayed straight.

"First the bad news," said the chief, facing Jonathon. "Because of your actions yesterday and the fact you discharged your weapon in the performance of your job, it is department and city policy that I must relieve you of your duty. You're not the only one and this is not a punishment. This is just procedure. So, effective immediately, you are on administrative leave with pay until further notice. The internal investigation into this matter should only take two or three weeks. Maybe sooner. Okay, that's the bad news. Now, the good news.

From the preliminary reports and witness testimonials I have been reading, you have nothing to worry about. I've also spoken to some of the victims from the museum. The one notable discussion was with Christopher, the employee who was in the restroom with you."

"Yes sir."

"He heard your conversation with the dispatchers and felt you acted in a very professional manner in dealing with this crisis. This is what I like to hear from the public. Officer and dispatch reports also concur with this. This was a nasty situation, by the book, and one that had no perfect solution. However, with how fast events were moving, the victims and our officers walked out and the bad guys did not. This was a very acceptable scenario for me. Any questions so far?"

"No sir."

"Okay. Now, with the bad guys dead, we may never fully know why this happened. These guys have been identified and they were no strangers to trouble. Their residences are being searched for any reasoning behind this. More questions are coming about with answers leading into more questions. This part of the investigation, obviously, does not affect your leave. After we are done here and before you go home today, I will need you to write your report to add to the official record."

"Will do sir," Jonathon said, nodding.

"Okay, now this concludes the official part of this briefing."

"Official part?"

"Yes, there is more, but this does not concern the administrative record…well for the most part. Again, nice job Jonny! You did this department proud. This is a testament to the training and strong principles this agency wants to project to the public. So far, the news media and public opinion strongly supports the actions of the department. Hopefully this will hold as the facts about why this occurred come about, but goods guys alive and bad guys dead always make for a good story. Plus, when a officer is given a medal of valor, that helps too."

"What!" Jonathon exclaimed with surprise.

"Yes, Mayor Bradley wants to give you the city's highest honor that can be bestowed on a public servant. It appears that one of the children in the tour group yesterday was one of his grandnephews. In addition, his office has been flooded with praise from grateful parents. Some of these parents have used the term…hero."

"Hero? I don't think so, sir," Jonathon said, blushing. "Just an officer doing my job."

"That may be so, but Mayor Bradley is planning to make a big deal about this. You are going to be presented with the medal at a ceremony in front of the courthouse next week. The heads of other cities, the governor, and of course the media will all be there."

"Sir, isn't this a little fast and premature?"

"Perhaps, but Mayor Bradley wants to ride this wave and grab as much attention from this as possible. You know politicians; these things are like gold to them. Plus, I do think this is also a bit personal because of his grandnephew."

"I don't know, sir."

"Jonny, I know you are the modest type. However, regardless if it was just in the line of duty, you saved a lot of lives. I believe, too, this ceremony will also give the victims and their families a chance to thank you."

"All right sir. I'm just not used to so much… attention."

"I know, but get use to it. In the city's eyes, you're a hero."

Jonathon stood up straight. "Yes sir!"

The chief stood up and extended his right hand again. "I can't say it enough…good job!"

With Jonathon's right hand clasping the chief's, the two shook. Jonathon then turned to leave the office.

"Don't forget, Jonny, I need that report."

Jonathon twisted back. "I will have it for you in about an hour or so. Good day, sir."

"Good day, lieutenant."

Jonathon faced back to the front, opened the door and exited. Walking past the chief's administrative staff, he noticed all of them staring and smiling at him with admiration. A very uncomfortable Jonathon did not know how to react, so he kept walking.

Entering back into his office, he turned on the light, closed the door, sat down at his desk, and turned on the computer. Life around the department and perhaps the city was going to be different, not that this was a bad thing. He was just going to be uncomfortable with all the extra attention. However, he could not wait to tell Dana and his kids about the ceremony. They have always been his biggest supporters. Jonathon always did his job knowing he was creating a safer world for them and now he could share this moment of success with them. While his computer loaded up, he accessed the report processing program. Positioning his hands on the keyboard to start typing, he paused. *Where do I begin?* he thought. He started going through the events again and became overwhelmed. Sitting back for a moment he thought, *Once I do write this, I can be officially free from this. I can either choose to let this haunt me or I can embrace this as another episode of my life that I can learn from and appreciate.* Jonathon made his choice, leaned forward, repositioning his hands on the keyboard, and started typing.

CHAPTER TEN

CEREMONY FOR A HERO

"I don't know, Dana, this seems a bit much," Jonathon said.

"Jonny, you always say you want to make a difference in the world. I believe today is the world's acknowledgement. This…how can I put it… is a celebration, not just for you, but for Gulfside City as well. This is something everyone of this town can be a part of and proud. In some little way, everyone's lives here have been changed for the better…especially for all those children, including ours. I know, I know, you were just doing your duty. I have been hearing you mutter that for a week now, but for the rest of us it is so much more. I hope you can just go along with this. Whether you like it or not, you are a real life hero."

"Hero, huh. I just…don't see myself as that."

"I know, but here we are," Dana said, smiling. "A hero comes in many forms and at many times." Dana leaned over towards Jonathon and planted a kiss on his cheek. "Come on, mister, Adam is waiting inside with Kim and JR."

Jonathon and Dana both exited the van, feeling the warm sunshine on them. They were parked behind the courthouse, in a secured section reserved for the judges, away from all the commotion. Jonathon was in his ceremonial uniform, as were the other officers who were attending. As they were walking toward the rear entrance of the courthouse, one of the judges exited. He was about to just walk by when he noticed it was Jonathon. He immediately stopped and turned towards Jonathon.

"Officer Scott, isn't it?"

Jonathon and Dana likewise suspended their trek up the pathway.

"Yes, your Honor."

"Well let me congratulate you on a job well done." The judge held out his hand and Jonathon did the same. The two briefly shook hands.

"Judge Francis, this is my wife, Dana," Jonathon proudly acknowledged. The judge and Dana briefly shook hands.

"Connor…nice to meet you, Dana," Judge Francis said with a smile. "I bet you are so proud of him."

"I am very proud of him. I just need to figure out how to get him to be proud of himself."

Jonathon looked at Dana, blushed, and then looked back at the judge. "I was just doing my duty, your Honor."

Dana rolled back her eyes and shook her head.

"Well, officer, whatever the case may be…still nice job. I would stay for the ceremony, but I'm on my way to the depot to catch my train to a judges' conference I am chairing. Good Luck!"

"Thank you, sir," Jonathon replied.

Connor veered away and resumed his walk toward the parking lot.

"Well it begins," Jonathon grumbled to himself.

"I heard that!" exclaimed Dana. "This is a good thing, Jonny. By the way, did he call you officer?"

"He calls everyone officer. He calls the chief, officer. The chief hates that, but this is the way Judge Francis is and he is really not required to call any of us by our rank."

The pair, continuing their march, reached the rear door and entered into a hallway. After taking a few steps, they were readily greeted by the chief who was now leading them out to the reception area.

"How are you doing, Jonny?"

"Fine sir. I'm still trying to get used to all of this attention. Sir, if you remember, this is my wife, Dana," Jonathon gestured toward her.

"Yes, Dana, it is very good to see you again."

"It is very good to see you again…officer," Dana said, with a mischievous smirk.

The chief looked at Jonathon with a perplexed expression. Jonathon shrugged his shoulders and was blushing. "We ran into Judge Francis on the way in here, sir."

"Oh Jonny, you better watch out for her, she's trouble," the chief said with a hearty smile.

Jonathon glared at Dana. "I know, sir. She's been trouble from day one."

"Jonny!" shrieked Dana as the two men chuckled.

The trio went through a secured door and emerged into a large open reception area at the front of the courthouse. Normally, this was filled with guards, scanning equipment, and a small eatery, but today it was cleared and only filled with the hustle and bustle of all sorts of individuals there for the ceremony. By now, most everyone was slowly exiting out the front doors.

The chief angled toward Jonathon. "All right Jonny, the fun begins here momentarily," he said. "Mayor Bradley will be at the podium in front of the courthouse. I will walk out with you by my side and we will stand slightly behind and off to the side of him. He will give a short speech, then present you with the award. He will step aside and you will be expected to make a brief statement. Any questions?"

"Yes. How many people are here?"

"The whole town," replied the chief, smirking.

Jonathon stiffening up as Dana chimed in. "Jonny, just relax. I'm sure it's not the whole town. Judge Francis was on his way out. That's one less person." Jonathon gave Dana a sour look as Dana and the chief began to chuckle.

"Ah my husband, you will have to get used to the spotlight," she said.

"Okay Dana, while Jonny and I are with Mayor Bradley, you and the kids will be seated in the VIP chairs that are somewhat behind and to the side of us."

The chief's lead assistant, Suzie, walked up. "It's time," she said. "They're ready for you."

"Thank you, Suzie," said the chief. "Let them know we are on our way."

Suzie nodded, turned, and walked back toward the front. Dana and the men faced the same direction and began their march toward the front. The chief excused himself for a moment after being summoned by another one of his aides. Adam, with Kim and JR, walked up to Jonathon and Dana.

"Are you two behaving for Uncle Adam?" Dana asked.

"Yes, Mommy," replied Kim.

"Uncle Adam was telling us some jokes," JR added.

Dana glared at both Adam and Jonathon. Jonathon lowering his head and muttered, "Oh boy this can't be good."

"Don't worry Dana, they're kid approved," Adam said, claiming his defense.

"Hmmm…" Dana groaned.

Jonathon raised his head, attempting to quickly change the subject. "Well, at least it is not raining today, everyone will have a good view of me making a fool of myself."

Dana pointed at both Jonathon and Adam. "I'm going to have a little chat with you two later." Dana gave Jonathon another kiss on his cheek and then, with a smile said, "Good luck and congratulations. I know will do fine up there."

Both Kim and JR said, "Good luck, Daddy. We love you." Both ran up to him and hugged him.

He slightly hunched down to return the embrace. "I love you both, too. Thank you for being here."

The two let go of Jonathon as Dana gingerly took one of Kim and JR's hands. Turning around, they started walking towards the front. Dana, halting their trip outside, twisted herself slightly back toward Jonathon, released Kim's hand, and blew Jonathon a kiss. Jonathon caught it, of course. During that moment, he felt serenity like all was well in the world. Dana faced forward, clasped Kim's hand again, and continued to proceed outside to the staging area.

"Aw… isn't that cute," Adam said with a grin.

"Oh hush, you got us both in trouble."

"They were kids' jokes," Adam said, being descriptive with his hands. "Completely harmless."

"Yeah, sure," Jonathon said, sarcastically laughing. "Thanks to you, JR, for a week, was running around with that one about…"

The chief returned. "Stance, are you getting an award today?"

"No, sir."

"Then get your tail outside."

"Yes, sir. See you afterwards, Jonny."

"Bye, Adam."

Adam faced front and hurried toward the doors to outside. Jonathon and the chief, then slowly marched their way to the doors.

"This is it, Jonny," said the chief. "I know you are nervous about this, but this is no different than any assignment. You'll be fine."

The two proceeded outside where there was a rather large noisy crowd. The new ten story courthouse with it's large square in front, faced Ringling Boulevard and overshadowed its predecessor across the street. The old courthouse, which was what it was now called, was of Mediterranean Revivalist architecture. The elder structure was the site of law and order since the incorporation of the city and formation of the county. The old courthouse, which was only three stories, included a twelve-story bell tower that stood proudly and watched over the city all of its life. However, recently its slightly taller and more modern neighbors had blocked its watchful eye. Yet, the tower did still manage to peek through at certain angles and was able to be somewhat noticed despite Gulfside's progress.

A single ornate crosswalk spanned across the four lanes of Ringling with a flashing caution signal overhead. The new courthouse's manicured combination grass/concrete grounds were filled with citizens, officers, dignitaries, and, of course, the media to see Jonathon get his award. The middle of this square housed two flagpoles, one for the national flag and one for the municipal flag. In between the poles was a seemingly permanent addition; a rather tall, probably ten-foot, jade-colored statue of a man. Jonathon shook his head and thought, *Oh no, they didn't.*

The chief led Jonathon to his position near Mayor Bradley, who was standing behind a standard chest high podium, with a single microphone protruding out from the top. Mayor Bradley looked back and seeing the two there, adjusted the microphone and cleared his throat to get everyone's attention. The crowd quieted down.

"Good morning, ladies and gentlemen. Let me start off by saying that Gulfside City, hands down, is the greatest of cities, in our fair nation! It has been an absolute pleasure to serve as your mayor. With your support, I have seen many wonderful businesses grow and thrive here. Along, with this, more and more families move here and flourish. We have a vast amount of resources to properly fund our schools, offer subsidized healthcare, and provide numerous local recreational activities. Accordingly, our schools, healthcare, and recreation are the best in the country. Why? Because you, the people, are the essence of a community that works to succeed and excel not only in your own individual lives, but also for the betterment of our neighbors. These are some of the advantages of being a Gulfside City resident. Everyone here brings life to our city, which in turn brings life to us. One week ago, our home was rocked by what could have been a horrific tragedy. A heartbreak that would not have only taken lives, but adversely affected the many lives and the many families who make up this amazing town. However, as a result of diligent thinking and quick action, these families are here today to celebrate life. A hero stands amongst us. A gentleman who embodies the selfless spirit which prominently contributes to the prosperity here in Gulfside City."

The mayor gestured to the statue. "So it is with great pleasure for me to present to the people of Gulfside this commemorative statue of our honored guest…Jonathon Russell Scott. His courage and dedication is a symbol for all of us. Gulfside City is here to challenge all threats to its continuing prosperity and to stand the test of time."

A thunderous applause arose from the crowd along with shouts of cheers and the occasional whistle. Even with the overwhelming endorsement of the citizenry, this attention to Jonathon was still making him uncomfortable. Rubbernecking back to his wife and his children, both Kim and JR waved to their father and Dana, giving him a reassuring nod and thumbs up. Smiling, Jonathon faced forward again. The mayor raised his hands over the podium, and then gradually lowered them to quiet the crowd.

The noise abated with Mayor Bradley continuing with his speech. "With great citizens like you and him, Gulfside's continuing success and stature are guaranteed forever. It is a rare and sincere privilege for me, as an elected official, to present this prestigious award for valor." Reaching into the podium, he retrieved an object from a concealed shelf. It was a small closable case. Opening it, an ornate medal was nestled inside. Mayor Bradley held up the medal so the audience could see it. There was brief applause. Mayor Bradley turned around, faced and positioned himself in front of Jonathon, and removed the medal from the case, handing the empty case to the chief. The medal was attached to a lanyard which was patterned with the colors of Gulfside City's municipal flag. The mayor, lifting the medal, gently guided it to its suspended position in the middle of Jonathon's chest. Mayor Bradley stepped further off to the side, motioning for Jonathon to take the place at the podium.

Just as Jonathon began to move, the crowd began to clap again. Even though this ovation was more energetic and with more feeling, it was all he could do to resist the urge to faint. Stepping up to the platform, the applause intensified. Mayor Bradley took position next to the chief where Jonathon was. Jonathon, not sure what to do to quiet the crowd, tried smiling. Waving. A thumbs up. With each passing second, Jonathon grew more nervous as the crowd continued their applause. *How long has it been now? An hour? Two?* He had been up at the podium for only several seconds. Twisting back at Dana, she gave him a big smile and a wink. Gaining some composure, he again faced out to the sea of people. The crowd was finally lightening on the applause, and he knew it was now time to speak.

Jonathon cleared his throat. "Uh, thank you so very much for being here. This is a such uh… great honor." Pausing for a moment, he lowered his head to examine the award hanging around his chest. Reaching up, he held the medal between his thumb and index finger, lightly rubbing it. He then let go of it, beginning to feel the power and symbolism this honor represented. Lifting his head and focusing back to the audience he said, "I know I've heard the term 'hero' used a lot in the past week… and surprisingly it is being referred to me. That day I was scared like anyone else would've been. I didn't know how it was going to turn out. But, standing here today, I remember why I acted. Twelve years ago I took an oath to protect the lives of every citizen here in Gulfside City. Every family, including mine, I promised to defend. If I had just cowered in the bathroom and I would be lying if I said I didn't feel like doing that, I would have broken that promise. Because I stuck to my oath and honor, all our families are still here. This was not about an award or recognition.

This is about our community, our values, our family. Mayor Bradley is right. We live in a wonderful place and I'm proud to call Gulfside my home. Thank you!"

The assemblage, erupting into cheer, began to intensely clap again. Jonathon stepped away from the forefront, indicating to Mayor Bradley that he was done. Mayor Bradley returning to his former position as Jonathon regained his position next to the chief. Jonathon briefly glanced over to the chief, who gave him a nod and a grin of appreciation. The ovation was now tapering off as Mayor Bradley prepared to make his final remark.

"Thank you all attending, that concludes this event." Mayor Bradley said. "Everyone drive safely and cherish every moment. Thank you and good day."

The crowd very slowly began to disperse.

Mayor Bradley swung around and walked right up to Jonathon. "I wanted to personally congratulate and thank you, Lieutenant Scott. I'm hosting a benefit fundraising dinner and dance at my house on Friday and I would like you and your wife to attend if you can. I think this would be an excellent opportunity for more people to meet you and to show what Gulfside City has to offer."

"Thank you, Mayor Bradley, I will ask Dana."

"Terrific, I will forward the invitations to the chief. Good day Mr. Scott." The two shook hands, then Mayor Bradley turned to the chief. "Later today. Come by my office. We need to finalize next year's budget."

"I will check my calendar. However, I'm thinking around 3ish," replied the chief.

"Sounds good. See you then. Good day."

Mayor Bradley then strolled toward the courthouse, greeting others along the way.

"Well Jonny, see, you made it through," said the chief.

"Yes, at least this part, sir."

"What do you mean?"

"Well, now Mayor Bradley wants to parade me around to his political friends."

"It's just a fundraising benefit…yeah you're right. Eventually, all of this will cool down in a few weeks or so and you can then relax."

"I suppose. Thank you, sir."

"No Jonny, thank you. Because of your heroics, my budget is looking very good next year."

"Not you too, sir."

"Jonny, face it, you're a political gold mine for all of us," the chief responded with a chuckle. "See you later, Jonny. I will be in touch with you soon. Probably another week to sift through the rest of the investigative and bureaucratic mumbo jumbo. Hang in there. Good day."

"Bye sir and good day."

The chief turned and headed back into the courthouse. Jonathon turned to face the VIP area, and noticed Dana strolling toward him with a sway in her step and hero worship in her eyes.

"You see, that was not so bad, mister."

"Oh, it's not over. Mayor Bradley has invited us to attend some fundraiser thing on Friday."

"Sounds like it could be a lot of fun," Dana said, stopping in front of him and gazing into his eyes.

"What!"

"What do you mean what?"

"I really don't feel like being a trophy for the mayor." Dana pouted her lips and flaunted her puppy-dog eyes, in an attempt to convince her husband. Dana sometimes got her way with this method.

"You really want to go?"

"Yes, yes I do. A chance to mingle, hobnob, dine, and dance at the mayor's mansion. I thought I would never be able to do that, especially with a guest of honor." Dana now pulled out the big guns, and she started to bat her eyelashes. Jonathon usually caved in at this point.

"Okay, okay we'll go to the dinner."

Dana clapped her hands and hopped up and down like a little girl. "Yes! Thank you, Jonny." She stopped and stood still. "I need to go out and get a new dress now."

"Oh, boy," Jonathon grumbled. "All right gala girl, let's go find Adam and the kids."

"I think he said he was going to take them down to the ice cream shop down the block."

"He does this every time. He gets them full of sugar, he goes bye, and leaves us with the all of the excitement."

"Jonny, you know he loves to spoil them."

"Yeah, Yeah."

CHAPTER ELEVEN

REINSTATEMENT

In the station's locker room, Jonathon was getting ready for his shift, the night shift. Adam strolled in. "Hey, Jonny. I keep forgetting to ask you, how was dinner the other night?"

"Words just can't describe. My fingers still hurt from shaking so many hands. Dana had a blast, however. Dancing, talking to people, showing off her new dress."

"New dress?"

"Yeah. New dress. She wants to go to another one of these things again."

"Lucky for you, that will probably not happen again."

"Oh no, unfortunately for me, I'm on Mayor Bradley's permanent guest list now. He made so many new political contacts, he told me he would like to see me at more events. Dana, of course, was within earshot when he said this to me. We'll be at the mayor's mansion again in about two weeks. And… she's going shopping again!"

"Don't worry all this hype will eventually calm down."

"That's what I keep hearing, but it hasn't happened yet. Oh also, to add injury to insult, Mayor Bradley wants to start naming things around town after me. This is just going too far now."

"Yeah, I'd hate to have to respond to a disorderly conduct call on Jonathon Scott Boulevard," Adam said, laughing.

"Shut up, you're not helping."

"Have you seen the chief yet?"

"No, not yet. After I'm done here, I have to go see him to be officially reinstated."

"Not a moment too soon."

"Yeah, you briefly mentioned on the phone the other day about pulling some extra time…what's that all about?"

"Calls have been going through the roof ever since the museum deal. Nothing major, just numerous prowling, trespassing, and disturbing the peace reports. It's been all over the news."

"I've been so busy with the kids, I really haven't been paying attention."

"I know. That's why I haven't been around as much."

"You know you could have visited me at any time."

"Hey, I know there are weeks you don't really get to see them. I wasn't going to interfere with that."

"Kim and JR are growing up so fast."

"Yes they are."

"What's behind all the ruckus anyway?"

"We don't know. By the time we respond to the locations, the perps are gone. As a result, and in addition to myself, some have been pulling in some extra hours to help with coverage."

"Could some of this be related to the museum?"

"I don't know, nothing has been mentioned or suggested at the shift briefings. Oh, I've been put back on your squad."

"Okay. Good."

"Can I ride with you for a bit?"

"What happened to your car?"

"I ran into a tree last night chasing one of these shadows."

"Are you okay?"

"Oh yeah, but the car isn't. They say it will be about a week before it is fixed. With everything going on, there are no spare vehicles."

"I don't see that as a problem. However, I am going to insist on driving."

"Very funny," Adam retorted sarcastically.

Jonathon closed his locker door and walked over to the locker room mirror. Inspecting himself thoroughly, he made sure everything was in order before going up to see the chief.

Adam moved closer to him. "Looking good, Jonny."

"I feel good. I can't wait to get back out there. Well maybe… with the town going mad all of a sudden, I'll probably be eating my words." Jonathon glanced at his watch. "Okay, it's time for me to see the chief. I'll meet you out in the lot?"

"I was wondering if I could tag along with you up to the chief's office. This will give me an excuse to see one of the chief's assistants."

"Suzie?"

"Yeah Suzie, what do you mean?"

"Come on, it's obvious to everyone, including the rookies, that you like her. Why don't you just ask her out some time."

"I don't know if I'm ready to."

Jonathon rolled his eyes. "Adam, are we in high school?"

"Uh, no."

"Okay, then. Be a man and ask the pretty lady out. I'm sure she already knows you like her. You always make an ass of yourself when you are around her."

"I do?"

"Yeah, I told you everyone can see it. Once, didn't you spill her coffee on yourself when you were bringing it to her?"

"Oh yeah."

"Also, if I remember correctly, last month we were walking in from the motor pool, she came out the door, and you walked into a pole."

"Hey, that really hurt."

"And then there was the time…"

"Okay, okay, you made your point."

"Let's go."

Adam and Jonathon exited the locker room and they entered the same hallway connecting the access door to the lobby. Walking up to the elevator, Adam pushed the up arrow. While waiting for the lift, Jonathon took the opportunity to rib Adam a little more.

"You know, I am a little upset you did not tell me about her sooner," he said.

"Uh well…I was going…"

Jonathon chuckled. "Relax, I'm just messing with you. However, please tell me you are going to ask her…today? I can't bear to watch you walk into anymore poles. You will be doing yourself a favor… and the rest of us."

The elevator stopped and the doors soon opened. Jonathon followed Adam inside, and they both turned to face the open doors. Adam, closest to the floor control panel, did not push any buttons. The doors closed and there they stood.

"Uh, hello?" Jonathon sarcastically stated.

"What?"

"You're thinking about Suzie, aren't you."

"Yeah, why?"

"Unbelievable," Jonathon grumbled.

"What?"

"Would you be so kind and push three please."

"Oh, yeah." Reaching out, he pushed three. Jonathon shook his head and secured his hands on the rail behind him.

"Why are you shaking your head?" Adam innocently asked.

"No reason."

"I'm just not sure if I'm at that stage yet."

"How long has she been here?"

"That's not the point."

"Unbelievable."

The elevator stopped on the third floor and the doors opened. The two exited and they trekked toward the chief's office. Reaching the chief's section, they were greeted by Suzie, who was standing at her desk at the front of the area.

"Hey guys," she acknowledged. "Jonny, the chief is waiting for you."

"Thank you Suzie."

Sitting down at her desk, she started shuffling some papers around. Jonathon walked past Suzie and twisted back to glance at Adam. Jonathon nodded his head a couple of times in Suzie's direction, but Adam stiffened up and shook his head. Jonathon rolled his eyes, refaced the chief's office, and marched through the doorway.

"Lieutenant, please come in."

Jonathon walked up to the front of the chief's desk, then stood there straight.

"Okay, lieutenant. This will be very brief. I assume you read the investigative report and signed all your papers."

"Yes, sir."

"The meat of it, you were not found at fault for any wrongdoings. Nor were any of the other officers involved. So, effective immediately, you are reinstated to active duty."

"Thank you, sir."

"The briefings for your district were already done today, so tomorrow you will resume that responsibility. Any questions?"

"No, sir."

"All right, that's it." Jonathon relaxed his posture. "Jonny I need you out there. The whole town seems to be on edge."

"Has there been any pattern to all of this strange behavior?"

"I hate to answer like this, but I don't know. Everyone is working to the bare bone to get to the bottom of this. However, we were warned when the museum incident happened that there is a larger problem going on here. It could be related. There are just not enough answers. Most of these calls could be people seeing things that aren't there because they are still freaked about what happened at the museum. I don't know."

"Adam is riding with me while his cruiser is getting fixed. We'll keep our eyes peeled."

"Very well. Good day, lieutenant."

"Good day, chief."

Jonathon turned around, and strolled out of the office to the chief's administrative area. Surprisingly, Adam was talking to Suzie. Adam appeared to be telling her a story and was using his arms and hands to illustrate. Then all of a sudden, Adam knocked over one of Suzie's cups, filled with paperclips, onto the ground.

Adam, mortified at the sight of the paperclips scattered all over the floor said, "I'm sorry about that, Suzie."

"It's okay, Adam," she said with a grin.

She swiveled her chair towards the mess and slid out of her seat. Setting her knees on the floor, she bent over slightly forward. Recovering the cup, she began to pick up the clips.

"Oh, let me help you with that," Adam said.

He kneeled down, rested his knees on the floor, and bent over to help. As the two were grabbing paperclips, they both leaned in closer together. Adam then clumsily rammed his forehead into Suzie's.

Jonathon stood there in horror, thinking to himself, *This is a wreck. I can't watch anymore of this.*

Adam lifted his face to see her. "Oh Suzie, I'm so sorry for hitting your head."

"It's all right. It doesn't hurt that much."

Shifting herself back to sit upright, she began to feel around the spot he hit. Reaching up to her desk, she searched around for something. Clasping a makeup compact, she slid it down to her, opening it, and briefly viewed herself in the embedded mirror.

Lowering the compact to face Adam she said, "See, it's only a little bump." Closing the compact, she placed it back on her desk.

"Still, I'm so sorry."

She nodded with a smile, then leaned back down, cautiously resuming picking up the paperclips. Adam continued as well.

"Um, Suzie. I was wondering…would you like to go have dinner somewhere…sometime…I mean if you are hungry sometime?"

Oh the humanity, Jonathon thought.

Suzie looked up at Adam. "Are you asking me out on a date? At least…I hope you are. I do eat you know."

"Oh yeah, I know. Yes, I am asking you out."

Suzie straightened up while still on her knees. Adam did the same.

Suzie placed her hand on Adam's. "Yes. I thought you would never ask."

Adam, with the biggest grin said, "How about Friday?"

"Friday would be perfect," replied Suzie with a smile.

Adam rested his other hand on top of Suzie's and looked up and over at Jonathon. "Jonny, she said yes."

"I know buddy, that's great," he said with disbelief.

Done picking up the mess, Adam rose to his feet. He bent down, helped Suzie up off the floor, and retrieved the cup. With Suzie now on her feet, Adam carefully placed the cup back on the desk.

"We've got to go, Adam," Jonathon said.

Suzie turned toward Jonathon, while again feeling the lump on her forehead. "Jonny, say hi to Dana for me."

"Will do, Suzie." Jonathon moved towards Adam and grabbed his arm. "Come on you smooth talker."

Looking back at her Adam said, "Bye, Suzie. Again, sorry about the mess and your head."

"Bye, Adam," she said with a smile.

Adam turned and moved with Jonathon. Jonathon let go of Adam, feeling it was safe to do so. Adam, with his new freedom, quickly snapped back to look at Suzie again. Jonathon veered with the walkway, but Adam did not. Crashing into one of the main area desks, he knocked it over.

"Oh, for crying out loud!" Jonathon exclaimed. "I can't take my eyes off of you for one moment."

Helping Adam compose himself, the two promptly picked up the workstation, returning it to its original state. Jonathon bent down to retrieve the items that fell from the desk.

"Yeah, you are definitely not touching the steering wheel of my car."

CHAPTER TWELVE

BACK ON THE JOB

Jonathon and Adam were out on patrol, randomly driving thorough various neighborhoods looking to see if there was any trouble or concerns. The call load was lower than normal for daytime, but they knew this was more than likely to change after sunset. Most of the unusual activity Gulfside City had been enduring lately was occurring at night.

It was about an hour away from sunset. The sky was clear of clouds and a hint of evening red and pink started to replace the blue of day.

"It really looks like it's going to be another great sunset," Adam commented.

"It sure does. Dana adores sunsets. She tries to get outside most nights, even if it's for only a few seconds, just to get a look. She absolutely loves nature. She feels society disregards its splendor in favor of other unworthy pursuits."

"I've noticed lately, she has been lashing out at technology."

"You've picked up on that, huh."

"Yeah…well…she has mentioned a few times, how I spend too much time at my apartment watching TV. She once suggested, I should go volunteer at the arboretum." In a mocking tone, he continued. "You should get a good look at some real vivid and stimulating colors and get away from the digital ones rotting your brain."

"Yeah, that sounds about right. However, she's just saying that because she cares about you."

"I know."

"Dana has always made it a point to enjoy the simpler aspects of life, but it has been more pronounced lately. I think because Kim and JR are getting older, she is becoming more aggressive in trying to instill this quality in both of them."

"In an age of video games, digital music players, tablet computers, and cell phones, it is very difficult to keep kids on track with school and different activities. From what I can see, you and Dana have done a terrific job keeping Kim and JR engaged with their schoolwork."

"Dana deserves all the credit for that. She has been taking them to places like the aquarium, parks, and the new zoo. She constantly teaches them that all of their gadgets and gizmos are no substitute for the natural beauty of the world going on around them. I don't watch nearly as much television anymore. Yet, when I do get a chance to watch a program, I barely get through a half-hour show before she has a hint for me to do something more constructive. She'll recommend that I take JR to the beach and fly a kite, recently it was take Kim to the museum, or take the kids to that farm store in the rural part of the county."

"Oh is that…"

"Yep. The same one my grandfather used to take me to. I'll pick up some fresh fruit and a jar of that apple butter we like so much when we trek out there. I follow her instructions, not only to avoid an argument, but this does allow me to fully enjoy my time with my children."

"That's great Jonny. I know I say this a lot, but…I hope I can have a family like yours someday."

"I'm sure you will."

"I'm real excited about going out with Suzie."

"I know you are. The entire department is happy for you. Just do me a favor, let her drive and handle all of the beverages."

"Whatever."

They both started to chuckle.

Jonathon and Adam had been close friends for years. It was almost like they were long lost brothers. Adam was an only child. His mother died when he started high school and his father died shortly after he graduated. It was a very difficult time for him and it left him isolated and alone. This void in his life is what prompted him to join the police department. He had hoped by serving the citizens of Gulfside City, he would have a sense of belonging.

The first day of training, he met Jonathon and the two formed an instant friendship. Jonathon, Dana, and the kids accept Adam as a member of the family. Adam was never bitter. He embraced the challenges in his life and was very thankful for his surrogate kin. Adam could see Jonathon would always watch out for him and Jonathon could count on Adam always having his back. It was not a common practice in the department for close friends to work directly together in a supervisor and subordinate position, but because they always worked so well with each other, this fact was never an issue and overlooked. They both had the same amount of time in, yet had different goals. All Adam wanted to do was work patrol. It is what he liked, it was what he was very good at, and to date, he had won more awards and citations of service than any other officer in the history of the department. At the behest of Jonathon, Adam took and easily passed the tests for advancement in the department. Adam qualified for the rank of lieutenant, same as Jonathon, but had turned down the official position. Jonathon, on the other hand, had it in his mind he was going to be chief someday. The two recognized from the beginning they both had their respective strengths and weaknesses. This understanding long ago had allowed them to thrive and succeed in both their duty together and friendship.

"Hey, Jonny, look."

"Yeah, it looks like a little lover's quarrel."

Jonathon and Adam passed by a man and a woman in an obvious verbal disagreement. She appeared to be in distress, but at a distance they were not able to determine for sure. Jonathon slowed down and Adam grabbed the communication radio receiver.

Adam raised the device to his mouth. "Dispatch, this is unit 14, we are responding to a domestic dispute on the north side of the roundabout section of Colorado Street at the 2500 block of Ringling."

"10-4, 14. We are sending another unit your way."

CHAPTER THIRTEEN

THE CHASE

By now, the sun had set and it was dark. The faint glow of nearby streetlights shone onto the roadway. Adam and Jonathon were standing at the rear of their patrol car as there backup left the scene.

"Those two were unbelievable," Jonathon said.

"Good call on arresting them both."

"Yeah it was for their own safety. Hopefully once they cool off, they'll be more civil."

"It was nice of Ricky to take them in for us."

"Yes it was. Let's get back out there and see what else we can find."

"You got it, Jonny."

Adam split away from Jonathon as they scrambled to their respective sides of the car. Jonathon paused, then stood for a moment, and faced downtown Gulfside City. Gazing at what skyline he could see, he then looked farther up at the clear night sky, thinking about Dana. He normally did not mind working this part of the shift rotation, but tonight he despised it. Every six months for three months, everyone in the patrol division was required to work a night shift. During this interval, he did not get to spend much time with his family. This is when Jonathon felt the most detached from his kids. For the most part, when he was asleep, they were awake. When he was awake they were asleep. Between all of the schedules, it was challenging enough. To add to the difficulty, if he had to appear in court for any sort of testimony, it was on his time in addition to his shift time.

If his kids got scared in the middle of the night, he was not there to protect them. Sure Dana was there, but that was not the point. His cause to be a police officer was one he never regretted, but one effect was the time he had to spend away from his loved ones. He generally comforted himself by whispering out loud, "I am making the world a better place for my children." But, for some reason, it was not working tonight. He felt so alone, too. This was nothing new either, but more than usual, and he did not know why.

"Hey, you okay out there?" Adam asked through the slightly open driver's window.

"Yeah…sorry. I was just taking a moment for myself."

About to open his door, something beyond in the darkness caught his attention. He believed he was seeing a human figure prowling about near one of the homes in the adjacent neighborhood.

Jonathon softly spoke. "Hey, two o'clock."

Adam peered out the window in the direction Jonathon indicated and quietly replied, "Could be one of our prowlers."

"I don't want to shine a light over there. He…she…it may take off."

"Good idea. We maybe can sneak up on him and grab him before he can react. This could be the break we've needed. We have not been able to get a physical sighting."

Jonathon waved his hand back and motioned for Adam to come back over by him. Adam, wasting no time, reached over to the center console and pushed a button to disable the interior light. Carefully opening the car, he gently swung his feet onto the ground. Gently closing the door, he glided along the car over to Jonathon. Jonathon kept an eye on the mystery figure. It seemed to be oblivious to their presence as it scurried across the nearby side street to a house directly in front of them, visible from the far end of the roundabout. It started to slowly circle the house, almost appearing to study the structure. Adam moved closer to Jonathon, and they both watched the body move to the side of the dwelling, where it paused.

At this time several cars were approaching, but this did not seem to scare it off. The cars, staying on Ringling, passed by unabated. Once the commotion ceased, it continued on, to the rear of the house.

"Weird," commented Adam.

"Okay, we're going to try a long shot. I want you to take the car about two streets over."

"Davis street?" Adam asked.

"That should be fine. I'm going to get as close to him as I can. If he runs off, I will try and flush him to you. Hopefully we can try and corner him. If I catch him, then you can just come back to assist me.

Use the screen in the car to track the satellite signal in my radio. Try and position yourself straight ahead of me if you can. I hope he will run straight into you, if it comes to that. Switch your uniform radio to channel three. This way you and I can talk with each other. Channel three will also relay our conversation to dispatch."

"What if he doesn't run straight?'

"We probably should get some help. We'd better hurry, though. He's moving to another house."

Jonathon reached up and removed his wireless radio receiver from a clip on the upper part of his uniform. Quietly opening the driver door, he slipped his hand into a small compartment in the dashboard. Seizing a wireless earpiece, he knelt down beside the cruiser, pushing a button on the earpiece and sticking it in his ear. Holding the receiver close to his mouth and softly speaking into it he said, "Dispatch this is Lieutenant Scott with unit 14. Stance and I are still on 2500 Ringling with a possible prowler sighting in the Ringling Oaks subdivision. We are about to pursue, however, please send units to assist and coordinate with Stance on unit 14's radio."

"10-4 Lieutenant."

Jonathon stood back up. "They're going to send some backup to you. Direct them wherever you need them."

Adam circled around Jonathon and seated himself inside the car.

"Start the car on the hybrid battery motor," Jonathon continued.

"Oh, good idea, it makes very little noise."

"Okay, here I go. Good Luck."

"You too."

Jonathon reattached the receiver to his uniform shirt and hurried toward the prowler but not too much, so he could us as much stealth as possible. The figure moved farther in, but was still close enough to currently be seen from the road. Adam drove away, keeping the headlights off to be as inconspicuous as possible. Jonathon kept a watchful eye on the prowler and considered crawling up to it, but decided against not to. If for some reason it attacked, he would be in a vulnerable position. Jonathon quietly hiked up to the yard it just vacated and hid behind the neighboring house, peeking around the corner. He could see nothing out of the ordinary, other than it circling around the side of the house visible from his vantage point. Clearly finished, it quickly flowed into the next yard.

With a silent pace, Jonathon inched into the next door yard it vacated, keeping close to the house and slithering along its outer wall. Stopping at the corner bordering the adjacent residence, Jonathon was more exposed this way, but could get a better view of the interloper. It must have still been unaware of Jonathon's presence as it still proceeded about its course without delay. All of sudden, though, it paused. It was positioned near what appeared to be an electricity meter panel on the side of the house. It reached up to the panel, then snapped it back, resuming motion onto the next house.

With the area clear, Jonathon tiptoed up to the electric meter to get a look at it. Other than the ambient lighting from the streetlights, it was too dark for him to see if anything had been altered.

"Jonny I'm in position, I'm ready when you are," Jonathon heard in his earpiece.

Jonathon did not respond, fearing the prowler would hear him. He knew Adam was tracking him and the need for quiet. Jonathon continued his pursuit of the mystery guest, slinking over to the next yard. Maneuvering himself into another risky viewing position, he found the human figure at the next home's power meter. Again, it reached for it, then pulled back. Done with its task, the shadow now advanced to the next house.

Okay, that's enough. I don't know what the deal is with the panels, but I do not want to give the prowler any more opportunities to continue. Once captured, we can investigate this further, he thought.

Jonathon silently passed it and jogged to the house to what he thought was the next domicile on the intruder's course. He was going to wait for the silhouette to come to him, positioning himself to where it would not see him until it was too late.

The figure, now done with its current house, progressed to Jonathon's. Jonathon waited on the east side of the yard and next to the meter, while the prowler moved onto the west side of the property. Jonathon inched to the southeast corner and waited just before the edge. The prowler circled around the corner and Jonathon stepped in to apprehend it. The shadow quickly noticed him, turned about and took off running straight ahead.

Jonathon chasing after it yelled, "Police! Stop!"

It kept running unfazed. Jonathon, no slouch when it came to running, was having difficulty keeping pace with the prowler. A track star in high school and deemed the department's fastest runner, he was falling rapidly behind this incredibly quick prowler. Jonathon made it to the next block of houses and barely could see the figure now, but could see it was already at the next street down.

"Adam, it's coming for you," Jonathon said.

"I see him…Shit! He just jumped over the car," Adam radioed.

Jonathon approached Adam's former position, as Adam was back in the car speeding off, quickly turning south on the cross street. Jonathon maintained his foot pursuit.

"Jonny, Buchman is another street down. He is going to see if he can flush him back to either you or I."

Jonathon slowed down to catch his breath, concerned with what he witnessed so far. *Who is he?* he wondered. *His speed...his agility."*

"Buchman forced him back to me, I'm moving to intercept. I may have to send him back your way."

Jonathon stopped completely to further recoup, wanting to be ready. *Maybe I can try in force it back to Adam and Buchman, hopefully trapping it at that point,* he thought.

The prowler came back at him, and Jonathon started yelling and screaming while charging at it. It worked. It was now running south again and towards Adam.

"He's running back to you Adam," Jonathon said.

The prowler, with a commanding lead, ran through the dividing yard ahead, quickly veering east as it made it to the next street. Jonathon chugged along and entered the side yards in front of him, when all of a sudden he heard something hit the ground.

"Got him!" Adam exclaimed victoriously.

Jonathon passed through to the subsequent front yard and noticing Adam sitting on the body.

"Jonny, I stunned him!"

"Great Job!" Jonathon reached the two and quickly removed his handcuffs from his belt. Kneeling down on one knee, he bent over, handcuffing the now apparent ordinary man. Other than smelling very bad, there so far seemed nothing unusual about him.

"Oh, now you don't resist," Jonathon stated in frustration as he fastened the cuffs on the man's wrists behind his back.

Adam was still on top of the man. "Whew, buddy you stink."

With all of the commotion, some people started to come out of their homes.

"He's cuffed," Jonathon said.

Adam removed the front section of the stun weapon and placed it on the ground as he stood up. Jonathon stayed on the ground and further secured their prisoner. Adam returned the stun gun to his belt and vacillated in the general direction of the homes.

"Folks, please go back inside for your safety," Adam said.

Some complied and some did not. Adam turned to the street, to see headlights of an approaching car, "Oh good. That's Buchman."

"Adam, he's not moving...at all," Jonathon stated with concern.

"You're right."

"Call for a medical unit. Then run over to Buchman and come back with a flashlight."

Adam complied, speaking into his radio and ran over to Buchman at the edge of the yard. Jonathon removed the stun gun probe from the man's back and set it on the ground next to him. Placing his index and middle fingers on the man's wrist, he could feel a pulse. He also determined the man was breathing normally.

Jonathon was relieved, but still was concerned. “Hey, buddy. Can you hear me? Wiggle your fingers or something.” There was no response whatsoever.

Adam came back with the flashlight. “How’s he doing?”

“I don’t know. He’s breathing and got a pulse…which is good, but he is not responding to my verbal commands.”

“He could just be giving us a problem.”

“Yeah, that’s possible. Let’s get him on his back.”

Adam moved closer to the man’s side, opposite Jonathon. Both in position, they carefully flipped the man over. Adam switched the flashlight on, and shone it at the man’s face. His eyes were wide open, not squinting or even blinking.

“Jonny what’s going on here?” Adam asked.

“Where’s medical?”

At that moment, they heard sirens in the distance.

“That’s probably them, Jonny,” replied Adam

Buchman walked up and next Jonathon. Adam diverted the light away from the man’s face and directed the beam to the man’s chest and abdomen. More and more people were coming out of their homes, advancing onto the scene.

“Buchman, get these people away from us,” Jonathon ordered. “They’re making me nervous.”

“Sure thing,” Buchman said.

He strolled towards the residents and began to work crowd control. Two officers hovering over a person in the middle of a yard was not a common sight in Gulfside City. The siren noise was getting louder.

“Should we give him CPR?” Adam asked.

“I don’t think so. He’s breathing normal and has a pulse. I don’t know what else to do.”

Jonathon waved his hand over the man’s face, snapping his fingers a few times in front of the man’s eyes, eliciting no response. The medical unit drove up and parked head to head with Buchman’s car. Two paramedics exited their vehicle. They swiftly retrieved some gear from the truck and advanced up the lawn to the hovering officers. Jonathon and Adam stood up and stepped back.

“Hey, Jonny, what’s going on here?” asked one of the arriving men.

“Artie, we chased this man throughout this neighborhood. We incapacitated him with the stun gun and as far as I can tell, he is breathing and has a pulse, but he is unresponsive.”

“Let’s get a look.” The other medic, holding a light, switched it on then rose it up a bit. This light provided better overall illumination than Adam’s flashlight. Adam stepped further out of the way, keeping the flashlight shining at the motionless man's chest.

"Wow, this is a smelly one," Artie commented. Bending down, he set a portable medical case on the ground next to him. Opening his kit, he removed out a pair of rubber gloves, sliding them on. He then selected a stethoscope and inserted the earpieces into his ears. Placing the circular probe on the man's chest, Artie moved it several places on his chest. With no expression, he lifted the probe and took out the earpieces. Laying the stethoscope back into the holder, he then selected a small flashlight and tongue depressor. Removing the wrapper, he placed the sterile stick in the man's mouth and shone his light into the same area. Moving the light around, he then moved the depressor further in and then quickly removed it from the man's orifice. Placing both objects on the ground, he looked up at Jonathon.

"This is real weird, Jonny," Artie said. "I shoved the thing far enough into his mouth to gag him and nothing. His heart is beating strong and normal and he is breathing normal. I checked his throat to see if there were any obstructions and it is clear."

Artie glanced back at the man and moved one of his hands in front of the man's face, near his eyes. Lowering his hand, he placed it over the man's lifeless eyes. Gently swiping his hand down to close the eyelids, Artie moved his hand out of the way and the man's eyes reopened. Artie, shaking his head, picked up his small flashlight, and vacillated the beam into the man's eyes.

"No blinking, no squinting, or even full closure," said Artie, with a curious tone.

Leaning in a little farther, he momentarily examined the lit eyes a bit further. Backing off, he removed the light.

"His eyes have normal dilation for the amount of light we're throwing at him, but no reaction to any other stimuli."

Switching off the light, he packed it into the kit, along with the rest of his belongings and refuse. Closing the case, he picked it up as he stood up. Artie glanced over to his colleague.

"Let's take him in, Joe. I do think we'll have the doc get a look at him," Artie said. "I think he's okay, but when we get him in the truck, let's get his vitals."

Joe switched the light off and headed back to the ambulance with it.

Jonathon, moving to Artie, asked, "Could he be just screwing with us?"

"If he his, he's damn good."

Artie faced the ambulance and strolled down to it. Placing his gear back into its compartment, he then moved to the rear to assist his partner. Rolling a stretcher out the rear of the ambulance, Joe pushed a button allowing wheeled legs to release as he pulled it from the van. He set a small manual brake with his foot. Artie at the front of it, pressed another button, freeing the upper bed from the lower supports. With Joe at the rear, they carried the bed up the lawn.

The paramedics lined the bed next to and parallel with the man, and bent down at the knee. The two set the stretcher on the ground, unbuckled the safety restraints and straps, and then scooted over to their respective ends of the man. Jonathon and Adam stepped even farther back, to give them ample room to do their job.

Hey could one of you help us for a moment?" Artie requested.

Adam immediately volunteered. "Sure."

Positioning himself on the side of the man opposite the stretcher, he bent down at the knee to match the other two.

"Before we move him on the stretcher, were going to turn him a bit so you can get the cuffs off of him," Artie said. "We will secure him in the stretcher."

Adam nodded, quickly retrieving his handcuff key from his belt. The two medics subsequently turned the man slightly on his side. Adam swooped in, and removed the cuffs. The man's arms did not move with gravity.

"His arms should of fallen," Artie commented.

Adam scowled at the man. "What's going on here, buddy?"

Adam returned the key back to his belt and placed the cuffs on the ground. He wrapped his hands around the man's wrists, separating them a bit. Adam then released them and they still did not move.

Artie was somewhat frustrated. "We'll adjust them as we get him on the stretcher," he said.

The medics gently rolled him on his back while Adam, again grabbed the man's arms, maneuvering them around and placing them on his abdomen.

"Thank you," Artie said.

"Of course."

Adam picked up the pair of handcuffs and then stood up. Jonathon moved over to Adam and retrieved his handcuffs. Folding them up, he placed them back into the holder on the rear of his belt.

Artie stated to Joe, "One…two…three."

The men stood up part way and smoothly shifted the motionless prowler onto the stretcher. Artie and Joe wrapped restraints over the man's chest and legs, fully securing him.

"He's not going anywhere now," Artie noted.

Releasing their hold, they both clasped the handle grips of the stretcher at their ends, lifting it upward. Joe carefully moved backward to the ambulance as Artie guided them. Stopping at the rear, they set the bed onto the support housing and locked the bed into place.

The medics loaded the man into the rear of the ambulance. Joe hopped inside, making sure everything was secure.

"You good to go?" Artie asked.

Joe gave Artie a thumbs up and sat down on a narrow bench seat lining partway up the interior side wall of the truck. Artie closed and secured the two rear doors and started walking back toward the officers. Adam picked up his stun gun magazine, and carefully wrapped up the probe.

"The car is around the block," Adam said. "I'm going to go get it."

Jonathon nodded and Adam started jogging away.

Artie approached Jonathon. "Do I need an intake report?"

"Yes. I'm going to have him booked. As soon as Adam comes back, we're going to drive over there. I'll write the report then. Plus, I'm curious to see what is going on with this guy."

"Yeah, me too. This whole thing is bizarre."

"Yeah, to say the least. Just from your expertise, could the jolt from the stun have done something?"

"It's possible, but I don't think so. I think he's okay, but I've never seen a reaction like this. Hopefully, the doc will figure it out."

"Who is the doc tonight?"

"Mayers."

"Oh great. He's going to give me an earful," Jonathon said, sarcastically.

"Yeah probably," Artie chuckled. "I'll see you at the infirmary."

"All right. See you over there."

Artie faced the ambulance and marched along the grassy yard. He opened the driver's door, pulled himself in and started the engine. After closing the door, the medical vehicle, with its emergency lights still flashing, slowly drove off.

Jonathon roamed over to Buchman, who was still talking to some of the residents. "Excuse me, but Adam and I are going over to the infirmary."

"Oh, are we done here?"

"Yeah. I've got to write up a report for this, so I might as well craft it up over there. Plus, I'm just curious as to what is going on with this guy."

"All right, Jonny. I'll finish talking with the residents here and then I'll get back on the road."

"Thanks for your help."

"No problem."

Buchman resumed his conversation with the curious bystanders.

Jonathon walked down to the street to wait for Adam. *What a weird night,* he thought.

Standing there, he faced downtown. His thoughts shifted back to Dana and the kids. He could not shake it. For some reason, he was having trouble keeping his mind off of them. Maybe it was because this was his first night back and he was just missing them more tonight. Or maybe this was his first night back after his close call and he was questioning his priorities. Again, Jonathon loved his job, but he loved his family, more. Generally the two had never clashed to a high degree, but that may have changed. He was getting older. His kids were getting older. And time…once it is gone it's gone.

Every now and then, he tossed the idea of going back to school to advance his criminal degree further to go onto something else, however there was that pesky time factor again. Between work and family, he barely had any free time as it was. To add to his dilemma, he had been recently offered a teaching job at the police academy. During the mayor's function, he was approached by the director of the academy and offered a job to become an instructor there. At first, he thought it was a joke, but a few days later a small package was delivered to him with detailed literature about the position. His current criminal degree and experience was enough to qualify him, but he would still have to go through a specialized training certification program to teach law enforcement procedures. This certification was a key requirement to be an instructor. He could still assist the other trainers with certain duties and functions until he earned that certification, which was conveniently offered by the academy. There would be always something to do.

The academy, which was administered by Gulfside City, was not just for Gulfside. It served as a training facility for about two dozen law enforcement agencies in the region. He enjoyed his life on patrol…but…he was not sure now. In the past, he would have rejected this gracious offer right away. However, he had not formally done so yet. The window for the position was waning though. This offer in question was a 9 to 5, Monday through Friday job. His weekday schedule would be much more in sync with his family's. Weekends and holidays would be a guarantee for family time. In addition, the prospective job was still technically with the city, but a different boss, different pay, and responsibilities. He would still have the same benefits and retirement plan.

Jonathon enjoyed being out in the community doing something different everyday, not cooped up inside for any length of time. Nevertheless, this freedom took him from his family quite often. Generally, Dana put on a good act and strong face, but she did worry about him especially now. He had not told her about the academy job. She, in her own creative way, would subtly hint for him to accept the offer.

I guess there is no harm in finding out more information, Jonathon thought. *I should gather all the facts and leave it at that for now.*

Jonathon shifted his attention to down the street as he noticed Adam approaching.

Driving up in front of Jonathon and speaking through the open window Adam said, "Sorry, that took so long. I was cornered by a curious citizen."

"No problem. Let's head over to the infirmary. I've got to write up an arrest report for our latest catch."

Jonathon stepped up to the passenger door and entered the car.

"I called everything in, but you should probably update dispatch with us going to the infirmary," Adam said.

"I will do so…wait."

Jonathon glanced at himself sitting in the passenger's seat. "Please. Get us there safely. I think I've had enough excitement for one night."

Adam chuckled. "Whatever."

He shifted the car into drive and drove away from the scene.

CHAPTER FOURTEEN
AN ODD DISCOVERY

A joint venture between the municipality and the sheriff's department allowed the creation of a full service medical and surgical hospital inside the jail. This infirmary was not a public hospital. It served the medical needs of the county's prisoners and detainees. It also served as a clinic for county and city workers, department and law enforcement staff, and any other public servants. Minor ailments, on most days, could be treated without an appointment. More complex issues, such as surgery, were by appointment only and would depend on the service load for that day. This worked out great for anyone working a late or night shift. The infirmary, like an emergency room, was always open.

This dedicated facility eliminated the need to transport a prisoner to a general civilian hospital in case of illness, to assign an officer to guard said prisoner, and allowed costs to be managed in house. Plus, this medical staff was specifically trained to render aid to even the most difficult of patients. They could still have a pleasant bedside manner and be concerned with making them comfortable. On the other hand, if a detained patient became belligerent, their extended training provided them the ability to subdue and control this behavior and allowed them to do their jobs without delay.

One of the physicians working here was a good friend of Jonathon's. They met in high school, but had different career paths afterwards. Jonathon, of course, was interested in law enforcement. He joined the department and went to school for criminology. Jason Mayers, in contrast, had an intense love of biology, anatomy, and general science as a whole, but did not know what he wanted to do with that. When he started college, he never had thought about becoming a medical doctor. In his first semester, one of his professors was a retired physician who decided to teach. Jason and this professor, at first, did not see eye to eye on a lot of things. Yet, as the semester went on, Jason came to respect his educator and the teacher became quite fond of his student.

At the end of the school year, Jason's professor was extremely impressed with how dedicated Jason was to his studies. He volunteered his time to help and assist Jason with whatever questions or difficulties he may have had. Jason often overloaded his school schedule. He worked and studied hard with his schoolwork and moved at an accelerated rate. As time went on, upon earning graduate and postgraduate degrees and at the urging of his now mentor, he decided to go to medical school. With his mentor's help, he graduated at the top of his class.

Jonathon and Jason talked and wrote regularly with each other over the years. Jonathon informed Jason, who happened to be looking for his first job, that the city was opening a new type of hospital. When Jason heard that Gulfside City was opening the infirmary at the jail, he soon thereafter submitted his resume. Jonathon, of course, put in a good word. Jason was the first interview on day one, and was hired on the spot.

Jason, who was now the chief doctor, was on staff tonight and just finished examining one of the biggest challenges of his career. After finishing another, but brief, call, Adam and Jonathon walked into the main booking lobby, a section that was accessible to the public, but not prisoners.

"Adam why don't we take our meal break now," Jonathon said. "I want to go back and see what is going on with our guy."

"Sure. If you don't mind, I want to take the car and go to the diner down the street. I can bring you back something if you would like."

"Yeah, that sounds good."

"Anything in particular?"

Jonathon shrugged his shoulders. "Nope. Surprise me."

"All right. I'll update our status with dispatch. See you later, Jonny."

"Bye, Adam."

Adam turned and went back out the access door. Jonathon proceeded up to the booking desk and filed his arrest report with one of the booking officers.

"Ah, this must be for our John Doe," stated the sergeant.

The sergeant hunched over and began to write in a log book. Jason then came storming out to the lobby to greet Jonathon. The two shook hands.

"Jonny, what in the world did you bring me?" Jason asked.

"Good to see you too, Jay."

"You know, it was a quiet and peaceful night until your latest work came in."

"Well, I've got to keep things interesting for you."

Jason smiled. "Yeah thanks. Come back with me, Artie told me you wanted to know what was going on with this guy."

The two walked toward the infirmary.

"Did you find something out?" Jonathon asked.

Jason did not answer right away. He indicated he would answer in a minute. They reached the entrance to the infirmary. Jason pulled out an access card and swiped it through a reader on the wall. The doors opened inward and the two proceed through. As they walked passed the nurses' station just on the inside of the entryway, the doors closed behind them. Jason stopped the both of them at the end of the now vacant station.

"I would not openly tell anybody this, but I don't know what is going on with this guy. So far, the few tests I have run, show all his body functions as normal. Yet, he's not responsive to any external stimuli. It's as if the lights are on but nobody's home. The only other oddities are some weird scars, possibly surgical incisions, all over his body. I'm also trying to figure those out."

"Jay, before we took him down, I had trouble keeping up with him. Adam said that he jumped over the car. He was very active until Adam zapped him. Could the stun have anything to do with that?"

"If something were physically visible I would say yes. There is nothing physically wrong with him, other than the smell. So at this point, I would have to say no. I've got one of the technicians running an MRI on him now and then we are going to test for brainwave activity. Thanks to some grants, we just got new equipment in here. These tests won't be long. How are you doing? I haven't talked to you much since what happened at the museum."

"I've been okay. I ended up going to that fundraiser dinner I was telling you about."

"Oh, really. Let me guess, Dana pushed you."

"Yeah, something like that."

"Oh, so you are now Mr. Big Shot, huh?"

"It's nothing like that, you know I hate all of this attention."

"Yeah, I know. I've just got to give you a hard time. How is Dana doing with all of this?"

"She, for the most part, is all right. She has broken down a couple of times, but overall she seems to be handling it well. Far better than I am."

"You just said you were doing okay."

"Yeah, I say that. But, I'm having trouble moving past this. I've been thinking about Dana and the kids a lot tonight. Not that I didn't before, but it's different now."

"Well, I think that's to be expected. You just think about the people who bring you comfort."

"It's more than that. While I was on leave, I got a taste of what it was like to spend some real time with my family. Breakfast, lunch on the weekends, dinner, and of course all the time in between."

"I know you love your job and all, but I told you long ago that family and career would butt heads eventually."

"You're right. I hate to admit it. I haven't told Dana this…I have been offered an instructor's position at the academy."

"Oh, Jonny, that's great."

"Well, I haven't responded yet. In fact, I don't know if it's still available. I'm going to look into it though, but I'm still on the fence about it."

"Since I have known you, being a police officer is all I ever heard out of you. You've done it for a long time…much longer than I have been a physician. If you are having second thoughts about continuing, it is probably time for a change. I know you love your job, but I suspect you love your family more."

"Of course I love them more."

"Then what more is there to think about?"

"Well my grandfather…"

"Jonny, your grandfather is an awesome man. I am sure he is very proud of you and would want you to spend more time with your family. Didn't he do that for you?"

Jonathon thought about it for a moment. "You're exactly right, Jay. I can't believe I had forgotten that. Life just takes hold of you sometimes and you forget about the most special things."

Jason patted Jonathon on the shoulder. "I know you will make the right decision. Does Adam know about any of this?"

"No he doesn't and I'm not sure how he would react."

"He is a good friend. He'll support you no matter what."

"You've got to tell him and Dana."

"Like I said, I'm going to check further into this. I want to get more info and details before I make any decisions or tell anyone for that matter. There is no sense in getting everyone worked up if I decide not to take the job."

"You'll take it."

A technician approached Jason. "Doctor we've got some results on John Doe."

"Oh, terrific, Stewart. Jonny come back with me. I may have some more questions for you."

All three individuals walked farther back into the infirmary. They entered into the MRI room and went up to the restrained and unresponsive patient. John Doe was undressed and covered with a blanket up to his waist. The motionless man was still on the MRI table, but was completely out of the scanning apparatus. They were standing on one side of the table at around his feet. The tech went across the room, picked up a medical chart, walked back to Jason, and handed it to him.

As Jason read the reports, he showed no facial movement or emotion as he read. He then walked behind the glass wall of the observation and control area for the MRI machine. Stewart followed. Jason sat down at a computer terminal and started looking at the screen. Jonathon could hear various mouse clicks. He surmised that Jason was looking at the MRI images. Stewart was moving about in the control area and appeared to be shutting off lights except were Jason was sitting. Stewart came out of the control area, then left the room.

Jonathon moved around the table to get a better view of the John Doe. He really never got a full and complete look of him outside in the dark with partial light. It was very bright in this room. Mr. Doe appeared to be an average man, except he had several scars on his shaved chest, torso, and arms. Jonathon briefly lifted the blanket around John's legs and found some scars on them as well. It looked like someone had at one point shaved in and around those areas too. The man appeared to be in his thirties and did not have a muscle tone consistent with his ability to run and jump the way he did. His hair was somewhat long. It looked to cover the rear of his neck. With this guy lying on his back though, Jonathon couldn't be sure.

"What in the world is going on here?" Jason exclaimed.

"What is it?" Jonathon asked.

"Come over here and take a look at this."

Jonathon hurried across the room and into the control area with Jason. He looked over Jason's shoulder. Jason was still clicking through images and looking at the screen.

"Those scars all over his body are definitely surgical incision points. According to these images, there appears to be objects of some kind that were inserted at every one of those points in his body."

While clicking through multiple images, he pointed to several examples for Jonathon to see.

Jason turned and looked up at Jonathon. "I have no idea what these things are and that concerns me." He turned back toward the screen and resumed view the images.

"Do you have any guesses?" Jonathon asked.

"Nope not a single one."

Jonathon could see Jason was getting agitated. He was not sure though if it was because it was something he didn't understand or that this was really getting more and more strange.

Jason stopped on another image and pointed to a section of it, again with agitation. "What is this now?"

"What is it Jay? What's going on?"

Jason was still looking and pointing at the screen. "There appears to be something on the back of his neck…and it looks like it might be externally visible." Jason turned to Jonathon. "I physically examined him when they brought him in here. I did not see anything out of the ordinary."

"Do you want to get another look?"

"Yes. Do you mind helping me?"

"Of course not."

Jason got up from the chair and the two walked out from behind the wall and headed back over to the motionless man. Jason, on the way, took possession of a wheelchair that was in the room.

As Jason and Jonathon were placing the man into the chair, they discovered John had no tendency to fall. It was as if he was balancing himself with every move. Jason gently pushed John's chest and Jonathon helped guide the man into the wheelchair. The man, with the help of the two, voluntarily assumed the sitting position. With the man safe in the chair, the two let go of him. Jason placed his arms on the armrests, then knelt down, swinging the foot supports of the wheelchair down, pulled and maneuvered the man's feet up off the floor, and rested them on the supports.

"For someone who is supposed to be unresponsive, he made that easy for us," Jason said. He then moved behind the chair. "I want to get a good look at the back of his neck."

Standing behind the man, Jason placed his hand on the man's head and gently pushed it down. Jason looked down at John Doe's neck. Jonathon angled himself to get a peek too.

"There's nothing here," commented Jason.

Jason then began to examine the area more closely by tapping certain areas. He moved up the neck region into the hairline. He continued tapping until he hit something hard. "What in the world?"

"Is there something under his hair?" asked Jonathon.

"I think so. Can you lift some of it out of the way?"

"Sure."

Jonathon moved in a little, placed his hand in the man's hair, and lifted up. "I feel something too."

Jason looked down. "What is that?"

Jonathon looked closer at it, too. "It looks imbedded into his neck."

Jason reached into his coat pocket and pulled out a small flashlight. "Don't move, Jonny."

Jason turned the light on and shone it at the object. It was small and square shaped, protruding slightly out of his neck. "It looks like it was surgically implanted. But, it doesn't look anything like any medical device to me. It looks like it could be connected directly to the brain stem. I'll have to look at the MRI images more closely. I might have to do some more imaging, specifically on these areas with the scars."

"What would be the purpose for this thing or things?"

"I'm not sure. I have never seen surgical devices or implants in these locations before. If this one is attached to the brain somehow, it is far more advanced than any surgical procedure I've ever seen. It's very likely that whatever these objects are inside of him might all be connected together. I need to study this further."

"Do you need anything else from me? I've got to get back out on the road."

"No, but I know how to get a hold of you if I do."

"Before I leave, I'm going to have one of the booking techs come in here and get his fingerprints. It would be nice to know who he is. Maybe, that might help answer some questions."

"What if there are no records found for him?"

"We'll hope that won't be a problem. Most fingerprints in the database are collected when most individuals are or were children. This is usually done to make it easier to locate and identify a lost child. As you know a fingerprint, for the most part, does not change. We, at the least, have a person's basic information on file for as long as it is needed. How long do you think you'll need to study this?"

"I don't know. I'll let you know when I find out more."

"All right. See you later, Jay."

"Bye Jonny, thanks for all of this," he replied, with sarcasm.

Jonathon smiled as he left the room.

CHAPTER FIFTEEN

A SPECIAL PLACE

Jonathon drove Adam to his apartment at the end of their shift. They put in some extra hours to help with coverage. The morning light, with reds, oranges, and blues was already replacing the night sky.

"Hey, do you want to get a bite later today?"

"I was thinking of going by the school today and having lunch with Dana and the kids. I really missed them during the night."

"Oh, okay. Say hi to everyone for me."

"Yeah, will do. Have a good day."

Adam swung the car door to close it, but stopped it partway. He reopened it and leaned into the car. "Is everything all right, Jonny? You've been somewhat reserved since I picked you up from the jail."

"Oh, this thing with the prowler has me unnerved a little." That was not what was bothering Jonathon. He, of course, did not want to tell Adam just yet that he was thinking about going to the academy. He was not sure when or how he was going to tell him.

"Yeah, from what you told me, those things in his body do sound creepy. Don't worry about him. He's not going anywhere now, especially in his current state."

"Yeah, I know, it's still weird."

"See you later, Jonny. Get some rest."

Adam, with a smirk on his face, shut the car door and proceeded to stroll up the walkway to the stairs to his apartment. Jonathon shifted the car into drive and went toward home.

Jonathon's house was a short way from Adam's. Just from the little amount of time he was at Adam's, the sky had become brighter.

After leaving Adam's complex, it was a quick drive over the causeway bridge. For the most part, the only real turn he had to make was the one into his neighborhood. As Jonathon drove, he was tossing the idea of getting some sleep before he went to the school. He then thought about maybe tackling some of the items on his honey-do list. His thoughts then shifted to what he was going to do for the next few days.

As it happened to be, he and Adam had the next three days off. This was great for Jonathon only one night back to work and he was due for time off. Adam always liked to do something when they had time off together, but all Jonathon wanted to do was spend as much time as he could with Dana, Kim and JR.

He drove into his driveway and put the car into park. He reached into his pocket and pulled out his personal set of keys. He had a small remote control for the garage door on the ring. He held the device up and pushed the open button. The door slowly opened. *Damn, I missed them,* he thought.

Jonathon's car was there, but Dana's van was gone. They had all left for school already. Jonathon was not in the mood to walk into an empty house.

He sat in his cruiser for a moment, contemplating what he was going to do. Was he going to suck it up, go inside, and go to sleep, or tackle that list? No. His mind was racing too much to sleep and the list, "Yeah…right." He pushed the close button on his remote, watched the garage door travel down to the ground, and shifted the car into reverse. He pulled back out onto the street, shifted the car into drive, and drove away from his house.

He decided he was going to the beach. The specific beach he had in mind was about two miles away from his house and was a straight drive over a another smaller bridge and through Merchant's Circle, a large roundabout housing a business and tourist area. Jonathon was going to go for a quick walk to help clear his head. When Jonathon was a child, his grandfather would take him to this same spot every time they went. Jonathon would build his sand castles, dig holes until he found water, or bury his grandfather in the sand up to his head. Jonathon liked to go to this place as well, to think, when he had had a rough day. He also brought Kim and JR there, too. It was a rewarding experience for him to share and build new memories with his own children. He hoped that someday Kim and JR would bring their children there as well.

Approaching a cross street exit, he followed the curve toward his beach. Now at the last intersection just before the shoreline, he could see beach goers and lifeguards making their way to the powdery sands past the motels and hotels lining the coast. Left or right was his only option at this point, so without hesitation, Jonathon veered to the right, maneuvering his way down a small access parking lot, the same one he and his grandfather went down. Not much had changed on this very narrow strip of road over the years.

After removing his uniform shirt, shoes, and gear, he was left with an undershirt and his pants. It was about fifty feet until the actual beach. The path was burrowed through some trees and natural foliage.

Jonathon remembered being so excited when his grandfather held his hand walking him out onto that pristine shore. Of course, when Jonathon was older he became aware of the fact his grandfather was also a pack mule carrying a cooler, blankets, a pail and shovel, and any other toys young Jonathon wanted out there with him.

Jonathon emerged from the path and gazed out along the vast sandy beach that stretched out to the gulf water. The sand was clean and felt like powder on his feet.

He missed those times with his grandfather. His mother and grandfather moved away from Gulfside shortly after Dana gave birth to JR. Jonathon's mother was offered a new position with the company she worked for. It was her dream job, but in another country. After a quick thought, she did accept it. His grandfather went with her. Time had not been kind to him. He had become so frail, requiring a lot of assistance and care. Jonathon did offer to take him in and watch over him, but his mother felt that it would not be fair for either of them. Jonathon and Dana already had their hands full with their toddler and new infant. Jonathon was working crazy hours, and Dana was getting her teaching degree. Jonathon's mother was concerned that his attention would be focused on his children, as she understood it should be, and there would not be enough time for her father. She knew that Jonathon was sincere in his offer, but probably did not realize all that was involved with caring for a partially disabled man. Part of her salary included a health support plan for parents needing aid. With this, someone would come and stay with him when he needed help or was alone for long periods for time. This meant she could keep him home with her. It just made better sense for him to go with her. Besides, he had to sacrifice for her bad choices in the past and was never really there for Jonathon. She wanted to do this for her father who helped her through the good times and the bad, and not interfere with Jonathon's life and family. It was as if she was returning the favor to her father and would be able to spend more time with him.

Jonathon talked to his grandfather on a regular basis and thanks to technology, he could see him, too, with video telephone and the Internet. His grandfather had been able to watch his great grandchildren grow up over the years. Dana sent pictures to him constantly, and Kim and JR talked to him too. Now that the kids are getting older, Dana and Jonathon decided for their family vacation next summer, they are going to fly overseas and visit him. When they told him that news, Jonathon's mother had trouble keeping him calm. She conveyed to Jonathon she had not seen him that excited about anything for a very long time. With his grandfather so far away, coming to the beach was Jonathon's way of being close to him.

As Jonathon walked, he began to think about the crossroad he had approached in his life. *Do I stay on the same path or take a new one?* He still was going to go with his intuition, find out more about the job and then decide.

Well, he thought, *today would be a good day to do it.*

Jonathon needed to figure this out. By delaying this further he was just going to drive himself nuts. The job may no longer be available and that would be that. Another possibility: It may not pay enough for Jonathon to meet his family's financial obligations. Then there was the scenario where the job would be available and it would pay enough, and he would be back to square one trying to decide. Yet, why was he having trouble with the decision? Maybe it was the museum? Maybe that was enough to unnerve him. Of course, a new job meant more time with family. Jonathon also considered the possibility he may not like the job after he took it. He was afraid he might regret his decision, then, as a likely consequence, start to resent his family because they were the reason why he made the change in the first place. This round and round was not productive.

Looking at his watch, he guessed that if he went to the academy from here, he would have a couple of hours open to talk to the operational director, ask around, and gather whatever information he needed. Depending on how long this took, he might even be able to take a shower there as well. Jonathon always kept a spare change of clothes in the car. After that, it would be time for him to go by the school for lunch. Jonathon felt a little better with having a plan. He was not sure how he was going to feel later, but at least he was doing something about this. He had about ten more minutes before he had to leave, so he continued to walk.

CHAPTER SIXTEEN

A MYSTERY MUST BE SOLVED

Jonathon had a wonderful lunch with his family. Kim talked about her dancing, JR showed pictures he drew in art class, Dana shared that the students in her class presented her with a "Thanks For Being A Great Teacher" award. He did not say anything to Dana about going to the academy. However, she had to throw in a subtle comment about them growing up so fast, and that he might miss a few things along the way. She was still making this hard for him.

It was going to be a few more hours until the end of the school day, so Jonathon stopped over by the jail on his way home to see if there was any new information about the prowler. He walked into the main lobby and was immediately summoned by the officer working the front desk.

Jonathon went up to him to see what was going on. "Lieutenant Scott, the doc has been trying to get a hold of you for the last couple of hours."

Jonathon realized he had left his radio in the trunk with his uniform shirt. He went into his pocket, retrieved his phone, and looked at the screen to find out he did not turn it on. Although he was off-duty, he thought it best not to draw attention to these minor oversights. The radio was off, but it goes into a standby mode that could be used as an alert pager to get a hold of someone in case of an emergency. All officers, including off-duty one's, were required to carry these at all times.

"Is everything okay?" replied Jonathon.

"Yes, the doc said he has some info for you. I'll buzz you in."

"Thank you."

As he entered the infirmary, a duty nurse approached him. "Jonny, Dr. Mayers has been looking for you. I'll take you back."

"Thanks Jenna. Did he ever go home?"

"I don't think so. He was here when I started my shift earlier this morning."

"Oh, that's Jay. When he gets onto something…"

"Here we are."

They arrived at Jason's office. She knocked on the door.

"Yes," Jason answered.

"Doctor, he's here."

After a few moments, the door opened. "Jonny, I've been trying to get a hold of you!" Jason exclaimed. "Thank you, Jenna."

"Sure thing, Doctor."

She turned and went back toward the nurses' station.

Jason motioned for Jonathon to enter. "Come in, please."

Jonathon walked into the room and went by Jason's desk. Jason closed the door behind them. His office included an examination area. The prowler was there, lying on his back on a mobile bed with an intravenous line in his arm.

"What's going on, Jay?" inquired Jonathon.

"I've found out some more things. First of all we have a name."

Jason walked over to his desk, picked up a file, and handed it to Jonathon.

Jonathon read and paraphrased the information out loud. "His name is Albert Stevens. Age 38. He was born here. He is currently listed as homeless with his last address at a residency about five years ago. He has no known family or next of kin. He has no felony arrests, but a few misdemeanors. Trespassing, open container, disorderly intoxication. All resulted in no convictions."

Jonathon handed the file back to Jason. Jason laid it back on the desk.

Jason faced Jonathon. "I ran his ID in the medical database and found no records for ever having surgery. Of course that doesn't mean he didn't have some back-alley procedures done. But, for someone who is homeless, how could he afford even that?"

"He could have had money at some point in his life."

"True, but it looks like these things were put into him only months ago."

"Were you able to ascertain what these objects are?"

"No. I took more MRIs, but all I can get are images of the outsides of the objects. Either these things are solid or the MRI just can't penetrate them. However, the devices appear to be connected to nerve pathways all over the body. The one in the neck is connected to the brain. Without knowing what their functions are, I don't know why they are in there and what they're for. For the heck of it, I called one of our information technology guys in here to see if he could determine what they might be. I had him examine the MRI images as well as the device sticking out on his neck. He said without being able to take the devices apart, there was no real way to make a determination. He couldn't even tell if these things are even on."

"Why not take one out?"

"Legally and morally I can't. He is alive. Other than being non-responsive and slightly dehydrated, he is in good health. Removing one could do some real harm or even kill him. Unfortunately, there is nothing more I can do with him in his present state."

"How long do you think he will live?"

"With the right care, years, even decades, I presume. He is breathing normally, but he needs to be fed through an intravenous needle."

"Okay, then this may seem like a stupid question, but what would happen if you took the IV out?"

"He would die from lack of nourishment."

"Ah. That is not an option then?"

"No. In some cases, if someone is on a respirator and if certain legal procedures are done, the respirator can be removed by the permission and direction of a family member or designated next of kin. The person will then die as a result. This can be done with an IV line for sustenance as well. However, he has no family or next of kin listed. Therefore, the process gets a little more tricky. Not to worry, I'm not giving up on him. I want to make him right again. This is a man's life here. Nonetheless, I'm limited to what I can do and I can't spend all my time on this. Yet, I don't like leaving a mystery unsolved. I know this is going to bug me."

"I know the feeling. It goes along with starting something and not finishing it. It was probably a year ago. JR has this remote control car that means the world to him. His favorite parts about it are the headlights. He just loves it how they light up every time he drives it. Then one day, the lights stopped working. Oh my, you thought it was the end of the world. So, out to the garage with it I go. I put it on my workbench and I took it apart. I replaced the bulbs. Nothing. I checked all of the connecting wires. They're fine. I must have spent hours on it. Of course, I want this thing to work for my son, but what was really chapping my ass was I couldn't figure out this problem. Dana came out a couple of times, hinting at me to stop and not obsess over this. I think I growled at her once. I did, eventually, stop. I convinced myself to get some sleep and continue fresh the next morning. That didn't really help. I laid awake half the night still thinking about it. When I did finally fall asleep, I ended up dreaming about cars and headlights. So yeah, I understand about leaving a mystery unsolved. Sorry, I went on a tangent."

"That's okay. Did you fix the lights?"

"Well, I decided to read the manual. I probably should have read it in the first place. I read that the battery has two sections to it. One part operates the motor and a smaller part works the lights. I never heard of something so ludicrous, but apparently it was not holding a charge. So, I go marching off to the store, buy a new battery, replace it in the car, and sure enough everything works fine. Mystery solved."

Jason gave Jonathon a thumbs up.

"The cool thing is he still plays with it to this day and with no problems," Jonathon proudly stated.

"Those remote control cars are neat." Jason added. "I bought Josh one for his birthday next week. I'm keeping it under my desk here. If I bring it home before then, he'll find it. He's a snooper. It doesn't have the lights, so I won't be tearing my hair out over that."

"Did you get a car or truck?" Jonathon asked.

"Here let me show you."

Jason bent down, reached under his desk, pulled the toy out, and placed it on the desk.

"Wow, it looks very much like your car right down to color," Jonathon said.

"Yeah, I thought that was neat. He's going to think that's cool, too. He'll have a car to match Daddy's. I saw it, picked up the box, and bought it without thinking."

"Jay, have you been playing with it?" Jonathon inquired with a smirk.

"Why do you say that?" Jason asked, his face turning bright red.

"Where's the box? You just said in came in a box."

"Well, you know, it's got all those twist ties and such. I didn't want to spend twenty minutes at his party trying to open it."

Jonathon just stared at Jason.

Jason gave in. "Okay, okay you got me. I took it for a little spin around the office here a couple a days ago."

"Uh huh. A doctor…really."

"I had to test it out for my son…to see…"

"It's okay, Jay. Your secret is safe with me."

"It's real nice. Plus, I bought a separate remote controller that has an indoor setting and an outdoor setting."

"What's the difference?"

"The settings control the speed. The controls are preprogrammed to allow it to go up to a certain speed indoors. The car, no matter how much juice you give it, does not have enough power to knock over or break anything. Switch it to outside mode, then the controls are a little more sensitive allowing the car to go very fast."

"So, this is what your research has revealed?"

"Hey, this could benefit you, too," Jason said with a red face again. "The controller has universal settings which can be used with most remote-controlled vehicles like JR's. Here, look."

Jason picked up the car, turned it on, and placed it on the floor. He then picked up the remote from the desk. He pushed a button on top of it to turn it on.

"I've got this on the indoor setting," he said.

Jason put his thumb on the controller stick to move the car. He pushed up and all of a sudden the unresponsive patient briefly jolted.

"What was that?" Jason asked.

"Jay, do that again."

Jason repeated this motion. Again, the man briefly jerked.

"I think I need to get the tech guys back in here," Jason said.

"Yeah, good idea."

CHAPTER SEVENTEEN

HE STANDS

It had been about an hour since Jason called the facility's information technology personnel. Jonathon removed himself from Jason's office to give everybody room to do their assessments. Jonathon was concerned. Reports of prowlers had come in from all over Gulfside City. A couple of them were from his neighbors. Was this the work of this one man or were there others out there just like him? There were no other prowler calls after they stopped this guy, so maybe the problem had been solved. Jonathon decided to phone in this update to the department. As he turned to go out the door, Jason came running out of the infirmary.

"Jonny!" Jason motioned for Jonathon to go back with him. "You've got to come look at this."

They hurried back to Jason's office. Upon entering, Jonathon immediately noticed Albert was standing.

"Is he awake?" Jonathon asked.

"No. Something in his body is giving him the ability to stand," stated an unknown male voice.

Jonathon turned to see who else was in the room. A man approached Jonathon and Jason.

"Jonny, this is Michael, our computer guy," Jason said.

Jonathon and Michael shook hands.

"Nice to meet you, Jonathon."

"Likewise, Michael."

"I know it's a little belated, but congratulations. I was at the ceremony where the mayor gave you your award."

"Well, thank you. It was an honor to receive it, but I was just doing my job. What's going on here?"

"When Dr. Mayers initially showed me his patient, I could not figure out what these devices were. With them inactive and no way to take them apart, I couldn't even make an educated guess. Now, that's changed."

"These devices are connected to the nerve impulses in his body," Jason said, turning toward Jonathon. "When I used the remote, the signal from it activated the devices and stimulated the nerves."

"Huh. What?" Jonathon sputtered with confusion.

"Jonathon, I don't know much about medicine, but I do know machines," Michael said. "From the way this guy is reacting to the controller, I think these devices are designed to receive communication signals. More specifically, the one on the neck is actually tasked with receiving the signals. It then transmits and relays its data to the rest of the devices."

"Let me see if I follow this," Jonathon said, still with confusion. "Are you saying he is being remote controlled?"

"In a sense, yes," Michael answered.

"Jonny, this somewhat makes sense to me," Jason added. "This type of biological and mechanical interaction has been done before, but with insects. As far as I know, this type of merging has never been done on a mammal at least this elaborate or on a human. The nerves are far more complex. This type of bioengineering is extremely advanced."

"Okay, okay," Jonathon said. "I'm not sure if I believe what either one of you is telling me, but why hasn't whoever or whatever is controlling him moved him out of here? Or away from the scene last night for that matter?"

"We've been trying to figure that one out, too, but until I can take something apart…I can't answer that right now. Maybe it has a limited range. Maybe him being indoors interferes with the signal. I don't know."

Jonathon looked directly at Jason. He seemed to be deep in thought at that moment.

"Jay, what is it?" Jonathon asked.

"You zapped him," Jason said. "You said Adam shocked him with the stun gun." The men continued to look at each other.

"I see where you're going with this doctor," Michael said. "A stun gun delivers a powerful burst of electricity designed to impair and disrupt the nerves. It is possible that it disrupted the connection from the devices to the nerves in his body, vice versa, or it damaged the transmitter's ability to receive the master signal from wherever."

"Could it be the latter? Jonathon asked. "You two got him to stand."

"Oh, that," Jason said. "Before I came out and got you, we

physically stood him up ourselves. The device in his neck, which we now think is the main component of this artificial network, is connected to the brain stem. The brain stem controls basic functions in the body like breathing. The devices appear to be regulating these involuntary functions. I wanted to see if it aided any voluntary functions like standing. It seems like it does."

"I'm theorizing, Jonathon, that even without a signal, these implants are programmed with basic information to assist with the basic body commands like sit, stand, and such," Michael said. "It is the same way a computer would act with just basic programming and with no external input. Essentially, the computer is on but does nothing until someone utilizes it. In the case of our friend here, without the external signal giving the instructions he is motionless. We can physically make him perform some actions like stand. More complex functions, like walk or run, well those instructions have to be received through some sort of transmission. So with that said, it appears the outside signal is what was disrupted. Yet, it could also be just the higher functions disrupted. It depends on how these devices are constructed."

"It may not seem like it to you, but this is actually very interesting, Jonny," Jason said. "However, without further study and more tests a lot of this is just theoretical. With him standing, even though we performed the function, the corresponding devices knew where, when, and how much to access and manipulate the nerves to stiffen his legs, allow his arms to hang down, and give him balance. Again, I need more tests to see how all of this is working. Hopefully, I can get these interactions to register on something."

Jonathon just shook his head. "All right you two, my head is spinning. Whatever. Nonetheless, good work. At least there is more then just a lifeless man. Well, I guess lifeless might be inaccurate. Jay, is he alive?"

"Yes. Physically, anyway. As far as free thought, free will...I don't know. When these things were put into his body, that part of his life may have ended. Without knowing the research behind this, I may never know. I still can't take them out to see if he snaps out of it. A scary version is he is aware and conscious, but no longer can do anything about it. It would be like he's being held prisoner in his own body. I hate thinking about things like this, but it's a possible reality."

"I'll be right back guys, I've got to check in with my office." Michael turned and exited the room. Jason, at this point, was looking at Albert. Jason had a worried look.

"Are you okay, Jay?" Jonathon asked.

Jason composed himself. "I'm a healer, I don't like the thought of anyone suffering. I hope he isn't suffering. I don't know what to do except keep Albert as comfortable as possible."

"I can't think of better hands for him to be in."

"Thanks, Jonny."

"I hope you get to the bottom of this though. There might be more like him out there."

Jason looked at Jonathon with trepidation. "More?"

"Yeah, we've been chasing shadows in the dark for some time now. He might be related to all of that, we're not sure. However, last night the prowler calls stopped when Adam and I captured him. It's doubtful, but he may have been it. Until last night, anybody responding to these calls always found nothing."

"Well, I hope you get to the bottom of this then."

"You should have seen this guy run. I could not keep up with him."

"That would stand to reason. One of the devices appears to tap into the adrenal gland. This would give him a boost in strength and other abilities, like running and jumping."

"Another odd thing I noticed last night, too, was he was encircling houses and attaching something to what looked like the electric meter panels on the respective houses. I couldn't see what it was, it was dark."

"That's strange."

"Yeah, I included that in my report so the investigators can go and check it out. Sorry to say, I don't think he is the only one."

Jason turned and looked at Albert for a moment, staring and contemplating.

He then turned and faced Jonathon. "If Albert here is a remote controlled man, as Michael is suggesting, then who is doing the controlling?"

Jonathon, who hadn't really thought about that, did not answer. He shook his head and shrugged shoulders.

"I can stomach a lot of things, but this really has me concerned," Jason reluctantly acknowledged.

"I guess, when you can, write up a report for me," Jonathon said. "I'll need something to turn in so this can be investigated as well. Be as detailed as possible. This could be a prelude to something bigger and pose a significant danger to the city. It might even have something to do with what happened at the museum. A lot of weird things are happening around here lately."

"I will. I should be able to release all of my notes. Especially, because the welfare of others could potentially be in jeopardy."

Jonathon gently grabbed Jason's arm and guided him outside of the office and into the hallway. Jonathon reached for the door and closed it.

"What is it?" Jason asked.

"This could be me over thinking, but it is a cop instinct. Could whoever is or was controlling him be listening to everything we're saying?"

Jason looked at Jonathon with alarm. "That's a good question and point. I'll ask Michael. But, to be on the safe side, we should probably refrain from saying anything in front of him that could compromise safety and security."

"Yes, please have something in writing soon."

"I will."

Jonathon looked down at his watch. "I've got to be getting home. I was going to meet Dana and the kids at the school before they left, but I don't think I'm going to be able to get there in time. Plus, I'm tired and haven't slept all day."

"So, you decided to hang out here with us. Are you working tonight?"

"No, I have the next few days off."

"I bet Dana is happy with that."

"She is, but she will be happier to know that more time will soon be permanent."

"What?"

"I took the job."

"Jonny, that's great!" Jason said with a big smile. He reached out his hand to shake Jonathon's. Jonathon reached out, too, and the two shook.

"Congratulations!" Jason said with excitement.

"Thank you. I'm still kind of nervous. Yet, when I see the smiles on my family's faces, it will just validate I made the right decision."

"You did this all today?"

"Yep. After some thought this morning, I felt I needed to do this as soon as possible."

"When do you start?"

"That's the thing, in a few months and that's because of budget constraints. The position I was originally offered was filled. As luck would have it though, another instructor there is retiring at the end of this year. The director wants me train with this person until he leaves. I will also be going through a required certification process during this time as well."

"I know you are going to go back and forth with this in your mind. There will be times you are going to wonder if this is the right thing to do. It's all rubbish. You are doing what is necessary for you and your family. Enjoy."

"Thanks, Jay"

"Are you telling them today?"

"Yeah. I was going to meet them at school and take them all out to dinner, but I'll just do it at home."

Jason, with a smile, started to push Jonathon down the hallway and toward the exit. "What are you doing standing here then? Go. Go."

CHAPTER EIGHTEEN

THE RETURN

Jonathon and Adam were easing into their shift. They were patrolling their assigned district in their cruiser, looking for anything amiss. Adam was his normal self, while Jonathon was reserved. Jonathon tried very hard to hide this and be more upbeat. He laughed along with Adam's jokes and was somewhat talkative. Yet, his mind was elsewhere. He was not into the jokes or the conversation. Jonathon was worried how Adam was going to react when he told him he was leaving the department. They had been friends for many years and knew each other's mannerisms very well. Adam would be all right with the news in the end, but it would still will be hard for him to accept.

Jonathon could tell Adam was getting a little concerned with how he was acting today. There was just no way to hide it from him. Dana was an easy sell on the job switch. She leapt into his arms and hugged him for what seemed like forever. It was the happiest he had seen her since the day at the museum. The children were equally filled with glee, especially now that he would be more available to see all of their events. Dana, elated, let Kim and JR stay up a little later to help schedule these plays, recitals, games, and such. She even suggested that on Jonathon's first weekend off, they should take a little trip. There were so many possibilities now, and they were all so overwhelmed with joy.

Now, Adam was a whole different scenario. Jonathon wanted to wait for the right time to tell him, but Adam was getting anxious.

"Did I do something to upset you?" he asked. "I didn't see you at all while we were off and today you aren't very chatty. What's up?"

It was now or never for Jonathon. If he did not fess up now, it would make this harder in the long run.

"I've just been thinking about the future," Jonathon said. "Kim and JR are growing up so fast and Dana…well…I really don't get to see her. She's either at work or off doing something with the kids, and I am either at work or asleep. I just don't get enough time with them."

"Yeah, I guess that's hard. But, it's never bothered you before, at least, that I've noticed."

"It's always been an issue, but it really has flared up since the museum."

Adam paused. "Oh."

"Yeah. Lately, when I do see Dana, she is not her chipper self. The kids have been a little on edge, too. Kim is old enough to know what's going on and JR is asking questions and giving me gifts for extra protection. It's got me thinking about my future."

"Hey, I'm not going to sit here and tell you I know how you feel because I don't. I don't have a family growing up in front of me. What I do know is that everyone in your house adores you. I can only hope to have a family…"

"Attention Unit 14, suspicious activity reported at the Lakes District automated power substation. Redirect and investigate."

Adam picked up the car's receiver. "10-4 dispatch. We're on our way."

Jonathon turned on the cruiser's emergency lights and accelerated around traffic.

"Dispatch, what type of activity are we dealing with?" Adam continued.

"14, the electric company called and stated they caught someone, on one of their cameras watching the facility, jumping the security fence and now appears to be tampering with the equipment."

"10-4 dispatch." Adam put the receiver back in its holder.

"If I recall correctly, that fence is ten feet high," Jonathon said.

"Looks like the prowlers have returned."

"I hinted to Jason the other day, about the possibility of others. Depending on what we find there, we may have our answer."

"The question then is why now and why the power station?"

"The one we captured was interested in those meter boxes on those houses."

"Investigations noted on their log that all they found was a single piece of tape affixed to each of the meters we reported and then some. We'll have to ask about that when we get back to the station."

They approached a busy intersection. The signal light up ahead was red. Jonathon merged into the center turn lane and then the opposite side of the road. Fortunately, no one was coming their way. Jonathon moved with haste. When they got up to the intersection, Jonathon activated the audible siren and cautiously drove through. The cars, yet to enter the intersection, stopped to allow them to go by. Jonathon drove back into the lanes of flow in their direction and accelerated again. He kept the car in the inner lane.

"Traffic is bad tonight," Adam said, holding onto the door grip.

They traveled straight for a few hundred more feet. Jonathon merged into the outer lane and then turned right. Jonathon and Adam were now on a two lane road. Jonathon was still driving at a high rate of speed, but not as fast as before. They came up to the section of road in front of the Lakes District School. Jonathon slowed down. The school was hosting parent and teacher meetings. Dana was there with all of the other teachers. Kids were not required to be here, but Kim and JR were.

As they passed the school nestled away from the road with tall oak trees surrounding it, the substation was in full sight past the trees of the heavily wooded adjacent lot separating the two. Jonathon crossed the road and parked in the grass in front of the substation, which was about two hundred feet away. The lot was heavily lit, and they could see someone moving about inside the fence line.

"Looks like this one isn't worried about concealing itself. That could be a problem," Adam said as he opened the door and exited the car.

Jonathon subsequently got out too. "Adam, call this in and request a K-9 unit. He'll probably run the moment he sees us or considers us a threat. There is no way we'll keep up with him or track him for that matter. It's too wooded here for us to even think about capturing him without help."

"Got it."

Jonathon started toward the power structure. It, like the school, was surrounded by trees. However, the trees were cut away from the substation to give it room. There were no trees in the front of it facing the road. As Jonathon got closer the prowler stayed concentrated on its tasks. Jonathon removed his stun gun from its holster. It worked last time he figured. He hurried up to the access gate for the surrounding fence.

He stepped in front of the keypad for the gate. "Dispatch, I need the code for the Lakes substation."

"10-4."

While he waited, Jonathon watched the intruder fumble around with various equipment. The prowler was accessing control panels, pushing buttons, and flipping switches.

"Lieutenant the code is 779287."

"10-4."

Jonathon pressed the corresponding numbers on the pad and the gate unlocked. He pulled the gate open and went inside of the fence. He now lost sight of the intruder. He went on the side of the power array where he observed it meddling with the equipment. Still, there was no sign of him. He went back to the front and around to the other side of the array. Nothing. He inched through cautiously and slowly as he moved toward the other end. He held his stun gun up in a firing position.

I better not miss or I'll barbeque myself, he thought.

As he neared the end, he heard some rustling from the other side. He hurried his pace and reached the end of the fence line. He was about to go around the corner, when the prowler jumped over the fence and landed in the grass behind. The prowler stood up, turned, and stared right at Jonathon for a couple of seconds. *What are you doing?* Jonathon wondered. The prowler then turned and started running without looking back. He went into the woods and out of sight.

Jonathon hit the fence with his hand. "Damn it!"

He turned and put his weapon back in the holster.

"That was creepy, though," he added, muttering to himself.

He maneuvered around to the other side to see what this guy was up to. He observed the chaos the prowler left behind. He poked around somewhat further and then walked back to the entrance. He went outside the fence line to find Adam walking up.

"What happened?" Adam asked.

"He got away."

"Jackson is on her way with the dog."

"Thanks. Let's check around here for anything. He made a mess in there. Someone from the power company is going to have to come out here and see what he did. I can't make heads or tails of what he was doing."

Jonathon and Adam walked the outside perimeter looking for anything out of the ordinary. Adam pointed toward something that was behind the substation.

"What is that?"

"I don't know. It has a fence around it. It might be part of this station. Let's take a look." Jonathon replied.

Jonathon and Adam continued toward the object in the still open area.

"Did you see him at all?" Adam asked.

"When I got inside past the gate, no. I didn't see him until he was outside the fence line."

"These things are getting on my nerves."

"Yeah. Before it took off, it stood and stared at me."

"Weird."

"Yeah, you could say that."

They got closer and had a better idea what it was.

"This might be an access and shut off point for the gas line," Jonathon surmised. "It does have no smoking and open flame warnings posted all around."

It was about a six-foot span of pipe aboveground with both ends going into the ground. They looked through the fence to see if anything was out of place.

"Do you hear that hissing noise?" Adam asked.

Jonathon listened. "Yeah, and does it smell a little funny around here, too?"

"Yep, I noticed that when we walked up."

"Looks like our friend might have been tampering with this as well. I can't see anything wrong, but that does not mean anything. We need to get someone out here."

Jonathon reached for his radio. "Dispatch, contact the power company. Tell them to send someone over to Lakes substation to check on their equipment."

"10-4 Lieutenant."

Jonathon and Adam started to walk back to the substation, when Jonathon paused.

"Wait a minute." Jonathon reached for his radio again. "Dispatch. When you contact the power company tell them to shut the gas off to the Lakes district and have the fire department come out here. We have a gas leak and may need to evacuate the surrounding area."

"10-4."

"Good call," Adam said.

Both of them resumed walking. "I'm probably overreacting, but it is better to be safe."

"With the prowler ransacking the station, we don't know what he did."

"Exactly. Let's go back in and see if we can find anything ourselves, before the power company shows up. I'd like to tape the whole thing down, but we can't deny the electric personnel access. They need to do their job."

"Maybe when Jackson gets here, we can collect some evidence."

"Lieutenant Scott be advised, the electric company ETA is 45 to 60 minutes."

Jonathon looked at Adam and asked, "Why so long?"

Adam shook his head and shrugged his shoulders.

Jonathon spoke into his radio again, "Dispatch, do we know why the delay?"

"Electric company advised…their call load is heavy today with power outage reports all over the city. They did also say the gas will be shut down shortly."

"10-4 dispatch. Please send an investigator out here in the meantime then. I'm turning this into a crime scene."

"10-4."

Jonathon and Adam, by this time, reached the entrance.

"Apparently they're not that concerned, so we'll let the pros collect what they need," Jonathon said. "However, I find it strange that someone was screwing with this substation and the city has been having power loss."

"Could be because of the tampering here," Adam said.

"True, but it sounded to me that they have been dealing with the outages prior to this. Come on let's take another peek in here. Did they say how long Jackson was going to be?"

"No. But, she was finishing a call herself. She is the only canine unit on tonight. It probably would have taken longer to call someone else in."

"I guess it doesn't matter now anyway. The prowler is most likely long gone. Plus, with the gas leak, the search is off now, too."

Jonathon and Adam made their way inside the fence line. They went over to the area with the most mischief. Adam moved closer to a cluster of control boxes.

"Looks like he was in just about every panel box here," Adam said.

"What was he after? The power still sounds like it is on. Unless his plan was to hurt this thing."

"In that case, doesn't the power company have the ability to monitor and remotely shut this down at any sign of trouble?"

"I thought so. I don't know."

Jonathon made his way over to what looked like a system monitor. "Over here, maybe this can tell us something."

Jonathon opened and swung the small door to the side. Jonathon removed a protective panel to find a blank screen with a small keypad in front of it. He placed that panel on the counter next to the video monitor.

"Looks like that may operate this display. Touch one of the buttons," Adam suggested.

"They're blank, what does what?" Jonathon asked, and then went ahead and pressed one. "Nothing happened." He pressed some of the others and still a blank screen. "Nothing."

Jonathon knelt down and noticed a sliding door underneath the counter for the monitor half open.

"Maybe he disconnected it for some reason," Jonathon said.

He slid the door fully open to find a bunch of wires. He felt around inside the opening and found what seemed like a switch. He flipped it and sure enough a light illuminated inside the area under the counter. He looked at the wires and noticed some were spliced and attached to some other device.

Adam crouched down. "What in the world is that? It looks to be spliced directly into the monitoring system. Why?"

"This is only a guess, but someone could be using that to manipulate the signals going to the power company's central receiving center. As far as the power company is concerned, nothing is wrong. That's probably why they are not in a hurry to get out here."

"Good point. I bet they probably didn't know about the leak until we said something. Of course, now the question is what's wrong here."

Adam stood up, turned, and went looking around the array. Jonathon continued looking at the wiring. Adam went back to the panel boxes. He looked at each of them trying to learn more about what the prowler was doing.

Jonathon eventually stopped tinkering around with wires. He stood up and went toward Adam. "Someone with computer knowledge is going to have to look at the device. For all we know, it belongs to the power company. Let's go out and wait for everyone to get here."

"All right."

Jonathon and Adam walked back to the entrance. As they were walking out the gate, a marked patrol SUV pulled up.

"Jackson's here" said Adam.

All of a sudden, they heard something hit the fence. They both ran back in and over to the side to find a prowler standing a few feet inside the fence line straight ahead of them close to the other side.

Jonathon grabbed his stun gun and said, "I think he is the same one."

Adam grabbed his electric weapon. "This can't be good, if he came back."

The prowler stayed for a moment, appearing to stare at them. He then turned to face the fence. Jonathon started running, trying not to knock into anything. Adam followed. The prowler ran, jumped the fence back to the other side, and ran again. The two stopped.

"Damn it, he did it again!" Jonathon shouted.

They both put their weapons away. Just then the prowler stopped by the fence of the pipeline. He picked up something on the ground next to the fence and then jumped over and landed inside.

"What is he doing?" Adam asked.

"I don't know, Adam, but Jackson is here. Let's get the dog to run him down."

As the two were about to turn Adam noticed something new on the ground where the prowler was previously standing.

"What's that?" Adam asked.

"It's appears to be a small metallic cylindrical object…Shit! Run!"

Adam turned and started running out. Jonathon was right behind him. They made their way back though the obstacles, turned the corner, and out the gate they went. The new officer was out with her dog, walking up to the substation.

Jonathon shouted as they ran out. "Jackson, get back to your car and get out of here! Call the bomb guys when you can and try and block the traffic!"

She immediately turned and started running back.

"Jonny, how much time do you think we have?" Adam asked.

"Probably seconds," Jonathon replied.

Jonathon and Adam picked up their pace. Jackson got back to her truck and hurried the dog in. The canine hopped in, she closed the door, and ran around the truck to get to the driver's door. The fire department then pulled up behind Jonathon and Adam's car.

The fire personnel started to exit their truck when Jonathon shouted, "Get back in! Get out of here! There's a bomb! Block traffic if you can!"

They immediately climbed back into their truck. Jackson pulled away and out on to the road at a high rate of speed. The fire truck then pulled out and away as fast as they could. Jonathon and Adam ran up to their car. Jonathon put his finger on the thermal reader on the driver's door. The doors, after a brief delay, unlocked. Jonathon opened his door, got in, and slammed the door shut. Adam ran around to the other side. Jonathon started the car. Adam opened his door and got in. Before he could shut his door, Jonathon put the car into reverse, turned his head, and stepped on the gas. Adam eventually got the door closed.

"Sorry!" shouted Jonathon.

"Don't worry about. Go, go, go!"

"I hope there is no traffic coming."

Jonathon was doing is best to keep the car straight. They were passing the school when all of a sudden a plume of fire and smoke shot up into the air from the area of the substation. This was followed by a concussion blast. Jonathon turned his head for a moment to look, lost control of the car and backed into a concrete utility pole. He smashed the rear of the cruiser, disabling it. The fire was advancing on them. After the initial shock of hitting the pole, both of them quickly exited the dead hulk.

Adam turned and started running. Jonathon stood there for a moment and saw the wooded lot engulfed in flames and the subsequent shrubbery near them catching fire. He turned to follow Adam when the school caught his attention. It was on fire, too. In fact, a section of the building had collapsed.

"DANA!" Jonathon yelled.

Jonathon started to run toward the school, even with the fire still spreading. Adam noticed Jonathon wasn't with him so he stopped to see if he was okay. He turned and saw Jonathon running into an area that was about to become overrun with fire.

"JONNY, NO!" Adam screamed.

Jonathon continued to run for the school. The fire department showed up and Adam pointed toward the school. One of the firefighters jumped off the truck and ran toward Adam. The fire truck turned into the parking lot and headed for the school.

"Captain Parsons, Jonny is at the school. His wife and children are in there, in addition to some parents and the school's staff."

"Shit!"

Parsons turned and ran toward his crew, who were suiting up and rigging hoses. Adam followed.

"All right, guys, we have people probably trapped inside. Do what you can to get to them. We also have a police officer somewhere around trying to get into the school to get to his family."

The firefighters finished setting up and went to work. The hose crew aimed and started hitting the fire with water. Another firefighter went around the school, where he could, trying to assess the situation. More sirens could be heard in the distance.

"Adam, I called in two more companies and some ambulances when the power station went up."

"We should have more people on the way, too," Adam replied.

"What happened?

"Jonny and I were investigating a prowler call at the station. During the course of this, the prowler dropped what looked to be an explosive device of some kind."

"It must have been some explosive."

"I think it was near what was a gas main."

"Oh, the main was most likely ruptured during the blast. Looks like the damage was severe enough to reach the school."

More fire trucks arrived, along with ambulances and police cruisers. They pulled in the lot, with the exception of most of police vehicles. Some stopped in the street, with a couple of them zooming past going down the road.

"We need to get the gas shut off," Parsons said.

"In the course of our investigation, we found a gas leak and called it in to be shut off."

"That will make our jobs a little easier."

The arriving crew exited their vehicles. The firefighters were already geared up and went right to work. The hose crews began setting up their equipment to assist with battling the blaze. The medical personnel removed stretchers and medical kits from their vehicles. They stood by, ready to go in when they got the word. The police officers began to set up to block the street and surrounding areas. The fireman brought the flames in front of an entrance down to a point to where a scout could go in. The brave man ran in, with fire still scorching around.

From inside the building he yelled, "I found an officer. He's unconscious. The suppression system is still working. There is no fire in here."

The captain turned and motioned for the medical staff to go in.

"He has been hit with ceiling debris," the firefighter inside added.

Another hose crew joined in at the entrance and contained the fire further for them to enter safely.

"Get him out there and be quick about it. The rest of this building is probably unstable and could collapse at any moment," stated Parsons.

The two medics, with a stretcher and a med kit, went through the tunnel of water.

"Do you have any idea where the school's staff or Jonny's family is?" Parsons asked.

"No. It's some sort of parent-and-teacher thing tonight."

"Are there more children?"

"I don't think so. Jonny's wife is a teacher here, but she had their kids."

Parsons had a grim look on his face. "We'll do our best to find and get everyone out."

Adam knew that look. He turned to find Jackson walking up.

"Where's Jonny?" she asked.

"This is Dana's school." Adam replied. "He went charging inside. He didn't make it too far, he was knocked out by the ceiling."

"What about everyone inside?"

"We don't know."

"What's going on here, Adam? What caused all this?"

"We responded to a prowler call. When were arrived we found him messing with the station. He ran off when we entered the fenced area. After a bit, he came back with what would seems to be an explosive bomb. As soon as I get my bearings, I'm going to get a report in as quick as a can. These prowlers should now be considered dangerous and we are going to have to find a way to deal with them."

"Could you ascertain what he was doing to the substation?"

"Jonny and I found some sort of device spliced into the monitoring system. We think it had something to do with silencing trouble signals. The electric company did not know there was a problem here. From what we understand, the city has been dealing with power outages today. This could have been related." Adam shrugged his shoulders.

"That doesn't make sense. Why go through the trouble of putting something in there, just to blow it up moments later?"

"It was just a guess. The device could be something that belongs…belonged to the electric company. We didn't get a chance to investigate further. Hopefully, we can still figure this out."

"I'll give a brief report to the chief. He's been calling trying to see what happened. Word of this has already hit the news and he is trying to keep a calm posture. I'll be right back, I've got to see if the roadblock at the other end is secure."

She turned and ran out onto the street. The medics emerged from the building with Jonathon on the stretcher. The fire was now gone from this entrance and the hose crews were progressing at other parts of the building. The medical crew made their way toward their ambulance. Adam ran up to them and recognized it was Artie and Joe.

"Artie, is he alive?"

"Yes, he is alive, but he took a bad blow to the head. We're taking him back to the infirmary."

CHAPTER NINETEEN

AWAKE

"I love you, Jonny."

"I love you, Dana."

"Our new girl is just beautiful."

Dana was in a hospital bed, cradling their hour old newborn.

Proud father Jonathon standing by her side. "She is just wonderful. She looks so much like you."

"No, she doesn't. She's got your...okay, maybe she looks like me a little," she said giggling. "Jonny, I've been difficult lately. I'm so sorry."

"Why are you apologizing? I understand you've been dealing with a lot, being both physically and emotionally drained."

"Not once did you ever raise your voice to me. After long days at work and school, you came home and I barked orders at you. You cheerfully complied without any moaning or groaning. Thank you for putting up with me for these last few months. I feel like I've been a horrible wife."

"Why would you say this? Listen, you acted the way you should have. A month after you were pregnant, you were nauseous. A couple of months later the strange requests came in. You wanted a salami and peanut butter sandwich; you got a salami and peanut butter sandwich. The following months your back hurt, your legs hurt, you couldn't get comfortable enough to get a good night's sleep. Then today, the realization of pushing a football through...well it didn't seem pleasant. I'm surprised you weren't meaner."

With a smile she said, "Thank you."

"There you go again. I love you. Happy Mother's Day."

Jonathon leaned over and kissed Dana on her forehead.

"What. What's going on? My neck is so stiff." Jonathon, groggy and dazed, tried to ascertain where he was. It was dark, he could barely see, and he was still very disoriented. "Dana?"

"Jonny."

"Who is that? Adam?"

"Yes."

"What's going on, what are you doing…where am I?" Jonathon was rapidly becoming anxious. "Adam? What is this thing in my hand? It hurts."

"It's an IV."

"An IV? Why do I need an IV? Dana just had the baby, shouldn't she have one?"

"What are you saying Jonny?"

"What's happening, where am I?"

"You're in the infirmary."

"The infirmary? Babies don't get delivered at the infirmary. Adam, stop talking nonsense."

"You're in the infirmary."

"Where's Dana? Where's my baby?"

Adam stayed silent.

"Answer me! Where's my family?"

Jonathon began to wiggle about. Adam placed his hands on Jonathon's shoulders to keep him still.

"Jonny, stop moving around, you're going to hurt yourself. I'll get the doctor. Please just with bear me."

"Where is my family? My wife, my daughter…my son…that's right I have a son. What's going on, help me!"

"I'm trying too. Let me get the doctor."

"What does the doctor have to do with my family?"

Jonathon stopped fidgeting for a moment. Adam kept his hands on Jonathon. He was concerned that once he removed them, Jonathon would start back up.

"Let me up."

"Are you going to stay still for a moment and let me get the doctor?"

"Okay."

Adam removed his hands and marched to the door.

Jonathon continued. "You and I have been friends for years, why won't you tell me what's going on? Why am I here…the school."

Jonathon, with his free hand, touched the back of his head. "Ouch." He put his hand back down. "How long was I out?"

"Three days."

"How long have you been here?"

"Three days."

"Three days? You've been here the whole time."

"Yes."

He sat still for a moment. He looked at Adam, puzzled. He struggled to comprehend this situation. Something was just not right. He began to move his body again.

"Jonny…"

"I'm not going to hurt myself."

Jonathon squirmed around, then reached his hand up to the railing and pushed a button to raise the head section of the bed.

"What happened at the school? I was running into the building."

Jonathon, more focused, was now propped up. "Where's Dana? My children? What's going on?"

Adam turned away from Jonathon and stepped a few paces away.

"Why aren't Dana, Kim, and JR in here?"

Adam started to tear up.

"Why won't you face me?"

With an eerie calm Adam said, "Please, let me get the doc."

"The school…part of it collapsed when area exploded. Please Adam, I want to here it from you. What happened?"

"Part of the school did collapse. Some on impact from the gas line explosion, some when the weakened structure gave out. The fire was contained, but… no… no one…came out."

Adam, with tears now running down his face, turned back toward Jonathon. Jonathon, with tears in his eyes, looked at Adam.

"Jonny, I'm so sorry."

Jonathon hunched forward, placing his hands over his face. With a quiver in his voice he whimpered, "No…No…No. This can't be happening. My children." He stayed still, sobbing, lost in sorrow. The happy serene moment he felt minutes ago was now being washed away with utter despair. His world was slipping out of his hands with the tears running through his fingers, crashing onto the ground. Adam walked up to Jonathon, leaned down, and embraced him.

CHAPTER TWENTY

GHOSTS

Two months went by since the memorial service for everyone lost at the school. Adam moved himself into Jonathon's house to watch over his dear friend. Jonathon insisted he did not have to do that, but Adam gave him no choice. Truth be told, Jonathon liked the idea. He hated being alone, in the empty house. Jonathon was progressing, but not very well. He found it difficult to fill the days and even more difficult to fill the nights.

In light of his recent heroic service, Mayor Bradley decreed to Jonathon an extended leave of absence. Normally, Jonathon would have fought this. Keeping busy with work would have been ideal. However, he just did not have the strength. Plus, he was aware that with his present emotional state, it could make a bad situation with an alleged criminal worse.

The department offered him counseling services, which he rejected. Several Gulfside support groups offered services to him as well. He just shrugged them off. In his state of mind, talking would not bring them back. Adam, concerned, never pushed the issue with Jonathon. Living at Jonathon's house gave him the opportunity to evaluate his grieving buddy. At the first sign of trouble, he could act. But Jonathon, so far, had not even come close to that point. He was just quiet and detached.

Jonathon and Adam barely spoke. Jonathon rarely stayed in the house by himself. He heard noises when Adam was not there, sounds that physically should not have been there. He would hear the stomping of feet running through the house, the clatter of pots and pans of dinner being prepared, scratching of crayons on paper, or the back door opening and closing numerous times.

While Adam was at work or out with Suzie, Jonathon would go for a stroll in a park or to the beach and sit or sleep. He read books at the library. He tried fishing, bowling, cycling. He volunteered a day or two a week at Gulfside organizations. Yet, in the end, he finished his day coming back to the house.

At night, in bed, was the hardest. Adam would be asleep on the sofa bed in the living room and the house would be very silent. This black hole of sound was what bothered him the most. His mind had a tendency to race during the long late nights. Images and thoughts were rampant. Dana, Kim, and JR were always there. He was grateful of the happy memories. His family loved him very much. This brought some comfort. On the contrary, when the reality set in of never holding and hugging them ever again, this brought him back to harsh loneliness and pain. *Something has to change,* he thought. *This just is not getting any easier. Maybe it's the house, laying in the empty bed, or walking by the vacant rooms across the way void of laughter.*

Adam had switched to days during all of this, but within a few weeks he would be reassigned to the night shift to assist with coverage. Adam was temporarily put in charge of Jonathon's squad and was already working long hours. Most shift times and lengths were adjusted to help compensate for the increased activity. The situation with the prowlers had worsened with increased activity, which included two high-profile incidents. These were not violent or heinous incidents, like the one that happened at the substation, but they were still otherwise disruptive.

Both occurred at night. The water treatment facility was attacked, shutting down service to half the city for little more than a day. No one was injured. The second involved the transportation grid. Most of the traffic signals and streetlights in the city were turned off. The outages were not reported until rush hour at daybreak. Several access points for the system had been tampered with the night prior. But again, no casualties. There were also the calls from frantic citizens about seeing shadows in their yards. These increased to the highest level since the museum incident. Who or what was behind this, had still yet to be ascertained.

While dealing with his grief, Jonathon was also trying to manage his anger. *Someone is going to pay somehow, someway*, he often thought. This affirmed it was best for Jonathon not to rush back into service.

Adam, originally, was due to go on a late morning to evening shift. His reassignment was necessary for the department. He was deemed as the officer with the most active experience and familiarity with the prowlers and the only one to catch one of these enigmas. Because all of the activity was happening at night, his presence during this time was essential. It was also suggested, by the chief, that Adam may head up a new task force specifically trained to deal with the prowlers. This team would be assigned to nights along with a regular shift. Adam was worried about how Jonathon would react to this change in schedule. He was also apprehensive about leaving Jonathon home alone late at night. He was very much aware of Jonathon's difficulty with the late nights.

Adam concluded it would be better to inform Jonathon sooner than later. This would give them enough time to make whatever arrangements might need to be made. Adam sat Jonathon down for breakfast on Adam's first day off since he was informed of reassignment. They sat across from each other at the dining room table. Adam brought Jonathon up to speed with everything going on, including the shift change. This was the first time, since Adam had moved in, the two had an in-depth talk.

"Wow, this is a shock," Jonathon said. "I thought I had three more months before you went back to nights. I was hoping to be back on my feet by then, too, and ready to go back to work. This way I would be back on nights as well."

"I'm so sorry," Adam said.

"No, please don't be sorry. Duty is duty. They are right. You are the most experienced to deal with this crap. Plus, I'm glad to see you in a leadership role."

"It's only temporary. I'm giving the job right back to you when you return."

"We'll see about that. You are probably doing a fantastic job. They'll demote me and put me under you."

"Yeah, that'll be the day. I'm not the one that will have half the city named after me."

"Don't start with that again. I really don't want to think about that."

"Again, I'm sorry for the change." Adam took a bite off of his plate.

"This is beyond your control. I understand and agree. I hate to admit it, but having you here has helped. It may not seem like it, but it has."

"I know this has been very difficult for you. I can see if I can find somebody to stay here at night with you."

"No, I don't want to be a burden to anyone else. I already feel I've interrupted your life."

"Jonny, it's been my honor to be here for you. Especially, when you tell me it has helped in some way."

"Just you being here seems to keep me in balance. I don't know what that means, but it appears to be working."

"Hey, whatever we need to do for you, I'm all for it."

"This divergence in the schedule may be a blessing in disguise, for both of us."

"That is probably the most positive statement I've heard from you in a couple of months. I like hearing it. We should embrace this moment. If I may ask, though, so I can follow your train of thought, how is this a blessing for both of us?"

"Well, I've been doing a lot of thinking. First, let me ask you a question. How are things with you and Suzie?"

"I wasn't sure if it was okay to discuss Suzie with you."

"Why would it not be okay? Because of…?"

"Well, yeah. I wasn't sure if it would be too awkward or inappropriate a subject to talk to you about. I just did not want to come across as being insensitive to your feelings."

"Don't be worried about that. I may be distressed, but I still want to know what is going on with you two. So, again, how are you two doing?"

"Everything is just great," Adam said with a big smile. "We have so much in common. Apparently, I am not the only one who walks into things when they are nervous. On one of our dates, she dropped a spoon on the floor and did not want me to know that for some reason. She distracted me and discreetly bent down to get it, knocking over a waiter with a tray full of food in the process."

Jonathon smiled.

Adam pointed and gestured to Jonathon. "I haven't seen you do that for a awhile. On a different date we were eating ice cream and window shopping. Suzie dropped some chocolate on herself and again, did not want me to see. While cleaning herself, she walked into tree."

Jonathon chuckled. "Why didn't you warn her?"

"I was too busy not paying attention to her. She and I laugh so much when we are together. We are getting to the point in our relationship to where she calls me just to say that she has been thinking about me and I find myself doing the same thing with her. I think it is love."

"That's just awesome. I really am happy for you two. Just so you know, if you need any advice, please don't hesitate to ask."

"Are you sure? It won't be out of line?"

"Of course not, you're my friend. I want to be there, whatever way I can, the same way you have been for me during this dark period in my life."

"I will be around as long as you need me."

"I know. Nevertheless, I do not think I can impose on you any longer."

"I just told you, I will be here as long as you need me. My life is not, in any way, being hindered."

"Well, like I said, this shift change is a good thing. Do you still have your apartment?"

"Yes. I still have a few months left on my lease. Why do you ask?"

"Like I said, I've been doing a lot of thinking. This house is a big problem for me. There are too many ghosts here. Granted, there are a lot of happy memories all over, but they are also constant reminders of what I lost." Jonathon set his silverware down on his plate and sat back in his chair. "I've decided on two things. First, I'm going to get myself into counseling and the support groups soon. I don't think these will do any good, but I will try. The second, and you will do this as my friend...I'm giving you the house."

Adam had just taken a bite of food and almost choked on it. He dropped his fork on the table, picked up his cup, and took a gulp of his drink.

"Are you Ok?" Jonathon asked.

Adam nodded. He put his cup back on the table.

"You're doing what?" Adam asked with puzzled expression.

"I'm giving you my house."

"Whoa, Jonny. Why would you do that? Please forgive me, but that's crazy."

"This house is haunting me. By letting it go, I feel it will help me, hopefully, move on. I'm sure some people might call this crazy or extreme, but it's my choice and it is what I want to do. Plus, what makes this decision easier is knowing this house is going to someone who deserves it, will appreciate it, and start a family of his own in it."

Adam just sat still. He then slowly shook his head. "I'm speechless. I'm at a loss for words."

"You don't have to say anything. This house needs a family and a family belongs here. You and Suzie, or whoever, will start that family."

"I'm overwhelmed with this. So please forgive me for saying what I'm going to say next. I realize it is way too soon to be thinking this, but what…"

"…If I want to start another family?"

"Yes."

"Then I will, but in a new home with new memories. The way I feel right now…probably not going to happen. Nonetheless, my grandfather always believed it was good to plan and think for the future. He always added that you should plan for that future to change several times before you reach it." Jonathon began to tear up, raised his chin, and turned his head away from Adam. "He was right.

I always thought Dana and I would grow old together. Kim would grow up to be the dancer she was trying to become. JR, well, I could see it in his eyes every time I put my uniform on. Sure, that is probably a father's narrow view of his son following in his father's footsteps." Jonathon put his head into his hands.

"Jonny, I don't think this is what your grandfather meant."

"Then what did he mean?" Jonathon asked, with weakness in his voice.

"I don't know, but not even he could have expected this."

"Adam, I feel so alone."

"You will never be alone. Always remember that."

CHAPTER TWENTY-ONE

THE MOVE

Intermittently for a week and after a slow pace, Jonathon made the transition over to Adam's apartment…his new home. With the exception for quick sporadic trips, Adam had left the apartment vacant the entire time he was at Jonathon's. The dust was somewhat thick, so Jonathon had to thoroughly clean. The timing was good. Adam was assigned as chief officer to the new night prowler task force. The physical move was good for Jonathon. It kept him busy. Adam removed what he considered sentimental. He also took his clothing, toiletries, a computer, and some knick-knacks, and left all of his furnishings at the apartment. Jonathon gave his furnishings and whatever else he could not deal with to Adam. This was a good portion of the household content. He brought with him only his personal effects, some pictures, and a few mementos.

Adam was going to take care of the rest of the stuff Jonathon left behind. Jonathon instructed Adam to keep, donate, yard sale, or throw out at his discretion. Adam exercised his new responsibility and rented a storage unit. He stored all of Jonathon's late family's possessions in there without Jonathon's knowledge. He planned to keep it for a few years in case Jonathon began to regret getting rid of something special.

Jonathon, during this time, hired a lawyer to handle the paperwork to transfer the house to Adam. There was no mortgage involved, so it was a relatively easy process. When Dana and Jonathon got married, Jonathon's mother bought them the house, as a wedding present. He initially refused this gracious offer, but his grandfather insisted they take it. His grandfather felt this was his mother's way of trying to make it up to him for working all those years and not being there for him. He told Jonathon that she wanted him to be there for his family and not worry about working all of the time just to survive.

Jonathon, for many years, had an issue with her working all the time. She didn't do it for the money, even though she made an abundance of it. She just liked working more than she liked being a mother. This fact just did not sit well with Jonathon when he was old enough to comprehend the situation. His grandfather, on the other hand, loved being a parent and grandparent. Jonathon loved his grandfather very much and valued his judgment and advice.

He had been speaking with both of them on a regular basis for the last few weeks. His mother conveyed to Jonathon that his grandfather was not doing well. She took time off from work, a shock to Jonathon and a first, to be with his grandfather around the clock. Jonathon's mother feared her father's time was near.

"Jonathon, I will keep you updated, dear," said his mother on the phone.

"Thanks, mother."

"How are you doing?"

"As well as could be expected. I finished moving into Adam's apartment…I mean my new apartment today."

"That was a difficult, but excellent decision. We are both proud of you. You know, if you want, I can send you a plane ticket to visit us."

Jonathon pondered for a moment. "I would like that. I can't fathom why I didn't think about visiting you guys sooner."

"Your head is somewhere else. It's understandable. I didn't mention it sooner, because I wasn't sure if you were up to the trip. You seem better."

"I guess."

"I'll make the arrangements and have a flight for you, hopefully, the day after tomorrow. I think this will be the earliest flight I can get."

"Mom, I can take care of it."

"Nonsense. You will be our guest here and it will be my pleasure."

"All right, I won't push the issue."

"Good. I will let your grandfather know you're coming when he wakes up. It will be morning here in a few hours. I'll send all of the info, when I get it."

"Thank you."

"Goodnight, dear."

"Goodnight, mother."

Jonathon hung up the phone and sat it down next to him. He sat motionless for a moment. He was apprehensive about the trip. This would be his first trek alone and out of the country. He tried not to dwell on that and focused on the notion that going somewhere else for a while would be good for him. In addition, he had not seen his grandfather since he and his mother moved away.

"This is going to be good," he said to himself. He got up off the couch and walked over to his small pile of boxes. They were in a small nook off to the side by the front door. He, so far, had only opened a couple of them. Just about everything he needed, Adam left for him. Silverware, dishes, glasses these were already here. Jonathon bought new towels, sheets, and a bedroom set. Jonathon and Adam traded living room and dining sets. They also traded televisions. Adam got the better end of that deal as Jonathon's television was barely used. Dana made sure that everyone kept busy and did not spend it sitting "lifelessly" in front of the glowing cyclops.

Jonathon mainly brought his clothes, police gear, books, computer, and such. There was one box, smaller than a shoebox, which he taped very well that contained some family photos and keepsakes. Jonathon was going to place this somewhere safe, out of sight, and would only open it when he was ready. A whole lifetime condensed into that one container.

He stacked the other boxes neatly and out of the way. Jonathon looked around his new home, void of familial objects. He was on his way, attempting to start over. Now that his day had slowed down, he took note of the relative silence. No radio, no television, no running appliances, no running water, and no voices. The only subtle noise was the ticking from a nearby wall clock, Adam had left for him. Jonathon stood there, listening to time move on. *Am I moving on with time or am I still suspended somewhere in the past?* Jonathon reflected. Even with this drastic change in his life, he still felt unsure of himself. This was a huge change in a relatively short amount of time. He shrugged it off as maybe needing time to get adjusted to his new surroundings.

He wandered aimlessly though the apartment taking in everything. Jonathon had been here many times over the years, but only as a guest. He walked into the bedroom. He looked at all of his new stuff but still could not shake the feeling of being pulled toward something. As much as he tried, he could not get his family out of his mind. The quiet was too much. He walked back to the living room and sat down on the couch. He picked up the phone and contemplated calling his mother back. He had hung up with her, just minutes ago, but he had felt somewhat comforted talking to her.

"I'll talk to both of them in the morning. No sense in disrupting them," he told himself.

He reached across to the coffee table and stood the phone up there. He subsequently picked up the television remote control. He leaned back, holding and examining the remote.

For so many years, Jonathon had been programmed to "fear" this device. Dana disliked television and made sure everyone in the house did, too. She did not do this to be controlling, strict, or overbearing, and it was not that they were never allowed to watch. They had their regular shows, some with educational value and some not so much. Dana just did not want the object to consume their everyday lives. She wanted the family to experience the many other facets of life, which she felt had been neglected by civilization for some time. It was Dana's hope the children would remember their own events, accomplishments, and achievements, and not simply watch and remember someone else's.

Jonathon stared at the remote. *Would Dana be upset if I just sat here watching television for a little bit?* he wondered. Dana did her job well. The children were involved with so many different activities. Kim had her dancing, which brought so much joy to her life. Jonathon had no coordination when it came to dancing. But it was important to Kim so he helped her whichever way he could, whether it be was being a stationary partner for her to establish a rhythm or just be there to watch and critique. No matter what, Jonathon put his whole heart into it.

JR was still trying to find his niche in life. He was still very young. Dana and Jonathon let him try what he wanted to gain experience. He tried some sports. He did not care for sports. He tried martial arts. He somewhat liked that. He really liked building things. When Dana and Jonathon got JR a new bike for his last birthday, it was in the box. JR helped Jonathon put it together. Dana and Jonathon, half a year ago, purchased a new desk for Kim. It was JR, following the pictures, who directed his parents with the desk's assembly. As a result, JR had a considerable collection of model cars, planes, and boats. Jonathon enjoyed assisting JR with his hobby. Jonathon's hobby was his children and he spent what time he could with them, most of which was not in front of a television. Dana was right. He had many wonderful memories interacting and loving with his family. Now, he did not know what to do.

The days were already hard to fill. The nights were more of a challenge. His first instinct was to find something constructive to do. Physically he was tired and emotionally he was once again drained. However, his mind was still racing and causing him not to want to sleep. Right now, his only escape seemed to be into the world of television. He did not have to do anything, including sleep. He pointed the remote at it and pressed the power button. The TV came on and Jonathon was immediately bombarded with an advertisement. He pressed the up arrow and began to cycle through the different channels, searching for something to catch his attention. He halted at a channel from a local station that broadcasted Gulfside area news around-the-clock. The current segment was a piece on the growing prowler problem. Jonathon turned the volume up to listen.

"…Gulfside police still do not seem to not have a solid grasp as to why there continues to be an insurgency of these enigmas who are frightening our neighborhoods. Police Chief Randall Dunbar continues to state that they are, in fact, exploring many leads and will find the cause behind this. Citizens around Gulfside are still reeling from the hostage takeover at Washington Museum and the explosion in the Lakes district that destroyed a power station and school. All perished at the school. Police state they are following numerous leads with these crises, but maintain these are still active investigations and will not be releasing any information until they are concluded. It has been speculated by some independent think tanks these incidents could be related to the increased prowler problem. Police investigators have had no comment. Citizens, who once hailed the department as a success in deterring and fighting crime, now question its ability to handle this ongoing quandary and future effectiveness. Chief Dunbar has assured the public that the department is regarding this matter with urgency. He further stated a new task force has been formed to solely deal with this burgeoning menace. As more develops on this, Gulfside News Now will be the first to bring it to you. Jack."

"Thank you, Donna. It has been warm one out there lately. Let's check in with meteorologist, Leslie Sands, and see if we will get any relief soon."

"Thank you, Jack. We might be…"

Jonathon lowered the volume. He did not like the thought of the public losing faith in his department. On the other hand, he understood why. A lot of people around the city were simply nervous, worried, and scared. Jonathon had confidence this would eventually be resolved. Adam was on the case. He was resourceful and knowledgeable, and he would get to the bottom of this. Yet, Jonathon was not sure and concerned with how he would react if Adam did find out who was behind this. Whoever it was, was responsible for the death of his family. He hoped he would act accordingly with his duty.

Jonathon avoided thinking about this other aspect of his feelings. His energy had been focused on his grief. However, Jonathon had some time now to really evaluate what was going on with his mind. He surmised he would not be able to bury his other prominent feelings for much longer. Anger was an entirely different emotion.

Was he angry? Yes. Sure he was. He was trying so hard not to acknowledge this. Amongst his deep anguish ran a vile river of rage, but his logic and reasoning kept this torrent from escaping. Sifting through the thoughts in his mind was not an easy task. He, one day, would have all of the answers. It did not matter what they were. They could have been simple things like the color of the paint on the wall to a more serious topic like life and death. But he would feel so much better with a certain solution. Jonathon had a solid direction and was not drifting haplessly. But then, on another day he would, for no reason, second guess those answers and tailspin back into uncertainty and despair.

Jonathon hated this back and forth, and repressive course with his emotions. This was not productive at all and was now too much for him to handle. There was no reason for him to be out of work for this long. Sure he was grieving, he was not going to dispute that, but he kept going back to how he would react with a difficult suspect. He imagined he would be patient at first, but then every scenario beyond that had a violent outcome. This was not good.

His darker feelings were on the brink of overwhelming him, not that he would have admitted that openly. Jonathon was going to give the counseling and group therapy an honest attempt. He detested having these internal struggles with himself and had to do something. He still had it in the back of his mind that none of it would probably work. *So much for that honest try, Jonny,* he thought. Still, he believed he needed to try or else he would regret it in the bigger picture.

He identified he should have done the counseling a while ago, but he would have most likely disregarded it as poppycock. *Maybe waiting was a good thing,* he thought. He was so resistant to counseling for so long. Maybe it hurt him. Maybe it did not. He was now, at least, receptive to going. He now had fervor to get going on this as soon as possible.

Fortunately, he retained the phone numbers given to him the by the department and was resolute on calling in the morning to set the necessary appointments. Relieved he had taken a moment to work this out, Jonathon was feeling somewhat at ease. Not much, but more than he had in a long while. Maybe it was because he had a plan. Jonathon liked plans. Maybe, deep down, Jonathon had some hope for the therapy and did not want to concede to that either. Acknowledging this conflict within himself, he was hopeful. Hope, for him, was in short supply. Regardless of his own shortcomings, he was ready to take what he could get.

Slouching down into the couch, he adjusted himself to get more comfortable, and to watch more TV. The news was too intense, so he started to flip through the channels to find something else. Scanning for something to catch his eye, his eyelids became heavy. This was a sensation he had not felt in a long while, either.

CHAPTER TWENTY-TWO

BEYOND THE BRINK

What is that noise? Jonathon wondered. Dazed, confused, and groggy, he could not ascertain what and where this horrific high pitch sound was. It seemed to be intermittent. Jonathon sat up in the couch and casually looked around the room. Even though the blare was very annoying and troublesome, Jonathon was finding it difficult to gather the strength to get up.

The tone would sound five times, with a brief pause in between, and then start again. He was hoping it would just stop on its own, with no intervention on his part. After a few cycles, the shrill seemed to stop for good. He was still lethargic, but came out of his fog and tried to gain his bearings. He was exhausted from his lack of proper sleep over the last couple of months. The TV was still on. *I must have dozed off,* he thought. *Huh.* Jonathon was surprised he had nodded off with ease. Lately he had been forcing himself to sleep, only to find that it would make it worse for him in the long run. At night, images and thoughts would just pop in his mind. The more he tried to not think about anything, the more he dwelled on it. He did eventually sleep, but after agonizing hours of telling himself he needed to sleep. In addition, his sleeps did not last long and were poor in quality. The stress he put on himself did not allow him to reach the deep recuperative state necessary to function normally.

For a moment, Jonathon forgot where he was. He looked around the room and felt like a guest in someone else's home. Then it hit him. He was home. Whether it was the TV or the new residence, he was glad to get some rest without a fight. Of course, the loud and almost painful noise disrupted this. Nonetheless, the spontaneous loss of consciousness was a positive sign to Jonathon. He stood up and stretched. He slowly maneuvered around the couch, stumbling his way into the low lit kitchen.

Jonathon went over to a cabinet and selected a drinking glass. He stepped up to the nearby faucet, filling it to the top with water. He gulped the clear liquid down without a breath. "That hit the spot," he said as he set the empty vessel on the counter.

Jonathon was becoming more focused. He stood there thinking about whether he wanted to try to go back to sleep, watch more TV, or find something to do. All of a sudden, the noise returned. "What is that?" He hurried back out to the living room and over to the couch. The sound stopped again after five short bursts. *Okay, this is getting on my last nerve,* he thought. He began to sit down on the couch when the noise sounded again. He shot up again. He glanced down on the table and saw a light flashing, on the phone, concurrently with the awful sound. "The phone is ringing?" He reached down and picked up the wireless handset.

Jonathon and Adam traded phones as well. Jonathon was confused. He heard Adam's phone ring numerous times and he did not recall his ring being so obnoxious. *What was Adam thinking of, choosing this ring?* He quickly searched for any button that would enable him to answer the call. *Hmm, I don't remember this phone.*

He located and pressed the "talk" button, then positioned the earpiece on his ear. "Uh, hello?"

"Jonny."

"Adam?"

"Yeah."

Jonathon realized it was late, but did not know how late. He looked back at the wall clock, but the lighting was too dim for him to determine where the hands were.

"What time is it?"

"It's 3 am. Is everything okay? Why haven't you been answering the phone?"

"I didn't realize it was the phone making that dreadful shrill. I never heard that ring before."

"It's a new phone. Sorry."

"Why on Earth would you buy this or select that tone?"

"I needed a loud ring to wake me up."

"Well thank you for that!" Jonathon retorted sarcastically. "Why are you calling so late?"

"You need to call your mother right away."

"My mother? Did she call you?"

"Yes."

"I gave her the number here, why didn't she call me here?"

"She did, but you did not answer the home phone. I think she called your cell as well."

"I…I have no idea where my cell is and I had no idea that was the home..."

"It sounded very urgent."

"She didn't tell you what is?"

"No, but she seemed to be distressed."

"All right, I will call her now. I wonder what's wrong? I spoke to her hours ago."

"Let me know what's going on, okay?"

"Will do. You at work?"

"Yeah. It's slow tonight, a first in weeks. If you're at work, how did she call you?"

"A while ago, you gave her my cell number, in case of an emergency. Now, call you mother."

"Yeah, yeah."

"Have a good rest of your night."

"You, too."

Jonathon pulled the phone away from his ear and hung up. He dialed his mother's number from the caller ID, filling in the international code. While the phone was ringing, he thought about what time it might be over there. It was definitely light there by now.

"Hello," his mother said on the other end.

"Mother, is everything all right?"

"No," she said, with an obvious quiver in her voice. "I don't know how to tell you."

"Tell me what. What's wrong?"

"I really hate to do this to you. You've been doing so well, but you need to know. Your grandfather passed away sometime during the night."

Jonathon stood motionless.

She continued. "He usually wakes up at daybreak. I went into his room to check on him and found he was gone. I'm so sorry dear. I know how much he meant to you."

Jonathon was calm and emotionless. "To both of us."

"I'm sorry dear, I've got to go. I've got a doctor here, police, I think a coroner. It's very hectic here."

"Okay."

"I will check on you later once things calm down. Once this all sinks in, I'm sure I'll want to talk."

"Okay."

"Bye, dear."

"Bye."

Jonathon lowered his arm and held the phone by his side. At a time like this, Dana would help console and comfort him. But she was not here. Jonathon felt more alone now. More, since someone else he loved and cared for had now slipped away.

Still motionless, he was unsure how to react. He was not sad or upset at his loss. It was more anger but not at the world or anything like that. He directed his anger at himself. At squandered time. He was furious for not going over there to see him sooner. Not once did he go visit since they moved away. He always made the excuse that his family and job kept him busy, and he simply did not have the opportunity to leave. He continued to beat himself up over this. His grandfather always made time for him and not once brought up the issue of Jonathon never visiting. Jonathon, on the other hand, did bring it up a few times and apologized each time for not going over. His grandfather, always understanding, never complained or pressured him.

Maybe it was not anger Jonathon was feeling. Perhaps it was guilt and perhaps he now comprehended the lost time. This had been nagging on him for a while, but he had convinced himself that he had all the time in the world. Now, he had lost the chance to rectify the situation and it hit him.

Jonathon fell onto the couch, dropped the phone, and buried his face in his hands. So wrapped with grief, his emotions once again overwhelmed him. "No…no…no," he whimpered. As the tears filled his eyes, deep anguish and sorrow filled his heart. He now felt adrift in what seemed to be an endless sea of sadness. One by one his world was being taken away from him. He felt broken and appeared there might be no one left to put him back together. Sure there was Adam, but he had his own life. His mother, well, she was not much of a mother when he was a child. He could not count on her now. Jonathon did not want to be dependent on anyone anymore. However, his strength was gone along with those who gave him strength. *Why am I going through this ordeal?* he wondered. *Why are such wonderful people succumbing to terrible fates?* Jonathon did not know and did not want to know.

He lifted his head and tried to compose himself. He pulled himself up and shuffled somewhat to the kitchen. At the edge of the living room, he glanced over the area. No, it was more like stared into nothing, which was what his life was becoming without his family. As he stood there, he began to think about his childhood and the things he and his grandfather had done together.

One particular moment stuck out to him. It was right after Jonathon graduated from high school.

His grandfather approached him after the ceremony and held out his hand. "Hey there Mr. Graduate. Congratulations."

Jonathon stretched out his, shaking his grandfather's. "Thank you, Pop. I don't think this would have been possible without your help."

"What are you saying? You did all the work yourself. I just helped you study now and then."

"No, that's not what I meant. What I mean is from day one. My mother, let's just say it, really was not there for me. You were. You raised me to the man I am today and I will always be thankful and grateful for this."

"No thanks are necessary son. The best reward for me is the success and honor you will bring to you, our family, and your own eventual family. You've got a great future ahead of you. I like that girl of yours. She'll keep you on your toes. That's what every good man needs. You two will have your difficult times, but you will be there to pick each other up. Plus, I am just a phone call away. But remember, I don't change diapers anymore."

The two briefly chuckled.

"Thank you, Pop."

The two men gazed toward Dana, who was some distance away, being congratulated by her family.

"She's one in a billion, Pop. I'm so glad she transferred to this school. She was much happier here and did very well as a result…all A's all year. I am so proud of her."

"She had such amazing support from you. You are a shining light for her. You remember that. Always guide and take care of her."

Jonathon faced his grandfather. "I will."

His grandfather faced him. "Good man."

The men leaned in and embraced each other with a hug.

Jonathon revered that moment in his life. It represented a perfect start to a wonderful life and now it was gone.

Jonathon stepped up to his pile of boxes and searched for a particular one that was marked "police" and "careful." He shuffled and restacked the boxes in his now desperate quest. Finally locating it, he set the small box on top of the nearest stack. He reached his hand in between the flaps and forcefully pulled up to break packing tape. Jonathon reached in, removed some foam insulation packs, and pulled out a metallic case. He carried it over to the living room table.

He sat down on the couch and placed the case on the table. It had a roll type combination on the top lid. He turned the dials to reveal the code, then swung the top open. Jonathon paused. He began to tear up. He reached into the case and removed a revolver from the internal form fitted foam insulation. With his hand grasping the handle grip, he threaded his index finger through the trigger guard and lightly placed it on the trigger. He raised the gun toward his head and paused.

Images of his departed family: Dana, Kim, JR, and even Pop intervened with what he was about to do. Jonathon quickly placed the firearm on the table. *They wouldn't want me to go this way*. Jonathon hunched forward on the couch, buried his face in his hands, and began to rock and cry. "I don't know what to do!" he screamed out. He lifted his head. Tears ran down the sides of his face. He picked up the gun again, placed it back in its groove inside the container, and closed the lid. He slid the box away from him.

Jonathon leaned back in the couch, wiped away his tears with the sides of his hands, and stared forward at the wall in front of him. He sat in total disbelief at what he almost did. He was overwhelmed. He just could not take this anymore and he did not know how to go on. Doubt set in again about the counseling and therapy. He was right back to where he was after Dana and the kids were taken from him. *I can't do this again,* he thought. *Someone has got to be able to help me.* Jonathon was uneasy and unsure, but the counseling and therapy were all he felt he had at this point. He tried so hard not to dismiss these forms of treatment. He had not even tried them. What did he know? Maybe there were other suggestions or courses of action he had not thought of and these people could direct him to them. Jonathon knew it was vital to be optimistic. With what just happened, he had to be or he would end up doing something stupid again.

He rested the back of his head on one of the couch pillows. He closed his eyes, wanting to just go to sleep. The sound of the television was in the background. The program on was a nature show, like the ones he used to watch with the kids. Normally, this would have bothered Jonathon. Another reminder of once was, but tonight it soothed his senses. He just listened to the sound of the narrator, with her soft serene voice, discussing the beauty of the world around.

CHAPTER TWENTY-THREE

A COURSE OF ACTION?

Jonathon, lying down on the couch, awoke to a light shining in his eye. It was a bright stream emanating from the rising morning sun. It was streaking through a small opening from a nearby window. Jonathon squirmed around on the couch to move out of the blinding beam. He found a position that was out of the path of the sun's ray, but the room was still somewhat bright. *It was nice while it lasted,* he thought. Jonathon was so grateful for the sleep he did get.

He sat up, swung his legs onto the floor, and faced the television. It was still on, when he dozed off. He watched the program, which appeared to be a commercial of some sorts. It was for a research company providing long term sleep. Jonathon had seen this ad before, of a woman standing in the foreground with multiple images of people living their lives behind her, but he never gave it much attention. It looked interesting. Jonathon reached down toward the table and picked up the remote for the TV. He raised the volume so he could hear better...

"Our process will allow anyone to sleep days, months, or even years in an almost suspended state where the aging process will virtually cease. No matter how long you sleep, time for you will stop, and the future could be yours with ChronoSleep. Do you want to see your grand or even great-grandchildren all grown up? Do you want to invest money in the market and have it grow without having to watch the ups and downs? Or do you simply want to wake up and go for a drive over the countryside. ChronoSleep: the next best thing to time travel! At ChronoSleep, we are conducting long term trials for extended sleep. Call or email us today to see if you qualify for this once-in-a-lifetime opportunity."

Jonathon, very much intrigued, noted the information displayed on the screen. He got up and ran toward the kitchen to find a pen. Adam always kept a bunch in a junk drawer near the kitchen entrance. He opened it and there were plenty to choose from. There was also some scratch paper. He pulled the pen and paper out and wrote the information down.

He set the pen down, stared at what he had written, then shook his head. *This is crazy! Science fiction nonsense.* He crumpled up the paper, walked to the other end of the kitchen, and tossed it in a nearby trashcan. *Just absolute nonsense.* He went back into the living room, approached the couch, and sat down.

Jonathon stared at the gun case on the table and thought, *What the hell was I thinking?* However, for some reason he felt very good this morning. He was not sure why. Nevertheless, he was not going to fight this feeling. Jonathon did not want to be cooped up all day, so he decided to go out to the beach. This was the closest way now to be near his grandfather. It was their place, where they laughed, talked, and bonded. He wanted some time out there to say goodbye.

CHAPTER TWENTY-FOUR

THE BEACH, ALWAYS

It was not very busy, Jonathon arrived at the right time. There was a light wind blowing, the temperature was just right, and the smell of the soothing salt filled the air. He walked along the shoreline getting his bare feet wet from the gulf water, every now and then, as the current rode in and out. His thoughts were all on his grandfather.

This place was more special to him now. He was at peace with his grandfather passing. Probably because he was in the place where they shared some of the happiest moments of their lives. In some way, Jonathon strongly sensed his grandfather's presence here. It was crazy, but he was not going to dismiss it. This was a wonderful state of being.

"Thank you, Pop, for everything. I'm going to miss you very much. Please say hi to Dana, Kim, and JR for me. I guess now that you are there to watch over them for me, maybe I can rest easier now. It is still very hard for me, but I know I have to carry on some how...some way. All of you coming to me last night, I guess, is an indication I have more to do here. Physically you are gone Pop, but you have bequeathed a wonderful gift for me here. I can for years and years now come to this place and hang out with you whenever. That's cool. I will talk to you whenever."

Jonathon stopped to face the water. The waves coming in were smooth and calm for the most part. Seagulls squawked above him searching for their next meal. A nearby man stood in the gulf, casting a fishing line. A child with her family hopped beside them in the sand.

"Life is going on," Jonathon said. "I guess I need too, as well."

CHAPTER TWENTY-FIVE

A PERSISTENT... WHAT?

Jonathon had a great day. It was long overdue. He talked to his mother. She seemed to be okay. He talked to Adam and brought him up to speed. He called and made his appointments with the counselors. He unpacked all of his boxes, arranged the apartment to his liking, set aside some things to be donated, changed the ring tone on the phone to something less stressful, and finally sat down to eat his dinner.

He set up a small portable table in the nook near the living room and kitchen. This was going to be his dining table until he could find something more permanent. The gourmet prepared himself some spaghetti that he heated up in the microwave. Dana did all of the cooking the entire time they were married and Adam took over that task when he moved into his house. Jonathon always wanted to learn how to cook better and was now a little more motivated to do it.

As he ate, the sun was setting and, again, he became more anxious. It would be night soon. Jonathon equated the night with loneliness and silence. The silence for him was deafening. The loneliness was unbearable. No kitchen clean up with Dana, no homework with Kim, and no "what was your favorite part of the day" with JR. He set his fork down on the plate and focused on the only sound available to him at the moment; the ticking of the clock. Time was going on by without him again. *I did so well today, why am I still having difficulty with this?* he wondered. He continued to think about Dana, Kim, and JR. Then Pop, and he was swept away with a wave of sadness.

Jonathon sat there for the moment sifting through his thoughts and emotions, realizing he was sabotaged once again by his own mind. He was coming to the conclusion that he was driving himself nuts. He composed himself as best as he could. He desperately wanted to get on with his life, but he kept getting pulled back to a place of despair and ruin, over and over.

He was happy at the beach, but the mere thought of it was now bringing him down. *To think of it, the drive this morning to and from the beach was not easy.* Many of the emotive landmarks along the way were formidable strong reminders of his former life. When he was at the house and went for walks or did something to keep himself busy, he was constantly bombarded with familiar scenes and places that would snap him back to his family. He worked through this or at least convinced himself he had, because he needed to stay occupied with something.

Jonathon, knowing he needed a fresh start, surmised that is was probably the house and hoped moving into a new home would make a difference. Now, he was considering it might not have been just the house. It might be Gulfside. There were familiar settings everywhere, but he did not want to jump to any conclusions. It had only been one day in the apartment, but an eventful one. Going back to work, he conceded, might not be easy as well. The streets would be the same streets. The buildings, the same buildings. And the people…they would be the same people…with their "how are you holding ups." Or, "time heals all wounds." Or, his personal favorite, "there is someone else out there for you." This was all rubbish to him.

His mother had offered again to buy him a ticket to visit, but he was reconsidering the trip. The primary reason he wanted to go was to see his grandfather. Now, what was the point? He did not have that deep of a bond with his mother and he was content with just talking to her on the phone. What about the change of scenery? It might have helped, but he kept telling himself that he was going to be back in Gulfside and still surrounded by the endless monuments of his past. *Maybe I need to leave...for good,* he thought.

Jonathon never considered leaving Gulfside City before. *All I would have to do is find a new home and job.* He did not have to worry about selling a house and with his credentials he would not have any trouble finding a department to hire him. *But, I grew up here. Gulfside is my home…a home with far too many emotional attachments, possibly screwing up my recovery. I fucking hate this. But, I have got to do something. I can't go through a repeat of last night. And…all I've been doing is killing time…and for what? No meaningful contribution to society or least myself.*

This conundrum he trapped himself into was an injustice to him. He did not want to leave Gulfside, but in order to move on he needed a more drastic change. Then there was this ChronoSleep. *Go to sleep and wake up in the future,* he thought. *Could it be that simple? It's like something out of science fiction. Or maybe nonsense. Or an absurd possibility.* Here he was again, thinking about it. *It has merit, right?* The more he tried to brush this ridiculous thing off, the more it kept rearing its persistent head. *I need a change of scenery, but I do not want to leave Gulfside. I could wake up in a different time with different buildings, cars, people, style of clothes, and maybe a way of life. Who knows what changes in society will take place 20, 50, or even a 100 years from now. The changes in transportation, communication, economics, social behavior, production, and warfare that occurred from 1900 to 2000 were just phenomenal. Today, in the age of computers, society is moving faster and faster, and is on the cusp of another change; the world of cyberspace. Paper documents, banking, entertainment, communication, and even war are making the transition into this digital medium. What will the world of tomorrow look like?*

Jonathon was fascinated with the prospect of leaving the Gulfside of today and moving to the Gulfside of tomorrow. Jonathon loved his mother and was very grateful for a friend like Adam, but Jonathon was convincing himself to let go of everything tying him down to his departed family. Jonathon decided he was going to look into this. *No harm in checking,* he thought. He was still going to give counseling and more time a shot, but if nothing improved and if he liked what he researched about ChronoSleep, then he would consider this unorthodox and seemingly ludicrous option. Jonathon picked up his fork to resume eating. He held up the fork in front of him and looked at it with a childish expression of wonderment and thought, *I wonder if they will have forks in the future?*

CHAPTER TWENTY-SIX

TIME FOR A CHANGE

After several weeks of counseling and group therapy, Jonathon noticed no improvement in himself. He was still anxious and restless at night, and going out in the day was becoming emotionally draining now. When he went to the beach to be closer to his grandfather, each visit was more and more distant. Jonathon did not know why this was happening. He wanted to keep the speculation to a minimum, as he feared he would fall further back and this time, it could be a bottomless pit of depression with no escape. He reluctantly conveyed this to his counselor and she wanted him to reason it all out and not bottle it up.

Jonathon was, of course, very skeptical. However, he complied. *No harm in trying,* he thought. One explanation was that he was getting used to the idea of his grandfather being gone and the emotional euphoria he was feeling at the beach was wearing off. Another, a not so logical one, was that his grandfather's spirit had moved on; *Whatever that means.* For his nights, when he was home, this was usually when he spent the most time with his family. This was when he would perform all of his household responsibilities as well. The absence of those moments and tasks were exasperated by the lack of noise and sounds which they generated. Yes this has been the problem all along. Nonetheless, it was moot whether there was a plausible explanation or not. His family was not here and they were not coming back.

The group therapy was not much of a help, either. Yes, he was able to interact with others enduring the same hardship. They all had suggestions on how to help one another and some of the individuals were showing signs of improvement, but Jonathon was just not warming up to treatment. It was not for him. His counselor, a licensed psychiatrist, recommended anti-depression medication. Jonathon begrudgingly took some of these, too. Nothing worked.

Jonathon labored to remain upbeat, but his optimism was fading. He was not sure what the issue was. Was it him? Was he, on some level, being difficult and resistant on purpose? Or, were the therapy sessions not clicking with him? All he knew was he was getting inpatient and time was running out. This was not good. He did not ever want to find himself pointing a gun at himself again. Jonathon never mentioned this to the counselor, his mother, or even Adam. He was ashamed that episode ever occurred.

Maybe it would help to talk about it or maybe not. Not talking about the gun event could be what was derailing the therapy altogether. But Jonathon strongly felt that he shouldn't say anything, so he did not. Jonathon recognized this could be him being stubborn, but it did not matter. He did not want to ever speak of it or acknowledge it to anyone else, ever. It was a reaction to him missing his family and that was that.

Jonathon now turned his attention to ChronoSleep. He did a considerable amount of research from his computer and was definitely very interested. Sure there were many risks, but he felt it would be worth it. That is, if it worked. ChronoSleep was taking volunteers to study the long-term process and effects. Jonathon had filled out the application and had to submit other forms, such as medical, dental, and any psychological records, to get him into the pool of candidates. Right now he was vying for the last spot and he was one of the top finalists. He was expecting a call from them any day now.

He knew that having this option on standby could also be contributing to the ineffectiveness of the counseling. Jonathon was careful when he filled the psychological portion. Losing his family, he thought, might hinder his chances. So as far as ChronoSleep was concerned, he was single and never married. He was hoping that he had all of his bases covered. He did not want anything to get in his way. This was an avenue he wanted to explore further, yet, he needed to be selected. At this point all Jonathon could do was wait. His mindset: "*If I'm chosen, then I am meant to go down this road. If I get rejected, I'll have to figure something else.*" The good thing for Jonathon was that he was aware of how fragile he was, however, he just had to be careful on how to proceed with either path.

It was nearing sunset and Jonathon, on cue, was becoming anxious. He finished dinner and started picking up after himself. While cleaning the kitchen, he was preparing for his nightly battle: how to pass the time.

"Let's see, go watch a movie? See if Adam wants to go bowling again? Go listen to music downtown? No…to all of that. I really don't feel like going out anywhere. However, I don't want to stay in either. Okay Jonny. You've got to do something. Maybe, I'll just watch TV and see how I feel in a little bit."

In the past, every now and then, Jonathon would find himself uttering a phrase or two…to himself. Recently, he has noticed this babbling had become more and more frequent. Jonathon figured as long as he did not respond and have in-depth two-party conversations with himself, he was safe. This was something else he was withholding from his counselor, but this time he uneasily decided to mention it at his next session.

Jonathon finished wiping the counter down, folded the small towel he used, and gently placed it next to the sink. He left the kitchen and headed over to couch in the living room. He was about to sit down when the phone rang. Sounds of a classical melody now filled the room, much more pleasing than Adam's previous selection. He picked the phone up from the table, bringing the receiver up to his ear.

"Hello," he said.

"Is this Jonathon Scott?" a female voice asked.

"Yes…yes it is."

"Hi, I'm Amy Weiss from ChronoSleep. How are you doing today?"

Jonathon prepared himself. This was probably the acceptance or denial call. He nervously answered, "I'm fine."

"That's good. Well Mr. Scott…Jonathon, first of all, I want to apologize for calling so late. I'm calling from the west coast where it is still late afternoon."

"Oh, that's fine. Not a problem."

"The reason why I'm calling you, we reviewed your application and profile and have selected you as a candidate for our long-term sleep study."

"That's great!"

"What I need to do now is schedule a time to meet with you in person."

"Uh, okay. Do I go to you or does someone visit me here?"

"I personally will be going to you there in Gulfside City. Our policy is that we conduct a face-to-face interview for a final evaluation. This is just a formality. I, myself, have not rejected anyone at this phase of the process. Just by one of us making the in-home visitation means we are very serious about our selections. This, too, provides the opportunity for us to explain our science, technology, and techniques in greater detail than what is provided by our website and informational literature."

"Oh, okay."

"Then, if after that point you are still interested, I will have you sign the consent and waiver forms. Any questions?"

"Yeah, just one for now," Jonathon said, somewhat uncomfortably. "Why would someone, hypothetically, not be interested after the face-to-face visit? I sense in your voice that this has happened. And I guess another question would be, how often does that happen?"

"Very good questions. Our technical procedure, or to be more accurate, series of procedures can be visually and physically daunting. This is an experience that I can guarantee you have never remotely seen, heard, or even thought of. This is one of the reasons, too, why we conduct the face-to-face. To answer your second question, from time to time, after viewing our video, audio, and printed presentation, some have declined to proceed further. Now, you are probably wondering what it is that could be so horrible to compel someone to change their mind and you would like me to explain it in further detail on the phone?"

"That's right," he said, somewhat taken aback.

"Another reason for the face-to-face interview. There are some aspects to this that are very difficult to explain over the phone without some form of visual reference. I'm sorry that I can't clarify this for you."

"That's fine. I understand. I'm still very interested."

"Good. Now, I was thinking that I will fly out and meet with you on the fourth later this week."

"Sounds fine."

"Great. Is all of the information like address, email, and so forth still current?"

"Yes."

"Okay then, I see you submitted your info to us via our website, so I will send you an email later this evening with all of the specifics. Well Jonathon, I look forward to meeting with you in person. This is an exciting time for us here and we are glad you are going to be a part of it."

"Thank you, Amy."

"I will see you soon and have a good evening."

"Thank you. You, too. Bye."

"Goodbye."

Jonathon set the phone back down on the table and stood there for a moment to reflect. He could not believe he was actually going to do this. If someone asked him months ago if he would ever consider doing something like this, he probably would have just laughed and told whomever they were idiotic for asking and ChronoSleep was drivel. Nonetheless, when circumstances and priorities change, so do views and perceptions. For Jonathon, the loss of his family caused him to reevaluate his own priorities. What those might be is what he was trying to figure out and, perhaps, was another stumbling block in his healing process. Dana, Kim, and JR were his priorities and purpose for all of his adult life. Now they were gone. His sense of purpose vanished with them, which was more of the problem with moving on.

The last few months, all he had been doing was drifting along, finding no anchor to keep him still. This was just not sitting well with him. Even in childhood and in his teen years he always had a plan. Dana had a taste of that when they were in high school. He was very much aware that plans sometimes didn't always go according to schedule. Nonetheless, at least there were still goals to achieve. Jonathon has no plan, no goals, and with that, no purpose. He was on unfamiliar ground.

Jonathon's counselor pushed for him to set some goals for himself and he understood why. This part of the counseling he responded and agreed to. The only problem he encountered with this was the goals were often hollow, artificial, and mainly symbolic. These superficial goals were based on an illusion that Jonathon believed he could never fully achieve, a world and a life without Dana, Kim, and JR. This was why Jonathon felt he was doing the right thing with ChronoSleep. This was a plan that would take him to a world where he could be free and move on. It made no sense, it was not logical, and it was crazy, but he felt at peace.

Jonathon was eager to get this process moving, but he knew he had to be patient just a while longer. What about Adam and his mother? Both of them would probably be very critical, wary, and just flat out against this. Jonathon decided it would be best that neither of them knew what he was doing. This was an extreme, eccentric, and, perhaps, foolish choice, but it was his and nobody else's. He did not want to hear their opinions or, what he assumed would be, objections. It was his life and he was prepared to live with the consequences, if any. He was going to act normal, for him, and just slip away quietly when the time came for him to go through the process. Other than Adam and his mother, he really had nothing else to leave behind. The house he had given to Adam. He had a decent amount of money in the bank, which he figured he should take with him. The only thing left of importance to him was the small box of family mementos. The reason why he was doing this was to get away from his family, or the reminders of his family, but he felt he would regret leaving these mementos behind. Jonathon was not sure how quickly the ChronoSleep process worked after the interview, so he wanted to have all of his business wrapped up by the time of Amy's visit.

"Okay, Jonny," he said to himself. "It's time to move on."

CHAPTER TWENTY-SEVEN

THE INTERVIEW

It was the fourth. Jonathon was tense, but ready. He had been preparing and waiting for today. He finished everything he had on his to-do list. He cleaned his apartment from top to bottom, and made sure he was clean-shaven, and well dressed. He bought a small sturdy table and chairs to put in the nook, so that he and Amy had a place to talk and for her to conduct her presentation. He had a counseling session scheduled for today, which he rescheduled to avoid drawing attention to himself. He was not sure if he would be going back. Jonathon was concerned that further counseling could confuse him more at this point. Plus, with ChronoSleep, there might not be any more time anyway.

He got his money from the bank and placed it and his mementos in a secure and sturdy attaché case. The tiny box of memorabilia was small enough to fit inside the case. He was hoping not to have to open and sort it. What Jonathon had done in the last few days was the most he had accomplished in months.

It was near time for Amy to arrive. She sent the exact details of her visit in the email, like she said she was going to do. Jonathon was preparing a pot of coffee. He placed the carafe in the maker when he heard a knock at the door.

"This is it," he said.

He walked out of the kitchen and to the front door. He quickly turned to give the apartment one last quick inspection. Everything looked in order. He refaced the door and swung it open inward. A plume of warm air rushed in. Standing in the doorway was a woman in a business suit holding in one hand what appeared to be a laptop computer bag.

"Jonathon?" she inquired.

"Yes, I'm Jonathon."

"Hi. I'm Amy with ChronoSleep." She reached her free hand out. Jonathon reached out and the two shook hands.

Jonathon motioning said, "Please come in Amy."

"Thank you."

She stepped up and entered the apartment.

Jonathon motioned again. "I have a small table right here where you can set up whatever you need."

"Oh, this is perfect."

She proceeded to the nook.

"Is there anything you need, Amy?" he asked.

"No this area is perfect. I just need a few moments to set up."

"Okay. I have some coffee brewing, would you like a cup?"

"Yes, that would be great. Thank you."

Jonathon walked back into the kitchen and opened the cabinet above to fetch a couple of mugs. He selected two plain mugs, then placed them on the counter near the maker. By this time, there was just enough coffee for two servings. He poured the steaming liquid into the mugs. He set the carafe back into the maker, then carefully wobbled out of the kitchen taking care not to spill the hot beverages.

At this point, she had placed a small laptop computer on the table. "Hey Jonathon, may I attach a screen to your wall here?"

"Sure."

Amy retrieved and straightened what looked like a rolled up bath mat. She began to affix it to the wall over his new table.

As he approached the table, he asked, "Would you like milk, sugar, or anything?"

She looked over at him and smile. "Yes, creamer please." She shifted her focus back to the screen.

Jonathon placed the mugs on the table, then started back toward the kitchen. "Do you need any help with anything?"

"Nope. I've done this so many times, I can do this in my sleep."

Jonathon took the creamer from the refrigerator, grabbed two spoons, and some napkins. He turned the corner out of the kitchen and noticed Amy had just finished setting up the screen. Jonathon sat down in his seat next to the table. He placed the creamer, spoons, and napkins down as she continued to get herself prepared for the presentation. She then sat down in her chair on the opposite side.

She opened her laptop screen, immediately placed her hands on the keyboard below, and started typing.

"I will be just one more moment, Jonathon."

"Take your time."

Amy continued moving her hands about on the keyboard. She

paused and started pushing on the monitor display. She then grabbed the sides of the computer and repositioned the rear of it toward the screen. She continued to tap on the display. In an instant, a square blue image from the portable PC projected onto the screen. While still sitting, she reached down into the bag again and placed some papers near her on the table.

"We're almost ready, sorry for the delay," she said, while looking at the computer monitor.

"That's okay, this looks really involved," he said.

She typed for a quick second, then stopped. Amy picked up a packet of paper, faced Jonathon, and handed it to him.

"All right Jonathon, this packet contains all of the information I'm about to go over with you. This is your copy to have and refer to if you want. Some of this information you've probably seen from the website. I apologize if some this seems redundant, but I still want to give you an overall overview nonetheless."

Jonathon nodded.

Amy continued. "Okay. What is ChronoSleep? Who are we? ChronoSleep is a private corporation formed about 20 years ago tasked with the study and implementation of induced long-term or extended sleep. The purpose of this is to seek the feasibility of induced sleep on manned space missions to Mars, the moons of Jupiter and Saturn, other solar system interests, and beyond. So with that, our primary source of funding and revenue has been from the government. Unfortunately, over the last few years, the government's role in our research has been significantly reduced and marginalized due to budget cuts. ChronoSleep's future and longevity, at one point, was in question. Then, like a ray of light, private space companies became very interested in our work. They began to fill the budgetary gaps that were vacated by the government. In addition, many physicians and hospitals have recently become drawn to our work to use for medical applications. The financial support we've been receiving from them has tremendously enhanced and accelerated our research. Any questions so far?"

Jonathon shook his head.

Amy nodded. "What makes ChronoSleep unique and of interest to these groups kindly giving us money? Our induced sleep procedure greatly slows the aging process to the point that any aging that does occur is negligible. This is of significant value to the space industry because of the amount of time it would take for a spacecraft to reach its destination. For instance, the nearest star to our solar system, Proxima Centauri, is four light-years away from Earth. What is a light-year? A light-year is the time it takes for light to travel from one point to another in one calendar year. Light travels at roughly

186,000 miles per second."

"That's pretty fast."

"Yes it is. At our current technological level we don't even come close to that speed. No one on a mission to Proxima would live long enough to see it. In fact, we may not reach the capability to go that fast for a thousand years. But, if a space traveler were to be put into ChronoSleep, they would make it. He or she would wake up in some future generation, but they would make it."

"Wow, that's fascinating."

"For the medical industry, when they diagnose somebody with a terminal disease or some sort of life-threatening ailment or injury, the physicians would like to present to their patients with the option of putting them into ChronoSleep to cure or treat them in the future."

"That's an interesting concept."

"It is. However, unlike the space industry, it is not that simple. In addition, to slowing the aging process for the human, we need to slow the spread of the disease as well so it does not kill the patient while they are in ChronoSleep. Only a handful of maladies so far have shown promise with our techniques."

"I guess a handful is better than none."

"This is very true. We're still working on more though. We have not been working on the medical application nearly as long as the general one for the space industry."

Jonathon nodded his head with acknowledgment.

Amy continued. "Okay, with that said, this brings us to where are we now. ChronoSleep is at the phase to conduct extended tests on human beings. These are tests which exceed five years."

"So does this mean you've done tests on humans for less than five years?"

"Yes," Amy replied, with a confident tone and expression. "These we've classified as long-term."

"What were the results of these tests if you're able to discuss them?"

"I can," she replied, still with confidence. "No one died, if that is what you are concerned about."

"Well, yeah. I think it is a huge concern."

Amy smiled. "I know and I understand. That is the most common question I get at this point."

"Then, I guess my next question is…are there any side effects?"

Amy looked down at her computer screen for a moment, then looked back up at Jonathon. "This is one of the primary reasons for the studies and testing. We have three areas of focus to answer our questions and theories. The first focus is, of course, can we put someone in long-term or extended sleep? The second is, what are the physical side effects, and the third is, what are the mental and emotional side affects? For the less then five-year mark, we can answer yes for the first focus. The second focus, the main physical complaints are bruising and rashes sustained directly from the process. Some complained of minor, but temporary, muscle atrophy. We've had a few individuals vomit from nausea after waking and one person had a nosebleed for about a day after waking. Others experienced an insatiable onset of fatigue."

"Fatigue after a long sleep?"

"As strange as it sounds, yes. The body has been dormant for so long, it does not know how to process energy efficiently. This ill effect usually lasts for a week, then the body corrects itself and functions normally. Any other questions?"

"No, not right now."

"The third focus, there were no major episodes of emotional or psychological trauma. The chief concern here was most individuals had to get caught up with all of the past events and just get use to the idea that time had passed. The third focus is what we are concerned about though for the extended trials."

"Oh, why?"

"Well, let's go back to our space traveler. He is sent on that mission to explore Proxima. Hypothetically and for simplicity, the trip there takes 50 years. The computer wakes him up. He conducts his studies and communicates his findings back to Earth. He is so far out, person-to-person transmission is not possible. He goes back into ChronoSleep and comes back home, which takes another 50 years. A whole century has passed since he initially left. The world, culture, and technology will be so alien to him. He'll be home, but it won't be. Do you follow what I'm saying?"

Jonathon quickly thought to himself, *That's the idea.*

"I see your point, Amy," he responded. "Your guy in the story might not be able to adjust due to how much time has passed."

"Exactly. Any questions?"

"No not right now," he said, shaking his head.

She looked away for a moment, wrestled through her stack of papers, and pulled out what appeared to be a document that may have been three to four pages.

She looked back at him. "Okay, before we proceed with the visual part of this, I want to review your profile. I have some questions for you."

Jonathon then looked away from her. He was concerned what those questions might be. He grasped his coffee mug, took a sip, and placed the mug back down. He felt he should play it calmly.

He looked back at her. "Okay, go ahead."

She looked down at the report, paraphrasing. "Let's see. You are 30 years old and in excellent heath with no known ailments. Your occupation is...police officer. Just for the record, you will be the first police officer to join the program." She flipped a page. "Okay, now this is where I have the question. Under marital status, you answered single. Yet, we obtained records that you are married?"

Shit, Jonathon thought.

"Actually, I'm widowed," he said. "My wife died several months ago."

"Oh, I'm sorry to here about that."

Jonathon stiffened his tone and tried to control his emotions. "It hasn't been easy."

She looked up with care. "Sure, I understand. It's not easy dealing with that type of loss. We can take a break for a few minutes."

"No, I'm okay," Jonathon said, now more relaxed.

Amy nodded and looked back down at her papers. "Okay. Our investigations also found that you have two children." Amy looked back up at him and sensing that this was another delicate issue asked cautiously, "If I may ask, where are they?"

Jonathon, again, had to fight with his emotions. "They both died with their mother."

"Jonathon, I'm sorry for your loss and I am sorry for having to bring this up, but like I said, we are needing to know how people are going to react to this process psychologically. I'm a psychiatrist. That is a reason why I conduct these meetings. I will say this is not necessarily a deal breaker. Otherwise, we would not have chosen you and conducted this visit."

"Even after the false info on the application and going through the ordeal of losing my family?"

"Yes. Actually, this is what caught my interest. I was able to get your psychological evaluation from your therapist." Jonathon looked surprised. "You signed a consent form to release any and all medical, dental, and psychological reports. We were able to get everything we needed through your insurance company. Don't worry...no one knows why...I'm just a therapist, with your consent, who requested them."

Jonathon nodded. "You guys are very thorough."

"We have to be. If I may ask, how did your family pass away?"

"It is related to something that happened while I was on duty. The investigation is still active, so I can't really talk about it."

"I see."

"The only thing I can say is that they died as a result of a criminal act."

"Okay. That's fine. Actually, that is all I really need to know about that. Your therapist reports that you are having a difficult time moving on."

"Yes, that's correct. In fact, this is why I applied to ChronoSleep in the first place."

"Interesting. So you are saying that you would be okay with waking up in a different time?"

"Yes. I feel I can still be home here in Gulfside, but it would be different enough and not have so many familiar surroundings for me to move on."

"I have to say, this is the first time I have encountered a response like this. This definitely, in my opinion, makes you a prime candidate. We are concerned with how people will react with waking up in a different time. The volunteers going into this are eager, but still somewhat anxious about adapting to the changes that occur while they are asleep. This is only natural and again, a reason for the studies. You, on the other hand, look forward to a new world."

"Yes, for me it is a solution to an imperfect and impossible situation."

"Well, again, sorry for your loss."

"Thank you, Amy."

"Your view…going into this…is something of valuable interest to ChronoSleep. Of course, when you do wake up in the future, you still could have difficulty adjusting to your new surroundings."

"Oh?" Jonathon asked, with a puzzled expression.

"I'm not trying to dissuade you. I just feel I need to mention it is a possibility."

"I understand."

"Now with all of this out of the way, I am satisfied and relieved with your response to this slight discrepancy. Other than one test I'll give you after the presentation, we can move on. Okay, duration of the sleep. The designated time slots we planned for this round are for 10, 20, 30, and 50 years."

"I was thinking the longer, the better. So I guess the 50 then."

"Well, good, seeing as how the 10 through 30 years are filled up. Now, I can give you 50, but I do have a 100-year slot that we are going to offer when we do our next round in five years."

"Five years? I don't think I want to wait five years."

"Good. Neither do I. I presented the board with enough good raw data to proceed with the 100-year study this cycle, but I need a viable candidate as well. I believe you are that person. We will have to do some further testing here and at the facility, but you've got it if you want it." She smiled.

"Well yeah, I would rather do the 100 if you can do it now."

"100 years it is then. I still have some arm-twisting to do when I get back, but I will get this. Any questions?"

"Yes. After the presentation, we do everything we need to do today and you get your approval, how long until I go and get set up with the procedure?"

"We can have you out to the facility as early as next week if you would like. We generally allow individuals a month though, to get their affairs in order."

"I'm ready now. I took care of everything already."

"Okay then, let's plan for next week. Before I leave, I will book the flight out to our facility on the west coast."

"Does it have to be a plane? I'm not that crazy about flying."

Amy smiled. "That's fine. There is a train depot half a mile away from the facility. I will get a train ticket for you. When you get there by the train, we can pick you up from the station."

"Great."

"Oh, there's one more thing. The compensation."

"Compensation? I thought this was strictly a volunteer deal. I don't remember seeing anything about compensation on the website."

"Exactly right. You didn't see it on the website. We wanted to make this look like a volunteer project to assist and prevent our processors from being overwhelmed with crackpots just trying to make a buck. We are grateful for the research and to help with integration back into society, we feel it is best for our volunteers not to go back into society penniless. Some qualified individuals may have some assets, while some don't. So we will set up a trust fund that will mature the day you wake up. It is not a lot to live off of for the rest of your life, but depending on the length of your sleep and if you are frugal, you could theoretically live without acquiring more money for about a year."

Jonathon nodded with amazement.

"Plus, we will pay for medical coverage for you during the process and for two years after you wake up."

"This may seem like a stupid question, but why do I need medical coverage while I'm a sleep?"

"A very good question. Our liability insurance requires it."

"Well, it's still amazing ChronoSleep does all of this otherwise."

"The fact is, most of our volunteers don't think about how they are going to live after they are awakened. We feel it is not right to burden society with that problem. In addition, the ones who do think about it don't need the added stress on them when they are induced into sleep. So Jonathon, are you ready to proceed with the rest of the presentation?"

"Yes. I have to say I am very excited and hopeful for this."

"Good," Amy said with a smile. "We are excited too. It makes the process easier for us. Okay, what I am about to show you are the daunting images I was telling you about on the phone. If you can, please hold your questions until I am done. Like I said earlier, everything I am going to show you is in the literature I gave you. You and I can go over it in more detail when I'm done. Are you ready?"

Jonathon nodded. "Yes, let's do this."

"Great. Here we go."

Jonathon turned his chair to better face the screen. Amy reached over and pressed a key on the keyboard to wake the computer. Then she pressed another to project the first image. She turned a bit too, to face the screen. The first was a graphic of what appeared to be a piece of medical equipment.

"This first picture is one of three probes we will be inserting into your body." She pressed a button to change the image. "This is where that probe goes."

Jonathon cringed.

CHAPTER TWENTY-EIGHT

TRAVELING DAY

This was it. This was the day Jonathon makes the trip to ChronoSleep. He had been up all night. He could not sleep, but this time it was not because his family was haunting him. It was more like anticipation for today. It did not matter. He figured after today, he was going to be getting a lot of sleep.

One-hundred years, he thought. *A lot can and most likely will change in 100 years. What can I expect from the 22nd century?* This was not a worry or a pressing concern. Not even uneasiness...or was there? This was a major life-changing event. The inevitable changes were always there, even sought after, but the reality of the process was now hitting him. Nonetheless, he stood by his choice with enthusiasm. Maybe leaving behind everyone he knew was starting to weigh on him. He spoke with Adam earlier and had to play it off like nothing was going on. He even made plans to do something with Adam the day after tomorrow. Maybe it was guilt for not saying "goodbye" to Adam.

Jonathon, fearing Adam's reaction, still did not want to tell him what he was doing. For the last week, he wrestled with what the effect of silently slipping away might have on Adam. Adam, more than likely, will wonder what happened. He still had a key to the apartment and would probably check it first to find nothing, fueling speculation with wasted time and energy in a vain search. *He needs to know,* Jonathon decided. *I'll put it in a letter. I'll tell him everything in a letter. My overwhelming despair. My brush with suicide. My struggle...to find normality...my place in the world...to be at peace. All of it, except ChronoSleep. He doesn't need to know about ChronoSleep. He does not need to know where I'm at. Just to know, I'm safe. This letter is a good idea. I'm glad I thought of it. Hopefully he can grasp the anguish...give some insight to exactly how much pain I'm in and understand why I'm going away.*

This letter also gave Jonathon the opportunity to give Adam his car and thank him for being a wonderful friend, for always being there. *This is good,* Jonathon thought. *I feel a little better about this. I have an hour before my ride to the train station, so I better get started on this now.* He sat down at the table to compose his thoughts. *This is not an easy thing to do. To tell him...my dear friend who stuck by my side during all of this...goodbye. But, this is absolutely necessary.*

Jonathon left the letter on the table, with the key and title to his car next to it. *I guess that is that.* Jonathon packed a duffel bag with clothes, shoes, and such. He was not sure what he was going to need, but he was going to be as prepared as possible. Jonathon set the bag down by the door. He walked over to the table, to get his packed attaché case. While it was still open, he glanced in to see if there was anything else he needed. "I think I have everything." Before he closed it, he made sure his gun was secure in its holster and stored safely in a pocket, "I hope I won't need this where I'm going."

He closed the case, then glanced around the apartment. He had not been here at the apartment long, but a little part of him was still going to miss it.

For the moment, standing there, he was in complete silence with the exception of the ticking of the clock on the nearby wall. Jonathon was again listening to time moving on without him. However, now defiant, he turned to look up at the clock.

"I've got you now, time," he said. "I've found a way around you."

After this brief battle with the clock, there was a knock at the door. He stepped over to it, swinging the door open. A plume of warm air rushed in. A man wearing a dress shirt and khaki pants was standing in front of the doorway.

"Jonathon Scott?" the man asked.

"Yes."

"Mr. Scott, I'm Dennis. I'm here to take you to the train station."

"Oh, great."

"Do you have any bags you would like me to get for you?"

Jonathon motioned to the bag, by the front door, "Yes, I've got one here." Dennis nodded. As Jonathon stepped back, the driver stepped up and into the doorway, leaned in, and took possession of the bag.

Dennis stood up and slung the strap over his shoulder. "Okay, Mr. Scott, I will take it down to the car."

"Thank you very much."

The man turned out of the doorway and shuffled down the open breezeway. Jonathon took one last glance around his home. *I can't believe I'm doing this,* he thought. He stepped over to the table, grabbed the handle of the case, and proceeded to and out the door. Jonathon did not want to look back. So as he walked out, he pulled the door closed. He turned around, locking the door with his key. He placed his hand on the handle to confirm that it was indeed locked. "Okay…that is that."

Curving to the breezeway, he made his way to the stairway. He firmly grabbed the handrail with his free hand, then began his descent down. *There is plenty of time, no need to rush,* he thought. He took each step slowly, one by one. *It wouldn't be good if I broke my leg or something now.*

Jonathon stomped out onto the hot asphalt, locating Dennis who was only a few spots down from him. Jonathon hurried to Dennis, who was standing next to the opened trunk of a running black full-sized sedan. As Jonathon approached, Dennis reached out his hand.

"I'll take the case for you," Dennis offered.

"Oh, no thank you. I'll keep this with me."

"Very well."

Dennis turned, reached up to the trunk lid and pulled it down closed. He stepped around Jonathon to get to the rear door. He pulled on the handle, opening the door for Jonathon.

"Thank you," Jonathon said.

Jonathon proceeded into the roomy and air-conditioned back seat. He sat on the plush leather seat and laid his case down on the vacant position next to him. The air inside had a pleasing light vanilla scent.

"Are you in okay, Mr. Scott?"

"Yes, thank you."

Dennis smoothly closed Jonathon's door, took a step forward, and maneuvered himself in the driver's seat.

"Are you comfortable back there, Mr. Scott?"

"Yes, thank you."

Dennis shifted the car into reverse, backing out of the parking space. He shifted the car into drive, beginning their trek to the depot. Jonathon leaned back and thought, *Will these apartments still be here in the future?*

Jonathon looked out the window as they traveled, passing by the same reminders he was trying to get away from. There was the restaurant he took Dana to on their first date after their first meeting at the festival. Then there was Gulfside Tower, a unique glass-mirrored building where Kim took her dance lessons. Just beyond this was the arcade where he and JR played games. This was only one block. The whole town was full of memories like this, keeping him stuck in the past. Jonathon closed his eyes. This was the last time he had to deal with this. Jonathon estimated it would be about 10 minutes until they arrived at the station. He was a little tired, so he kept his eyes closed just a few more minutes.

"Mr. Scott we're here."

"…What?" Jonathon was still in a daze from his unexpected nap.

"The train depot, Mr. Scott."

Jonathon looked up at Dennis, who had the door open and was hovering over him.

"Yes, of course," Jonathon acknowledged.

He looked around to get his bearings. They were parked in what appeared to be a loading zone in front of the depot.

"I must have dozed off there, sorry. I'll get moving."

"Mr. Scott, take your time. I'm in no rush. I just don't want you to miss your train."

"Right."

Jonathon stretched his arm over to his side and claimed his attaché case. Dennis stepped back and out of the way. Jonathon slid it across the seat as he slowly exited. Still groggy, Jonathon cautiously stood and made no quick movements until he maintained a comfortable balance.

Jonathon, staying close to the car, slowly stepped out of the way of the door to allow Dennis to close it, which he did. There was activity buzzing about, other cars and people going on about their business. Jonathon swiftly woke up, so he didn't do something stupid like walk out in front of traffic.

"Okay. I guess I'm okay. Where is my bag?"

"I already brought it inside and checked it in for you."

"Oh, I must have really been out of it. Well Dennis, I guess this is where we part ways. How much do I owe you?"

"The service was paid for by your company already."

Jonathon thought, *My company? Oh yeah, ChronoSleep.* "Then Dennis, let me give you something," he said.

He reached into his pocket with his free hand and immediately felt a loose bill. He removed it from his pocket and took a quick glance at it. It was a 20. "Here you go, Dennis, thank you for everything."

"Oh, thank you, Mr. Scott." Dennis reached up and graciously obtained the money. "You have a safe trip, sir."

"Thank you, Dennis, take care."

Jonathon began walking to the entrance. He stepped up off of the asphalt lane onto the concrete walkway. He quickly located the doors to get in and walked a couple of more steps, then paused. The depot was built on a small hill on the land of a former park. It arched over a cross street, then descended down to the actual platform. The front door and drop-off area faced downtown. Jonathon turned around. Dennis had entered back into his car and slowly drove away.

From where he was standing, he glanced toward the fledgling skyline of his beloved hometown. *So much has changed since I was child,* he thought. He briefly reflected on his life and the city's life over the years. Gulfside had cradled him all of his life. Even though the city was much older than him, with all of Gulfside's recent growth, it was almost like he and the town had grown up together. Now it was time for them to part ways, to find their own paths and become better entities for each other in the future. *Am I saying goodbye or see you later?* he wondered. *Perhaps it is a little of both, maybe neither. In either event, the future holds something different… hopefully. What does the future hold for you Gulfside? What new world is going to greet me when I wake up?* "I guess I will find out," he said, mumbling to himself.

He turned back toward the station, proceeded to the doors, and walked in. It appeared not to be too busy, but the station was still abuzz with people going about their business. He looked around to find where he needed to board.

"May I help you sir?"

Jonathon quickly noticed an attendant approaching him.

"Yes, I'm trying to figure out where I need to go to catch my train to the west coast,"

The man pushed a button on what appeared to be a wrist watch, then gestured to the floor. "Just follow the yellow line on the floor here. It will take you to platform two. This is the only west-bound train we have today."

"Thank you very much."

"You're welcome."

The attendant walked past him and out the front doors. Jonathon glanced down at the floor, which now had a yellow line illuminated and embedded within it. *Neat,* he thought. As he followed his electronic guide through the station, he looked around.

The train services came to Gulfside almost two years ago, so this was all new to him. Dana had never been on a train before and she was so excited when these came to the city. She continuously hounded him about when and where they were going to go.

"It will be a nice family thing to do," she convincingly explained.

"I will see about getting some time off from work," he often responded.

Of course, that never happened.

Damn it, Jonny, stop that! he thought. Jonathon focused back onto finding his train. The line on the ground eventually curved over to a small counter. Behind it was a large access door. Luckily, there were no other people waiting so he walked right up to the front of the line.

Another attendant, who was standing behind a computer terminal behind the counter, greeted him. "Hello sir, are you boarding train 121?"

"If it's the one going to the west coast, then yes."

"It is"

"Terrific, but I don't have a physical boarding pass."

"That's okay, we can look up your pass here in the computer. Your name please?"

"Jonathon Scott."

She typed his name in and then started clicking around with a computer mouse. Sensing he probably needed a photo ID, Jonathon reached into his pants pocket to retrieve his driver's license.

"May I please set my briefcase up on the counter here for a moment?" he asked.

"Of course."

"Thank you."

He lifted his arm and then gently slid the case onto the surface.

"I see your reservation in here, Mr. Scott. I just need to see some sort of official photo ID please."

He gingerly handed it to her. She set into some sort of scanning apparatus. She then began typing and clicking again.

"Okay, Mr. Scott. I see one bag has already been checked in for you and you have the one case here. Anything else?"

"No."

"All right. We have you in a private cabin."

"Private cabin?"

"Yes, that's what the reservation is for."

"Hmm…very nice."

"I have you listed as a law enforcement officer, do you have any weapons with you?"

Jonathon was surprised at first, but then remembered he had

signed a national registry for law enforcement personnel. This was to allow authorities to quickly identify who was real and detain those who were not.

"Yes, I do."

A security guard approached Jonathon. "May I scan your right middle finger please?"

"Absolutely," Jonathon replied.

The uniformed man held out a portable finger reader. All of Jonathon's fingerprints were on file with the National Law Enforcement Register. The first part of the two-step procedure was to ask for a random finger. Jonathon inserted his finger into the reader. The device scanned his print. Jonathon then removed his finger. The second part was to get a retinal scan.

"Now may I scan your right eye?" the guard asked.

"Yes. Of course."

The guard flipped the device and very quickly illuminated his eye. The officer flipped it to another side, reading what appeared to be a small screen. He then faced the attendant.

"He's confirmed." The guard returned his attention back to Jonathon, "Thank you for your cooperation." The guard then nodded to two other nearby guards. All three walked away.

This procedure was primarily put into place to detect potential risks. Random checks were performed on anyone coming through the door, but anyone with a weapon was automatically detained. Law enforcement personnel were the only individuals allowed to carry weapons on this mass-transit system anyway, so as a result, they were often the ones getting stopped the most to verify their identities. Jonathon refaced the attendant at the counter.

"Okay Mr. Scott, with your identity as a law enforcement officer being confirmed, I cleared your firearm for travel."

Jonathon was confused. "How did you know it was a firearm?"

"Security detected it the moment you walked through the entrance door. They had you under surveillance the entire time."

"That's right. I remember now."

"Okay, Mr. Scott, everything is in order. Your bags will be delivered to your cabin."

She clicked a few more times with the mouse. She reached below the counter, then slid a credit card shaped item toward Jonathon across the counter.

"This is your pass and cabin key," she said. "Just show it to any of our concierges beyond the doors here, and they will assist you from there."

Jonathon took the pass off the counter.

"I've unlocked the doors behind me here, so you're ready to go.

Have a nice trip, Mr. Scott."

"Thank you."

Jonathon reclaimed his case, slid it off the counter, and held it at his side. He walked around the counter to the narrow walkway to the access doors. As he approached, the doors slid open with a muffled rumble. Jonathon proceeded through and out to a massive set of escalators descending to the train platform. This area was covered, almost like an outside warehouse. He carefully stepped on to the conveyor, making sure to keep his balance. As he rode the contraption down, he could see the tracks, which split into three rows with a train parked on the nearest set.

"I guess that's my train down there," he mumbled to himself.

The train appeared to have been sitting there for awhile. No one seemed to be leaving, just boarding. Jonathon reached the end of the line, carefully stepping off to avoid getting caught by the teeth of the metal lip at the foot of the device. Glancing around he thought, *All these people. Where are they going? What are they doing? People living their lives in their own worlds, moving along with time. Well, now I'm moving along too.* Picking up motion, he neared the train and was immediately greeted by a concierge with "Louis" on his nametag.

"Hello, may I help you?" Louis asked.

"Yes, I have a pass here for a cabin."

Jonathon held out the pass.

Louis took possession of it and briefly glanced over it. "Looks like we have you in cabin K7. Follow me. I'll be happy to take you there."

"Great! Thank you."

"No problem."

Louis turned, guiding Jonathon toward a train car and an access stairway. He ascended up the stairs, with Jonathon behind him. They entered into a general passenger car. It had some people sitting in seats, but it was not anywhere near full yet. They passed through the main aisle to get to the next car. Louis manually opened the sliding connecting doors for the cars and passed through them. Jonathon was about to close a set of doors behind him.

"Oh sir, you don't need to close them," Louis said. "They will close by themselves in a moment."

They proceeded around a corner, into a corridor of a cabin car. As they passed a door, Louis pointed to the next door.

"Hmm K7…here we are."

Louis inserted the pass card into a reader below the cabin number plate and quickly removed it. The door slowly and automatically slid open. He went through the narrow foyer, entering the room with Jonathon in tow.

Jonathon looked around the small area. "Cozy, thank you."

He reached into his pocket to find more money to give to Louis. He pulled another bill out of his pocket and noticed it was another 20. *Damn is that all I have? Oh well, it doesn't really matter anyway,* he thought. He gave it to Louis.

"Thank you, sir. If there is anything else you need, you can reach me through the switchboard."

Louis gestured toward the phone on the wall. He then gave Jonathon the card. "To open and close the door from the outside, just feed the card into the reader. From inside, just push the button. Have a great trip."

"Thank you."

Louis left the room.

Jonathon stepped to the door, pushed the button, and the door closed. He walked in toward the window opposite the door and sat down. He set his case and the card on the seat next to him. His mind began to wander. His thoughts drifted to Dana and his children. He never really gave it much thought about what they would think about all of this.

"Dana…Kim…JR…I don't know if you can hear me, but here goes…I miss you all so much. I feel so lost and alone. I'm not strong without you and I'm not strong enough to move on. I just don't know what else to do. I don't know how to move on without you. I have to leave this place...this time. Hopefully, the answer is waiting for me in the future. I love you all…goodbye…I'm sorry."

CHAPTER TWENTY-NINE

ARRIVAL

"Jonathon welcome to ChronoSleep."

"Thank you, Amy, it's great to be here."

Amy had come outside to greet Jonathon as he walked up from the covered drop-off in front of the complex. The main building itself was a massive tall and long building, with a silver blue metallic futuristic look. They made their way to the entrance.

"May I take one of those for you?" she asked.

"No, it's okay. I've got them. Wow…this place is huge!"

"It has taken a long time for us to get to here. Each day of progress brings us further along. Thanks to you, Jonathon, we will begin another important chapter of our research."

They approached the outer translucent reinforced double doors, which slid open with a muffled rumble. Amy and Jonathon proceeded inside and were immediately acknowledged by two security guards sitting behind a desk. The guards were in all black, wearing almost military style uniforms. Amy and Jonathon stepped far enough in for the doors behind them to automatically shut.

One of the guards got up from his seat and came around to greet Jonathon. "Welcome, Mr. Scott. I will take your bag and case to our security area to be processed."

Jonathon looked at Amy with hesitation.

"We have to log them in, so they can be stored properly and safely while you are asleep," she said with assurance. "However, they will be brought to your room for you to have before the procedure."

"Okay."

Jonathon handed his case to the standing guard. "I have a revolver in there, just so you know."

"Charlie, I think I put in the reception file that Jonathon is a police officer from Gulfside City," Amy explained.

"Yes, ma'am you did," Charlie replied. "For that, we deactivated the door alarm for you. There was no need for you to hear it."

"Thank you," responded Amy.

Jonathon slipped his bag off his shoulders and handed it to Charlie, who in turn slid it on his shoulder.

"We will log these for you and have them in your room shortly, Mr. Scott," Charlie said, looking toward Jonathon.

"Thank you very much."

"You're welcome."

Charlie stepped toward a closed door near the security desk. The door opened as he advanced to it. As Charlie went in, another guard came out and went behind the security desk. The new man sat down and started conversing with the other guard. Amy motioned for Jonathon to continue through the access way ahead of them. They passed through the threshold into what appeared to be the main foyer. It was a very large open modern and futuristic space. The vast room was mostly quiet, but he could hear dampened voices echoing throughout. Jonathon paused, and Amy stopped as well. He slowly looked up. Each floor above them overlooked and encircled this area. Jonathon counted five floors, including the ground. In some instances, Jonathon could see people moving about.

"This place is amazing Amy," Jonathon said, still gawking.

"I'm glad you like it here. You will be really impressed when I show you our research division, but first I need to take you to our intake room and get you checked in. Follow me, please."

She gestured ahead, toward a bank of elevators. Jonathon gathered himself, continuing to walk with her. He still took brief peeks at anything that caught his attention, but was mindful not to pull an Adam and trip or bump into something along the way. They walked around a quick corner and stopped at the elevator doors. The two stood there, waiting. Amy did not press a button to call the lift. In fact, Jonathon promptly noticed there was no button to push.

"How are you going to get the elevator to us?" he asked.

"It is motion activated. Many things here are automated. We try to make this facility as ahead of its time as possible to get our minds in that way of thinking. You see, everything we do here is about the future. That is where we want to be."

"I see."

The sound of an elevator car was now audible. The doors opened, allowing them to enter. Amy motioned him to go in. It would not be gentleman of him to go first, but this was her place and he did not want to create an uncomfortable situation. So Jonathon obliged and stepped in with her behind. They both swiveled themselves to face the front of the lift. He took note again that there were no buttons or numbers to push but there was what looked to be a card reader.

"What level please?" asked a monotone computerized feminine voice.

"Level four," answered Amy.

The doors swooshed closed and the elevator commenced its rise up.

"How many floors are in this building?" Jonathon asked, curious from his prior observations.

"Five."

Maybe it was nerves, maybe it was reality sinking in, maybe it was a little of both…Jonathon started to have an uneasy feeling in the pit of his stomach as he watched the floor indicator count towards their destination.

The lift slowed and jolted briefly as it set into place on four. The doors opened to reveal a short narrow arch-like hallway that curved to the left and right. The walls, which were sparsely decorated, and the ceiling were metallic silver. The floor was black granite. The lighting was very calm, emanating from a continuous row from where the curves met in the ceiling.

Amy stepped out first with Jonathon in tow. As they flowed to the right, the corridor widened a little. There were some dark gray doors that lined both sides of the now-straight hallway, but there were not many of them. The air was very cold; it almost gave Jonathon a shiver. Amy and Jonathon walked past some of the doors before stopping at one. A number five was on a wall plate to the right of it about eye level to him.

"Here we are," Amy said.

The single door quietly slid open. Amy went in. Jonathon followed. The small room had the same silver walls and black floor, and was cold. Cold had two meanings here. The first was physical temperature. The second, the room was so sterile it lacked warmth and character. Jonathon was not an interior designer, but this room had no personality, as if it was almost lonely and lost. *Perhaps I'm projecting myself into the room,* he thought. There were no decorations. Only a futuristic looking desk and chairs, computer, some office supplies, and other odd equipment. Amy maneuvered around the desk.

"Please have a seat, Jonathon," she said.

He picked one of the two chairs stationed in front of the desk, sitting down as instructed. The door closed behind him. Amy sat down across from him in her corresponding chair. She reached under the desk top, taking out a tablet computer.

"Okay, this is just an informal meet," Amy said. Motioning to the tablet, "We of course have all of your information, but need to make sure the file is up to date as possible. Specifically, are there any changes in medical history or medications? Do you still want to go through with this? Stuff like that."

Jonathon smiled a little.

Amy had a bit of a smirk herself. "I know it seems redundant, but we are required by law to ask."

He nodded in agreement.

"I know what you are going to ask and the answer is, yes," she said, with a conciliatory tone. "We have had a few people walk out on us from here."

"Oh, well, that's only natural. This is a big deal. So to answer your questions, no, no, and yes."

"Well then, good," she said, now smiling. "I thought so, but again, I had to ask. Okay, are there any lingering questions about the procedure?" she asked a little more seriously.

"Nope," he answered while shaking his head. "I think I'm a little nervous…to be expected I guess, but I am still ready."

"All right. What happens from here? We have assigned a room for you to sleep in for the next couple of nights. Tomorrow morning, we will take you into the lab for a tour. You will be able to see everything up front. We have someone scheduled to be prepped for ChronoSleep. In the afternoon, we will have a look at someone who has been in ChronoSleep for under a year and an individual who has been in for almost five. Again, any questions you have during the tour, please ask. Also, if you're uneasy at any point, you can still leave. Looking at pictures and movies are a lot different than seeing this up close and personal. Surprisingly, we've had no one desert us during or after the tour."

Jonathon nodded.

"The day after tomorrow is your day. You will be prepped, hooked in, and on your way into ChronoSleep. Any questions?"

"Nope."

"Okay, we're done."

Amy picked up the tablet as she stood. Jonathon got up as well. They walked out of the room. He matched her stride as they marched further down the hallway.

"Your room is just a couple doors down here. It is just like one you would find at a hotel. A private bath…bed…television."

They stopped in front of a door with a number seven by it on a wall plate.

"You're free to roam around the complex," she advised. "The

only restriction is you cannot go onto floors two and three. Those are the ChronoSleep chambers and lab. When you get hungry, there is a small cafeteria on the 5th floor. All meals and beverages are complementary to everyone in the building. Security is very efficient with their process, so your belongings should already be in here."

Amy reached into her pocket, pulling out an access card.

"This is the key to your room."

She gave him the card.

"Now, don't lose this key because this also is a data card for you," Amy instructed.

"Data card?"

"Yes, it will be inserted into your ChronoSleep chamber, while you are in there. It will record information such as brainwave activity, blood pressure, and all your vitals. This allows us to go back, if we have to, and analyze anything at anytime and anywhere. If for some reason we find there is a problem, we can readily go back and see if there were prior abnormalities that we may not have picked up on in real time. If a minor correction is needed, we can make an adjustment or two accordingly."

"Okay."

"In addition, it provides a constant link to this computer and our master control room. We can access the information we need at anytime, anywhere. You will be under constant surveillance the entire time you are in, either by me or by someone in the control room. We will be watching over you very closely."

Jonathon nodded with more understanding. "I think I remember this now from the literature. This is so you don't have to wake anyone up unnecessarily."

"Correct."

"Have you ever had to wake anybody up before their time?"

"In the beginning of our research, yes. As time went on, with the amount of information we have gathered, we now know what to look for. We can determine normal versus abnormal. With that said, the last group of five-year ChronoSleepers went through their full term. And, so far so good, the current individuals are all doing fine."

"I'm glad."

"We will show you the process from start to almost finish. Again, we have someone going in tomorrow. You'll see him getting prepped and inserted into his chamber. Then you will see him and others being observed by our monitoring team. Finally, we have someone coming out of ChronoSleep in a few days. We are actually beginning the wake-up process tomorrow, but you will be in ChronoSleep by the time she wakes up. Exciting. Absolutely exciting."

Jonathon felt the pit in his stomach again. It was weird, how the last part was described. *I will be in ChronoSleep when the other person wakes up.*

"How long was this person in for?"

"She'll reach five years in a few days. She is the last of her group. They all did spectacular. Everyone going in the next couple of months are going for ten years or longer. I can't say it enough, this is an exciting time for us." Amy smiled. She held her hand out to shake. Jonathon reciprocated and shook her hand. "If you need to reach me for any reason, I'm in the phone directory. Anything else, refer to the directory. There is a map of the complex in your room to guide you around. Have a relaxing rest of the day, Jonathon. We will have a very busy day tomorrow. I'll be here at 7a.m. sharp.

"Thank you, Amy."

"See you later, Jonathon."

Amy walked by Jonathon going back the way they came in. Jonathon inserted his card into the reader next to the door. The door quietly slid open. He went into the room, taking a few steps past the door. The door automatically shut behind him. Jonathon closely examined the relatively good-sized room. The main living area was just inside the entrance door. It was furnished with a couch, a recliner, and a television. The bedroom and bathroom appeared to be through an open doorway off to the side of the room. On the opposite side, was a little dining nook complete with a square table and two chairs set across form each other. The room was very much like the rest of the building, very sterile with the same silver walls, same black floor. However, the ambient lighting was far more warming and calming. There did not seem to be any exterior windows.

The sofa, recliner, dining table, and chairs were futuristic looking. The television was a flat screen mounted to the wall opposite the couch. Jonathon walked into the bedroom. The bed frame, nightstands, and dresser were all of a futuristic design as well.

"I guess they were going for the futuristic look in here, too," Jonathon mumbled. Jonathon did catch a break in here though. The black alarm clock on one of the nightstands did have a green display. "Ah, color," he said.

On the bed were his bag and case.

"Oh, good. They are here," he said. "Who are you talking to Jonny?"

He shook his head in annoyance with himself. He went over to the bed and picked up his case by taking hold of its handle. He walked back out into the living area, walking towards the dining table. Jonathon gently set the case down and then sat himself down in front of it in on one of the chairs. He gripped the case with his hands, placing a thumb on the combination lock. One by one he thumbed through each sequential number, entering the code. With the last number set in place and hearing the click of it unlocking, he placed his hands on the side of the top, slowing swinging it open.

The first thing he noticed was that the gun was still snug, right where he placed it. Then he grabbed his box of mementoes, removed it from the case, and carefully placed it in front of him on the table.

"Why are you doing this to yourself?" he said, staring down at the still-unopened box.

He placed his hands on the lid, gently removing it from the small box. After setting the lid down, he looked inside. In a place with no feeling or emotion, Jonathon was surely feeling an abundance of them emanating from the contents. For some reason, he needed to view these select cherished family keepsakes.

He reached in, first removing a silver necklace with a solid silver heart pendant. He gave this to Dana the first time he said, "I love you." Jonathon held it in the palm of his hand, lightly brushing the pendant with his fingers from his other hand. To anyone else, this was just a trinket. To him, Dana's heart, being, and soul were in this tiny object. It radiated her beauty. She wore this necklace more than any others she had, but on that day, she didn't. *Why?* he wondered. He carefully laid it back into the box and selected another special item.

The second was a green and yellow plastic whistle. Why this seemingly worthless piece of junk? This belonged to Kim. She won the whistle at a founder's festival a few years ago. It was the first thing she had ever won and she treasured it immensely. She would constantly run around the house, blowing into it, producing its high-pitched shrill.

"Kim, stop blowing that thing in the house," he would often tell her.

The sound drove him crazy, but now he missed hearing it. He set the whistle back in the box and removed another keepsake.

The third object he possessed was a small model car. It was plain ugly. There were glue runs everywhere, the pieces were not flush with each other, and it was unpainted. However, this was the first model he and JR had put together. JR had an extensive collection of models, but could only display a few at a time on his little shelf. He rotated them out constantly, yet this one seemed to always have a permanent place on that shelf. JR never expressed why. Jonathon never asked. He could now only surmise that this must have meant a lot to JR. Jonathon picked the car up and placed it back in the box.

Jonathon selected and removed one final valued item, a police badge. He examined it in his hand. This was his grandfather's first badge. He gave it to Jonathon, the day he graduated from the academy.

"We have no real traditions in this family, so I would like to start one now," his grandfather said. "I want to give this to you as a symbol to the start of a long and brilliant career. May you have great luck and success as I did. Some day, when you have a son, and when he graduates from here, you can give him this and the one you now have proudly on your chest."

Jonathon vividly remembered that day, every day. The future was so unpredictable. *Never did I think I would be here alone, about to take a journey like this. I've only one regret…taking for granted the little things. I thought there would always be more time to spend with my family. More time to watch them grow. More time to teach them about life. I can't go back. All I have now is this uncertain future world. Hopefully, I'll find what I'm looking for.*

CHAPTER THIRTY

CHRONOSLEEP

Amy, in hospital scrubs and a mask, was standing and hovering over Jonathon.

"Are you comfortable, Jonathon?" she asked.

"As much as one could be."

He was lying on a table in an examination room to be prepped for the ChronoSleep process. There were technicians buzzing about, organizing and assembling instruments and devices in the bright sterile soulless room.

Jonathon was relaxed, surprisingly after seeing this done on someone else yesterday. What he witnessed was daunting, barbaric, unimaginable, and probably, somewhat vulgar. Yet despite all of that, he had the knowledge of why they put what where and who were the ones who carry this out. He knew he was in good hands here.

"Any last-minute questions, Jonathon?" Amy asked, with a comforting bedside manner.

"Nope," Jonathon replied. "Let's get this going."

"All right then, this is where I say goodbye and good luck. I will leave you a video message for you when you wake up. I wish I could be there…hey, who knows?"

"Thank you Amy…for everything."

She placed her hand on his shoulder and gave him a quick thumbs up with her other. "Good luck."

She looked up and away, nodding to someone in the room. She removed her hand and stepped back.

A man with a surgical mask approached, hovered, and looked down at Jonathon. "Are you ready, Jonathon?"

Jonathon nodded.

The man looked away briefly, obtaining what looked to be a clear oxygen mask. However, thanks to yesterday, Jonathon knew this was the anesthesia to put him under.

The physician placed and secured the mask over his mouth. "Okay, Jonathon, please count backwards from 100."

"100…99…98…9…"

CHAPTER THIRTY-ONE

A WORLD GOES ON

"...Staying in touch with you, today is August 17, 2019. The Koreas played another game of cat and mouse. North Korea sent scores of troops into the heavily fortified Demilitarized Zone, which divides the North and South, only to have them do an about-face and return to their home territory. This is the third time, in as many weeks, the North has done this, possibly in response to the South's increasingly aggressive behavior. No exchange of fire in all three instances. U.S. and South Korean troops are not authorized to use force unless fired upon or the North crosses into the sovereign South. As a response to this last incident, the new South Korean government sent troops into the DMZ to up the ante, but short of violating the North's territory. Many world governments have issued statements to both sides, to remain calm and not to escalate an already tense situation. The Koreas technically remain at war as the conflict in the 1950s ended with only a ceasefire truce."

"...September, 3, 2019. At 5:39a.m. local time on the 80th anniversary of the start of World War II, World War III may have begun. A nuclear explosion leveled the inner city of Pyongyang, North Korea."

7:20a.m., "...The unthinkable has happened...I don't know what to say...A nuclear explosion has devastated the city of Seoul... I...I can't believe this. What's happening to us...the world..."

8:00a.m. "...The leaders of multiple nations have issued statements for calm, but otherwise have been mobilizing their militaries for other possible aggressions."

11:01a.m."…September 5, 2019. After sporadic fighting broke out between various nations, the leaders of these nations are withdrawing their militaries from the multiple theaters of conflict, fearing for the future existence of the human race…"

"…September 6, 2019. The world financial markets opened up for the first time since the horrific events of the last few days. There was definitely fallout from this. Massive sell-offs have all but decimated the financial world. Many companies have rapidly found themselves without operating capital to function and reduced their ability to pay for their financial obligations…Many stock and shareholders not reacting quickly enough now hold worthless pieces of paper…"

"…November 1, 2019. Multiple volcanoes continue to erupt without explanation all around the globe. The ash is so thick in many cities, those officials have advised their people to stay indoors if they can. In addition to the drastic rise in respiratory ailments due to the dust and smoke being spewed into the air, ash continues to fall to the ground now choking many areas of fertile farmland and soil."

"…December 29, 2019. Many northern hemisphere countries are still gripping from the intense and damaging winter. New York City reported fifty inches of snow this morning. Berlin, London, Moscow, and Paris reported record snow amounts as well. Contact with Iceland has been lost. Overloaded power grids have succumbed to the unrelenting winter storms. With transportation at a complete halt, supplies in most cities are running low…"

"…April 15, 2020. The sun has been partially blocked for a few months, slowing the photosynthesis process for plant life. Hopefully this will abate soon…"

"…May 11, 2020. With the prolonged winter, many food crops were destroyed, had low yields, or planting was delayed for the new season, forcing food prices to rise to record levels. The hope here is that the sun will fully return and the southern hemisphere has a mild winter to compensate…"

"…October 1, 2020. A record number of natural calamities around the world have further strained the already-fragile food chain. Fuel shortages have also been reported, forcing record prices, while record low temperatures have claimed the southern hemisphere… changing and inconsistent weather patterns continue to be a major stumbling block for recovery."

"…March 17, 2021. Many restaurants and bars are empty on what is normally a busy night for these owners… 'Cash-strapped people are making it another night at home. I can't blame them. Besides, barley is hard to come by these days. Before too long, I will be staying home as well,' said Suds at the Pub owner Daniel

James…"

"…June 22, 2021. More anti-technology demonstrations were held in cities around the globe today. The indication here is that they are becoming more organized and this sentiment is not going away any time soon…"

"…August 1, 2021. Most of the automobile manufacturers have announced that they will not be producing any cars for the rest of the year. This is no surprise to financial experts as catastrophic declines in sales continue to plague the industry. With current strict loan guidelines, reduced incomes, and record energy and food prices, no one can afford to make a big purchase. As a result, more and more people are putting an emphasis on maintaining their current vehicles. Right now, many consumers state that it is more practical to fix them. One manufacturer recently tried to self-finance cars, without a bank, but this was described as disastrous. Another stopped producing cars earlier this year, just focusing on producing replacement parts and providing more trained service personnel. Many experts thought this was a bad idea. Even though it was very meager, that company, right now, is the only one in the industry making a profit…"

"…January 3, 2022. With the 2nd Great Depression enveloping the world, which appears to be rapidly eclipsing the one almost a century ago, the nations of the world have scrapped the failed policies of the past. After almost two years of agonizing, painful, and ultimately successful negotiations, the ONE council has been formed. The One Nation Earth assembly is tasked to work together to avoid another Korean incident and unite the world. To this date, no one knows who was ultimately responsible for those heinous acts. ONE's mission is to create an understanding, awareness, and tolerance of all cultures, and to address the deteriorating economic and environmental climate. Electing a chairman is going to be difficult, but trust is building and everyone is eager to get to work…"

CHAPTER THIRTY-TWO

GULFSIDE CITY (2030)

By the spring of 2030, the ONE council was working well overall despite some differences of opinion and slow progress. The world, as a whole, was better off than it had been in years. Nations were talking, not screaming. Nations were strategizing on working with each other, not against. Acts of war and terrorism were at the lowest levels seen in decades. However, economic policies were still taking much longer than hoped. This was due to the fact at the local level, cities around the world were still reeling from chaos and internal strife. Local economies were in ruin. Unemployment was rampant. Food was in short supply. Health calamites were on the rise. Desperate people did desperate things to feed, clothe, and shelter themselves and their families. With local governments' resources stretched very thin and beyond, there seemed to be no end in sight.

Gulfside City was not spared this insanity. Many of its coveted programs were cancelled due to a shrinking tax base. Rising crime rates and baseless lawsuits overwhelmed the once-mighty police department. Its beauty was ravaged by graffiti and neglect. With neighbors turning on neighbors, all of Gulfside's community associations worked harder than ever to try to put a stop to the horrible nightmare despite the sense of hopelessness now surrounding the city. Adding to the angst, Gulfside City had another white winter mired with fallen ash. Sure before the madness, Gulfside had seen snow before, but those were twenty years apart and then the snow would melt the next day. This year was worse though. It was the end of April and the snow was still sticking which made the mood around town much more ugly. The recent white winters were not consistent, so when snow equipment was purchased, it was usually sold after a winter or two of no snow. Gulfside could not afford to sit on it. The city was playing a short-sighted game, making the bigger outlook worse each year. This year, there was no money for the equipment, compounding existing problems and challenges.

People improvised, but it slowed down any business that was left. As far as transportation was concerned, citizens mainly walked. This was becoming the norm as high gas prices, high cost of car ownership, and high insurance made walking and bike riding, as well, the primary modes of travel around town. The city's bus service was cut about three years ago. Taxi service was still present, but there were only two small companies, one of which just filed for bankruptcy. High fuel costs, which led to high fares, was leading to low usage. The remaining cabbies were now charging for services up front, because people would often take rides and not pay for them at the end. They would report the crime to the police, but would often find there would be no response as officers were busy with more serious crimes. If someone was arrested, prosecuted, and ordered by the court to pay restitution, there was no guarantee they would ever get it. The situation was dark, the outlook bleak, but Gulfside may have an opportunity to see the light at the end of the tunnel.

Associates of Sydney Ryan Grant, the world's only remaining billionaire, has recently approached the mayor with a lucrative and grandiose proposal to revitalize Gulfside. Grant wanted to not only move his home to Gulfside City, but his business headquarters as well. This, of course, was not without some concessions on Gulfside's part, but an offer to help make the city great again was hard to ignore. However, some of the provisions of the plan would anger the communal nature of Gulfside City, which is what made it thrive in the past. *Some personal liberties are going to be infringed upon,* thought the young naïve mayor. *Perhaps with some creative rewriting of the city's charter laws and a declaration of emergency status, this could work. This will work. Everyone is tired of the condition we are all in now. It's a risk, but I think everyone will welcome it. Maybe I should think about this a while longer? Of course, how much worse could it get.*

In a difficult time in history, this leader had to make a choice to determine the future course for his people and city.

CHAPTER THIRTY-THREE

JONATHON AWAKES, BUT WHEN?

"I now pronounce you Husband and wife. Jonathon, you may kiss your bride."

Jonathon turned toward Dana, and she to him. He lifted her veil, gazing into to her love-filled eyes. Everything was right in the world. Perfect weather. Perfect day. Perfect life. He leaned in with her moving in part way. He tilted his head to the side, pressing his lips against hers. He moved his body in closer to her, wrapping his arms around his loving wife. She in turn, returned the embrace. In Dana style, she lifted one of her legs, bent at the knee, behind her. The two of them, stuck in time, did not hear the applause of their family and friends. It was just the two of them in their perfect secure world.

"…Where is she?" asked Jonathon with a firm grip on the man's chest.

"She's across the bridge on the island."

Jonathon, with his free fist, struck the man with all of his might in the face. The man went limp from the force of the punch. Jonathon let him go and the man fell lifelessly to the ground.

"…Adam, I'm going in…"

"…Jonny, go get her. I've got this…"

"…I know you are disorientated sweetheart, but the place is crawling with Guardians. We've got to go…"

"…Adam the system is going haywire…"

"…He's emerging from stasis…Jonathon Scott…heart and pulse rate are stabilizing. Body temperature… returning to normal …"

"It's…cold," Jonathon stated with a weak raspy voice.

"You'll feel that way for about a half an hour," answered a gentle kind male voice out of the darkness.

"Why?"

"Your body's external temperature was at 40 degrees."

"Why would it be that low?"

"It's part of the procedure."

"What procedure?"

"ChronoSleep, sir."

"That's right. Wait. Why can't I see?"

"That will subside in a few minutes. Your body is basically rebooting itself. Please be patient."

"Okay."

Jonathon figured he had no strength to argue. He just laid there, listening to the commotion and movement around him. He heard the sound of shoes striking the floor. He heard voices in the background, but he could not ascertain what anyone was saying. This was unsettling to him, not knowing what was going on and not being able to see. However, the room was now getting brighter. Or, more accurately, Jonathon's vision was coming back to him.

"This is a weird sensation," he mumbled.

"Hang tight, Jonathon. Doctor, he is becoming more coherent now."

Jonathon heard the sound of hard heeled shoes knocking against the floor, getting louder with each step.

"Very good," replied a familiar feminine voice. He saw a distorted figure emerge, hovering over him. The voice asked, "What is your name please?"

Still weak and raspy Jonathon said, "Uh…Jonathon Scott."

"What is your date of birth?"

"August 31, 1987."

"Very good. Where are you from?"

"Gulfside City."

"Very good. Okay, Jonathon, please be patient with us. We have a delicate process to go through. However, you are in excellent health and everything appears normal."

"May I ask where am I?"

"You are in the ChronoSleep research facility."

"No…no. It's more like when, I guess? Is this the 22nd century?"

His vision became more clear. The figure bent and hovering over him was definitely a woman, but everything was still out of focus.

"Dr. Weiss, can you come and take a look at this for a moment?"

"Yes, of course," she said. "Just a minute, Jonathon, okay?"

He lethargically nodded his head. She then moved out of his field of view with the thud of her shoes moving away. Jonathon could hear better now, too.

"I noticed this, what appears to be, an abnormality in his brain scan," said another male voice.

"Hmm…I think…" the feminine voice paused. "Ah…yes. As you can see here, this is normal for Mr. Scott, but a very good catch nonetheless."

"Thank you, doctor."

The shoes, once again, approached. The woman reemerged in his sight. She leaned back down, facing him. She was more in focus now, well into her 60s, but definitely familiar.

With more strength, but still somewhat hoarse Jonathon asked, "Is everything okay with me?"

"Yes, Jonathon. All is going according to the specifications of the process."

"Your voice. Your face. Amy?"

"Yes, Jonathon."

"What happened? How are you here?"

She reached down, placed her hand on his shoulder, then bent down to be more level with him.

"Did you ChronoSleep here, too?" he asked.

Still making eye contact she said, "No, Jonathon. We had to wake you up earlier than planned. I'm sorry."

"Why?"

"We'll go over that later, but you are in excellent shape. Nothing is wrong with you."

"What year is it?"

Amy stood back up and removed her hand. "It is the year 2047. You've been asleep for almost 30 years. I'm sorry, I know you wanted much longer."

His first instinct was to be upset, but for some reason he was fine with this. "It's okay, Amy. Just please help me through this."

"Of course I will. I will be here every step of the way."

"Thank you."

"If you excuse me though, I have a lot of data to examine before we can get you out of this room. It will probably be another hour. Afterwards, we will transfer you to a more comfortable room. As strange as this may be, you will probably feel like sleeping a lot for the next day or two."

"I think I remember you telling me."

"Very good. Do you have any questions?"

He shook his head.

"Okay. Let us get through our procedure and we will talk soon."

Amy smiled at him and then moved out of his sight. He closed his eyes. There were still the sounds of other people moving about the room. Her shoes became so faint, it was as if she had left the room. He wondered what was outside? What was the world like? He thought of images of a utopia awaiting him. Slowly his consciousness slipped away.

CHAPTER THIRTY-FOUR

GETTING BACK TO REALITY

Jonathon awoke and appeared to be in a room similar to the one he stayed in when he first arrived…30 years ago. It was dark, but a light from the blue display of an alarm clock somewhat lit up the room. Jonathon was on his stomach. He lifted his head off of the pillow, looking up.

"What..." he said.

He flipped to his side, took hold of the covers, and threw them off him toward the foot of the bed. He swung his feet off the side of the bed and sat up in progression. He looked down at himself and noticed he was wearing a pair dark pants and a light tee shirt.

"I don't remember putting these on," he said.

He slowly leaned back slightly and let out a big yawn. He straightened out then started to glance around the room, with his eyes more adjusted. "Hmm…I think this is the same room."

Jonathon slipped off of the bed and placed his feet on the bare cold floor. "It's the future, you would think the floor would be heated. Let's go check out the TV and see what's going on in the world. Okay, Jonny, who are you talking to again?"

Jonathon carefully walked around the bed toward the living area, when he paused. "Wait a second, let's see how I look after 30 years."

He redirected himself, stumbling toward the bathroom. His legs were weak and sore, but still tolerable. Once in, he turned on the light. The bright light raced into his eyes, so he quickly closed to give them a chance to adjust. He slowly opened them to match his comfort. Looking into the mirror, he saw a distorted image staring back at him. His eyes focused in better and the reflection became clearer. "Wow, she was right. I have not aged a day."

He rubbed his jaw, feeling the stubble he was seeing in his mirrored image. "I need a shave."

He walked back into the bedroom, then continued on out to the living area. "Where's the light switch out here?" Just then, the ambient lighting slowly illuminated. "Okay, never mind."

He paused, scanning the room. The layout was exactly the same with one obvious exception. "Where's the TV?"

His attention then focused on the dining nook. "Oh good, there are my things."

His case and bag were on the table. He continued his march, now specifically to the table. In addition to his personal effects, there was also a small white boxlike container, too.

There was a note on top of the box. *Hello, Jonathon. Hope all is well. Here are a few items you may need. When you are ready, give me a call at extension 112. I'll come by and give you an overview of what's going on. With regards, Amy.*

Jonathon set the note on the table, then opened the box. It contained travel sizes of body soap, shampoo, shaving cream, toothpaste, a toothbrush, mouthwash, and a razor. There was also some bottled water.

"That was nice. I didn't think to bring any of this. Hmm, that's weird. All of these products are all from the same company… SYNRG. Huh, almost sounds like synergy. Maybe it's just from a company that packaged this. Okay…again, Jonny, who are you talking to?"

Jonathon shaved, brushed his teeth, and showered. He dressed in some of his clean clothes, which he packed…years ago. He selected a pair of blue jeans, a tan tee shirt, and a pair of white sneakers. A moment ago, he had hung up with Amy who had stated that she was on her way. He wanted the table clear, so he packed up everything and placed the bag on the sofa. He stood his case upright next to the table. As he was standing up, a two-tone chime sounded.

"That must be her."

He hurried over to the door, locating the button to open it and pressing nervously. The door slid open. Sure enough it was Amy, dressed in very simple attire of blacks and whites.

"May I come in?" she asked.

"Please."

Jonathon motioned for her to enter. "Would you like to sit

down at the table?"

"Sure. Thank you."

Amy was carrying the same tablet computer she had years ago. She went around the table to the chair on the far end. She placed the computer on the table as she sat down. He sat down as well on the opposite chair. Amy tapped the screen of the tablet before resting her arms on the table.

With a smile she asked, "How are you feeling today, Jonathon?"

"Very well," Jonathon replied with an upbeat tone. "I don't feel any different than before the ChronoSleep."

"Good. Okay then, I know you must have a million questions, so go ahead."

"Thank you. I guess I will start with the date. The TV is gone, so I have no idea what today is."

"It is May 17, 2047."

"Wow."

"Sorry about the television. I had it removed so you couldn't see what is going on."

"Oh?"

"I wanted to give you some of the more notable events myself, first," Amy said, with a conciliatory tone. "It is a very different world and I thought this was the best way to ease you into it."

"Okay, that's fine. You know what's best. I guess my next question is, why only the 30 years? What happened to the full term?"

"Well, that kind of ties in with what's going on in the world. We'll get to that in a moment, but for us here at ChronoSleep, our funding has been completely severed. The private companies giving us money back when you went in no longer exist. When we did find someone else interested in our work, either they could not afford to help us long, they were taken over by someone else, or went out of business. The remaining support from the government was recently cut. We survived this long because no one realized we were still getting the subsidies. They just simply forgot about us. We filed reports regularly, per our directives, but no one must have been reading them. For the last twenty years, we've been operating on a shoestring budget and everyday was a gift."

"What do you mean?"

Amy unclasped her hands, reached down to computer, and slid it across to Jonathon. He grasped it, setting it in front of him. She leaned back in her chair and refolded her hands on the table. He examined the info displayed on the screen.

Jonathon glanced through articles about the Koreas, economy, anti-technologists, ONE, and the deteriorating climate. Amy sat patiently as he read, not hurrying or rushing him, allowing him to take his time to learn and digest about the decline of civilization and the world outside.

Jonathon slid the tablet back to Amy. It was all he could absorb for now.

He sat back in his chair and looked up at Amy. "What a mess."

"I'm so sorry to have woken you up now."

"Please don't apologize, there is nothing you could have done," Jonathon said, with gracious understanding. "From the sound of things, I'm grateful to have woken up to something. Do you have any info about Gulfside?"

"I'm sorry, I don't. We can try and get something before we leave."

"Leave?"

Her face was stern. "We have to go today…in fact soon."

"Why is that?" Jonathon asked, sensing pending doom.

"There is a rather large anti-technology mob, rioting, outside the building."

"What?"

"The world has gone crazy, Jonathon. This movement is getting out of control. They believe the world's problems are the result of rapid technological advancements. Maybe they're right, maybe they're wrong, that's not for me to judge, but ChronoSleep, even today, is still a technological marvel. We are…what these people hate."

"You tried to keep me in ChronoSleep as long as you could, to get me as close to my goal as possible."

"Yes. You and a few others. The money we have left was going to last until the end of the year, with my hopes of finding another source of revenue. But, this damn group showed up two days ago. That is when I decided to wake you up. They've been trying to get in ever since, like barbarians trying to storm a castle, but our fortified building here is slowing them down considerably. They broke through the outer slide doors, but we have a more secure blast door in place."

All of a sudden they heard a dampened explosion reverberate throughout the building, followed by a brief rattling sensation, almost like an earthquake.

"What was that!" Jonathon exclaimed.

Amy was eerily calm in her posture. "I don't know where they got them from, but they have been detonating explosives on the door. That was the third one in two days. I suspect they are the reason my funding got cut, but there is nothing I can do now."

Jonathon shook his head. "Unbelievable. Why are they trying to get in?"

"They gave us an ultimatum to stop our research by the end of last month or they would do it themselves. We obviously ignored them."

"What about the police, why aren't they stopping this?"

"They are stretched thin as it is, but this building has a helicopter pad on the roof. They've been flying us out, intermittently, the last two days. You and I are part of the last group to leave. In fact..." Amy looked at her watch. "...I lost track of time...the last one is going to be here soon. I'm glad you called when you did, or we were going to have to wheel you out of here. We have to go, now. I'm sorry this is so sudden."

She stood up from her chair.

Jonathon did the same. "It's not your fault. Let's just get out of here safely."

Jonathon went over to the sofa to get his bag.

Amy grabbed the computer. "The helicopter is taking us to the airport, which is not far from here. We'll get out there and then go by car to the train station. I assumed you would probably want to go back to Gulfside."

"I guess that will be the logical place for me to go," Jonathon said with his bag on his shoulder.

He maneuvered back to the table and grabbed his case. Amy came from around the table, darting for the door. Jonathon quickly followed. She opened the door, then marched out into the hallway with Jonathon in tow. All of a sudden there was the sound of another explosion. The building shook again, with lights flickering this time.

"We better hurry, I don't know how much longer the door will hold. I put the elevators and stairwells on card access only, to slow them down further if they did make it in the building."

Amy hustled down the hallway with Jonathon following suit.

"If it will be easier, I will fly on a plane if I have to," Jonathon said.

"Well, it's not an option. There has not been a domestic commercial flight in almost a decade. You either travel by a chartered plane, which most people can't afford, or on the overworked under funded rail system, which is very popular these days. Also, if one is lucky to own a car, then they have that, but of course it's not fast like a train or plane."

Amy and Jonathon reached the elevator at the end of the curved hallway. The doors opened. Amy slipped in, with Jonathon struggling with his stuff to get in. He managed to wiggle himself in, turning and backing into one of the rear corners to give Amy some room. The door shut, but nothing happened. She went up to the reader by the door and then inserted and quickly removed a card from the reader.

"Level please?" asked the machine.

"Roof access," answered Amy.

The lift began to move and she placed the card into one of her pockets. Within moments the car slowed, jolted into place, and the doors slid open. The light of a hazy setting sun shone right into their eyes. Jonathon was expecting warm air, but it was cooler than the air conditioning they had just came from. Amy exited, with Jonathon clumsily following.

"What's the deal with the cold air? I thought you said this was May?"

"It is May. This is part of the ecological problems. Nobody can explain if this is one problem or part of another. I can't remember the last time we had a daily high temperature much above 80 degrees."

They hiked up a walkway from the elevator then swayed to the right and onto the roof. The helipad was just ahead, on an elevated platform with five people standing around it. All of them are holding some sort of bag or piece of luggage. Amy stopped and then faced Jonathon.

With the ruckus of the ambient sound, Amy spoke with a slightly raised voice. "We have a few minutes before our ride arrives. I will be on the same train as you for most of your trip back to Gulfside. So if you have or think of any more questions, I am more than happy to help, answer, guide you as best as I can."

"Well, thank you."

"Sure, of course. After we get settled on the train, I have some money to give you…the compensation I mentioned before you went in. It's not much, especially after the financial meltdown. I had it removed from our investments before they took the worst of the beating and I have been holding on to it for almost 28 years for you."

"Thank you so much."

"I don't know how far you will get, but you will quickly find out what's more and what's less. We can go over more on the train. I wish there could have been more."

"Thank you, Amy, it is greatly appreciated. Any amount is sure going to be a big help."

"When I give it to you on the train, keep it as hidden as possible. People are desperate and will do anything to get it if they know you have it."

The sound of an approaching helicopter was becoming more pronounced from the distance.

"Excuse me, I've got to make sure we were the last to get out," Amy said.

"Yeah, sure."

Amy ran toward the group of people. Jonathon looked around

him and quickly noticed he was standing somewhat near the edge of the building. Curious about the world, he walked over to the railing. He put a hand on it and glanced over the horizon. ChronoSleep was out in the middle of nowhere, away from the hustle and bustle of society.

"Everything looks the same," he said.

Then he leaned a bit over the railing, noticing the large mob of people below. They were away from the front door and crouched down.

"What in the world are they doi…"

Abruptly, there was a flash of light, followed by smoke and the sound of an explosion, which was subdued by the now-closer helicopter. Jonathon gripped the railing as hard a he could as the building shook again, coupled with the increase in wind speed. The people below got up and started rushing for the door. Some of them looked up and pointed up at him. He could tell they were yelling at him, but could not hear what they were saying. More and more of the group seemed to be pouring into the building.

"Shit…they got in."

Jonathon quickly leaned back, then turned himself around. Amy was motioning him to come closer. He, as best as he could, hurried to her and the group. The force of the surrounding wind was now greater and the noise deafening, as the aircraft made final maneuvers to land. He marched right up to and next to Amy.

"I think they got in," he said, almost yelling to compensate for the racket.

"It will take them a bit to get through the labyrinth below," she said at the same voice level. "We'll be long gone."

The wheels of the helicopter touched down onto the pad. After a couple of seconds, the main access door slid open with one of the vehicle's operators jumping out and swiveling down a set of entry steps.

"We're ready, when you're ready," stated the man.

The five individuals ahead carefully climbed up the small set of stairs onto the platform, making their way up to the helicopter, stepping up and filing in one by one. Jonathon and Amy followed.

"You first." Jonathon offered.

"What a gentleman," she replied.

Gripping a handle bar just inside the craft, she ascended up the small step and in. Jonathon gripped the bar, and pulled himself up and in. Quickly selecting a seat near Amy, he secured his bag below it as best as he could. He sat down, gripping his case on his lap.

"Everybody in?" inquired the man. Jonathon gave a quick thumbs-up, but did not pay attention to anyone else's response. He hated flying and this was his first time in a helicopter. He leaned his head back and closed his eyes. He heard the man jump in, swing the steps up, and slide the door close.

Jonathon sat there, in somewhat of disbelief, at what was happening. *Am I dreaming? I'm still in ChronoSleep. This is a bad dream. That's it. This is a weird and bad dream. In fact, I will wake up and Dana will be saying good morning to me.*

The aircraft began to rise. Jonathon's little jump into fantasy was dashed as he got sick to his stomach. The helicopter was swaying, changing direction. Then began the forward momentum. Jonathon stayed still.

"Are you okay, Jonathon?" asked Amy.

"No."

Jonathon opened his eyes, looking out one of the nearby windows. He really could not see anything. *Probably just as well. I really haven't liked what I have seen so far.* He closed his eyes again.

CHAPTER THIRTY-FIVE

ONWARD TO GULFSIDE

The airport was not far from the station, which was not far from ChronoSleep. It was out in the middle of nowhere and there was no change from 30 years ago. Even the cars were models he recognized from before. Older, but familiar.

The train depot was pretty much the same, but it was much more rundown and filthy. Jonathon had a brief snag with security concerning his gun, but it was eventually resolved. Jonathon, for some reason and by luck, was still listed as an active-duty officer. This allowed him to keep his gun and prevent him from being detained.

The train itself, had a makeover or two, but there was nothing futuristic about it. Amy and Jonathon were in the dining car at a tall table for two with a pair of drinks in front of them. Other than another couple several tables down and the waitress, they had the room to themselves. The ambient light was subdued, creating a warm and comfortable environment. The room was quiet, even with the sounds of the train wheels rolling and knocking against the tracks softly muffled in the background, the waitress taking an order, and Amy's tender voice.

"I'm surprised, we have this place pretty much to ourselves," she said.

"Why do you say that?" Jonathon asked.

"Usually, you have to push your way through people just to move around. Of course..." Amy looked at her watch, "It is late... very late. How are you feeling with all of this?"

"I'm fine I guess. Now that things have slowed down a bit, the reality is starting to sink in. Thank you again, for everything."

"Sure."

Amy reached into a shirt pocket and pulled out a small business sized card. She gave it to Jonathon, then gestured to it. "This is my contact information. The best way to reach me would probably either be my mobile phone or by email. The work number is no longer valid. As of today, I guess I'm technically unemployed now."

"Oh?"

"Yeah, well I can only imagine what those people are doing to my building right now. Plus, with no fresh capital, the project is doomed anyway." She grasped her glass and took a sip of her beverage. "Maybe someday, I can start this up again…I managed to save all of the data and research. The physical equipment, not so much."

"If I may ask, did you start ChronoSleep? You just seem to have a passion about it."

"Oh, no. Not by a long shot. But over the years I've overseen so much of the program, the board of directors made me the facility director. In essence, I have become ChronoSleep. Yet, the last few years it's been more like cheerleader and fund-raiser than researcher. I spent more of the last few years out of the office soliciting money from anyone willing to listen. I have been on so many trains. I think I'm now an expert on the rail system. That's why I'm surprised. There are hardly no people here tonight, but I don't think I have ever been up this late on a train. I would usually just stay in my cabin. That's no more now."

"What are you going to do now, if I may ask?"

"Of course you may ask. I'm going to my sister's place. When I do get there, I will look over more of your data in full detail. Under normal circumstances, I would have like to have kept you for a week for observation to make sure there are no weird abnormalities, but you know how that turned out. Do you feel anything out of sorts?"

"Physically, no. With everything slowing down, I'm starting to think about my family again."

"Well that's only natural. For you, no time has passed. I know you did this to get away from that feeling, but…"

"I know. You, in a roundabout way, tried to warn me I might still have issues."

"Well, no physical abnormalities are good. Just be aware though, some side effects may manifest later. I'm a phone call away to help you through any of them. The emotional ones, I can help with, too. Call me day or night. I will be involved as much as or as little as you want."

"Well, thank you. I guess it did not help dreaming about Dana and our wedding when I was in ChronoSleep."

"What?" Amy said with surprise.

"I dreamt about Dana. Is there something wrong?"

"Well, no, I don't think so. It's just…you should not have been able to dream. You are the first one to report dreaming."

"Should I be concerned?"

"No, I don't think so. Just out of curiosity, was that the only time?"

"No. I remember a few others. A couple were with my good friend, Adam. Then there was one with me punching out a man. Oh and there was another one with a woman."

"Weird," she said, shaking her head. She looked back at him and he seemed concerned. "I'm sorry, Jonathon, I don't mean to react this way, I'm just a bit caught off guard."

"It's okay. I would like to note though, to possibly add to your dismay, the one dream I had with Dana, I obviously remember experiencing and living it…exactly as it happened. The ones I had with Adam and the man, I don't ever remember going through. And…I never met the woman. Or at least, I don't remember. Is this strange?"

"No not at all. With dreams, there is a random pattern to them, sometimes based on past experiences, but set in different ways. I would not be worried. As far as dreaming at all during ChronoSleep, my gut tells me to not worry about that either. I promise, when I get to my sister's, I will scrutinize your data very closely for anything that shouldn't be. Okay?"

"If you're not bothered by it, than I won't be either."

"Good, give me a few days and I will contact you…or give me a call. When you get settled in Gulfside, get me some contact info when you get a chance."

"Will do."

The two of them sat quietly for a moment. Jonathon sat back listening to the train. She took another sip of her drink.

"Do you know where you're going when you get to Gulfside?"

Jonathon shook his head. "No. I guess I need to figure it out and soon. If he's still there, maybe I will look up Adam. It will be bizarre though."

"How so?"

"He'll be what…60?" Jonathon said with a brief awkward laugh. "And you…"

"Yes, older as well. It's okay. I'm just glad to still be alive."

"I guess the world had a close call, right after I left."

"It was tense there, for those couple of days, after the nuclear explosions. I didn't sleep at all during the whole thing."

"You were worried."

"Yeah, but I think it was more like, I did not want to go to sleep and then...nothing. I wanted to be awake when the end came. Fortunately, our leaders came to their senses and stopped what could have been much worse. In the short-term ,we were safe, but then the real nightmare soon began after."

"The breakdown of society?"

"Yes. In a way you were lucky not to have gone through the meat of it. It's a little better now, but we still have a long way to go."

"Weeks before my family died and right after I stopped what would have been a horrific act of violence, I stood outside my house wondering what kind of world my children were going to live in. I don't want to say maybe it's better they are not here to see this, not at all, but what quality of life would they have had?"

"I understand," Amy said, with comfort.

"Do you have your own family?"

Amy casually turned her head away and appeared to tear up a little.

"I'm sorry, I should not be so meddlesome," Jonathon said.

She wiped her tears away. "No, it's all right. We all make our choices," she said with a regretful tone. "My sister got married and had two wonderful children, a girl and then a boy. Both are terrific. Both are doctors now, like their aunt. I married ChronoSleep. I literally lived there. ChronoSleep was my home. I felt safe there. I hated going on those trips to drum up support, to no avail I might add. I did not feel safe, but I always had my home to look forward to. I felt the trade off of never settling down and having a family was the best decision for me. Now, ChronoSleep is gone and I'm now running to my baby sister for safety. I was the one always watching out for her, when we were little, but how the tables have turned. I feel so vulnerable now."

"Your lost," he muttered under his breath.

"What was that?"

"I'm sorry, I did not mean for you to hear my drivel."

"No, please continue."

"You feel lost. After my family…I felt lost…maybe displaced. I went through a lot of long lonely nights to figure that out."

"I know my situation is not as severe as you losing your…"

"Perhaps, but you still lost your sense of purpose, your world. With my family gone, I have no purpose. No world. I'm a drifter, without a home. I may have physically had a home, but it was no longer home, when they died. You just witnessed your safe haven being ripped apart, so of course you feel vulnerable."

"Yes," she said, nodding her head.

"Are you close to your sister?"

"Very."

"Good. I don't have and siblings, but Adam was like a brother."

"Is."

"Huh?"

"Is like a brother."

"Right, I need to think he is still there. He would have done anything for me, including putting his whole life aside for me."

"It's what good siblings do."

"I did not want my misfortune to become his misfortune. He still had his whole life ahead of him."

"What did he say when you wanted to go into ChronoSleep?"

"I didn't tell him. I know Adam. He would have done his hardest to persuade me not to do it. And, I could not go on allowing him to take up any more of his life for me."

"So you just left?"

"I left a letter, just explaining how I was going somewhere safe and I could not take up any more of his life."

"Your 'letter' could have done more harm than good."

"I wasn't thinking very clearly on a lot of things, but sitting here, talking with you, I think the main reason I did ChronoSleep was not for me, but for me to release Adam."

"Yeah, you could be right."

"I still needed to get away from the familiar things around Gulfside, though. This may seem strange, especially coming from a former police officer, but I don't think I would have felt safe in any other town. Not while feeling alone and vulnerable. That, too, is what pulled me to ChronoSleep."

"I remember. Being home, but not having the familiar surroundings."

"Yeah, I guess I will see how it is going to go. Well, in a sense, you and I are starting over. Do you have any idea what you are going to do now?"

Amy shook her head. "No. My sister said I can stay with her forever, if need be, but hopefully it won't come to that. I have a lot of thinking to do."

"Of course, I understand. When I get things sorted out in Gulfside, finding a place, job, and such…I'll send you my info. Maybe you can come visit. Gulfside is such a wonderful place."

"I hate to spoil the mood here, but please be careful when you get there," Amy said with a grimaced expression. "I don't like being pessimistic, but you are going to have to lower your expectations of your hometown. The world is very different. Gulfside was most likely not spared what the rest of the world is going through."

"You mean the economic meltdown, unpredictable environment, and such."

"Yes. Among other things."

"Other things?"

"There have been reports of very odd behavior out of some cities. But not all." She shook her head. "I'm sorry, I wish I could explain further but…I really haven't been paying any attention to anything lately other than ChronoSleep."

"I guess I will find out one way or another."

Amy glancing at her watch again, said, "Phew…it is late. I'd better get some rest. You probably should, too. It has been an exhausting day to say the least. I believe the train will reach my transfer point in the late morning."

"Thank you, for everything, Amy."

"No, thank you, Jonathon. Just talking here, with you, has made me feel a little better. I can't wait to be at my sister's tomorrow, though."

Amy got up from her chair. Jonathon did the same. She walked up to him, taking him by surprise, and embraced him with a hug. He returned the embrace.

She then picked up her computer. "I will look over your info when I get to my sister's. If you need anything at any time, give me a ring."

"Will do."

Amy pointed to the table. "I will take care of the bill for the drinks."

"Thank you," Jonathon said with a nervous chuckle.

"You're welcome. Good luck," Amy said with a smile.

"You, too." Amy turned around, and headed for what looked like a cashiering station. The waitress took note and moved in that direction. Jonathon grabbed his beverage and gulped the remainder of the liquid. He set the empty glass back on the table.

He was about to sit back down when a clock on a nearby wall caught his attention. "It is late. It's time for me to get some sleep."

CHAPTER THIRTY-SIX

ARRIVAL AT HOME?

This is it. Gulfside City, Jonathon thought. *Home.* Jonathon was anxious, but ready to see his town...to see what was different…what might be the same, if anything. He changed clothes before leaving his cabin. He was not sure how long of a day it would be, so this was the best opportunity to do so. He put on another pair of blue jeans and another tee shirt. He also put on a black soft leather jacket, expecting it to be cool outside. As a precaution and just in case, he strapped his revolver to his leg above his ankle. He was ready.

Jonathon, with his case in hand, stepped off of the train and onto walkway below. He was immediately met by a guard, dressed in an all-black uniform and a beret styled black hat. He pointed down the way.

"Lets go, keep it moving," stated the man.

Jonathon complied and literally went with the flow of a few others who departed the locomotive. There were several guards, dressed very similar to the first one, at various points directing and corralling everyone down the way. So far, the station was very different.

The track platform was now enclosed, not just covered. The train he just got off of was on the first set of tracks, so he could not tell if there was the same amount of rows. Keeping pace with the pack, he wondered where they were being sent to. They passed through a chain-link fence line and into a large open space. There were now guards pointing and directing everyone toward four rows of escalators with a standard set of stairs in between. The two closest to the stationary set were working, the outer ones were not. It was just as well, there were not that many people around to use them.

Marching onto the metal plate, Jonathon stepped onto the moving conveyor and up he went. He took the right-side escalator while the others in his group, uniformly, took the other one. No one went up the non-moving stairs.

"Okay. I did shower," he grumbled to himself.

Jonathon arrived at the top first. He stepped off the machine and was now facing multiple stations set up similar to a customs checkpoint.

"What the..."

Jonathon was motioned toward a station. All of the stations, or booths rather, were uniform in shape and color. The stalls themselves were enclosed, similar to a ticket stand, large enough to seat two individuals comfortably. All had protective glass in front overlooking a small shelf. Sensing he would need his identification, he reached into his pocket for his wallet. He walked up to the window with a female attendant on the other side, who was dressed in the same uniform as the others.

"Your name, sir?" she asked with a flat tone.

"Jonathon Scott."

"Please put your middle finger in the reader," she said.

"Okay."

He pulled his hand out of his pocket, placing his middle finger as instructed on the cold glass-face plate in front of the window. The scanner read his print with a glow.

Glancing down at her screen, she began randomly touching it. "Remove your finger."

He promptly took his finger off the reader.

"Okay, Lieutenant Jonathon Scott, your finger print is a match and I can confirm you in our system."

Why was all of this necessary to just get into the city? he wondered. He figured he better not ask, to just go with it, hope for the best and find out later. *At least I'm in their records. That is a good thing,* he assumed.

"Your purpose here in Gulfside City?"

"I'm returning home."

She began touching her screen again.

"Do you have any weapons on you?" she asked.

I better be truthful, he thought. "Yes, I have a revolver strapped to my leg."

Still with a flat tone, she said. "Thank you Lieutenant Jonathon Scott. I will deactivate the scanner so you can go through. If you have any property with us, please check with the concierge inside.

"Okay. Thank you."

"Please proceed through the scanner now."

Jonathon turned and proceeded to the scanning area, and discovered a line in front of him. A male guard on the other side of the device waved him over. Jonathon moved out of line and hurried to him. Glancing over to the others in line, he expected to see or hear some grumbling. However, there was not one peep. In fact everyone in that line just kept staring straight ahead in unison, almost oddly vacant. Jonathon went by the luggage scanner, then the guard waved him through the body scanner partition without incident.

Is it supposed to be this easy? he thought. *I just need to go with the flow.*

"The concierge is ready for you, sir," said the guard with a flat tone as well.

The depot, as a whole, was not the same building as before.

Jonathon passed the guard, then headed up to the nearby counter. As he approached, the attentive, yet, indifferent man placed Jonathon's bag onto the counter.

"Here you are, Lieutenant Jonathon Scott. Do you need help with those?"

He thought for a moment. *I don't know where I'm going. I really do not feel like lugging these things around. I have my money on me so…*

"Actually, I think I'd like to store these somewhere if a can?" he asked.

"Of course. There are lockers around the corner from me."

With his belongings stored safe, Jonathon was ready to venture outside. He marched to what he believed was the way out. As he walked, he began to take note of his surroundings. There was something odd to him, something out of place. *Okay, this is the future, there are bound to be some unsettling changes. But what is it?* he wondered. The station seemed to be ordinary, nothing radical. Rows of counters lined the wall of the corridor in front of him. They were all unmanned at the moment. *Okay, nothing to be alarmed about.* Looking back at the massive corridor lockers, *Nothing out of the ordinary there. What is it?* As Jonathon approached the doors to get him outside, he paused for the moment. As he braced for what awaited for him on the outside, he began to be more conscious of the people shuffling around him. It was more noticeable to him, there was something missing. *The station is not very busy. But busy enough.*

He heard the sounds of footsteps…the rubbing of clothing… wheels of luggage rolling on the floor. *Talking?* There was not much talking. Not even on phones. Other than the voices being exchanged by the security check-in, which required interaction, there were no real conversations going on. Couples walked with each other but were not engaging in any meaningful contact. People with children were also quiet. In fact, the children themselves were oddly hushed with no emotion. *Texting. Texting was very popular in my time.* There was no texting here either. Everyone seemed to be content with staying silent. They were just lost in whatever it was they were doing.

The clothing styles were equally as bewildering. Colors and fashions were very drab and plain. Black was the prevalent color. Some had gray accents, some silver. Others had white patters and designs. Jonathon was the only one in blue jeans. In spite of this, no one either noticed or cared. Not one glance. Nothing.

Hats, some people had them. Some did not. Again, they were basic black, gray, silver, and white tones, with basic styles, shapes, and sizes. Strangely this almost was uniform. No brown, no tan, no other colors, no sports teams, or clever sayings. Just plain. Those not wearing hats had very short hair, including women. *None of the women have long hair,* he thought. *That's different.*

The world was moving by in such a stoic, maybe dystopic, manner. *I guess I shouldn't question this.* From Amy's ominous warning about the condition of society, he was imagining people to be more belligerent. *I haven't gone outside yet…probably more to come.* Yet there he stood, stationary, immobile. It was time to move on, but he remained in place, paralyzed again, by time. He did not know what to expect. He was nervous, perhaps a little afraid. Nonetheless, he could not go back. His only choice was to go forward.

"Well, this is it," he mumbled.

He took a deep breath and on onward he filed. The doors slid open with an eerie silence. Jonathon walked through and out, onto the concrete sidewalk of the drop-off and pick-up zone. The air was cool, as he now had come to expect, even for May. Not as cool for a jacket, but it was nearing evening. The area was covered, yet it probably would have made little difference as the sun struggled to peer through the haze.

The haze, however, could not conceal the colossal metropolis, standing in the distance, where downtown Gulfside City should have been.

"What the…" he said, with astonishment.

Jonathon felt a cold shiver radiate through his body, a rush of adrenaline, and great wonder. He also felt an extreme sense of solitude as he became lost in the view in front of him. "It can't be."

He knew this was home, but it was now all grown up. Massive skyscrapers dominated the skyline, in shapes and sizes he could have only imaged in his dreams.

"Oh Dana, what have I done?" he said with trepidation.

As he viewed this majestic marvel, he felt more alone now, more isolated, than he ever did. "I hope this was not a bad idea. I can't just stand here, but I can't seem to move."

He could not find the strength to go. It was as if he was holding himself prisoner in a trance, wrapped in a dream. He continued his gaze…at the skyline…at nothing…at home.

"Can I help you, sir?"

"Huh?" replied Jonathon, as he wrestled to get out of his stupor. He turned to see an older man, in a gray uniform of sorts, standing near him, facing him.

"Did you need a ride somewhere?" asked the man.

A little more coherent Jonathon said, "Yeah, that's probably a good idea."

"Where to?"

Jonathon pointed to downtown.

"You got it, let's go."

The man turned, marching down the sidewalk toward a lone automobile. Jonathon finally collected himself and followed. This guy did not seem to fit the norm around here. Although subdued, his mannerisms did have emotion. He was detached maybe, but at least there was a little spark of humanity.

As he walked, he noted one other oddity. This car was the only car in this entire driveway through the depot. Nonetheless, it was in exceptional shape and appeared well taken care of for a car of its age.

"What part of downtown?" asked the driver.

"I don't know. Just take me to the heart of it all."

"Uh, okay. No problem."

The man removed a small finger scanner from his pocket, similar to the one security was using when he left.

"Please place your index finger on the screen. This is so I can pre-approve payment."

"Oh? We haven't gone anywhere yet."

The driver seemed perplexed at Jonathon's statement. "I apologize sir. Per company and industry guidelines, I must take payment upfront. It's standard practice, of course."

"I'm sorry, it has been a long time since I have had to hire a ride."

Jonathon complied, gently placed his finger as instructed.

"Okay, you can remove you finger." the man instructed.

Jonathon removed his finger. The man read the information on the device.

"Oh, you're a Gulfside citizen. Then…" He tapped the screen a few times. "…this is on Gulfside's tab and free to you."

"Thank you."

"You're welcome, sir."

"I'm sorry, I did not catch your name?"

"It's Dennis, sir."

Jonathon, closely examined him and wondered if he was the same man. Sure enough it was, just older. *How odd,* he thought. The same guy who brought him here so he could get away from the past was now here to take him into his future. Jonathon found this eerie and unsettling on so many levels.

"Nice to meet you, Dennis."

Jonathon offered his hand to him, but this seemed to baffle the man.

Dennis, with obvious hesitation, returned the small computer back to his pocket and politely reciprocated. "You too, sir."

Jonathon continued his study of the man, which was making Dennis uncomfortable.

"Everything okay, sir?" Dennis asked.

"Yes, I'm sorry. I haven't interacted with many people lately."

"I understand, sir."

Dennis looked away, moving over to the rear door. It appeared as if Dennis did not recognize Jonathon. It was one ride, almost thirty years ago. Dennis opened the door to allow Jonathon to enter the dormant vehicle. Jonathon hurried over, now trying to avoid direct eye contact. He slouched down, entering the car.

Dennis gently closed the door. He walked to the front of the car. Jonathon sat in the relatively quiet space. The air conditioner was on and running, but the engine was not, as he could determine. The aroma inside was somewhat stale, like an old car would smell, especially if this was the same car as before. But, it was still clean.

As Dennis got in, Jonathon inspected the car. He looked around him. The interior was well maintained, but did have signs of being refashioned. *Is this...the same car?* he thought. From his understanding from Amy, new cars didn't exist. Besides, if it was a newer vehicle, why build, by today's timeline, an old model? Dennis had closed his door and was getting settled. Dennis then placed his index finger on a small black square plate near the ignition, where a key would go. The car started.

Leaning back in his seat Dennis said, "It won't be a long drive sir, but if you would like to read a newspaper or magazine, I've got a couple in the seat pocket in front of you."

"I think I will."

Eager to find out more of what was going on, he leaned forward and reached into the rather large pouch. He fumbled around, feeling for the texture of a newspaper or magazine. He just kept repeatedly touching a couple of items that were made of a hard plastic. He decided to pull one of the objects out to see what it was.

Holding the slim item in his hand, Jonathon examined what seemed to be a mobile tablet computer. "Hey Dennis, I think someone may have left their computer back here."

Dennis looked back to see. "Oh no, sir. That's the media device I just referred to."

"This is the magazine or newspaper?" Jonathon asked, with bewilderment.

"Yes sir," Dennis said with a smile. "I apologize for asking again, but are you okay? You just seem to be out of sorts."

"I'm fine, just surprised. I was expecting…paper, you know?"

Dennis, still smiling, refaced forward, shifted the car into gear, then started to drive. "As I'm sure you are aware, there has not been a printed publication around here for about 10 years."

"What?" Jonathon said, without thinking. *I'd better keep my circumstances hidden for now.* He quickly tried to divert Dennis's attention away from his obvious slip up. "You know, I try and avoid the news…it is always depressing." *Yeah, that was weak,* Jonathon thought.

"Yes, it is disheartening, sir. I hope at some point, something will turn around."

"Wow, 10 years, I guess it has been that long since…"

"I understand, sir."

Jonathon figured he should just shut up now and looked down at the tablet. Gadgets similar to this were very popular before he left his time. He was curious. Was this refurbished or a new version of those devices? Amy mentioned a rebellion against technology. He was not sure how old this thing was and was hesitant to ask, further risking his place in time. Jonathon located the power button and pressed it to turn the small machine on.

"Do you need help with that, sir?"

"I think I got it."

The screen woke up with a welcoming glow. A banner message trickled down the screen. "Welcome to Media Surge. Services, device, and network provided by SYNRG Technologies."

"SYNRG," he whispered, "I've seen that name before, but where?"

He shook his head. The main menu appeared displaying a list of options. *Oh, local news let me try that.* Jonathon lightly pressed the screen. A list of local publications displayed within an apparent radius around Gulfside City. He did not enter a search criteria, so he could only surmise that this thing was connected to some sort of global positioning system. "Gulfside Gazette." Jonathon pressed the option, and the "Gulfside Gazette" appeared for today, May, 18, 2047. He scanned through the banner headlines, listed in no seemingly particular order.

"Lice infestation under control?"

"Unemployment in Gulfside remains at less than 1%. Many cities around the nation and the world are still around 20%."

"Gulfside's agricultural division yields another monthly surplus for export."

"New bright star now visible in the north sky." *Let me take a look at that.* He pressed the selection on the screen and the full article appeared.

"Gulfside and the rest of the world seem to have a new neighbor. A new star has appeared in the sky and it has the nation's few remaining astronomers scrambling to figure out exactly where and how old the star is. 'Just because we can now see the light of this star, does not necessarily mean it is new or even nearby,' states veteran astronomer Frederick Haskel. 'Light travels at a fixed speed. The light from this particular celestial body could have started its journey a million years ago and just arrived at Earth yesterday. However, what makes this star more interesting is its ability to peek so brightly through the ongoing haze plaguing the atmosphere. Most cities where the haze is thicker, have not seen many stars over the years. Yet, no one seems to have trouble seeing this one. More time and more study will be required to pinpoint the exact particulars.'" *Hmm, interesting,* Jonathon thought as he tapped an icon to return to the main menu.

"Gulfside City police investigate another reported disappearance."

Jonathon tapped on that article. "Gulfside City police department, this week, announced it had no leads in the disappearance of another Gulfside citizen. Angela Leary, a spokesperson for the Opposition to Gulfside Oppression, had stated that she was appalled at this latest incident. Leary, with another cryptic statement: 'We know what you're doing, you won't be able to silence us forever. We are people, you can't control us.' Gulfside PD did issue a statement saying, 'We are still investigating. This is not a matter we take likely.' As for what Leary means, police have no comment…"

Jonathon tapped an icon to return to the main menu.

"Okay world news," he muttered.

He pressed the selection. The first publication was about ONE.

ONE, I've seen this before, he thought.

He pressed the choice, to open the article.

"This week during its quarterly meeting, the delegates of the ONE council unanimously voted to ban the further development of nuclear material to be used for energy or weapons. The council, still concerned with the environment, took the controversial move as many nations continue to struggle to keep the power on. A source at the conference stated, 'The world has been lucky not to be a victim of any other incidents of nuclear terrorism and we are not going to give anyone else the chance. By banning nuclear grade material, future generations will not have to worry about another Korea-like incident and will not have to figure out how to dispose of the growing nuclear waste generated from power plants.'"

"ONE is also still reeling from the unpredictable climate shifts around the world. The ash from the volcanic eruptions years ago still swirl in the atmosphere reducing the earth's exposure to the sun. Most have been dormant since the initial onslaught, but volcanoes, in and near Italy, are starting to show signs of life again. The Russian, Japanese, and U.S. governments report no increase in activity with their respective volcanoes, but continue to monitor them closely for any relapses. Authorities in Iceland are planning to finally start allowing residents to return to the tiny nation, but the streets and landscapes are still congested with ash, and are in the dark. ONE, officially, has no opinion on what caused these upsurges in volcanic activity. No solutions have been presented at this time to correct the aftermath. The world economy continues to erode the resolve of ONE. With the continuing rise of costs for basic necessities, due to lasting shortages caused by the looming colder weather and general resource scarcities, many individuals and families hold onto what little money they do have, careful not make frivolous purchases."

"ONE has been consulting with SYNRG facilitators for offers of help, but declined to comment on the specifics. SYNRG has stated it has no new plans to increase manufacturing for the next quarter..."

"This is just a giant mess." Jonathon stated aloud.

"What are you referring to, sir?"

"The bleak situation around the world."

"Yes, sir."

Jonathon continued to read, but became aware that the car had come to a stop. Dennis stopped several times, but each time was very brief. Jonathon realized they were motionless on the side of the street.

"Is everything okay, Dennis?"

"Yes sir, we're here."

"Wow…already, that was quick. How much do I owe you?"

"It's free to you."

"That's right. Well, thank you."

Dennis exited the car. Jonathon pressed the same button he used to turn the computer on to turn it off. He placed the device back into the seat pocket. Dennis opened Jonathon's door to allow him to exit. Jonathon departed from his comfortable seat, standing up on the asphalt on the outside.

The cool air swept across his face and hands, giving him a quick chill. The sun, now peering through the haze a little, warmed him up a bit. Jonathon's attention immediately gravitated upwards. *My God,* he thought. *These buildings must range from 20-50 stories.*

"Dennis, it's amazing, the strength of our little town here, to thrive like this through a global depression."

"Not so small anymore. We've been fortunate here, all thanks to SYNRG."

There's that name again. "SYNRG?"

Dennis reached his hand out and said, "I'm sorry, I can't stay. It has been a refreshing delight to meet you."

"Of course. Take care."

Jonathon reached his hand out and shook Dennis's.

"Bye, sir."

Dennis closed the rear door to the car. Jonathon stepped up onto the wide concrete walkway and swung around to face the road. Dennis walked around to get to the driver's side. Jonathon, now somewhat perched above the roadway, scanned around, noticing one huge discernible oddity, no automobile traffic. Focusing on the sidewalk he saw no foot traffic, either. There were no people, as well. It was completely deserted.

Turning back to the roadway, he noticed it was three lanes each in direction. However, the lanes were marked very differently. The outer lanes were marked with car symbols. The middle lanes were marked with a motorcycle symbol and the inner lanes with an obvious bicycle. Jonathon looked up the road, noticing Dennis driving away from a nearby speed limit sign of 25. Jonathon pivoted back to the sidewalk and was completely dumfounded.

"Where is everyone?" he asked, rambling to himself. "What's going on? I just can't stand here. Where shall I go?" With another passing sweep around he said, "I'll just walk for now."

He pushed his legs into a direction, moving down the sidewalk. He was not sure what direction he was moving, but he figured he was walking in the same direction Dennis was driving from the station. It was a straight shot from there, so this meant he was traveling west, toward the coastline. Looking back up, he randomly oscillated his view from side to side, up and around, and occasionally in front him, observing this new world around him. The buildings stretching upward drew most of his interest. This was the most radical and unbelievable change in his mind.

He went from building to building, taking in the shapes, designs, colors, and sizes as he wandered down his path. He was in complete awe with all of these structures now residing along the street. The buildings had a good distance between them, most of which were access points for parking, even though they seemed vacant at the moment.

"This is just astounding," Jonathon said.

He came to a large roundabout. "This was not here before."

He had no idea where he was. Rounding the giant circle, scores of people began to flood the sidewalks on both sides of the street, all eerily at the same time, emerging from the buildings. What seem to add to the peculiarity, they were all streaming out and going only in one direction, toward him. Some motorized scooters and cycles also appeared, but no cars or trucks were in sight at the moment. Bicycles also seemed to be flowing on the opposite side as well. In contrast to just moments ago, the sidewalks were now full of people walking, striding, and strolling, almost to the point of congestion, to wherever it is they were going to.

Much like the train station, the fashion was plain and drab with primarily basic whites and blacks. No one was wearing any jewelry of any kind. Hats again, were very popular, but very plain. More peculiar were the people not wearing hats. Almost everyone not wearing a hat, both men and women, had very short hair. *Is this a trend?* This seemed weird to him, but...*could very well be the style of the time.*

These individuals had no interaction with one another. They were not interested in texting, talking or having any extroverted traits whatsoever. This did not seem right to Jonathon, but...*could be just normal social behavior for this time.* It did not seem normal, but one thing was clear though: Jonathon stood out like a sore thumb with his blue jeans and hairy head. His hair may have been short, but it was still much longer than the apparent average length of today. What was even stranger than any of this, no one was looking at him. He obviously did not fit in, but no one noticed or seemed to care.

Scores of cyclists were now passing by on the opposite inner lane, with maybe two or three mopeds and scooters moving almost in unison along their side. There were still no cars, whatsoever. Jonathon cautiously stepped into the crosswalk and glided down a smooth incline onto the asphalt to pass through the intersection. There was a crosswalk sign, but it was more like a traffic signal with the red, yellow, and green combo. With the amount of people crossing with him on a green light, this was no surprise. The lane was being treated as part of the roadway, regulated by a traffic-control device. He continued staring over at the bikes, taking note of the styles. They were familiar and traditional designs and shapes. There was nothing futuristic or weird. Blacks, grays, and silvers dominated the color schemes, same with the motorized variety.

Jonathon cruised back up the ramp and onto the concrete sidewalk, curving along the remainder of the roundabout. "I just can't believe..."

He paused to catch his breath and to allow his body to catch up with him. His muscles were still a little tight, not used to all this physical exertion after his long slumber. Plus, he was just overwhelmed with all of this. Hordes of people were sweeping by him, just as emotionless and apathetic since his arrival in this seemingly soulless place. Still no talking. Couples were not engaging in idle chat. There was no hand holding, and no eye contact. Children straggled haplessly with parents. There was no crying, no whining, nor laughing. No emotion of any kind. He was among a sea of strangers, who rode with the current not deviating from their stupor.

At this point it was time to find the one person who could help him find his way.

"Adam!" he said. "You have to be here. The police department has to be here. I need your help."

But where, exactly, was the department from here? A man in his thirties, in a white tee shirt, black pants, and black newsboy hat was nearing him.

Jonathon raised his arm to get his attention. "Excuse me sir, could you direct me…"

The dead-eyed man just whisked right by Jonathon.

"Okay, then," Jonathon said.

A woman, maybe forty, in a long black dress was now nearing him. She was also wearing a plain cloche hat.

Looking directly at her he said, "Excuse me ma'am."

Without a gesture, nod, or any slight acknowledgement, she just rushed by.

Did she even see me? he wondered.

"You don't even register on any of their radar's, except to avoid you," said a voice out of nowhere.

Jonathon turned around, noticing a man in his thirties standing still and staring right at him. No surprise, he was wearing black pants, a white tee shirt and black shoes, yet he was not bald. In fact, his hair was slightly longer than Jonathon's.

The man drew closer to Jonathon. "You're not from around here are you?"

"I just got in today," replied Jonathon.

"Blue jeans? I haven't seen a pair…in years."

"Is that right."

"So, jean man, what brings you here talking to yourself."

Jonathon had to be careful how he answered. "I'm looking for someone, but I don't know where to go."

"Well, don't count on help from them, they are more interested in just blending in. You, on the other hand, not so much."

Jonathon did not respond.

The man continued. "I sometimes like to come out here, around this time, to watch the people all emerge, at the same time. They've done this all the days I've been here, and I don't know why."

Jonathon shrugged his shoulders.

The man shook his head, "I'm sorry, I don't speak out in public to strangers much. I don't mean to sound cynical. I guess I'm just a victim of my environment. I'm Bruce."

"I'm Jonathon."

"Let me ask you, Jonathon. Why did you not have that car drop you off at where…you know, at whom you are looking for? Or is that someone meeting you here?"

Jonathon became uncomfortable. "You noticed me with the car?"

"Yeah. I hid in the shadows, between buildings. You are an abnormality. You don't belong to this bunch swarming around us. I don't know what to think."

"Then I will be as equally candid. I don't know what to think about you."

"Fair enough."

"Good. I'm glad we got that out of the way."

"I'm still baffled by your blue jeans though. They look brand new…interesting."

"What can I say, I'm meticulous."

Bruce nodded. "Perhaps."

He intensely examined Jonathon. "I'm going to figure you out. I don't mean to sound distrustful, but…"

"Because of the world today?"

Bruce focused straight on Jonathon's face. "Yes."

"You just said a little earlier you were a victim of your environment. What environment would that be?"

"Very inquisitive, I like that. But putting this fact aside, you just don't belong here."

Jonathon felt if he conversed longer it would jeopardize his identity. "It was good to meet you, Bruce."

"There it is again…now sincere etiquette."

Jonathon turned to continue his trek, but Bruce was not going to let that happen. He hurried in front of Jonathon. "I'm not done with you. Etiquette from someone our age?"

"I said I'm not from around here."

"No, you stated you got in today. That's not the same. Plus…

because of the world today, you stated." Bruce looked down for a moment, snapped his fingers a couple of times and then looked back up, pointing at Jonathon. "You are a reminder of the past. From a world I read about. I bet you're an ice man, aren't you?"

"A what?"

"An ice man…from that place out west. What was that called?" Snapping, then pointing again he said, "ChronoSleep!"

"I've got to go."

Jonathon tried to sidestep around Bruce, but Bruce matched his every move, continuing to block his path.

"Listen, Jonathon. I don't care where or…when you're from, but why would you come here. This place is a lost cause."

"Why would you say that about Gulfside?"

"Because it is. Gulfside City is the model of the future…but don't concern yourself with that. What is your story?"

Jonathon glanced around him, as to see if anyone around was listening.

"Don't worry, nobody's listening and your secret is safe with me."

Jonathon was apprehensive, but knew he was not fooling this guy or going to get rid of him easily. "I'm from the year 2017. I went into an extended sleep almost 30 years ago."

Bruce, now with a big smile, "I knew it! My friend, you need to do better to blend in. Fortunately, everyone around here is so involved with themselves, you don't even matter to them."

"Thank goodness for that I guess."

"So ice man, where exactly are you headed?"

"The police station, that is, if I can find it."

"So far, you are going in the right direction. I'll be glad to show you the rest of the way."

Cautious, but not wanting to turn down the opportunity for help Jonathon said, "I guess, thank you then."

"No problem."

Jonathon resumed his forward march, with Bruce matching his step.

"Why ice man?" Jonathon asked.

"It is a term that has been generating around the last couple of years, since ChronoSleep came under fire by a group anti-technologists."

"I'm familiar with them."

"Well, I guess the name came about because they put you on ice, hence ice man."

Jonathon gave Bruce a nervous smile. "The procedure is far more complicated than that, but I guess I can see that."

"Why today…to wake?"

"Without boring you with all of the details, I was supposed to be in for a lot longer, but with circumstances being what they are…"

"I got it. And here you are. Where are you from originally… before the sleep?"

"Here, actually."

"Really."

"Yep, born and raised. However, all of this…here…was not here, thirty years ago. Are you from Gulfside Bruce?"

Bruce, obviously apprehensive himself said, "Yes. And I don't like what has happened here."

"I kind of got a sense of that."

"If I may ask, why did you do the ice thing?"

"Does it matter…I'm here."

"Don't want to talk about it, got it."

"Then Jonathon, may I ask another question?"

"Okay."

"Why are we going to the police station?"

"I'm hoping a good friend of mine is still there."

"I see." With a brief delay Bruce continued, "You're looking for a friend at the police station…probably a police officer. Let's see. A police officer disappeared shortly after the demise of his family…are you Jonathon Scott?"

Maybe this was not a good idea, Jonathon thought, Still hesitant he said, "I am."

"I'm sorry about your family, Jonathon. I don't know what to say."

"There's not much to say."

"However, this is kind of exciting for me."

"Why?"

"I remember reading about you in school. You were a legend around here."

"I was only doing my job. I'm no legend"

"Well the stuff named Scott this, Jonathon that, or Jonathon Scott something or other says otherwise."

Jonathon rolled his eyes.

Bruce continued. "You're a hero."

"I don't mean to burst your bubble, but where did it get me?" Jonathon retorted with disdain. "A dead family, no purpose, and now outside of time…" Jonathon stopped himself. "I guess I'm the one being cynical now, but here we are."

"I should not have brought it up."

"Don't worry about it, I'm here and I need to get on with my life, such as it is."

Bruce paused, then gestured toward an alley. "You have to cut through here. As much as this has been interesting, I need to make a few more stops and get home to my wife before nightfall."

"I don't mean to keep you. You have been very helpful."

"Good luck to you. Make sure you find a place to stay before it gets late tonight."

"Why is that?"

"I don't have time to explain. Just make sure you do, okay?"

"Will do, thank you."

"I hope you find what you are looking for, Jonathon. For what its worth, this world needs people like you."

Jonathon did not respond.

Bruce went on his way and Jonathon continued his trek down the alley. The surrounding light was somewhat subdued due to the sun being blocked by the structures he was passing by. Jonathon, alone and on guard for any surprises, examined the scene now enveloping him. He could see the light at the end of the path ahead of him, so this was not a closed lane.

Nearing the light at the end, the buildings to the sides of him were getting shorter. The one on the left was about ten stories and the one on the right was three stories, both seeming to face the street. The three-story building had a ten-foot concrete wall running along its side, curving in and running along its rear. The ten-story building was set a good distance away from him with its own small alleyway leading to it.

Emerging from the dark, Jonathon glanced around. To his left, was an open square with a single statue. It was a familiar statue, no less. On his right, the wall also curved into the three-story building near the front with a split secure access door built into it. The split door appeared to be wide enough for a car to pass through. Most everything about this street, like the statue, was familiar though. Paying more attention to what was in front of him now, he focused on the buildings on the other side of the street.

"Is this Ringling Boulevard?" Jonathon's focus gravitated to Gulfside City's now dwarfed and blind bell tower along with the dilapidated old courthouse. "This is," Jonathon nervously uttered to himself.

The street was seemingly the same, but the scenery around this small section was not. Taller buildings in the background lined the view behind the tower and around Ringling.

Jonathon stepped closer to the barren potholed roadway, to get a better view.

He turned to the right. Sure enough, it was the police department. The wall was throwing him off.

Jonathon, still trying to take all of this in, glanced around some more. Paying more attention to the characteristics of the road, which was in serious need of repair, he looked ahead to what appeared to be the now abandoned and boarded sheriff's building.

"What happened here?"

The jail appeared to have power, but seemed to be vacant and deserted, too. Facing the new courthouse to his left, it had the signs of being abandoned as well.

"Nobody around here either. What's going on? This used to be a very busy street."

Snapping back to the police department he said out loud, "The station looks to be in decent condition. All right, Adam. Please be here."

Jonathon hurried down the sidewalk to get to the entrance, which he located quickly as it had not changed. He curved up the walkway to the sliding doors, which opened as he approached them. Gliding through them he entered the lobby area. As he stepped in farther, the doors closed. The lobby appeared to be pretty much the same as before, but rundown. The front desk was empty with no one present. Jonathon gazed up to the display wall to find all of the art, gone. The pictures of the past chiefs were still there, though. He moved in closer, to see what had changed over the years. He advanced down the line to where the more recent replacements were. On the end, there was only the addition of one past chief, his, which was in sepia.

He shifted to the current chief, which was a black and white photo. "Weird."

He examined the photo. "No, that can't be him."

He read the nameplate to confirm the slightly older version of his good friend. "Adam Stance. You have got to be kidding me."

Strangely there was another picture to the right of Adam's. This was not of a chief, but an honorable mention. Jonathon was staring at a black-and-white photo of himself. To confirm, he read the nameplate, "Jonathon Scott."

He shook his head in disbelief. "This was your idea, wasn't it Adam?"

Just then, a woman, in her early twenties emerged from the administrative section behind the desk and approached the front customer service area. She was dressed in the same uniform style, as in his day, and wearing a small hat with a petite bill in the front.

With a slightly annoyed tone she asked, "Can I help you sir?"

Okay, sorry to disturb you, Jonathon thought. "Yes. Is Chief Stance in today?"

Apparently she was still annoyed. "No. He will be in on

Monday. Do you want to make an appointment? He's very busy."

"No. it's nothing important. Thank you."

Jonathon started to walk away.

"Wait a minute, sir," ordered the woman.

Jonathon paused.

"You look familiar," she said.

"Yeah, because my photo hangs above you everyday," he said, mumbling to himself.

"What was that sir?"

"I guess I just have one of those faces, I'm new here."

"Oh? What is your name?"

"Jonathon."

"Jonathon what?"

"I'm sorry, I'm in a hurry."

Jonathon resumed his march to leave.

"Hold on there!" she shouted.

All of a sudden a loud siren sounded.

"Shit," Jonathon said. He neared the door, but it did not open. Turning back to the desk, the access door by it quickly opened with three officers in full uniform and all wearing billed caps rushed out and rapidly surrounded Jonathon.

"You guys can't hold me here, you have no cause to do so."

"You are in our department, we can detain you if you want," responded one of the young officers.

"What?" Jonathon was about to further challenge them, but he figured it was best not to escalate the situation. He had no idea what was going on with this world.

One of the officers held out what appeared to be a fingerprint reader. "Sir, I'm officer Jamison Kohler. We are going to get your identification now. Place your right index finger on the scanner."

Jonathon reluctantly complied. He gently placed the requested digit on the cold scanner plate. He was not going to be able to hide who he was any longer. They were about to know everything in seconds. The device indicted it was done, so Jonathon removed his finger.

The officer read the displayed information. "Okay, sir, you are Jonathon Scott…59…you reside here in Gulfside City…What?"

Jamison looked down at Jonathon, then took a couple of steps back.

"It says I'm a police officer, doesn't it," Jonathon retorted.

The other two men closer to him looked at each other with confusion.

Jamison secured the scanning device to his belt. He then spoke into his radio receiver, "This is Kohler. Sergeant, I need you out here." Jamison nodded to the other two. "All right guys, move away from him."

As the two officers moved away, Jamison moved closer again. Jonathon did not like the attention of his heroics of the past, but he was going to use them now.

"Jamison, how much of Gulfside's history do you know?"

"Plenty sir. I was raised here."

"Good. Then you must know the significance of Jonathon Scott."

Jamison veered away from Jonathon and stomped to the other officers. He spoke into his radio again. "Sarge!"

The access door opened. Jonathon positioned himself, facing the new arrival. The older sergeant approached his men, whispering so Jonathon could not hear him. He was in his sixties and yes…familiar. The supervisor turned and moved toward Jonathon with the three younger officers in tow. The obviously experienced veteran was worn with time but still appeared sharp. He examined Jonathon up and down, without saying a word. He quickly paused, then stared right at Jonathon's face. Jonathon returned the gaze to determine who this guy was. He did not have a name tag on him, but it hit him.

"Buchman?" questioned Jonathon.

"It can't be…this is impossible…Jonny?"

Before Jonathon could respond, Buchman grabbed the upper arms of his former colleague and smiled. The other officers looked at each other, with bewilderment. Jonathon did not move. Buchman released Jonathon and took a couple of steps back.

"Jonny, you have not aged since…how could…"

Jonathon smiled, "It's a long story Buchman. Where's Adam? I've come here to see him."

Buchman was still in shock. "He's not here."

"Do you know where he is?"

"Home, probably?"

"Is he still living at my house?"

Buchman nodded.

"Good. I think I can find…well, on second thought, Gulfside has changed so much. Are you able to take me to him?" Jonathon asked.

"Sure Jonny, I'd love too."

Jamison moved closer to Buchman and tapped him on his shoulder. "Sir, are you sure this is Lieutenant Scott?"

Buchman twisted back to his subordinate. "Absolutely," Buchman said with a smile. "Return to your duties and speak to no one about this. Make sure to pass that on to the other two and Michelle at the desk. Then, you all get your tails home."

"Yes, sir."

Jamison returned to his previous position with the others and motioned for them to follow him. The three officers marched toward the access door.

"So, Sergeant Buchman is it now." stated Jonathon.

"Yeah. It's..." Buchman shook his head. "I'm sorry, I'm still shocked at all of this. I mean you have not aged a day. How is that possible?

"I can explain on the way. I'm real anxious to get to Adam."

"Sure, my cruiser is out back. Let's go."

CHAPTER THIRTY-SEVEN

AN OLD FRIEND

It was a quiet ride to Adam's. Jonathon did not talk. Even though Buchman was eager to find out more, he respected his former leader's desire for silence. Jonathon just absorbed the sights of the changes around him. Buchman weaved about Jonathon's old and now dilapidated neighborhood. The street was coarse with potholes and dips. The houses appeared to be either neglected by apathy or just outright abandoned. Pulling up to a clean house, Jonathon recognized it as his old one. He opened the door, thrust his feet out, and set them on the broken pavement. Taking a couple steps away from the car and balancing himself on its door, he stared at the house.

"Do you want me to wait for you, Jonny?"

"No, but thank you. Take care."

Jonathon gently pushed the door shut on the gas/electric hybrid, which was similar to his old cruiser. The front passenger window opened.

Jonathon turned to the car slightly. "Is everything okay?"

"I just wanted to say, it's really good to see you."

"It's good to see you too, sergeant. When I get my head straight, I would like to talk more."

"Good day, Jonny," Buchman said with a smile.

"Good day."

Buchman rolled up the window. Jonathon stood tall and watched Buchman drive away. Standing at the edge of the driveway, Jonathon watched the city, as he used to do so long ago.

"The view here is so different," he said. "I hope I know what I'm doing."

Jonathon turned back to face his former residence. Adam obviously had taken care of the house over the years. Adam's home looked brand new, unlike his neighbors. Jonathon perused around to some of the other homes within his view. They looked rundown with some of them possibly derelict.

"I lived alongside of most of these people for years," he said. "I wonder what happened to them all."

Jonathon began his march up the driveway, toward the walkway to the front door. This was the first time, since he moved out, he had been back here. He was not sure how Adam was going to react. *Would he be happy, angry, or hesitant?* he wondered. *Maybe, and probably, a mixture.*

He paused for a moment, taking in a deep breath, and released that anxiety into the air. "He's my friend, he'll be understanding."

He continued, curving, along the path through the covered porch and up to the solid front door. Jonathon stepped up to the door and knocked gently. He stood there patiently, waiting for Adam to answer. He looked to the side, and noticed the shrubbery had been replaced with small bushes, probably gardenia. The fragrance of the blooming white flowers was unmistakable.

"I hope he is home."

Jonathon knocked again, but a bit heavier this time. As the sound of someone unlocking the door from the other side filled this silent calm air, his heart pounded harder. His breathing became shorter. His muscles tightened, with the trepidation at who was about to come forth from inside.

The door swung open inward, and a woman emerged in front of him. She appeared to be in her late fifties, maybe early sixties. She was wearing all black and had very short hair.

"What is it?" she asked. "Who are you? My husband is a police officer and will arrest you for trespassing if you don't leave right now."

"Husband?" Jonathon muttered.

"Yes. You need to get off our property."

"Our property?" he said very quietly. He thought he would take a shot in the dark. "Suzie?"

With surprise she said, "How do you know my name?"

"Who's there, Suz?" came a voice from inside the house.

"Some weird guy who is not getting the hint to leave and knows my name."

"What!"

Heavy footsteps followed, hurrying to the front door. A man came into the light, subtly getting in front of Suzie. Jonathon stood there, speechless, staring at his recognizably older, grayer, worn-by-time friend. He had very short, slightly longer than stubble, gray hair. He also had some wrinkles, crows feet around his eyes, and a scar on his chin. He was wearing black pants and white tank top, which exposed his upper arms. On his right upper arm was a tattoo with initials, in a fancy calligraphic pattern.

"JRS," Jonathon muttered.

"Who are you, fella?" Adam asked.

Jonathon looked straight at Adam, and he returned the gaze. Adam quickly studied over Jonathon and then took a few steps back, almost knocking his wife down. Adam placed his hand over his mouth with a startled look.

"What is it, Adam?" asked Suzie, glancing at her husband and then back at Jonathon. "Who is this?"

Adam, completely bewildered.

"It can't be," Adam said. "This is impossible. You haven't aged a day."

Suzie stared back at Adam and was becoming anxious.

"What, who is this?" she asked. She glared at Jonathon and with a stern expression asked, "Who are you?"

"It's me…Jonny."

Suzie now placed her hand over her mouth, and with shock and surprise stepped back.

"I know this is out of nowhere, but I'm back," he said.

Jonathon oscillated back and forth between the two of them while Suzie and Adam just stood there, completely stunned.

Jonathon stepped back a couple of paces. "I know it has been a long time and I left without a proper goodbye…I can understand if you guys are upset with…"

Adam quickly advanced forward and down the front doorstep and leapt at Jonathon, wrapping his arms around him. "It is so good to see you, Jonny. It has been so long. I've missed you."

Jonathon returned the embrace. "I'm so sorry with how I left things."

Adam let go and Jonathon did the same, but both maintained eye contact with each other.

"It's okay," Adam said.

"It's just that when Dana and the kids died, then my grandfather following…I was in a really bad place."

Adam gently grabbed Jonathon's upper arms, looked directly at him, and with a smile said, "Jonny, it's okay. I have no ill will about this. I'm just so elated to see you…to know you are alive and well, but still the same?" Adam let go of Jonathon. "How is this possible? You haven't aged."

Suzie inched forward. "Jonny, would you like to come inside?"

Jonathon, with a smile said, "Yes, I would like that."

Adam gained his bearings and motioned toward inside. "Yes, where are my manners, please come inside".

Adam sidestepped out of the way to allow Jonathon to pass. Jonathon glided up through the threshold and into the house with Suzie looking on.

"Wow, you guys really changed a lot in here," Jonathan said.

Adam edged closer to Suzie, both of them still in shock. For the moment, they let Jonathon just be. Jonathon was standing in a dining room where his old television room used to be. He then wandered toward the kitchen, stopped before it, and stood there, taking everything in. The most noticeable difference was the kitchen itself, which was now an open area, exposed to the rest of the house.

What was once Jonathon's house is completely gone right down to the walls and floor. All of Jonathon's old furnishings and belongings appeared to be gone too.

"What do you think?" Suzie inquired nervously from behind.

Jonathon nodded his head. "Yeah."

He progressed a bit farther in and stopped about midway past the kitchen, discovering another amendment to the house. "You guys added on to the living room to make another room?"

Suzie slowly strolled up to Jonathon's right side. "Yep."

The former living room was now set up with sofas arranged for entertaining guests. The sliding door which led to the back yard was now an open archway leading into some sort of other room, he assumed.

The new room appeared to be across a somewhat long narrow hallway, as the two windows still had a good view of the outside. He was about to check this new room out when he paused and looked toward the old dinning nook, absent a table. There was one familiar piece of furniture, Dana's heirloom hutch, just as it was when he left.

Jonathon stumbled back a pace and then glanced over at Suzie. Holding back the tears and with a quiver in his voice he said, "You kept Dana's hutch."

Adam moved up to Jonathon's side and placed his hand on Jonathon's shoulder. "I kept everything. It's in storage. But this was too special to put away, so I thought it would be okay to keep with us."

Jonathon did not say a word.

"Was that okay?" Adam asked with an unsure tone.

"Of course," said Jonathon, glancing over to Adam. "This was the best home for it. It's just strange to still see it, after all of this time, now…here…in this time…in this same, but different home… I'm sorry."

Jonathon turned around, slowly stepping back into the new dining room. Adam did the same and followed, but stopped short of matching Jonathon's position.

"Jonny, what happened? How is it that you still look…or are still…young?"

"ChronoSleep."

"Huh?"

"I went into ChronoSleep."

Suzie came in closer to the men. "Are you talking about the sleep research place?" she asked.

Jonathon nodded to her. "Yes."

"Why would you do that?" Adam asked with confusion.

Jonathon kind of stared between the two of them. "It was my only option. I thought I was going to be able to run away from my past here."

"Why didn't you just move away from Gulfside?" asked Adam, becoming a bit riled.

Suzie tried to calm her husband down. "Adam!"

"Suz, come on. He shows up at our door out of the blue after thirty years."

Jonathon stared into nothing. "I'm sorry you two…I didn't know what I was doing…or doing. This is so confusing. I did not want to leave Gulfside, but I did not want all the reminders either."

"And you thought thirty years was going to make everything better?" Adam asked, more annoyed. "It just doesn't make sense."

"It was supposed to be a hundred."

Adam shook his head. "Thirty, a hundred years, it still doesn't make sense."

Jonathon retreated and slowly marched toward the front door.

Adam quickly overtook him. "Jonny, I'm sorry. I know I said I was okay with this. I'm still trying to process this. Maybe I do feel a little hurt, but this does not change the fact that I'm still very glad you are here."

Suzie approached the men. "Jonny, would you like something to drink?" she asked. "We have our own well, so I can give you fresh water if would you like."

Jonathon twisted back to her with a puzzled expression. "Water will be fine Suzie, thank you."

She smiled, then walked into the kitchen. Jonathon shook his head and refocused himself.

He faced Adam. "Suzie, huh? Do you still walk into things?"

Adam smiled. "No. That stopped years ago," he answered sarcastically. Adam motioned for Jonathon to go in the living room. "Do you want to go sit down?"

"Sure."

Jonathon gave the room another quick examination, then stepped toward the sofas with Adam in tow. Jonathon passed the kitchen area when picture frames on side tables caught his attention. He veered toward them. Adam continued into the seating area as Jonathon leaned in and examined the photos in the various-shaped frames. They were of children, or more specifically, of a boy growing up through the years. One photo was of the young man in a black graduation cap and gown.

"Here's your water, Jonny," said Suzie

She was standing by him holding an almost full glass of water.

He took the glass. "Thanks, Suzie."

"Sure, Jonny."

She walked over toward Adam. He was thirsty, so he took a hardy gulp and emptied the glass.

"Do you want more?" asked Suzie.

"No thanks."

He stepped just inside the kitchen area, and placed it on the counter. He steadily turned about toward the couple and gestured to the pictures on the adjacent table. With a slight smile he asked, "So you two, is that your son?"

Both of them nodded.

Jonathon pointed to the other side of the room. "And those pictures over there?"

"Our daughter," Suzie replied.

Jonathon, with a more stoic expression, stared off to the side.

"All grown up?" he asked.

Adam proudly responded. "Ashley is 28, a horticulturalist, and is pregnant with our first grandchild. Jake is 25, not married yet, and is a chip off the old block…he is with the department."

"That's wonderful you two," Jonathon said with a revived but forced smile. "I'm happy for you."

"Jonny, are you all right?" Suzie asked.

Jonathon faced away from them, but for the moment did not say a word. Adam and Suzie looked at one another.

Jonathon lowered his head a bit and began to tear a little. "I'm sorry guys…I am genuinely happy for you two. I'm happy this home heard the laughter of children again coming from the rooms at the end here. I'm happy the sound of children running, knocking into things, was heard in these walls…that a loving environment existed here once again."

He moved over and up to the hutch, and he put his finger on its side about a third of the way up. With a slight chuckle he said, "Kim put this gash here about a year ago with that scooter of hers. Dana played it cool…as always."

He removed his finger, now wiping his tears. "I guess it's been a little longer than a year ago now. I'm still processing this, too. I thought I could escape this, but I guess I was wrong. I feel more alone and out of place now than I did thirty years ago."

Adam inched toward Jonathon. "Jonny, you'll never be alone here."

Suzie matched Adam. "We are here for you, as long as you need."

Jonathon nodded. "I know, but I still miss my family so much. I don't know why I'm here now. I just feel lost…and with the time difference, now displaced." He placed his hand back on the side of the hutch. "All I have is a head full of memories and no purpose. I'm not a husband, I'm not a father, and I've come back to a grown, but seemly dead and soulless city. This future is...my future is pointless." He removed his hand. "I remember watching a couple of science fiction shows on TV where the future was so bright and hopeful. This place just…"

"Sucks…" blurted Adam. "Jonny, I would have helped you."

"I know, but what kind of future would you have had worrying about me? I think part of why I did what I did was so I didn't ruin your life, too."

"That is just silly nonsense."

"Perhaps, but here we are. You have your wonderful family."

Suzie came in closer. "Well, putting everything aside, if it weren't for you, Jonny, that wonderful family might not have happened or, at least, in the form we were blessed to have. You gave Adam a wonderful gift…giving him this house."

"The economy collapsed, much worse than ever seen, sometime after you left," Adam added. "More people lost their homes, credit was wiped out, and cash became hard to come by as prices of commodities spiked."

"Even with Adam and I both working, no prior debt, and good salaries, we still would not have been able to get a loan for a house," Suzie said. "There are many days I felt guilty, because of your circumstances, but this house probably saved us. So let me say now, whatever you need Jonny…we will help you no matter what we have to do!"

Adam agreed. "Yeah, Jonny. You say you didn't want me to help you then…well you don't have a choice now, we ARE going to help you now."

"I got a brief taste of the economic situation around here," Jonathon said, nodding. "You mean to tell me it never got better after all of that time?"

Adam shook his head. "No," he said, just above a whisper.

"Let's go sit down," Suzie said.

Adam waved his arm toward the seating area. "Yeah, come on, Jonny. Are you sure you don't want another drink?"

"No, I'm good," Jonathon said.

They all walked to the sofas. Adam and Suzie sat down on one and Jonathon sat on the opposite one. The couple leaned back, while Jonathon sat closer to the edge of his cushion.

"Chief Stance?" Jonathon asked with a smirk.

Adam's face turned red. "How do you know?"

"I stopped by the department before I came here. Noticed you on the wall of chiefs."

"Oh, then I suppose you saw the other part then?"

"Yes, I did. It was your idea wasn't it?"

Adam's face turned red again.

"So Suzie, do you still work for…the chief?" Jonathon asked.

"No. I actually manage the administrative section and front counter now," Suzie said, slightly chuckling.

"Was this because of Adam becoming chief?"

"No. Our chief promoted me to the position, which made things a lot easier when Adam took over."

"It's a good thing. It would have been very awkward if I had to fire my wife," Adam said with a quick laugh.

"You said you're in charge of the front desk?" Jonathon asked.

Suzie nodded.

"So is that lovely woman Michelle, I think that's what he called her, one of yours?"

"Yeah, why?"

"I almost ended up in jail today because of her."

Adam leaned forward. "What?" he asked.

"She recognized me, but could not figure out where, so I tried to leave in a hurry. She probably thought I was a criminal, so she locked the doors and your officers swarmed me. However, thanks to me still being on active status, I was released."

"Okay, Jonny, now that one was not my idea. The old chief could not bring himself to deactivate you. He was not going to be the chief to declare a hero dead or missing in action. Then, when I took over, I did not see the need to make any changes to your status."

Jonathon nodded with a smile. "Of course you didn't."

"Who ended up releasing you?"

"Buchman. I mean Sergeant Buchman."

"He remembered. Good."

"Yes, he did. In fact, he was the one who brought me here. From what I remember, he was a good officer. Now he's been then for a while."

"He's my longest veteran now. And yes, he is a very good officer. I rely on him heavily."

"You were so dead set about staying put."

Adam smiled. "Okay. So I changed my mind." He got more serious. "Things got real bad here for a while. The prowlers got worse, then vanished, never to be seen again. Then the citizens got worse after everything went haywire. The economic strain pushed good honest people into taking desperate actions to survive. When the chief announced he was retiring, most of the officers circulated a petition for me to take his spot. Well, you came up first. But with you gone, they turned to me. I couldn't say no." Adam leaned back again. "I really could have used a hero, Jonny. It may have prevented some of the carnage around here."

Jonathon shook his head. "I'm no hero. You were a better officer than I ever was. I'm glad you took the job, but how did you adjust to sitting at a desk?"

"I didn't. From day one, I made it clear I would not be confined to an office. I assigned myself to recurring patrols. I couldn't do it for the whole day, or even a half of a day for that matter, but as long as I got out of the office, I was happy. Plus, I had to work administrative hours, so I constantly had to figure out ways to dodge the phone. Being chief is very complex, especially with all the bureaucratic nonsense and all. As a result, I could not finish all my mundane chiefly responsibilities at first. But, thanks to my awesome wife here and her experience with our former chief, she helped me after hours at home."

Suzie lit up with a big smile. "I still help every now and then, but Adam has a good handle on balancing everything out now."

"I still go out regularly, but the time is much, much shorter. I've kept myself in great shape over the years, but time is starting to catch up with me a little."

Jonathon snickered a bit.

Adam continued. "Oh, you find that funny, huh? Wait till you get to my age…of course…in the past…I always envisioned us growing old and retiring together. But nonetheless Lieutenant, I could still use another good officer on the beat. And you are still on active status. I could have you on the street tomorrow if you want."

"Adam stop that!" shrieked Suzie.

"Well thank you, but...I don't know. I don't know what I'm going to do…with myself or…everything is so different and a little strange. Almost alien." Jonathon said.

Suzie gave Jonathon a reassuring glance. "Whatever you decide to do, Jonny, we are here for you."

"Thank you."

"Yes, anything," Adam said, also reassuring. "Do you have a place to stay?"

"No. I guess I haven't thought that far yet."

"You do now," Suzie said with assertion. "We could get one of the kids' rooms ready for you or the couch in the media room here behind us."

"The couch is fine, but I don't want to impose."

"Nope, we insist," Adam said firmly. "The couch is a good choice." He pointed his head toward Suzie, "I've had to use it myself from time to time."

Suzie playfully slapped Adam's arm.

Jonathon turned to Suzie. "I have a question for you Suzie…well it is probably more general, but it is an observation."

With enthusiasm she said, "Sure."

"If this is too personal, let me know. But why did you cut your hair off? I noticed a lot of people here, well those who weren't wearing hats, have very short hair. Is this some fashion trend?"

"Not exactly. Several years ago, Gulfside and many other cities experienced the start of a persistent and prolonged lice infestation. Due to the economy, there were no medicinal shampoos or special combs available. I read somewhere that mayonnaise might work, but that seem to piss them off even more. Back-alley treatments did eventually become available, but the side effects increased along with the costs. Plus, many think, this just added to the bugs' overall resistance. Besides, in a depression, when forced to make the choice between food and lice treatment, well I think you can probably guess what choice people make. The cheapest and less-risky solution was for people to shave their heads. Just what everyone needed to add to their already stressed, worried, and fearful lives. The problem is just now starting to correct itself, but I think everyone still shaves down out of habit, including Adam and I."

"Sorry."

Suzie was upbeat. "Don't be. With everything going on, it's just hair."

"I have another question."

Suzie was still very much accommodating. "Go ahead."

"I noticed clothing color is very bland."

"Another result of the economy. Henry Ford's old adage of you can have any color as long as it's black seems to be the theme of sorts. Synthetic fibers are the norm today, along with very streamlined manufacturing processes. In addition to blacks…whites, grays, and to a much lesser extent, tans and browns, are our color choices. Your blue jeans are a welcome sight. Where on earth did you get them?

Vintage clothes with any color are very rare."

"They went to ChronoSleep with me."

Suzie nodded. "Do you have any more?"

"Yeah, I've got some more in a bag I stored at the depot. When I started to take note of the color scheme, I thought, I was going to attract more attention, but everyone here seems to be in their own little world."

Adam moved to the edge of his cushion. "It's strange. No one wants anything to do with one another, it's bizarre."

"Is this a result of the economy?"

"That's a popular excuse, amongst those who are still vocal."

"But you don't buy that."

"Nope. This development started about five years ago. Long after the financial woes."

"It could be just weariness."

"Yes, it could, but what makes this more strange is…I'm not very busy."

"Busy?"

"The crime rate has dropped drastically."

"Really."

"I'm not complaining, but it is very peculiar. With the dehumanized pattern of behavior from the public, I expected everyone to be at each other's throat."

"Maybe it is the dehumanized behavior for the lack of crime. I mean, if no one is reacting emotionally with each other, that would stand to reason."

"A lot of actions are emotionally based, I guess. I don't know. It just seems there is more to it. But, as long as everyone isn't hurting one another, I should be thankful."

Jonathon suddenly hunched over, jamming his elbow into his leg and placing his hand on his forehead in an attempt to prop himself up. "Damn it," he said.

Suzie was alarmed. "Jonny what is it? What's wrong?"

The couple simultaneously sprang to their feet and rushed to Jonathon. Adam knelt down in front of him, with Suzie standing by. Adam put his hands on Jonathon's upper arms.

"Jonny come on…what's going on?"

Jonathon put his arm down, looking up at Adam, struggling to get the words out, "I believe it's a side effect of the ChronoSleep…an intense wave of fatigue."

"Are you in danger? What can we do?"

"You have already helped. I want to thank you for letting me stay here. All I can do now is sleep."

Adam looked up at Suzie. "Suz can you get the bed out?"

"I'm on it."

Suzie spun around, hurrying into the hallway to the new room. Jonathon rapidly became weaker. "You may have to move me. I don't know how much longer I got before I pass out."

"That's fine, whatever we need to do."

"I may be out for a while, I don't know what the guideline is for this..."

Adam shook his head. "Is there anything I should watch for?"

Jonathon was barely conscious. "Not that...that I know of. In my wallet, I have...have a contact card...someone at ChronoSleep. She can help..."

Adam caught Jonathon before he completely fell over and out of the chair.

"Suz, I need your help out here!"

CHAPTER THIRTY-EIGHT

AWAKE AGAIN

"...Jonny, it's time to get up."
"But it's Sunday. I thought this was my day to sleep in."
"Nope. Sorry ram boy, you have work to do..."

"Where am I?" Jonathon asked.

He sat up quickly in bed, and was dazed and foggy. "Hello!"

Gazing down he realized he had fallen asleep in his clothes. "What the..."

Glancing around the room as his eyes came into focus, he realized he had never been here before. Nothing was familiar. He was starting to feel uneasy. "What is going on? How did I get here? Is it Sunday? What day is it?"

It was somewhat cool, but tolerable. Still perusing around, he deemed this to be some sort of media room. There was a silver flat screen in front of the window across from him, but it did not look like a television. Off to the side was a desk with a computer and monitor on it. Scanning upward he saw a projector device, mounted to the ceiling. "Where is this?"

Tossing the covers off of him, he swiveled himself out of the bed. "Why can't I...that's right, this is Adam's house. I hope. Okay, Amy, we can add this to the side effect list...extreme disorientation. I passed out, shortly after I arrived here...at Adam's in 2047. Now, how long have I been out and what time is it? If this is the next morning, it would be a Sunday."

Jonathon searched around for a clock or anything which would clue him in, but nothing around could answer his question. "All right, let me see what is going on."

He pushed into his legs to gain momentum and advanced toward the only door in the room. He glided the doors open, revealing a long narrow glass hallway ahead. There was a set of slide doors on both sides of the hallway, which appear to access the outside.

Resuming his forward momentum, he staggered through the hall carefully, allowing his muscles to catch up. Passing through the threshold at the end, he entered into Suzie and Adams's living room. All was quiet, except for the sound of water passing through the pipes behind the walls.

"Adam! Suzie! Hello!" Jonathon shouted.

Adam ran out of the master bedroom wearing all black. With an elated expression he said, "You're up!"

Jonathon, still groggy asked, "How long was I out?"

"Probably twenty hours."

"Twenty hours, damn."

"I called Amy Weiss…the doctor on your card, last night, after I moved you."

"Was she able to…help?"

"Yes. She told me normally she would of liked to keep you longer to give you time to readjust, but due to…"

"Yeah, we had to leave in a hurry."

"Well she said not to worry, at least short term."

"Short term?"

"She said if you did not wake in twenty-four hours, I would have to try and wake you."

"What time is it?"

"A little after two."

"How is Amy?"

"She seemed fine. She was genuinely concerned about you. She offered to come to Gulfside if I needed her to. Does she need to?"

"I think I'm all right."

"Let me know, if there is anything wrong."

"Okay."

"Suzie is going to the festival tonight and I was going to stay here to watch you, but if you're feeling okay, I would like to go, too."

"Festival?"

"The Founder's Festival."

"The festival is still here?"

"It's not as grandiose as it used to be, but yes…every year so far. In fact it is still held at the same fairgrounds at the edge of town.

You're welcome to go with us if you feel up to it. Suzie volunteered this year."

"I think I would like to go. I've rested enough. I want to see more of the town."

"Great!"

"Do you think you could take me to the depot, so I can get my things out of the locker?"

"Yes, of course. We can go before we go to the festival. In fact, if you want a change of clothes now, I'll let you borrow something in the meantime."

"That would be great."

"You're in luck. Suzie was able to get me new underwear, still in the wrap. You're my friend and all, but…"

Jonathon chuckled. "Thanks."

The sound of the water ceased. "If you want to take a shower, you can in the other bathroom."

"That's probably a good idea."

"I believe there are clean towels in the closet in there. I'll put your change of clothes outside the door, so they will be there when you're done."

"Thank you."

"No problem. I'll let Suzie know you will be going with us. She'll be so happy."

Adam turned and marched back toward his bedroom. Jonathon faced the other end and was about to go take his shower. "Hey, Jonny."

Jonathon turned to Adam. "Yeah."

"I'm really glad you are here."

Adam stepped back into the bedroom, closing the door behind him.

Jonathon stood still, there in the silence of his former living room and glanced over to the hutch. "I'm glad you are…but I'm still not sure I belong here."

CHAPTER THIRTY-NINE

THE GUARDIANS

Suzie, Adam and Jonathon arrived at the fairgrounds. Adam was wearing his same outfit. Suzie was wearing black plants with a black and white striped referee's shirt, her "uniform" for the festival. Jonathon borrowed a dashing ensemble of a white tee and black pants. It was after seven o'clock, with the sun setting in the background behind the behemoth skyline of downtown Gulfside. The air was cool, but not enough to need a jacket. In fact, it was the warmest Jonathon had felt in this new world. The lit potholed parking lot was oddly barren, but this could have been the result of the lack of cars in this economy. Yet, foot traffic seemed to be lacking as well.

Suzie and Adam were one of the few fortunate to have a vehicle, even if it was Jonathon's old car. Suzie and Adam kept it due to it being a hybrid. It had signs of wear, but overall, it was still in excellent shape for a thirty-one year old. It was still very expensive to drive, which they could only do on a limited basis, but this was more cost effective than their former conventional autos. Replacement parts for it were costly, but the labor, for them, was not astronomical. Adam had a good rapport with the department's fleet mechanic, who made house calls as a means to make extra money.

They all approached the lighted entrance and stepped up off of the pavement onto the straight concrete path.

A man in his 40s, short hair, dressed in black was rushing up to the trio, more specifically, to Adam. "Chief Stance, it's good to see you again."

Jonathon glanced at Adam who was smiling, but Jonathon could tell it was forced and fake.

"Hi, Phil. Let me guess, he's a no show?" retorted Adam.

"Unfortunately, Mayor Fuller has a scheduling conflict."

"Of course," Adam said, with obvious sarcasm. "Well I know it must be very important, for him to miss this again."

"He is very sorry, but this was unavoidable."

"I see."

"Well, all of you have good time."

"Take care, Phil."

"Bye, chief."

The man passed by the three and walked away in an obvious hurry.

"I guess it's five years in a row now."

"You expected this," Suzie said in a calming voice. "You said this was going to happen."

Jonathon leaned in and asked, "What's going on?"

Adam took a couple of steps away.

Suzie answered. "Our Mayor is hiding again, ashamed to face the crowd, not making the annual speech."

"Oh. But, why is he getting so upset about it?"

Adam, stepping back to Suzie and Jonathon. "Because that asshole of a mayor sold the city out…damning it! He knows he screwed up and can't face us."

"What does that mean?" Jonathon asked, perplexed.

Adam stepped ahead again.

Suzie responded. "It's very complicated. Look I've got to get inside to start my shift, so let's relax a little. We can talk about this later." She patted Jonathon on his shoulder.

"Of course," Jonathon said, with understanding.

Suzie glided up to Adam and gave him a kiss on the cheek. "Bye, honey. I'll see you in there. Please just let this go tonight."

Adam gazed at Suzie with a smile. "Okay, Suz, do a good job."

"Hey Suzie, what are you helping with?" Jonathon queried.

"I think they have me on the ring toss," Suzie said with zest.

"Well then, I guess I'll have to strut my stuff for my gal," Adam said with a smirk.

Returning with a smirk of her own, "Whatever. You couldn't get a bicycle tire over a pencil. I'll see you guys in there."

She sped toward the main open gate and hurried inside.

Jonathon inched up to Adam. "She's right, you always did suck at the ring toss."

"Hey, no comments from the peanut gallery. I've gotten better over the years, you'll see."

"Is all the entertainment still free?"

"Yep, but the whole setup is very different than from our day.

The first one is obvious...usually this place was packed with people, but here we are. Plenty of elbow room. Unfortunately, this appears to be the lowest turnout yet. " Adam motioned toward the gate. "Let's go inside. I'll show you."

The two men slowly approached the open-arched gray metallic entryway, which was connected to a ten-foot-high chain-link fence surrounding most of the grounds.

"They took away the old entrance," Jonathon said.

"That rotted away years ago. It was cheaper to go with this."

The men passed through the cold sterile archway onto the mainly brown grassy landscape and into the main staging area, which had an abundance of ambient lighting from the adjacent light poles.

"Suzie volunteered this year, with the hopes this would be the turnaround year, but..."

The game stalls were arranged into three very long rows, not the staggered configuration as before. Jonathon and Adam angled toward the right-most lane. It was evident at this point, this was not very organized. It was opening night and there were still many individuals setting up the booths.

"Are we here early?"

"Nope. This is the way it has been for a few years now. The lack of attendance has been demoralizing, so there has been a lack of help, plus no one really is motivated to be in a hurry. Suzie's surprised they had as many volunteers as they do have."

"Where are the bumper boats? I think I'd like to go try them first."

"Another change...the boats are not here anymore. In fact, you won't find any water-based games at all here. We have very strict water usage restrictions due to the wacky environment."

"Water restrictions? Is this why you have your own well?"

"Yep. I can still access a good amount of clean water deep down in the earth without having to buy the expensive stuff from our desalinization plant."

Adam peered over at one of the stalls, spotting a couple of men struggling with placing a display booth. This caught Jonathon's attention, too.

"I think I'm going to help them real quick," Adam said.

"Oh yeah. Go ahead," Jonathon said with a smile. "If you don't mind, I'm going to explore on my own for a bit."

"Yeah sure, I'll catch up to you."

Adam dashed toward the men to assist. Jonathon faced forward and continued to roam through the lane. Examining the various booths as he strolled, he was quickly noticing another difference, none of the booths appeared to have any displayed prizes whatsoever.

"Maybe they are not out yet," he mumbled to himself.

In addition, nobody really decorated either. The kiosks were gray bare metal pole frames or white plastic pipe supports, with no coverings whatsoever. Basically the booths were skeletons without any skin.

"Okay, they are still setting up maybe."

Then there were those seeming to be done with their respective prep work, waiting for anyone to stop by. Reaching the end of this lane, he decided to continue on straight ahead toward where the stages used to be. He wanted to see, out of curiosity, if there were any shows. Jonathon had a fondness for these live acts, too. The dark night now dominated the sky, with no clouds of haze in sight. The stars shone abated above, with one overtaking the rest of them. The wind was calm and the air was a bit cooler, but still tolerable. There was lighting on ahead, but it seemed to be haphazard, as if nothing were ahead. In fact, the platform seemed to be abandoned and in complete disrepair. Around him now were the remains of some old wooden structures which appeared to be no longer in use. He did remember these from his day as he continued on the path to get to the now-defunct amphitheater.

"I guess that was it. This is just…"

He tried not to comment on the negative aspects out of respect for those putting in the effort to make this a happy occasion, but under his breath he slipped, "This is pretty sad."

"It is, but so is someone talking to the air," said a soft female voice from the shadows.

Jonathon paused, stunned to hear the voice.

Probing, he uttered, "Hello?"

Searching the area around him, he caught the glimpse of a female figure emerging from around the corner of the derelicts and approaching his side. She had full shoulder-long hair, with one side somewhat brushing over her left eye. She seemed to be in her late 20s, early 30s, and was dressed in a black buttoned long-sleeved shirt with charcoal gray pants and black shoes, similar to sneakers.

"Someone spontaneously talking…a rarity these days," she said. "Are you from around here?"

Jonathon instinctively wanted to keep his situation a secret for now. "No. I'm here visiting a friend."

"I see."

Jonathon kept his eye on her as she stared to his side, leaned down and in a bit, extended her arm as if to shake someone's hand. "Nice to meet you. I'm Angie."

Oh great, she's crazy, Jonathon thought.

She looked up at him and returned his stare, but with a wink and a smile. She stood straight up and retracted her hand. "Okay, that didn't go over well."

Jonathon understood now and smiled nervously at her. "Oh, you were joking."

"Another rarity these days, but I still try when I can."

She shifted herself to fully face Jonathon and extended her hand to him. "I'm Angie."

Reciprocating Jonathon said, "I'm Jonathon."

The two shook hands, but Angie did not release her hand at the appropriate moment.

"Did you fully comprehend the joke?" she asked.

"Yeah, I got it. I said I was visiting a friend. He obviously is not right here with me, so you were introducing yourself to my implied invisible friend."

"Okay, so you can appreciate the concept of a joke."

"Uh, yeah," Jonathon said with sarcasm.

"Good. I like you."

"Terrific. Glad to hear it."

She finally released his hand.

"So do you like hiding in the darkness, spying on unsuspecting marks?" asked a somewhat-suspicious Jonathon.

"Well. It wasn't dark when I sat down behind the building. I got here early, so I thought I'd sit down here for a bit. I really didn't sleep last night, so I must have nodded off. I woke up a few minutes ago and was gathering my bearings when I heard someone rambling to himself."

"Are you all right?"

"Yeah, for the most part." She obviously wanted to change the subject. "So Jonathon, is this your first visit to Gulfside City?"

"Yes, it is, but it's not what I expected."

"How so?"

"I come from a very different way of life, so this is just overwhelming for me."

"I see. You must be very important. It is very hard to get into the city."

Oh crap. This could be problematic, he thought.

He quickly tried to change the subject. "I do have a question for you…if I may?"

"All right," she said, nonchalantly nodding.

"I thought a festival would have more entertainment and prizes, is there more somewhere?"

"Well, unless you've been living on a deserted island somewhere, there is a teeny economic crisis going on."

"Okay, sarcasm. Great."

She lowered her head down a bit. "I'm sorry, I'm just trying to joke again."

"I'm sorry, too. I'm usually more jovial than this."

"Okay than we are both…just plain…sorry."

"Okay, I think I got that," Jonathon said with a chuckle.

"That you get!" Angie said with a big smile. "It was so lame!"

"What can I say, I'm lame."

Still with a smile, she just shook her head.

Jonathon continued. "Okay, no prizes due to lack of funds. Got it. I am surprised though, for a free event, such as it is, in the middle of a bad economy, there are not many people here."

"Ah, there lies one of the mysteries of today."

"You mean the anti-social behavior."

"So you noticed."

"Do you have any guesses as to why?"

"Nope. It just doesn't make sense to me. Everyone getting on everyone's nerves, then all of a sudden, nobody wants anything to do with one another. Well, let me clarify. It's not everyone, but it is a lot of people. What's even more weird, I have found it's only in certain places. Not all cities are like this."

"So I've gathered. It is weird."

"Then adding the enigma, these same people will be coherent but will still be very subdued at certain times, then they will be back to being completely oblivious at other times."

"Hmm, interesting."

"Hey, I think the mayor is going to be giving a speech in a few minutes, would you like to come watch with me?"

"I don't think the mayor is coming tonight."

"How do you know that?" Angie asked with a puzzled expression.

Yeah you moron, how would you know that? Jonathon thought. He quickly referred to the conversation with Adam and Suzie out near the parking lot. "I overheard this old guy talking to his wife, near the entrance, about it."

"Oh. The speech was the main reason I came tonight. Well then, would you want to hang out with me for a little while? I don't feel like playing any games now, but I don't feel like going home either. I mean if you're not doing anything or you don't have to go anywhere." Angie slightly shifted her footing and was giving him some sort of a puppy look. "You are the first live person I have met in a while who seems to be living."

Angie now more visible in the light, Jonathon was able to see her eyes; her grayish/blue eyes. He was not sure, but there was something oddly familiar about her. This naturally made him more curious.

"Sure, I don't have anywhere to go at the moment." he answered.

"Great!" she said with a smile. "I want to find out more about you, mister air talker."

Jonathon was more relaxed now. "All right, this should be interesting."

"Let's find somewhere to sit. I think there are some chairs, closer to the amphitheater here." She gestured toward the stage. Both of them started toward the theater.

"Are you from Gulfside?" Jonathon asked.

"Born and raised."

"If I may ask, how old are you?"

"Of course you may ask. Such manners…I'm 29. I'll be 30 in a few months."

Jonathon quickly realized, she was probably born around the time his life ended in the old Gulfside…before he went into ChronoSleep. *Great,* he thought. *If I couldn't feel more dated, out of place, and alone.* Traipsing into an area with very good ambient lighting now, they spotted numerous open plain folding chairs off to the side of the lane they were on. Among the sea of seats were two set close and directly across from each other as if they were waiting for Angie and Jonathon. The pair sat down, facing each other with Jonathon in the direction of the amphitheater. She leaned forward a bit as he set himself against the rear backrest.

"All right, now your turn, how old are you?" she asked.

Jonathon thought, *Probably around 60.* "I'm 30."

"I thought so."

"May I ask another personal question?"

"This is the most in-depth upbeat conversation I have had with someone in a long time. I mean, you have been more talkative than any of my good friends lately. I'll probably answer any question at this point."

"Well, please don't feel like you have to."

"Go ahead," Angie said with a smile.

"You have a nice head of hair there. Did you have a problem with the lice at all?"

"Strangely, no. I took all of the usual precautions in the beginning, like everybody else did. But these things became very aggressive and resistant. Most everybody caught them, through no fault of their own. I was very lucky, not one louse."

"That's amazing."

"Yeah, but I feel real bad for those who had no choice but to cut their hair, which was most of everyone around here. I kind of feel guilty, though…you know, because I didn't have to."

"You shouldn't. Who knows, maybe your body chemistry had something to do with it."

"Yeah, maybe. Though, you have nice hair yourself."

Jonathon changed the subject. "What do you do here in Gulfside?"

"I'm a farmer."

"A farmer?"

She gave him a playful smirk. "Yeah, you know…growing crops, fruits and veggies…living off the land."

Jonathon grinned. "I know what a farmer is, but in Gulfside?"

"Not in the central city of course silly, in the Outland."

"The Outland?"

"You really don't know much about this place do you?" she said, now with a full smile.

"I'm afraid not."

"I'll let you slide on that."

"You will huh, that's kind of you," Jonathon said, almost beaming.

"Please don't think I'm too forward, but you have a nice smile."

Jonathon paused for a moment, and looked off to his side.

"I'm sorry, I didn't mean to make you feel awkward," Angie said with regret.

Jonathon looking at her again. "I'm not. In fact, for some reason, this is the first time in a long while I have genuinely felt like smiling."

"I'm glad to hear it…me too. My friends are just being so weird right now, I never get to just do this…you know…talk and laugh."

"Did any of them have a traumatic experience or something?"

"I don't think so. It's so strange though. Why would all of them be so…out of it?"

"Yeah, you're right. It is strange."

"Initially, I thought they were mad at me for some reason, but then over time I noticed it was with others, too. In one way I was relieved, but in another I am still concerned. You said you are here visiting you're friend?"

"Yep."

"And he is normal?"

Jonathon smirked. "Well, for him."

She giggled a little. "Stop it."

"He is acting the way he should be and his wife is fine, too."

"Well, I'm happy they're fine."

"Yeah, me too."

"So Jonathon, what do you do?"

"Right now, I'm not working at the moment. I'm probably going to be moving to Gulfside soon anyway, so I'll figure out the job thing later I guess."

"Moving to Gulfside? Why?" Angie shook her head. "I tend to think out loud. I'll give you a heads up when I do that and you can stop paying attention to me."

Jonathon grinned. "I tend to think aloud a lot, too."

Angie smiled back. "Well, whatever you decide, you have a new friend now… if you want?"

"Of course."

"Good. Now, you have a friend here, what about any family?"

Jonathon was hesitant. "No, I don't have family here. In fact, I don't have family at all. What about you? You were born here, is your family still here, too?" She began to tear up.

Oh Crap, he thought. "What's wrong? If I asked…"

"No, it's nothing you did. I've been holding this in for so long, but there is no one I can talk with."

Jonathon, with a comforting tone said, "I'll listen."

"Both my parents died years ago. I was just eighteen when they passed away."

"I'm sorry."

"It's been so long now…I'm somewhat at peace with it. Every now and then though, I do have my tough days. What I'm worried about, is my brother."

"Brother?"

"I have a younger brother who was only twelve when they died. I essentially raised him. I know I was not our mother, but I cared and guided him as best I could. We had a huge fight about a year ago. He stormed out in a hurry and I haven't heard from him since. He has a fiancée, but she is just as incoherent as everybody else and is no help."

"You reported this to the police right?"

"Oh yes, of course, but they have no idea what happened, either. I don't know what to do anymore."

She was heavily sobbing now. She leapt forward off of her seat and wrapped her arms around Jonathon. He did not return the embrace. He did not know how to react or what to say. In his mind, he was the last person to offer comfort for this kind of pain. All he did was mutter under his breath, "I know what you mean."

She let go of him, sat back down, and rested herself against the rear of the chair. She gazed at him with the tears running down her cheeks and tenderly asked, "What was that?"

He gazed back. "I kind of know what you are going through…I can't believe I'm going to tell you this…"

"It's okay. Please."

"I have no family…period. I'm all alone."

Jonathon was still not sure what happened to his father and had not yet asked Adam about his mother. He assumed, at this point, they were both probably dead. "My wife and my children, who were my whole existence, were killed in an act of violence years ago."

"Jonathon, I'm so sorry."

"I have tried, for some time, to escape this…feeling…this feeling of sorrow and loneliness…but no matter what I do or what I have done, I feel more alone now."

"I know you're sad right now," Angie said with a kind tone. "But you are not alone."

"What do you mean?" Jonathon asked, baffled.

"You have a very strong, almost saintly, aura surrounding you."

This did not change Jonathon's expression. "I'm sorry, what?"

"You have such a strong energy surrounding you…I know you are probably thinking I'm crazy."

"Well, I would be lying if I said otherwise." Jonathon quickly realized, he was perhaps a little abrasive. "I'm sorry. I was out of line."

"Why are you apologizing? You are just being honest. My friends, well, when they use to talk to me, told me I was crazy, too. I don't know, I just feel these things. I just can't explain it."

Jonathon shook his head. "I don't believe in stuff like that, but that's me."

"It's all right."

Angie stood up to stretch her legs. "Thank you…for helping me."

Jonathon stood up as well. "I didn't do anything special."

"You did. You may not realize it, but you did. Or let's just say, I feel hope now. I miss my brother so much and I want to find him, but I feel a little better…since I met you." Peering closer into his eyes she asked, "Or have I met you before?"

Her eyes were strangely familiar, which coincided with the feeling of familiarity he had since the beginning of their encounter with each other. His logic and reasoning set in though, there was no way he could have met her prior to tonight.

"I can tell you that is impossible. I arrived here only yesterday. We have never met before," he said.

He looked over at her. Then toward the amphitheater, the same amphitheater, from the first night. "It almost looks the same."

She glanced over to the theater. "What, the stage?"

A younger Dana overwhelmed him. "I met her here, so long ago. She was so lost..."

Angie looked back to him with confusion. "What? You just said you've never been here. In fact how did you get into the city?"

"I shouldn't be here. This has been such a mistake. All this effort to hide, and I'm still faced with the reminders. Even with you for some reason." He abruptly walked away from her. "It was nice to meet you, Angie. I hope you find your brother."

Scrambling to get away from her, he stepped back onto to the path, hurrying back toward the festival.

Pursuing behind him, then passing him, she swiveled around to face him, forcefully placing her hands on his chest to stop him. "Who are you?"

"I'm just a broken man…lost in time."

"You're not making any sense. What do you mean?"

"It means nothing, because it is who I am."

"You are not nothing. Okay, maybe I don't know you. But I can tell, you have a kind heart and soul…someone who helps."

Jonathon shook his head with abhorrence. "What heart and soul? They died a long time ago. I'm just drifting...aimlessly…through time, which…I'm a prisoner and have no purpose."

"Jonathon, I'm going to tell you something that is probably going to freak you out, but I'm going to tell you anyway. Just please don't run off. I came here tonight, because I had this overwhelming feeling to do so…that my future depended on what I found here tonight. I thought it was to maybe confront the mayor on all the nonsense around here. To confirm my suspicions about what is going on with everyone. But now…I think, maybe it was you."

The sound of a faint turbine engine could be heard rapidly approaching from the distance.

Jonathon glared down at Angie. "What is that?"

"What time is it?"

"I don't know, probably eight by now. Why?"

The noise grew increasingly louder.

"It's too early," she said

"Too early for what?"

A bright white roving light supplemented the blare, which appeared to be almost on top of them. Evidently, the engine was now engines. The wind kicked up around them and multiple lights streamed and flashed around them as if there were in some sort of dance club.

Angie screamed up toward the sky. "It's not time yet!" She grabbed onto Jonathon's forearm. "We have got to go right now. I came in by bicycle, we'll make it work. Come on."

She started running, pulling him along. He figured it was best not to resist right now.

"What's going on?" he asked.

"Let's get to a safe place, then we'll discuss it."

Jonathon regained his senses. "Adam!"

Jonathon quickly reached up, grabbed her forearm, and then

hurried faster to lead the way. "You're with me. My friend has a car."

"He what?"

Guiding her with him, they both struggled to balance and fight their way through the dusty wind created by the objects above. Entering the middle lane of the gaming area, they could see the festival volunteers scattering to leave the area, carrying what they could. Angie and Jonathon continued to trudge forward, making sure not to hit anyone. In the distance Jonathon could see somewhat through the churning dirt, the figure of a male standing as if he was waiting for something.

As they got closer, Jonathon knew. "Adam!"

"Jonny, thank goodness!"

The two ran up to the older man as he waved them in.

Adam stiffened his posture. "Miss Leary?"

Angie had a surprised expression on her face. "Chief Stance."

"You know the chief?" she asked Jonathon.

"He's my very good friend."

"Jonny, is she with you?" asked a confused Adam.

"I guess. Is it okay?"

The sound of the ruckus above now lowered in volume, and the wind and dust began to dissipate.

Adam forcefully motioned them toward the lot. "We don't have time for this. Let's go!"

"Come on, Angie, it's all right."

All three of them were now running toward the way out. Jonathon firmly but gently held Angie's wrist to help her along to the archway. They passed through with great haste and ran out to Adam's visibly live car. The headlights were on, both driver side doors were open and Suzie was waiting inside, in the front passenger seat. Adam darted for his position, flew into his seat and quickly closed his door.

Angie hunched down and angled herself into the automobile.

Jonathon pausing, glared over toward the massive roadway. "What the hell is that?"

A battalion of soldiers appeared to be marching down the street. The troops, dressed in what seemed to be dark uniforms and beret-shaped hats, were all carrying military-style rifles slung behind their shoulders. The regiment altered course, faced them, and stepped up from the roadway on to the adjacent sidewalk ready to stream into the lot.

Adam shouted from inside. "Get in now!"

With haste, Jonathon complied. Swinging himself inside, he reached out and closed the door fast. Jonathon was about to buckle himself when Adam shifted the car into reverse, accelerated and swerved quickly out of the parking spot. The force pushed Jonathon into his door. Adam shifted the car into forward drive, once again accelerating rapidly, now away from the approaching mob. The car jostled on the uneven surface. Adam, with a sharp turn, maneuvered swiftly and cautiously not to hit anyone else trying to escape. This time the force flung Jonathon into Angie, who was belted in.

Angie wrapped her arms around him. "I got you. I won't let go."

Adam angled out of the lot, down a slight incline and onto a small street heading toward downtown Gulfside. Jonathon, resting against Angie, could feel and hear the engine racing to a higher velocity and then quickly slowing.

Adam made a sharp turn, followed by another quick jolt. "We don't have time to take her home."

"No, we probably don't," Suzie acknowledged. "It's better to be safe than sorry."

Adam continued to drive fast down the straight roadway, but was still being cautious nonetheless not to strike anyone. Jonathon struggled up to get a better look out the windows and could see them rapidly passing by those individuals on bicycles and scooters.

"These people better be going home," Adam said with annoyance.

Jonathon also noticed more of the soldiers lining up at equidistant positions on both sides of the street.

He straightened up as best as he was able, to get a better view. "What is going on, Adam?"

"Not now, Jonny!"

"There seems to be more of them again," Suzie chimed in.

"Yeah, I see that!" Adam responded. He sped up more. "I hope I don't hit somebody, but I don't think we have much more time."

Jonathon, feeling a little motion sickness, lied back down. With his head against Angie, he just looked up out the window. The streetlights streamed by as they hurried toward home. Adam slowed the vehicle down a bit and made his way around what felt like a large roundabout. Straightening out, he accelerated again. Jonathon felt a little better and decided to get up and get himself fastened in. Adam curved again going through another roundabout, but not slowing much this time thrusting Jonathon back into Angie as they rounded. Adam floored it once again, and they continued straight.

Angie looking out the window and uttering to herself, "Life should not be this way."

It was loud enough for Jonathon to hear.

Looking up at her he asked, "What do you mean by that?"

"Nothing," she said, shaking her head.

Adam slowed and made another sharp turn. There was a brief jolt of speed and then he slowed to make a smoother turn. Speeding again, they drove straight before curving slightly up an incline.

This must be the causeway bridge, thought Jonathon. He struggled up again, to see what is going on.

The bridge, at night, looked the same as it did thirty years ago. Looking back and to his left though was a different sight. The skyline of the city was far more out of place for him. At the apex of the bridge, Adam sped up, causing Jonathon to get that sinking feeling in the pit of his stomach. Slowing just a bit, Adam sharply turned into the subdivision. Jonathon, still not secured in, once again found himself in Angie's arms. Adam wound through the private road, with a quick turn here and a quick turn there.

"Suz, get the door!" Adam said.

Jonathon could hear her opening and wrestling in the glove box, searching for something.

"Okay, I got it," she said.

She pointed and repeatedly pressed a button on a garage door remote at the windshield as they approached Adam's house.

Adam confirmed the door was opening. "Great job!"

He directed the automobile into the driveway and cautiously rolled up to the door, which was not fully open but open enough. He rushed the car into the garage and stopped before hitting the inner wall. Adam reached up to his keys and shut the car off. The lighting in the room was reduced to a faint glow without the flow of the car's headlights. Adam leaned back in the seat, laying his head on the headrest.

"We're safe," he said with a sigh of relief.

Suzie and Adam opened their own doors, and exited the vehicle. The two closed their doors, with Adam slamming his and Suzie gently pushing in hers. Angie let go of Jonathon, who now was finally able to sit up straight without any jostling.

He turned to her. "Thank you."

"You're welcome," she said with a nervous smile.

"We should probably get out."

"I just want to sit here for a moment."

"Okay. Take as much time as you need," Jonathon said with a kind tone and smile.

He pulled the door lever to him and pushed the door open. There wasn't much of a change in temperature, but there was the usual smell of garage must. Jonathon waded himself out, planting his feet on the hard concrete floor below him. Taking a couple of steps away, he pushed the door in gently not to startle Angie.

Stepping to the edge of the concrete at the open end of the garage, he observed the view ahead. The street in front was quiet, nothing was going on. But in the distance, the scene over Gulfside was a much different story. Multiple aircraft buzzed about, hovering and flying around at various positions, shining bright lights throughout the city. These objects were moving so fast and due to the night sky, it was almost impossible for him to ascertain their shapes or sizes. The buildings were now eerily dark, but there was enough ambient light near the ground that he could see human figures, at certain points, sternly marching up and down the thoroughfares at the foot of Gulfside's massive skyline.

Jonathon was in such shock, he was finding it difficult to muster any words to utter any type of inquiry. Adam moved in closer to him, standing next to him watching the unfolding chaos.

Adam placed his hand on Jonathon's shoulder. "I'm sorry." Adam then gently patted his shoulder. "I've got to check in with my shift supervisors real quick, excuse me."

Adam removed his hand and walked toward the door leading into the house. He unlocked the door, then pulled it toward him. The inside glow of the interior lights added to the garage's ambient luminosity. He stepped up into the house, closing the door behind him, returning the brightness to its original level.

Suzie moved up next to Jonathon, gazing out to the city with him.

Jonathon, more lucid now, glanced over at her. "What is all of this? What is going on? Also, who is she? How does Adam know her…is there something wrong with her?"

"Adam will be done with what he needs to get done very shortly. I think it would be better if this is explained by him."

Jonathon timidly nodded as Suzie continued.

Suzie continued. "As far as she is concerned, it is complicated, but no…there is nothing wrong with her. Quite the opposite in fact." She briefly patted him on the back. "I'm going inside. Take a few more minutes to absorb and gather yourself. We have to close this door soon, so before you come in, would you please do that?"

Jonathon nodded. "Sure."

Suzie veered away from Jonathon and headed to the opposite end of the garage. Jonathon, once again, was lost in the frenzied panorama of Gulfside City. He wanted to speculate, to make some sense out of what as unfolding in front of him, but did not have any clue where to begin.

Still studying the cityscape Jonathon said, "I think I really screwed up, Dana. I should have never have done this." He looked up to the sky, seeing a bright star shining down to him. He closed his eyes. "I feel so alone now. I wish you were here."

Although the commotion in Gulfside was somewhat audible, all he focused on was the silence of his loneliness.

"Kimmie…Jonathon Russell, I guess this would have been your world. Let's go and find out why." Opening his eyes, he realized Angie was still in the car. "I'd better check on her."

He walked around and up to her door. Quickly peeking through the window, he could see she was sitting still. She had her face buried in her hands.

He gently pulled the door open, hoping not to startle her. "Angie, we're at a safe place. Let's go inside and talk this out. I need to know what is going on here, but I don't want to leave you here alone."

Slowly picking up her head, she wearily faced Jonathon. Tear trails streamed from both of her eyes. "Thank you for taking me with you. I don't know if I would have made it home. I'm so tired…I can't go on like this."

Jonathon recognized her tone. However, he had no real advice or comfort to give.

"Come on. Let's go inside. I don't know what history you have with Adam, but he is a good guy…I think he can help. He'll do what is right."

She nodded. "He is a good guy."

Angie slid out of her seat, but struggled to get out. Jonathon offered his hand, which she took. He gently assisted her out of the car and to her feet. She surprised Jonathon by lunging forward and wrapping her arms around him. Logically, he did not know what to do. Though, this time, he did return the embrace.

Trembling, she started to lightly cry. "It has been so long since anyone has hugged me. I am so lost."

"I know what you mean," Jonathon said very softly. "I wish I could help you, but I can't even help myself."

"I know we just met and this is going to sound corny, but you have already done so much for me."

Jonathon let go and stiffened his posture. She stepped back a pace, staring at him. He returned the gaze. It was strange. Her eyes were so comforting.

"What was all of that you were saying back there?" she asked.

Jonathon shook his head.

Angie continued. "Who are you?"

"I'm no one. Just a guy, like any other guy, trying to make it day to day…and my days are just getting more complicated, no matter what I do."

"I feel something in you, but I can't quite pinpoint it."

Jonathon became heated as his emotions swayed. "Stop that. You can't feel anything from me because I don't feel anything anymore. We need to go inside. Suzie told me to close this door. Why? I don't know why. But I'm going to do it. Why we had to leave the festival in the manner in which we did, I don't know why? But we did. I don't know what is going on or why. Quite frankly it is pissing me off a bit." Jonathon motioned with his head to the entry door to the house. "But, I'm going to go through that door right now and get some answers."

Jonathon gently clasped one of her hands, towing her readily along. He maneuvered around the side of the car and up to the door. He pushed the garage door button as instructed. The hum of the motor filled the room as the outer door traveled slowly down its tracks. Section by section, the door shielded them from the dismay of outside. Jonathon opened the door to the house, carefully guiding her out of the way so it would not strike her. The light from the house poured in once again. Jonathon stepped up, leading Angie into the house. As Angie passed through, she closed the door behind her. Suzie and Adam stood in front of them from living room.

"All right, Adam, I think I deserve an explanation," Jonathon said, agitated.

"You do."

Jonathon let go of Angie's hand.

Suzie walked toward Angie. "Miss Leary, would you like to get cleaned up a little?"

Jonathon looked over to Angie. She nervously looked at him. He nodded with assurance.

"Thank you, Mrs. Stance. That would be nice."

Suzie smiled and gestured to the guest bathroom. Angie walked over to Suzie then the two ladies strolled off. Jonathon stepped closer to Adam, as the women left the room.

"I guess before we get in to what is going on out there, what is her deal?"

"Miss Leary…Angie…is loosely connected to what is going on out there. It's complicated, but we will get into it in a little bit." Adam motioned to the couches. "Let's sit down."

Both Adam and Jonathon sat down across from each other.

"All right, Jonny, What do you know so far? It will help with where to start."

"Well, I guess shortly after I went into ChronoSleep, there was the nuclear detonations in the Koreas. Shortly after, the economy collapsed. To add to the dismay, the environment has been doing goofy things exasperating certain aspects of life." Jonathon shrugged his shoulders.

Adam, with an expression of acknowledgment, nodded his head. "Okay. I really thought what was happening in the Koreas was the end of the world, especially after the second detonation. I remember I was in the middle of a special shift briefing when the news of the second detonation came through. The chief, after the first explosion, ordered all available officers to active duty. He wanted to be prepared just in case there was mass hysteria and rioting. I blurted out, 'Who are the fucking assholes, using these things?' In my mind anyone stupid enough to set off one nuclear weapon would trigger other stupid idiots and boom…the end of the world. The second blast came and I thought this was it. Suz was pregnant with Ashley…either my daughter was going to be born in a radioactive wasteland or not born at all. I found myself hoping for the latter. As it turned out, we were all blessed with a miracle…the end did not come. We are still here, but it came at a huge price. The markets crashed, the economy collapsed, and everyone was holding worthless pieces of paper with useless numbers on them. Then the ash fell and food became scarce. Everyone went crazy, turning on each other. Rioting. Looting. Robbery. Carjackings of delivery vehicles. Levels of violence, nobody had ever seen. All of us were on duty, days at a time. The mayor declared a state of emergency, ordering a nightly curfew, but this did little to deter the troublemakers. It did keep everyone else out of harm's way though, but was not fair to them. So the mayor wrote and enacted stronger ordinances suspending the bond schedule for violent crimes. Many challenged these saying they were unlawful, but we were in a state of emergency and it did give us time to get a handle on things and give us some breathing room. The curfew was subsequently lifted and the emergency status ended. However, this rapidly led to another problem."

"Crowded jail cells?"

"Yes. Along with an overworked court system. We had turned abandoned buildings into makeshift jails, and had to hire people to staff these places. The cost to the city was staggering. Then, to compound things, because of the crumbling economy, getting steady deliveries of food, water, toiletries, and such was very problematic due to a lack of companies doing the supplying. In addition, the physical resources overtime began to reduce as well. When goods did make it here, the prices were astronomical."

"No one reigned in to stop that?"

"Nope. There were no price controls whatsoever. Politicians, were more concerned with stabilizing the world stage, leaving local governments to fend for themselves. Many local businesses failed along with the big guys as well. Food was a priority. Fortunately the neighboring cities around here formed a co-op to protect and develop local farms. Gulfside was part of a twelve-city collective which traded services and goods. The basic needs of the people were being met. This is what mattered until a more permanent solution could be found. However, it did not last long. The logistics were too much for the city leaders to grasp as some took certain elements too far. So back to chaos we went. Good people turned on good people to get what they needed."

"Unbelievable."

"Yeah. So here we go again. No matter what we did, there was always a problem and we just were not gaining any ground."

Suzie walked in the room from the guest hallway, then sat down next to Adam.

"How is she doing Suz?" asked Adam.

Suzie leaned back and faced Adam. "I don't think she has had good sleep in a while. I put her in Ashley's room. When I went into the closet to get some of her old clothes, she laid down and fell fast asleep. I let her be. She is so worried about James."

"I know," Adam said with a regretful tone. "Me too."

Jonathon asked, "Do you have any leads?"

Adam hesitantly responded. "Officially…no."

"What does that mean?"

"I have an idea…who might have taken him…Angie has the same idea, but I can't do anything about it."

"Why the hell not!"

"Well, it's complicated…it ties in with what is going on."

"Then go on."

"Now where was I? The situation was bleak. It was around early 2029 and Gulfside was at its pinnacle of the depression. The crime rate was at unheard of levels. The homeless just lined the streets of the metro areas along with boarded-up shops and businesses. And to make matters worse, the snow was just not going away."

"Snow?"

"Yes, snow. But not just snow. By this time the ash stayed in the atmosphere. But we still had plenty of it still on the ground. Snow and ash mixed together is not an ideal combination. And we were not equipped to deal with it. The newly elected mayor, who succeeded the very unpopular replacement to our old mayor, did not know what to do. He was young, idealistic, and full of hope…which is why he won. Gulfside was looking for a savior, and he was portrayed as one. But when it came to execution, he fell short. Very short. Then later in 2029 Gulfside was given a lifeline…when S-Y-N-R-G, pronounced as synergy, showed up."

"SYNRG, now I have seen the name before."

"I'm not surprised. They own and run everything. For the first time in many years, it looked like we were on the mend. Food assistance, housing, jobs, you name it they had it and they gave it, but only in cities where they had business interests. This was not enough to make people fully independent, but enough for SYNRG to look like the hero. These communities loved SYNRG, including us. Later, Gulfside benefited the most. One of SYNRG's founders, Sydney Ryan Grant, set their corporate headquarters here. All the buildings and growth here is all owed to SYNRG. Jobs flowed like wine around here during the cleanup and all of the construction projects."

"Wow."

"Now...wages were not high enough to make anybody rich, again consumable products were at sky-high prices, but it did provide for a more comfortable life than what everyone experienced the decade prior. Gulfside's future looked bright, but this was not without concessions from the city, which turned into consequences for the city."

"What do you mean?"

"In 2030 the mayor, in exchange for enhanced economic assistance from SYNRG, signed a contract with SYNRG essentially giving SYNRG the authority to act as the city's governmental body."

"Huh!" exclaimed Jonathon.

"It's complicated, but basically the mayor sold out the city as a whole to SYNRG. Now SYNRG's upright expansion was only the beginning. The philosophy for the city, more like a doctrine from SYNRG, was for it to become protected and self sustained. So a year later, SYNRG announced it was building a giant wall around the incorporated area. SYNRG flexed its muscles under its new power. Eminent domain became a way of life for those living on the border of the city. Relocation to the central city became the norm."

"Did people resist?"

"Surprisingly, no. Because it was getting expensive for people to drive cars and there was little to no mass transit, people were happy to move closer to their new construction and manufacturing jobs on SYNRG's dime. It was a win-win for both sides."

"Okay, let me get this straight. There is a wall around Gulfside, like a castle?"

"You didn't see the pair of fourteen-foot reinforced iron walls coming in?"

Jonathon shook his head. "No. I was probably in the bathroom on the train changing when we passed. Wait a minute, is that why I had to go through like a custom's check-in when I came in?"

"I'll get to that. Okay, SYNRG was on it way to securing the city. Now the self-sustained portion of its creed. Food and fuel were scarce. SYNRG does hold a vast amount of it, but there are still many independent outside sources, not under SYNRG's control. As a result, SYNRG's resources in this area were strained. To be more efficient, the plan of producing these assets here went into effect."

"I thought you said they owned everything?"

"Well, almost everything," Adam said, rolling his eyes. "So to execute their plan, they needed more land. Two years went by and they engulfed the entire county through a series of negotiations, meaning SYNRG bought the county, redistricting the area under incorporated Gulfside City."

"Gulfside is the county now?"

"More like the county is Gulfside."

"And no one stopped this?"

"There was not much resistance. The people had stable food and shelter. No one could stop this anyway as SYNRG has a knack for bending the rules to its favor. Eminent domain was executed on a massive scale. Entire neighborhoods were bulldozed, schools and shopping plazas knocked down, and malls and restaurants were razed to the ground to form and develop the new Outland…the area outside the wall."

"The Outland. Angie mentioned something about that. Okay, where did all of these people go?"

"Most went into the central metro Gulfside here. The remaining stayed to work on the new ash-free farmlands, wind and natural gas power stations, thermal power collector, a water extraction and reclamation plant, and some factories."

The development in the Outland took another two years and SYNRG wanted their new assets protected. So, up went another wall along the old county border. Now, going back to Angie for the moment. Her family, her parents in particular, were farmers in the rural sections of the old county. So when the Outland came, they were not affected at first. During the development of the Outland, the Leary's, along with the other farmers and ranchers, were utilized to produce the fledgling consumable food and materials needed for the new community. Angie and her brother, James, learned the trade during all of this. They were experts by the time their parents died. Once the Outland was finished and the local supply chain was better established, SYNRG wanted the remaining land. SYNRG was aggressive and most of these landowners did eventually capitulate. There was one holdout though."

"Angie."

"Right. However, SYNRG, at the time, was content to leave them alone. They were happy, SYNRG was happy, and the citizens were happy. Gulfside was on its way to becoming a utopia…a model for the rest of the world, but only one thing stood in its way."

"Crime?"

"Sort of. When SYNRG showed up, they not only came with their vast financial might, but they also came with physical strength in the form of the Guardians."

"Who are the Guardians?"

"The Guardians of SYNRG, originally, were the elite of SYNRG's small and fledgling security detail. They were tasked to… well…guard the emerging SYNRG's vital assets and core interests. Now they are a huge militarized protection force, essentially an army. No one, not even the world governments, knew how far developed the Guardians were until they arrived here. SYNRG's doctrine to protect the city did not stop with just building high walls…it was also to control the deviant behavior within. SYNRG did not like people stealing, cheating, and hurting one another. They deemed it as a destabilizing factor to Gulfside's new doctrine. SYNRG, with its substantial strength, had our puppet mayor declare a state of emergency, but this was not a typical suspend-all-liberties deal. SYNRG wanted the population to be appeased, not appalled. It is very important to SYNRG to have the population, as a whole. be willing and supportive."

"Or face a major uprising later, right?"

"That's kind of what I think. So during the day, there was no change. Life was normal, such as it was. However, a nightly dusk to dawn curfew went into effect with a stern warning from SYNRG not to violate this."

"Oh great, another curfew now?"

Adam shook his head. "This time the curfew was to be executed by the Guardians. No one, and I mean no one, was allowed out during the curfew time at all without SYNRG's permission."

"What about police, fire, and medical?"

"Nobody at all. Policing the city at night is handled by the Guardians."

"How did this stick?"

"SYNRG has its ways to manipulate a situation to its favor. Citing the benefits of reducing costs and strain on the beleaguered department, its highly trained elite was allowed to fill in as long as they did not violate the law."

"I know I keep going back to this…but it stuck?"

"There was a minor vocal opposition to this, but the people as a whole did not care who and at what time was doing the crime fighting. Many were sick and tired of being fearful. The opposition's pleas fell on deaf ears anyway. Remember, we were on our own here. Higher governments had bigger problems to deal with and the majority of citizens favored this new order."

"Now, what about a fire or medical emergency during the night?"

"You still call like you normally would, but it is routed to a

SYNRG call station. They clear and give permission to the appropriate service, but it is closely monitored by the Guardians. Any deviation not necessary to the task at hand is considered a violation of curfew."

"Wow, very strict. How did you feel about it?"

"I don't like the idea of someone, other than the our police department, keeping the order, but…here we are. They were given control of the city, by the legitimate governmental body of the city."

"How was the transition when the curfew started?"

"The homeless were the first to go, of course. With no available shelters to go to, they were swiftly removed."

"It must have been some morning when you went to work, processing all of those arrests."

"Yeah, it was some morning, but there was not one arrest to process."

"Come again?"

"The detention center, which was set up to house the detainees any Guardians apprehended, was empty."

"What happened to all of them? They had to have gone somewhere."

"Indeed. I investigated the oddity myself. I did check, to be sure, all of the normal homeless hangouts, abandoned buildings, and so forth, but there were no signs of them. So I contacted one of SYNRG's…'facilitators'…the public relations people for SYNRG. You know what he said to me?"

"What?"

"To help ease the burden on the city of prosecuting these minor offenses, the individuals seized were relocated outside of the city and outside of the Outland outer wall."

"You don't seem convinced of that."

"Nope. Plus, I asked about any violent crimes, and he responded that there were none."

"Really?"

"I would like to think there were none, but come on. I continued looking into the matter of the homeless, with negative results. I went outside of the wall to see if any of them happened to be nearby. Nothing."

"Could some of them have snuck back in?"

"The wall is very secure, with various security checkpoints, similar to the one you encountered. I don't know." Adam shook his head. "I don't know for sure, who was removed. However, going back through court records of some of our repeat offenders, we have come up with a list of possibilities. Their records all ceased around the commencement of the curfew."

"Interesting."

"I expanded the record search beyond Gulfside for these same individuals…nothing."

"They all decided to turn over a new leaf all of a sudden?"

"I don't know. What I do know, however, there is not one homeless person in Gulfside City."

"How is that possible?" Jonathon asked with confusion. "When did the curfew expire?"

"The curfew is still in effect. What you witnessed earlier tonight was SYNRG setting up for the night, but earlier than scheduled."

"I'm confused. We were well past nightfall. I thought it was a dusk to rise curfew."

"For the first couple of years it was. As the crime rate dropped, the weariness of not being allowed out at night grew, along with the minor opposition. The group, now known as the Opposition to GulfSide Oppression, became more vocal. SYNRG, who has no reason to back down from its policies, did. Again, keeping the populace somewhat happy seems to be important. As a compromise, the curfew would stay, but start later and end earlier. This was acceptable to the Opposition and the new curfew started at 10 at night, ending at 6 in the morning. This was in effect until about a year ago."

"What happened a year ago?"

"Nothing. SYNRG, without notice or warning, have been erratically moving up the start time for the curfew. Some nights it starts at the agreed time of 10. Other nights, like tonight, they begin it earlier without warning. The first few times they pulled this nonsense, those who did not clear the streets, probably thinking they were safe because they were before the 10 o'clock start time, disappeared. Again, no arrestees at all. I checked with the facilitators, and got the same response as I had been for years, that these individuals had been relocated."

"What happened to these people? Somebody at some point would have communicated with someone here. A friend, a family member, something?"

"I don't know what happened to any of them. The department was subsequently inundated with missing persons' reports. Not as much as I would have thought, with all of the introverted behavior and all. Nonetheless, this was the most action I had seen out of the townspeople in a while. This is when Suz and I met a very distraught woman named Angela Leary."

Suzie added. "I was helping the front desk with filling out those reports when she entered the department. She immediately caught my eye with her long flowing hair..."

Suzie exited the office area and went right up to the timid and obviously distressed woman.

"Can I help you miss?" Suzie asked.

"I think my brother is missing."

"What makes you think that, ma'am?"

Angie had tears in her eyes. "We had a fight last night and he stormed out. Minutes later, the Guardians came out. It wasn't curfew time yet, but they appeared to be on the warpath for some reason. I wanted to go after my brother, but I figured I had better stay out of the way. I tried calling him to let him know to avoid them, but I couldn't get a hold of him. Again, it wasn't curfew yet, so I did not think anything of it. When he calmed down, he would call me. As angry as he was, he would have called me by now to let me know where he is. I'm hearing now, SYNRG started the curfew early without warning."

Angie was more hysterical now. "Why would they do this? I don't know where he is...I'm so scared. He's the only family I have." She buried her face in her hands.

Suzie continued her story to Jonathon. "I don't know. There was something odd with her, but in a good way. I was so drawn to her. I wanted help ease her pain. I wanted to find her brother immediately. I decided to take her upstairs to get a detective to help her right away..."

Suzie led Angie out of the elevator. She tried to keep Angie calm by just having idle chats.

"This is our officer and investigations section. The investigative staff, along with the phone unit, were relocated up here several years ago to allow us to turn the second floor into a holding area for detainees after everything hit." Suzie pointed across the room. "The chief's office is straight ahead in the office down there. I can't see anyone up here, but I hear someone somewhere. Let's walk in a little farther and peek into some offices to see if we can find someone to help."

Suzie peeked into several offices, checking for any signs of life. Angie, with no expression, followed behind. As they approached the chief's office, the two men in the phone unit appeared to be talking on the phone.

Suzie stood there for the moment, with Angie haplessly by her side, contemplating their next move. "Hmm, I don't know where everybody is at."

Adam walked out of his office. "What's going on Suz?"

"Where is everybody, Adam...err chief, sir?"

"I've got everybody out in the field looking into this mess that occurred last night." Adam gestured to Angie. "Who is this?"

"I'm sorry I never got your name," she asked Angie.

In a soft quivering tone she answered, "Angela Leary...Angie."

"Her brother is among the missing. So I brought her up here."

Before he could give a generic and cold response, Suzie looked at him in a way a wife could, to get her husband to do what she wanted.

"She needs our help, Adam."

"Okay," Adam responded with a slight smirk.

Suzie gestured toward Adam. "Miss Leary...Angie, this is Adam Stance, chief of police. He'll get to the bottom of this."

Adam motioned to Angie, "Miss Leary, would you come into my office please, so I can get your statement."

Angie walked to, then past Adam and entered his office. Adam stared and smiled at Suzie, dumfounded at the aspect of just having received his marching orders from his subordinate employee wife.

"All right, Mrs. Stance, it's time for you to resume you duties."

With a big smile she said, "Yes sir."

Adam continued telling the story to Jonathon. "I interviewed her, taking her statement. I'm glad Suzie insisted. During the interview, I felt something about her...something very special, almost familiar. I knew her for some reason. I obviously take all cases very seriously, but with her...this, for some strange reason, was personal to me."

"Yeah, I felt a connection to her, too," Jonathon said with acknowledgment. "I don't know why. Maybe I helped her once...you know, on the job. But then...it's impossible! There is no way. She probably was not even born yet when I went into ChronoSleep."

Adam looked at Jonathon with a bewildered expression. "Well, putting this aside for the moment, I did something I shouldn't have done."

"What was that?"

"I promised her, with every fiber of my being, I would find her brother."

Jonathon leaned back in his seat. "Oh."

"Jonny, every day that goes by, I feel worse. A year has past, and nothing. Not one damn solid lead. It is getting to the point where I can't face her anymore."

"And I just brought her into your home."

"It's okay. But, I feel like I have failed her, though."

"You hinted earlier you may have an idea?"

"I have to be careful how I approach this,"

Jonathon nodded. "You think SYNRG has these people captive, don't you?"

"I have not officially or even unofficially suggested or acknowledged this to anyone, including her, because it would probably be the end of the department and the last line of defense for freedom here. Not that I can put up much of a fight anyway, but as long as I keep my mouth shut, at least everyone in Gulfside City gets to have the daylight, freely. But then, on the other hand, I'm failing my duty by not pushing the issue. To make matters worse, the more time that goes by, SYNRG gets that much more organized and stronger. They have been bringing in more Guardians. I don't know what to do. The citizens who are still coherent are getting impatient. In fact, it is what Angie and her brother were arguing about when he disappeared."

"What do you mean?"

"James was the leader of the Opposition. He hated SYNRG. Now don't get me wrong, I had and still have no problem with these people, but they take very unnecessary risks."

"Such as?"

"The main one is they break curfew. They go out at night. They hide in the shadows to avoid detection."

"Have any of them ever been caught?"

"Yes, unfortunately…never to be heard from again."

Jonathon shook his head. "Scary."

"The Opposition has grown louder and is becoming more vocal. Whatever SYNRG has planned for us, which may be nothing…we all could be overreacting, but if there is something going on here, this group, I think, is getting under their skin."

"What makes you say that?"

"The people who have been taken this last year, during the altered curfew incidents, are…or were confirmed members of the Opposition."

"Oh, come on. You have got to be kidding me. This is something you would read in a book." Jonathon quickly rose to his feet, stomping toward the kitchen. He placed his hands on his hips, arched his back, and looked up. "How could this have happened?"

Adam rose to his feet now and stepped somewhat toward Jonathon. "I hate to say it buddy, but this is the world we live in. It's not just a madhouse here, it's all over the entire world. And SYNRG has a firm grip. The Guardian numbers are also rising in the other cities they occupy."

Jonathon turned back to Adam. "How in the world did this SYNRG get this powerful?"

"With all of the chaos, it is hard to specifically pinpoint, but its seems they seized their opportunity at the beginning of the meltdown."

"By taking over other dying businesses, maybe?"

"Possibly, but it is probably much more complicated. I'm no financial expert, but those who once were, not in SYNRG's pocket, aren't sure what happened either. SYNRG guards its information and controls a vast amount of the world's information very closely and uses their benevolent programs as a shield. However, over the years, we have managed to get some facts."

"Then I guess the next question is, how did SYNRG acquire its fortune pre-meltdown?"

"SYNRG did not appear on the scene until right before everything happened. And I think the key to its origins is with its main founder…this Sydney Grant. When SYNRG came to Gulfside, my first question was…out of all of the places in the world…why here?"

"Did you figure it out?"

"Unofficially, I think so. I'm sure Sydney was born here."

"What?" Jonathon moved back to the couch and sat down. Adam, likewise, followed suit,

"His name is what drove me crazy. So, I played with arranging his name around. I got a hit from Grant Sydney Ryan…Junior."

"A prior criminal past?"

"No, actually a victim. More specifically a six-year-old victim, here in Gulfside."

"What was he a victim of?"

"Attempted murder."

"You said six right?"

"Right. The story is his father was a very wealthy industrialist. In fact, Grant Sr. was considered to be one of the world's top ten wealthiest individuals. He was also a philanthropist. Senior started the many charities and programs in Gulfside that formed the core communal groups which helped Gulfside thrive in our day."

"Yes, of course…Grant Ryan put Gulfside on the map. Okay it's coming back to me now. In addition to the many charities he headed, Grant Sr. liked to personally help people too."

"That's right. It was often, he'd bring some homeless people home, get them back on their feet, give them a job at one of his business, and send them back into Gulfside as a productive member of society. In fact, one of his top financial managers was someone he helped. Then, one day in 1992, the family's housekeeper came home from her daily errands and found the family, Grant, his wife, two sons and daughter, murdered. When the emergency services arrived, they did find one survivor however."

"Let me guess, Grant Jr."

"Yes."

"I remember this from the cold case files."

"Yep. When the housekeeper was interviewed, she advised that Grant Sr. did have a pet project, but the man vanished after the murders."

"This case was unresolved when I left."

"It technically still is. If you recall, all we had was the vague description of the man from the housekeeper and a set of fingerprints which did not result in any known matches."

"What about a name?"

"Still no name. We never got a break…until on a review of the case. I put two and two together on the names. Grant Jr. survived, but only after two major surgeries and a lengthy stay in the hospital for intensive care, both physically and mentally. Grant Sr. planned very well. Grant Jr. got everything, but because he was a minor, his assets were put into a trust. Grant Jr.'s shares with the company was assigned to a regent until he was of age. He had a living relative, an aunt, to whom was given full custody of Junior. But she was more interested in the house and the money she received than little Grant. She placed him in an out-of-state private boarding school, which apparently was an option in the will. Subsequently, the aunt sold the house and was never heard from again."

"I guess you can really count on family when you need them," Jonathon said with sarcasm.

"Fortunately, the school Junior went to was one of the finest in the nation, which his estate paid for. For him, under his circumstances, he was in a good place. In addition to the room and board and education, he received excellent medical care and counseling. He was there right up until he became an adult. I visited the school some time ago, or really what is left of it now, under the premise of following up on the investigation, which in a sense was true. I had access to all of his records for his entire life at school."

"How did he do?"

"Very well, academically speaking. Grant excelled in his studies, especially in physical science, biology, and mathematics. The school had to develop a special curriculum, just for him. He started college level courses at 14 and was working on doctoral stuff when he left at 18."

"Wow. How was he with…his emotions…dealing with what happened to him and the loss of his family?"

"Only he knows. He would not open up to the counselors at all. He was always very polite about it. Never angry or visibly upset, but often stated that he did not want to talk about it. He was happy to talk about anything else…schoolwork…hobbies, but never about the family. The school brought in specialists. They got even less. Socially, Grant was an outcast. His mannerisms were awkward. He was often bullied, which the school claims they intervened on numerous occasions, but his psychological evaluations told a different story. Yet, when he was younger, whenever the school had organized events, he persisted to be included. Nonetheless, as time went on and he got older, he became more withdrawn."

"Did Grant become belligerent at any time? I mean that stuff will wear on a person over time."

"Nope, he always kept his cool. The counselors just concluded he focused all of his energy into his schoolwork. In addition, he did make a couple of friends whom were also teased and ridiculed. The counselors added, having these friendships more than likely helped him. He maybe opened up to them, but they don't know for sure. He befriended the two, about a year after he arrived. The trio formed a strong bond. Grant talked fondly of his friends to the counselors, even making references to them being like brothers. This was significant, as this was the only reference to family he ever made. As Grant became more withdrawn, so did the other two. They often stayed to themselves, avoiding contact with everyone else wherever possible. Grant was happy with his friends, or brothers as he did later called them, but never discussed what they did. As a result, the other two excelled in their courses as well, but nowhere near the level of Grant."

"What happened to Grant Jr. after he left the school?"

"Well, Grant's friends left first. They were both from extremely wealthy families as well. In time, they took over their respective family businesses. When Grant received his inheritance, he signed his stake in his company to his friends, and was never heard from again."

"So just like that…gone."

"I cannot find any record of him."

"And now we have a Sydney Grant here in Gulfside. Photos? You had to have some photos. Maybe, from the school? Are there similarities between Grant and Sydney?"

"I do have photos of Grant, but no one has ever seen Sydney."

"How is that possible?"

"He is a recluse…never goes out in public. He is the majority stakeholder in SYNRG, but the day-to-day operations are overseen by two main individuals."

"Let me guess, his friends."

"Right again. They are the power behind SYNRG and are never seen."

"Wait…how do they conduct business then?"

"Direct contact with the public is managed through the facilitators."

"Wait a minute. I thought you said Grant…Sydney whoever, sold his company to the other two."

"Again, assuming Grant…Sydney are the same person, we aren't sure of the exact details, but I suspect the now-Sydney is behind the scenes making all of the decisions, with the other executing his instructions."

"This whole thing is just odd."

"You're right it is. If Grant is Sydney, which after visiting the school, I think is the case, they had a lot of time to plan and organize whatever they have in mind for us today. They were all inseparable at school, all brilliant, and seemingly devoted to their tasks."

"What tasks? And why all of this?"

"I don't know. Again, the details in the beginning are sketchy, but…it seems through manipulation, guile, and subterfuge…SYNRG was born. And like I said, not too long after you left. After the nuclear incident and the massive sell off in the markets following, SYNRG emerged victoriously as most of the world's companies fell one by one. SYNRG subsequently swept through the financial world like a tidal wave, wiping everything out that was left, in less than a year. By the time anyone noticed, it was too late. Then after the environment went haywire, they tightened their grip by becoming the chief supplier of food and now here we are."

"Still in a globalized depression?"

"The Opposition thinks SYNRG is keeping things this way on purpose, probably to maintain its virtual monopoly on the world. Some smaller businesses, like the Leary's, do exist, but have extremely limited capabilities and resources. SYNRG cities, such as Gulfside, have things a little easier…people have jobs…have shelter…food… medical care…but that is about it. Hardly any luxuries whatsoever, which doesn't matter anyway as most everyone seems to be disinterested in most everything. They go to work, then go home. In fact, another one of the mysteries now…what work? Sure there is plenty to do around here, but the vast amount of people here and jobs conducted don't seem to add up. Nonetheless the situation is more bleak outside the walls…hence the walls and checkpoints. SYNRG is very careful about who they let in. There are primarily three ways to get into a SYNRG city. One: If you are a citizen of the respective city. Two: If you are given permission to visit or even move to a SYNRG city. Three: If you are a government employee or representative, visiting for official business. We have had five world leaders here in as many months."

"Interesting. Why?"

"I don't know. Lately, I focus on what is going on here, but there are signs that SYNRG may be trying to break Gulfside away from the rest of the country, making the city an independent state."

"You mean, Gulfside as its own nation?"

"Yes. It is by far the largest out of the SYNRG cities and has the most access to resources."

"But why on earth would SYNRG…"

"They would ultimately answer to no one. Not that they really do now, but this way makes it official and absolute. And with the build up of Guardians in the last year and their erratic behavior lately…the Guardians first job was to control the crime. They did. The next was to keep who isn't allowed in, out. They do. And now we seem to be entering into a new phase, which could be for nationhood or for a far bigger plan."

"Does anyone know about the Grant-Sydney connection?"

"Because the case is still active, it's not public record. The school's documents are not public record. As far as the department is concerned, I have the file on lockdown, for the chief's eye only. The three of us here only know of the possible connection. I have a feeling, if this ever came to light, it might make things worse around here."

"I agree. Sydney…Grant…whoever….seems to have gone through the trouble of erasing his former self…I can almost sympathize."

"Jonny there is no reason for you to hide."

"I just feel so out of place…so vulnerable…it's best I…"

Jonathon leaned forward and rubbed his eyes. "I feel weak again. I probably need to get some sleep."

Both Suzie and Adam rose to their feet.

Suzie inched closer. "Do you need any help?"

Jonathon, struggling to his feet, steadied himself on the arm of the sofa.

"I think I'll be okay. It does not seem…"

CHAPTER FORTY

"LET'S SEE WHAT TODAY THROWS AT YOU"

"Good morning, lazy bones."

"It's morning already?" Jonathon said.

"Come on, Jonny, you're wasting time."

"How about ten more minutes?"

"How about no. This is another big day for you."

"What do you mean…I have nothing special planned for today."

Jonathon tossed himself onto his back to face his wife. Dana was so radiant and stunning. How could he just stay in bed? "God you are so beautiful."

"I know. Nice try. Flattery is not going to get you anywhere ram boy. Adam needs your help. Plus, he is your ride into town today. He has something to show you and it's going to be life altering..."

Jonathon, in a daze, tried to gather his bearings.

"Dana? Where did you go?"

Jonathon pushed himself up. "What game are you playing now?"

He sat up. "Dana? Where'd you go? Kimmie…JR? Are you ready?"

Still foggy and out of it, he perused around the room. This wasn't home. This was Adam's.

"What am I doing here?"

Then it hit him. There was no Dana rushing him. There were no kids to get ready. He was alone.

"Damn it, mind. Why are you doing this to me?"

Removing the sheet and blanket off of him, he casually swung his feet and legs to the side of the bed, allowing them to dangle off the edge. "I hate waking up with this pit in my stomach. Even if I were successful at changing my environment, my mind is just not going to let me be free."

There was a soft knock at the door.

"Jonny, are you up?" asked Adam.

Jonathon responded in an elevated intonation. "Yeah, I'm up!"

"Is it all right if I come in?"

"Oh yes, sure!"

The sound of the doors parting way entered Jonathon's welcoming senses. His loneliness, was about to get a short reprieve. Adam walked in, dressed in standard uniform. He stepped directly in front of Jonathon, who was smiling at him.

Adam grinned back. "What?"

"It's very good to see you, chief. It's a trip seeing you with those stars on your collar. It suits you perfectly."

"Thank you. What are planning to do today, that is, if you have thought that far?"

"No I really haven't."

"You can go in with me if you would like?"

Jonathon nodded, without hesitation. "I think I will…good idea."

"Good. I have some things I need to show you. First of all, do you remember Jason?"

"Of course I remember him. Does he still work…I mean here in Gulfside…for the county…city…whatever?"

"Yes. Sort of. He is working on something for me."

"For you?"

"Yes. And it is what I want to show you."

"What's going on?"

"You'll see. Let me get out of your hair, so you can get ready. It is going to be a busy day. However, before we go, Suz prepared some breakfast. Get yourself a bite to eat."

"Thank you. How is Angie?"

"She is still asleep. She has been in absolute misery over the last year."

"Because of James."

"Yes. I can't imagine what she is going through."

"I can. You live in a world where nothing matters. Your mind takes over, keeping you prisoner. You don't eat…don't sleep. All your basic necessities go to the wayside as your mind continually torments you on the one thing you try not to dwell on…yet all the while, hoping for a better tomorrow which does not seem to be coming."

Jonathon shook his head. "I didn't mean to go off on that tangent. I had a bad dream. It's got me messed up a bit this morning."

"It's all right."

"I'll get myself together here. You and Suzie have jobs to get to. You don't need a bum like me slowing you down."

"Well…Suz is taking the day off to stay here and watch over Angie, but I still have a job to do."

Jonathon took in a deep breath. "Right. Let me get myself together so we can go."

Adam smiled. "Great! I'll get another set of clothes for you to wear, so you can blend a little better with today's…trend."

Adam marched to and through the doors, closing them behind him.

Jonathon paused for a moment, before getting in motion. "All right, Jonny…let's see what today throws at you."

Jonathon followed Adam into the garage. Once inside, he paused and he shut his eyes.

Where am I? Jonathon thought to himself. *This is so surreal. What reality is this?*

He heard the sound of the opening garage door and the starting engine of his car. These normally routine senses overwhelmed his fragile psyche, bringing him to a place he once called home. However, now it was not. *All this time has past…but has it?*

"Jonny, you okay?" Adam asked.

Jonathon opened his eyes and regained his senses. "Sorry, I just got lost for a second."

Adam closed his door to the car as Jonathon made his was way to the passenger side. Jonathon subsequently got in. Adam set the car into motion, leaving the safe haven of the garage. Adam pushed the button to shut the garage door, then continued on their way to the station.

"Hey, chief. Why don't you have a patrol cruiser?"

"With cars and parts so limited and expensive, I could not justify having one sitting around when I'm not out on the road. Besides, most of the patrolling is done by foot, bicycle, or motorcycle now, and mainly in the Outland."

"What about the core city?"

"We haven't had a single incident or arrest from city dwellers in over a year. Everyone keeps to themselves. The Outland is tame now, too, but we still had about a hundred or so incidents last year…and about a dozen of those resulted in an arrest, all minor crimes and all dismissed, as time served, the next day."

"A hundred incidents last year? We averaged a hundred incidents, usually in a three or four days."

"Yeah, well at the height of the collapse, it was far worse. But when things tapered off, so did the department's budget. The city budgets enough money for three dozen officers, a half a dozen support staff, and a fair amount for equipment maintenance."

"We had far more officers than what you have and you have much more area to cover now. How do you manage?"

"With such little activity…fine. In fact, I'm expecting my budget to be slashed again."

"Scary."

"It is. So, I use my own car. However, I do split the cost of fuel and some maintenance with the department. It's a nice arrangement."

Angie woke. Sitting up in a panic, she desperately tired to figure out where she was. She whisked the covers off of her in a hurry, swung her legs to the side of the bed, and sprung quickly to her feet.

"I'm still in my clothes?"

Angie stood in a space between the bed and a desk. She noticed a bunch of picture frames on the desk, which ranged in sizes and shapes.

She inched closer to get a better look of the photos. "Who are these of?"

Examining them more closely, she realized these were photos of Suzie, Adam, and their children with a few exceptions.

"Who is this?" she asked.

Angie picked up one of the larger frames. It was of Adam and another male at what looked to be some sort of graduation, more specifically, a law enforcement academy graduation. A caption a the bottom said, "Graduation 2005." The two smiling men were each holding their framed certifications from the State in front of them. Adam's, of course, had "Adam Stance" in bold letters.

She then focused on the other male. "Jonathon?"

Panning down to his certificate she read, "Jonathon…Scott. 2005." She set the picture back in its place and selected another one, bringing it closer to view. This one was of Jonathon standing next to Dana, who was holding a baby, and Kim on the other side of Jonathon, holding his hand. All three were smiling proudly. The caption at the bottom said, "Welcome Home, Jonathon Russell-September 26, 2009." Angie set this one back in its place. She chose another, this one a lone picture of Jonathon. It was a copy of the same one hanging in the station. The caption stated, "Jonathon Scott may you find your peace; wherever you are."

She set this frame down. "Jonathon Scott? Why does this name sound familiar? And why does it appear, Jonathon has not aged?"

Angie opened the door, then hurried out into the hallway and into the kitchen and entertainment area. "Hello? Chief Stance? Mrs. Stance? Jonat…"

Suzie emerged from the master bedroom. "Hi. How are you doing?"

Angie stopped at the edge of the kitchen. "I think I'm okay, but just a little confused. Who is Jonathon?"

Suzie moved in part way, but still with a good gap between her and Angie. "He is a good friend."

"Jonathon Scott?"

"Yes."

"The one from history…on the wall at the station…the hero," Angie said, now realizing.

Suzie hesitated. "Yes."

"How is that possible? Some of those portraits you have are from thirty or more years ago...and he has barely aged."

Suzie was still very hesitant, but didn't want to insult Angie's intelligence, so she figured she better say something. "Let's sit down, okay?"

Suzie motioned to the sofas. Both sat down. Suzie thoroughly explained about Dana, Kim, and JR…the museum…prowlers…the school…Jonathon disappearing without a trace…him emerging from ChronoSleep just days ago…the house…the hutch.

Angie leaned back, and stared into nothing. "Okay. I did not expect…"

"Jonny is very sensitive, for whatever reason, about his presence here. Please keep this to yourself. I only told you because…Adam and I…well, care for you."

Angie looked back to Suzie. "You do?"

"Yes. Adam is really knocking himself out to find James."

Angie nodded. "I know."

"He feels so guilty, for not…"

"Mrs. Stance…I know."

"Suzie…you can call me Suzie…no need to be formal."

Angie leaned over and wrapped her arms around Suzie. "Thank you for being so kind to me."

Suzie returned the embrace. "Of course."

Angie stood up moving to the side.

Suzie rose to her feet. "I know you probably want to get home, but you can stay here as long as you like."

"Ever since James disappeared, I have felt very uncomfortable at home. I've even given up on the fields. It's been nice to talk to someone."

"Then stay as long as you need. Come and go as you need. We are here."

"With Jonathon, my lips are sealed."

"Thank you. Jonny is a good guy, but has never been the same after the loss of his family. But he still is a good guy…an upstanding guy."

"Why did he do the Chrono thing?"

"He says he was trying to escape his pain."

"I guess I can understand that."

Suzie smiled. "Adam gave me the day off, so I'm going to make use of the time and get some things done around here. Just relax. Our tablet is around here somewhere…if you want to read or something."

"If it is okay, I'd like to help."

"Thank you. Let's get started."

Adam and Jonathon arrived at the station. Jonathon was quiet the whole way. There was plenty of activity on the streets, almost like a normal day such as individuals who appeared to be on their way to work. *What work? What is a typical day now for everyone?* He valued the silence for the moment, so he decided he would just ask later. Now, standing at the elevator in the back hallway of the first floor, he had something more pressing on his mind…it was time to inquire.

"What happened to my mother?"

Adam looked over at him with his hand suspended in front of the call button. "I was wondering when you were going to ask me." Lowering his arm without pressing the button. "After the initial financial catastrophe, she, like most everyone else, lost her wealth. Soon she found herself without work. I offered for her to come back to Gulfside…I had a job for her, but she declined."

"It probably was beneath her…if you know what I mean."

"I didn't want to say anything, but I got that impression."

"How did she react when you told her I disappeared?"

"I think she was genuinely concerned, but you know your mother. She was emotionless about it."

"Yeah, sounds about right."

"I kept in touch with her as much as I could over the years. I had my hands full here with dealing with the crisis…raising a family…"

Jonathon nodded in agreement then braced himself. "What

happened to her?"

"She died five or six years ago...old age and in her sleep. She lived alone, so when I didn't get a response from her, I called the authorities over there and they were the ones who found her."

"So she died alone."

"Yes."

"Sadly, that is probably what she preferred. Thank you for letting me find out on my own timing."

"Absolutely. I've always said I'd be here for you."

Adam pressed the call button. The doors immediately rattled open, exposing a distressed interior. Adam gestured for him to enter, and Jonathon stepped in. Adam followed, then both turned around.

Jonathon noting the wear or the interior, backed up and grabbed the handrail. "Is this thing safe?"

"Surprisingly, yes. It still has no incidents," Adam said as he pressed the 2 button.

The doors clattered and screeched closed. Adam stood perfectly still, bracing himself as the car jolted into motion. Jonathon swayed a bit, but maintained his balance by holding on tight as the lift shimmied upward.

"You okay?" Adam asked.

Sarcastically, Jonathon replied, "Sure."

The elevator slowed, then seated into place with another slight jolt. The doors rattled open, revealing a darkened room to which Adam confidently marched with Jonathon eagerly following.

"I've got to get that light fixed," Adam stated .

Jonathon did not recognize the section they were in. "What is this place?"

"When the county was absorbed, we turned a portion of this floor into holding cells and a small detention area to make things more efficient. Adam pointed to the right. "Of course, like I said earlier, we don't use them much these days. The jail here is more for short-term holdings, for those with hearings and awaiting trial, if necessary. We have access to the jail across the street to house any sentenced offenders, but it is empty at the moment. The courtroom, with a judge's chambers, as well as the state attorney, public defender, and clerk of court, all have their offices through those doors, which makes for faster processing."

"Sounds cramped."

"It is."

"Why are we here?"

Adam stepped toward the left, with Jonathon in tow.

Adam pulled out an access card and slid it through the adjacent reader. "The medical quarters are here...and this is where Jason is...

and why I brought you here." Adam then pulled the door open. "After you."

Jonathon entered, the much brighter hallway. Adam tailed, releasing the door with it closing by itself. The hallway was long, lined with three doors on each side spread equidistant from each other. The gaps between the doors implied these were large rooms. Adam moved up to Jonathon's side.

"We need to go to the far door on the right."

Both Adam and Jonathon started walking toward it as Adam continued,

"Our evidence room is this first door on the left here."

"This is all so weird and...depressing."

"I know things look a little rough around here, but we barely have enough just for the essentials."

"It's okay. I'm just still a little taken back at these changes too."

"You have no idea."

"So Jason still works as a doctor here?"

"In a manner of speaking, yes."

"What does that mean?" Jonathon asked with confusion.

"Just wait...Ah...here we are."

The men arrived at the last door on the right. Jonathon quickly noticed this door needed an access card. *Weird,* he thought. Adam slid his card through reader. The door unlocked then he pushed it inward. Gesturing for Jonathon to enter, he then followed as Jonathon inched in. The door closed by itself.

The room was some sort of laboratory of sorts. An examination table was set in the middle of the room. In the far corner stood a black standard desk with a computer screen. Some disheveled papers adorned the desk's surface, along with a few strewn pens. This was the first wide use of paper Jonathon had seen in this future. A long rectangular black counter with an open bottom ran along the adjacent wall to the attached inner wall. Two powerful-looking black microscopes were sitting next to each other in the middle of the countertop, along with a couple of other, rather large, devices next to the rightmost one that he did not recognize. He also saw a few stacked tablet computers.

Tall and wide metal bookshelves occupied the closer left corner. Files, journals, and all sorts of medical-looking books were haphazardly stacked. Some appeared as if they would fall off at the slightest movement. There was a small workstation in the far left corner with more papers scattered about. In between the bookshelves and workstation was an opening to another room.

Adam called out. "Jason? Are you here?"

From the other room they heard, "Hey chief...be with you in a second."

Adam turned to Jonathon. "He is going to be in for a shock."

Emerging from the other room was a man in his obvious sixties, worn face, and walking with a distinguishable limp.

"We have a guest?" Jason asked.

"Hobbling up to Jonathon and extending out his arm he said, "Hi. I'm Jason Mayers."

Jonathon smiling. "I know. It is good, but weird, to see you so much older Jay."

Jason lowered his arm. "Jonny?"

"Yes, it's me."

"But how…how in the world?"

"It is amazing what a little ChronoSleep will do for you."

Jason nodded. "Of course. Jonny, it is so good to see you."

Jason inched closer, leaned in, and gave Jonathon a quick hug. Jonathon returned the embrace. They gave each other the typical guy pat on the back.

Jason then shook his head. "I'm sorry. I just can't believe you are standing here."

"Yeah, it took me a moment, too," Adam added.

Jason hobbled toward the workstation, pulling a stool out. Carefully he sat down. "Jonny, it really is good to see you. How long have you been back?"

"Just a few days."

"So what do you think of our world today?"

"It's a lot to take in."

"The understatement of the year, ay, chief?"

Adam smirked. "He doesn't know the half of it."

"So…why ChronoSleep?"

"After Dana and the kids, then my grandfather, I just fell apart."

"And ChronoSleep seemed the way to go?"

"At the time, it seemed to be the only way for me."

"Did it help?"

"No. I actually was supposed to be in for another 70 years. All the reminders I was running away from are still here."

"Ah. So, do you think if you went the full term, you would have been okay?"

"I'm thinking, probably not. I feel so alone now, I can only imagine if it were farther into the future."

"Hmm…well it would seem you still have some friends here. You will never be alone."

"I know. Enough about me, how are you? How are Beth and Josh?"

"Well Beth and I are divorced. After the shit hit the fan, medical services were lacking around here. At the behest of the mayor, I decided to help those who needed it. Of course, nobody could pay, but I was doing what mattered most. As it turned out, I was spending a lot of time at the infirmary…16 hour days, sometimes longer…7 days a week. This translated into not much of a home life. Never mind the fact, she and Josh still had a roof over their head and food on the table. I mean…there were many people doing with much less. But, I can't blame her I guess, for wanting more. She wanted a husband and I just could not be one at the time. We were cordial about it…or more to the point, I was cordial, especially for Josh. So I gave her everything in the divorce, including custody of Josh. She wanted it, she got it. She wanted Josh in her life and I wanted him to be comfortable and not suffer in a lengthy messy process. Beth eventually took Josh out of the city and moved in with her parents to start over. Josh is all grown up now, with his own family, struggling like everyone else."

"Does he live here in GulfSide?"

"No, and I rarely get to see him. SYNRG is very strict on whom they let in and I can't afford to travel. I wish I could do more for him. I don't even have a home…I live here."

"Here?"

"Yep. Adam is kind enough to let me stay here. My room is the next door down. I have my own commode, cooking facilities in the break room, and I use the shower downstairs in the locker room. I'm actually very blessed to have this…I have no salary."

Adam chimed in. "Again, SYNRG controls my budget would not approve a staff doctor because SYNRG provides free medical care now."

Jonathon shook his head. "This SYNRG seems to be a complete enigma. Curtailing freedoms on one hand with an apparent army, but giving something like medical care for free?"

Jason looked at Adam. "I think, chief, we need to show him."

"I agree. That's why he is here."

Jonathon, vacillating between the two asked, "Show me what?"

Jason continued. "I guess you noticed my limp."

"Yeah," Jonathon said to Jason.

"Well, I had a minor disagreement with a guardian a few years ago. Before I go on with that, let's go into the next room."

Jason struggled to get up.

Adam rushed over to assist. "How can I help?"

"I'm all right."

"You should be using your cane." Adam directed.

"I hate that damn thing! It just reminds me of this."

Jason limped at a good pace to the archway into the next room.

"Come on, Jonny, you are about to see our dirty little secret."

Adam motioned for Jonathon to follow. Jonathon followed right behind Jason with Adam in tow. The three crossed into the room and Jonathon's attention was immediately drawn to the center of the room. On two rollaway beds, which had a sizable gap between them, were the bodies of two men, both with their eyes wide open. The men were covered up to their chests with thin blankets. The man positioned near the door way was about Adam and Jason's age and the other appeared to be Jonathon's age.

Jason stumbled to a nearby rolling chair positioned at the foot of the lying men in the middle and sat himself in it. Jonathon moved closer to the older man and observed the two of them closer. The dormant men were connected to all sorts of monitoring equipment, but there were no wires. The machines indicated heartbeats, pulses, blood pressures and such. The room itself was pretty plain. The wall opposite the doorway was completely bare. The other two intersecting walls were lined with plain chest-high counters, with multiple drawers. There were multiple tablet computers strewn about the counter closest to the beds with another two stacked neatly near the edge in between the two dormant men.

Jason continued. "Okay. Medical care, before SYNRG. I was helping as many people as I could. It was a difficult time for me personally and for the world as a whole. I did the best I could though. However, despite all of what was going on, the hardest thing for me was turning people away. I was the only physician here, with a limited staff and resources. Things eased when we got volunteers, but we could not always rely on that. In the end though, we did a lot of good. After SYNRG came, they brought their own medical personnel. No one here was allowed to work with them without first going through their training program. In addition, as a condition of employment and to receive SYNRG medical services, an implant of some sorts had to be installed for medical monitoring. Everyone lined up. They didn't care. Either out-of-work doctors and nurses wanted a steady paycheck or the masses just wanted reliable and readily available access to the care. SYNRG was and is the sole provider for all medical services in Gulfside."

"What about you…you didn't want to work for them at the time?"

"What, and have some…thing, without a real clue as to what it really is, stuck in the back of my neck? No thank you."

Adam stepped up to Jonathon's side. "There are a few, like Suzie and I, who have never gone to a SYNRG clinic or hospital. In fact, it was Jason who delivered both Ashley and Josh. Of course that was pre-SYNRG, but all of our ongoing care is provided by the good doctor here."

Jonathon nodded. "So your entire family is implant free."

"You bet." Adam replied. "I did not like the idea of sticking mystery devices in us as well. The entire Opposition is made up of people with the same feelings about SYNRG. They have people from all walks of life including physicians and nurses. They take care of their own, and those who ask and can be trusted."

"What do you mean?"

Jason added, "SYNRG is the only medical supplier left in the world, amongst other items, but I have a plethora of what I need and…I will leave it at that."

"I see. How do you feel about that Adam?"

"Again, I have no problem with the Opposition, but they sometimes take unnecessary risks."

Jonathon nodded. "But they probably help in other ways too… don't they?"

Jason answered. "The chief, of course, on the surface, cannot confirm or have any appearance of favoritism to the Opposition whatsoever. He and I do both benefit from their activities, but they can be nuisances as well.

Adam continued. "I don't want to become judgmental, but on the other hand, I do answer to the mayor who is the puppet of SYNRG. I have been given instructions to find and arrest them for violation of doctrine, but alas, they are just to cunning for me."

"That's a shame," Jonathon said with a smirk.

"I just wish they would be more careful," Adam said with concern. "It is getting harder to come up with excuses."

"So Jay, do you still practice medicine?"

"Like I used to…no. I do the occasional checkup, but ever since the incident with my leg, it is hard for me do surgeries or anything complex as such. However, I was tapering off from medical care and giving focus to my new area of interest."

"What's your new interest?"

"Take a real good look at the man closest to you."

Jonathon inched over to the older man and examined him more closely. He had some visible scars on the portions of his arms which were not covered, but nothing else stood out.

Jonathon shook his head. "What's wrong with him, doc?"

"You don't recognize him do you?"

"Should I?"

"Yeah, well seeing as you and Chief Stance brought him to see me thirty years ago."

Jonathon took a step back. "This is the prowler…uh, Albert?"

Adam rested his hand on Jonathon's shoulder. "The same."

"He never woke up or became coherent?"

"Unfortunately, no," Jason said with a remorseful tone.

Adam removed his hand and gestured toward Jason. "He has, however, learned a lot about the devices in his body."

"Yes, I have. Like we discovered before, these implants are designed to work with specific parts of the body. The one attached to his brain stem is the brain, if you will, of the whole network of mechanisms. Now, after much deliberation, thorough study, and soul searching, I determined I could remove any implant I wanted… except the one on the stem. So I did. I removed one in his arm and one I found in his hand. These things are very complex with many intricate applications. In addition to controlling the nerves and impulses in the body, it appears they were designed to repair and restore neurological and cell damage as well."

"What are you saying, someone who is, say, paralyzed…could walk again?"

"Without any signs of ever having any ailments and even enhancing said person, like you two saw with Albert."

"Astounding."

"Astounding, breakthrough, marvel...you name it, but there is a very crucial trade off."

"You turn out like Albert?"

"Well Albert is the way he is, because he was removed from whatever was controlling him. But I suspect he was like this even when he was linked with the master signal controlling him."

"What would happen if you did remove the main device? Would he regain…himself?"

"He would die. It regulates his basic involuntary body functions like breathing, heartbeat, digestion, and such. As far as him regaining the essence of who he was, the device has created a lot of deep-level scar tissue for it, disrupting the engineering he was born with, in favor of its own inputs. There is absolutely no way I could ever correct that. At least with my knowledge."

Jonathon looked over to Albert. "Poor guy. He was robbed of his existence." Jonathon turned back to Jason. "Wait a second…these devices are still operational? Still powered?"

"Yes."

"How?"

"They are designed to convert the bio-chemical energy in the body to fuel them."

"Does he eat and go..."

Jason nodded his head. "To the bathroom? Yes. I have him on a feeding schedule like one would have with a newborn. Plus, I get them up regularly to give them exercise."

"Huh?"

Jason nodded to Adam. Adam moved to the stacked tablets, picked them both up, examined them quickly, and then returned one back to the counter. He turned to face Albert.

Adam tapped on the screen for a moment. "Here we go."

Albert began moving himself out of the bed. Swinging his feet from underneath the blanket out toward Jonathon, the man rose to his feet, and balanced himself as if he were doing it himself. Albert was wearing a pair of black shorts and still had the distinctive scars all over him.

Jonathon stepped back a couple of paces. "How?"

Jason explained. "I figured out how to decode the signal. Using an advanced artificial intelligence algorithm, I have been able to write scores of commands for him. He can walk, run, jump, and even go to the bathroom. I can execute multiple functions in a continuous loop, if I had to, all in a streamlined sequence to where he would operate independently without any input from me. I'm still not sure how the translation from device to human and vice versa works, but I can understand and utilize the end result."

Jonathon shook his head. "Uh Jay, I don't know what to say."

"It took a long…and I mean long…time to figure this out. However, I still haven't a clue as to the origin of the master signal. Without the main transceiver functioning properly, which was damaged from your initial contact, I may never know."

"Nothing else was damaged?"

"I don't think so. It appears there is a shielding around the devices to protect them from a catastrophic electrical discharge and as a last resort, designed to be channeled into the transceiver like a lightning rod. Probably for the designers, the transceiver was the easiest thing to fix. But I have no idea how. Without seeing it fully operational, it is very difficult to determine the full interaction it had with the host."

"His mind. Is it still active? I mean…on its own?"

"There is still brain activity, like anyone else, but as far as what is Albert and what is the machine…I don't know. Nonetheless, I feel it is important to keep his mind engaged, as well as his body. At regular intervals, we implement sequences to do that as well."

"Why would somebody do this?"

"Simple. To control a body."

"This is just cruel to do this to somebody…I mean why not build a robot of some sort if you have this level of technology?"

"The human body, when it comes right down to it, is the greatest piece of engineering of all. It is basic in some aspects and very complex in others. All our technical achievements like binoculars, hearing enhancers, even computers are useless without us. Almost like a city without a population, it would be empty, without purpose."

"I understand completely."

"Our bodies are capable of so much more and it seems like somebody may have figured out how to unlock some of that potential, but at a price."

"It would seem." Jonathon glanced over to the second individual. "Who is that? He seems too young to be a prowler."

Jonathon turned more toward Adam, "You said the prowlers disappeared."

"Yes, they did." Adam replied.

Adam tapped onto the tablet again. Albert twisted himself around, and maneuvered back into bed and down. Adam turned around to the counter and placed the tablet down. Retrieving the second one from the stack, he turned back to face Jason, who was now struggling to roll his chair closer to the second individual.

"Let me tell you about my leg. One night, a few years ago, I had trouble sleeping. So, I decided to go outside for some fresh air."

"Outside? At night?"

"I used to do it all of the time. The wall around this building is high enough, it kept me very well hidden and out of the way of the Guardians. But on this particular night, I was distracted. As I was outside, feeling the cool night air against my face, I heard some commotion just on the other side of the wall on the property here..."

"What was that?" Jason mumbled to himself.

Jason moved quietly to what he believed was the location of the ruckus. The rustling became more intense...more like a fight.

"Let go of me," shouted a male voice in the darkness.

Jason, without thinking said, "Hello?"

"He's got us pinned. Help!"

Jason hurried to the outer access door and pushed a button on the adjacent wall. The door rolled open. Jason rushed through the partition, veered to the left, and found three men struggling with a fourth. Nearing them, he noticed what appeared to be a hair-brush shaped electric stun gun on the ground. Quickly snatching the device, he ran up to them. At this point, it was apparent the upright man was a guardian...and he had just subdued the other three men.

"Shit!" Jason said, coming to his senses and realizing how he was now in violation of curfew. Coming about, he darted back to the open door. Just within steps, he felt something pounce on top of him, most likely the guardian. Jason fell to the ground and tried to break free. Pushing, thrashing and flailing did no good. The guardian was just too strong…

"I managed to get myself onto my back, which made little difference. To make matters worse, he reached back and struck my shin using his forearm with great force. Intense pain followed, as I was sure this piece of shit just broke my leg. By now, I thought this was it. I'm a goner. Oh, wait a minute. I still had the stun gun in my hand. He shifted himself and released my arm, so I managed to reach up and I jammed the electrodes into his neck, then zapped him. He fell right on top of me. I was very lucky it worked, but it came at a price. It took me almost a full year to heal, and I have never been the same."

"What happened to the guardian?"

Jason nodded to Adam. Adam held up this tablet in the same manner as before, and began tapping on the face of it. Then, as before with Albert, the second man was now moving. He sat up and swung his feet off the bed. Wearing the same style black shorts, he rose to his feet and balanced himself. Jonathon right away noticed there were no scars on his body consistent with the former prowler.

"This is the guardian?" Jonathon asked with a stern tone.

"Yes," Jason replied.

"He has no scars. Does he have the same implants as Albert?"

"Yes, but with some differences."

"Then the prowlers and Guardians…"

"…Are one in the same," Jason answered.

Jonathon turned away and walked to the opened partition, but did not proceed through.

Jason continued. "The three men were part of the Opposition, breaking curfew of course. When they came to their senses, they helped me back inside. They also dragged the guardian inside the wall as well. I called Adam to get here quickly, once the sun came up and the curfew ended…before anyone else arrived. He got the guardian up here without anyone noticing."

Adam stepped a bit closer to Jonathon. "Jason was so stubborn, he refused treatment until we got some answers. So I propped him up in a wheelchair and we went to work. I tried to wake the guardian, even though his eyes were open, but he was out. The same as our prowler. However, there was nothing protruding out the back of his neck. So with Jason's guidance, I did testing. We found the same devices…well almost the same."

"These are far more advanced than Albert's," Jason explained.

Jonathon still facing away asked, "More advanced?"

Jason answered. "Yes. As you noticed, he has no incision marks. The best I can determine is that these were injected into his body as a small microbe and grew into the devices he has now."

Jonathon turned around. "What was that?"

"These are living breathing machines. I mean…this is scary stuff. These things have grafted and intertwined themselves into this man's body. There is absolutely no way I could even remove one to see how it ticks."

"Who is he?"

Adam replied. "His name is Brent Kozolosky. He is one of the missing homeless. In fact, I believe he is one of the ones who disappeared during the initial days of the curfew."

"Okay, so if I'm following this right…this SYNRG is acquiring its army by abducting curfew violators and turning them into mindless remote controlled beings."

"I believe so. Of course, I think the curfew was a means to accelerate the process. They obviously have been doing this for a long time, well before SYNRG, but on a more reserved basis."

"Who knows about this?"

"Just the three of us here and I would like to keep it that way for now. I haven't even told Suz. This information, along with our friends here, is locked up here."

Jonathon was more enraged. "What are you doing about this?"

"Jonny, I don't know what to do about this."

"Well something needs to be done. You realize these bastards… these SYNRG bastards are the ones responsible for killing my family."

"I do realize this. I have been haunted by this knowledge ever since we brought the guardian up here. However, they are too strong…too powerful."

"Oh come on. You are letting them get this way by doing nothing."

"It is a very complicated situation…"

"You are letting them get away with murder!"

Jonathon stormed out through the archway, dashing for the door. Reaching out, he rested his hand on the handle lever, but did not push down. Shaking his head, he said quietly, "What are you doing? It's not his fault."

The thud of footsteps emanated and then rushed in somewhat behind him.

Jonathon let go of the handle, and turned around to face the only person it could be. "Adam I'm sorry. That was uncalled for."

"It's fine. How else were you supposed to react? This is some kind of situation we are in…and right now there is no way out."

Jonathon did not like hearing Adam expressing such defeat, but figured a cooler head was better than yelling at him half-cocked.

Jonathon shook his head. "Okay, first things first…how many guardians do you think we are dealing with?"

"I don't know for sure, but just going through our records alone, thousands. Possibly more…and that's just here. There are many other SYNRG cities around the world."

"Poised and ready to strike."

"It seems like it."

"Yeah, we need to stop this."

"I agree, but how?"

"You guys should have some sort of idea…I mean you have been studying these things for quite some time."

Adam just shrugged his shoulders.

"Oh come on…something? Anything?" Jonathon asked, slightly annoyed.

"Well, SYNRG must not be able to locate or track the missing guardians. We've had Albert for thirty years and Brent for at least three now. Putting Albert aside, Brent is more advanced. If they wanted him back, and I'm sure they would want to stop someone from obtaining their technology, we would have been swarmed with guardians certainly by now."

"That's good. Definitely a good place to start."

Adam added, "Oh, the power boxes. You know, from when we picked up Albert."

"What about them?"

Jason hobbled in and added. "They were placing what appeared to be ordinary pieces of tape on the outer housings."

"Let me guess, not tape."

"No way. Not even close. These pieces of tape actually contain very small, atomic-sized machines…relays actually, probably to assist with keeping in contact with or even coordinating multiple prowlers...now guardians."

"Why power boxes?"

"At the time, they directly tapped into the power lines this way. Which, we also think is why they were messing around with the power substation as well."

"Right." Adam nodded. "I find this tape at various points around the city almost everywhere now."

"So this means they must have solved the power problem." Jonathon deduced.

"It appears so," Jason acknowledged.

Jonathon turned away from Adam and Jason. "You know, going into this, I never imagined I would have ended up here in a situation like this. I had such high hopes. No matter what I do or what I have done, I can't be free. I don't want any of this, but it seems your future now was the start of my nightmare in the past. It would seem I'm going to have to go through this no matter what."

Jonathon turned to face Adam and Jason again. "Let's find a way out."

"Thank you," Adam said with a soft tone. "I think it will be good to get a fresh perspective on this. Listen…I have to go mind the store."

Reaching into his pocket, Adam pulled his keys out and held them out to Jonathon.

Jonathon inched up to Adam. "What's this?"

"My keys. So you can come and go as you please."

Jonathon grabbed the set. Before placing them in his pocket, he noticed a small shiny silver object. "Is this JR's gift to me?"

"Yes it is. It was on the key ring you gave me when…"

Jonathon nodded. "Right." Slipping the keys into his pocket, he asked, "Okay what should I do?"

"Jason has a lot more to show you…which is sure to be overwhelming, but try to get as much as you can. If we have time, we can always reinforce it later. I'll send Jason an access card for you in an hour or so. Again, no one knows about all of this. It will probably be best, for us, for you to keep up your low profile."

"All right. No problem."

"Gather more information about our secret from Jason. I'll be back later today. Good day, Lieutenant."

"Good day, chief."

Adam walked by Jonathon and marched to the door. Jason had gone back into the other room, so Jonathon stepped back through the archway. The men were back in bed, with the covers back on both of them. Jason was sitting at the feet of the younger man.

Jason, tapping away on one of the computers, looked up at Jonathon. "Sorry to burden you with all of this."

"It's a lot to take in. I'm sorry for my outburst a moment ago."

"Don't worry about it. There is plenty to worry about these days."

"It would seem so. Adam said there is more."

"Unfortunately there is. I can show you as little or as much as you want. I won't force it on you."

"Well, with time appearing to be short, I better get myself in the mode to absorb what I can quickly."

"I guess the first place to start is the Guardians' weapon."

"Would this be a rifle-style gun?"

"Yes, but these are no ordinary rifles."

Jason pointed down to a drawer near the heads of the men. "Open the bottom one there and let's have a good look at it."

"You have a guardian weapon?"

"From this guy here. Adam found it the morning he brought him in."

Jonathon approached the counter and crouched down to the drawer. He slowly guided the drawer, revealing the weapon. A primarily rifle-styled gun, about two and a half feet in length, nestled in some sort makeshift padding. With both of his hands, he reached in, gripping the weapon carefully near both ends and then lifting it out of its home.

"You can set it on the counter. It will be fine."

Jonathon rose and gently nudged the drawer closed with his foot. Gently laying the gun down, he leaned it somewhat on its side, which seemed to be enough support.

"This is probably as upright as I..."

"No that's fine."

"It's very light. Not much to it."

Jonathon quickly examined the gun. It was similar to a military grade rifle, but had a hook like piece on top which appeared to fit over a human shoulder. There was one other notable oddity. There where three small triangular tips where an open barrel should be.

"Where do the rounds come out?" Jonathon asked.

"There is no bullet, slug, or projectile of any kind."

"Is this a laser gun?"

"I don't know."

"How could you not know? You've had this thing for a while now."

"Yes. And in all of this time, I have not been able to get the weapon to discharge once."

Jonathon was slightly confused. "Oh...okay."

"Let me start with what we know for sure. It is not a projectile style weapon. It is very light, compared to a standard rifle. It is metallic."

Jonathon waited for him to continue, but Jason just stared at him.

"Come on. That can't be all you know." Jonathon said with frustration.

"I'm sorry to say, it is. The metal casing is made up of some sort of alloy, I think, which we can't penetrate. I used some of the hardest substances known to us as cutting tools, but they just broke or snapped off after being pressed against its surface. I just can't get this sucker open. Plus, the limited chemical tests I conducted also revealed nothing. So what the heck? I threw it into the MRI, hoping to get a break."

"Anything?"

Jason shook his head. "Nope. The material is impervious to any scan I can conduct. I even bounced SONAR off of it…it was as if the signals were absorbed. So the meat of it is, I don't know how it works."

"Do you have any theories?"

"Of course. You see the somewhat flat rounded bulge on top…it is about the size of a D-battery from our day?"

"Yeah"

"I believe it is the power source for this thing, whatever that might be."

"You don't know how this gun is powered?"

"Nope. Not a clue. I can't get it open. I also believe it acts as a short-range transmitter to interact with the active guardian."

"What do you mean?"

"The best I can theorize…the weapon is only active when the guardian is active…receiving the master signal from wherever. In turn, one of the implants inside of the guardian's body emits a corresponding signal to the gun, thus activating it. It is pretty ingenious when you think about it."

"Ingenious?"

"Scientifically speaking, yes. If someone were to happen to strip the gun away from a guardian…or in our case, find it laying on the ground nowhere near an active guardian, it would be out of range and would not fire."

"It is a nice safeguard…scientifically speaking."

"Like I said."

"Yet, you have been able to decrypt the signal to control these men."

"Yes I have, but they have different frequencies or codes, which makes me think each guardian has their own unique code…similar to a computer with its own IP address or more simply, a house with its own physical address."

"If you were able to crack the code for the Guardians, why not the rifle?"

"Again, this is only speculation, but the master signal may be transmitting a secondary universal code which activates the mechanism for the weapon."

"So if I'm understanding you correctly, there is a different set of codes for the guns."

"Sort of. It is more like a single separate cipher for all of the guns."

"I think I get it. The guns function off of this dedicated signal, which means any rifle will work with any guardian, as long as it is within range."

"You got it."

"Why do you think it is only the one code though?"

"From a logistics point of view, if there are multiple signals for the weapons, in an emergency, it would be too chaotic to change if a guardian needed to replace their rifle. Things happen."

"Okay, I see the logic."

"But again, this is just me…the technology is extremely advanced."

"Have you had any luck?"

"Oh, yes, actually. I think I'm close. While shooting the active signal I found for the Guardians, I have then been using a second computer to search for the gun code. Recently, I have been able to get some of those indicator lights to light up. Just out of sheer recklessness, one day I pulled the trigger, but nothing happened. Needless to say, the chief was a little perturbed."

"I think I kind of need to agree with him…you could have hurt yourself or blown out the wall."

Jason smirked. "Yeah."

Jonathon smiled. "You like being careless, just a bit."

"Oh, it was one time. We get so little pleasures these days. Anyway, when I do get all the lights on, we're going to transport everything to a now-abandoned gun range near the Outland."

"Do you have any thoughts as to what this gun fires?"

"No. Not without knowing any of what makes it tick. I haven't even seen the weapon in use, however, some in the Opposition have…and they've been nice enough to share with Adam and me. Adam may have his reservations about them, but without the Opposition, I would not have been able to conduct all of the research I have done."

"How has the Opposition seen the rifle in use?"

"Right. As mentioned earlier, to the chief's angst, there are those who break curfew. Not to cause trouble, but because they want to be free. Generally, as a rule of thumb, they travel in packs, staying off the main roads, hiding in the shadows. Guardians patrol the streets in pairs of two, so the coverage in the past was spotty at best. The trio wrestling with this guy here was part of a group of seven. The others apparently were not as fortunate…the other guardian…"

Jonathon nodded. "I understand."

"Guardians tend to favor using brute force, but on occasion will discharge their guns. The first such incident was about a year ago, after SYNRG became erratic with the curfew. A group of about twenty protesters, armed protesters, fired on the incoming guardians. The guardians responded in kind. Amid the bedlam and out of the twenty, only one managed to escape. The chief, Adam and I, interviewed the man. He described the scene as chaotic, of course, but he said prior to discharging, the SYNRG weapon makes a distinct buzzing hum noise with a burst of bright white light."

"A laser?"

"I don't know. Without seeing the damn thing work, I don't have a clue. According to the survivor, the discharge time is quick like a flash of light. And the cycle time between shots is very short too. Now this is where it gets interesting.

"More interesting than a ray gun?"

"It was only two guardians at the scene against all twenty protesters. Some of them with shot guns, hand guns, one had an old military grade rifle, but all of them had something. The guardians did not falter, stumble, or even fall once. With all of those shots being fired…I mean…"

"They all couldn't have missed."

"The man, as he escaped, saw the same two guardians beginning to drag the others away. Now again, this is all based on this one person's account."

"Were the others dead?"

"He didn't think so. The weapon seemed to have disorientated them enough to be captured. This initial action is what affirmed Adam's fear of the Opposition being too reckless."

"Adam is concerned that further hostile actions against SYNRG might trigger an all-out fight."

"Right. But they do so much behind the scenes…the benefits of their actions..."

Jonathon nodded his head. "Do you have any thoughts as to the Guardians' apparent invulnerability?"

"I do."

"Is it their uniforms? Are they made out of some bullet-proof material?"

"Yes it has to do with the uniform. No they are not bullet proof." Jason pointed to the guardian. "Those bastards beat me to it."

"Beat you to what?"

"Adam, fearing the worst, wanted a defense against a possible SYNRG takeover. Knowing we probably would have no help from the reduced and thinly stretched military, we needed something big to protect us from a massive occupation force."

"Wait a minute. Aren't you a medical doctor? I mean you are talking like you're a weapons designer now."

"Well after studying Albert for all of these years and now the Guardians, it has stimulated my general love for science. Plus, when you are homeless, have no family, and have no social life…I found I had a lot of free time."

"Jay, I'm so sorry…"

Jason shook his head. "Don't be. I made peace with it a long time ago. I'm here, alive, and of free will. You want to feel sorry…" Jason pointed individually to the two dormant men. "Feel sorry for these two, forever locked in a subjugated state."

Jonathon nodded. "Okay."

"Now, the Guardians. I started tinkering with a defense about five years ago, well before I acquired the rifle and Brent here. I won't bore you with all of the scientific bullshit, but using the Earth's electromagnetic field and the body's interaction with it, I theorized I could develop a defense. It wasn't to make something bulletproof, but to simply keep bullets and other lethal objects from making it to the person. I couldn't quite make it work, so I abandoned the project. Then the guardian showed up. After much study, I affirmed the key is the human body and the uniform does what I tried to do. At first, I thought the garb was reacting with the SYNRG implants."

"Was it?"

"To my delight, no. After some basic experiments and only after I was sure my theory was sound, Adam and I tested it…" Jason smiled big. "…And it worked."

"I'm sorry. I'm not quite following. What exactly worked?"

"The uniform forms an invisible protective bubble around the user."

"Like a shield?"

"More precisely, a deflector…repelling any small objects coming at it. Now this will only work with a living being wearing the uniform. It will not work by itself or covering non-living matter."

Jonathon shook his head. "This sounds like science fiction nonsense again."

"Really? We have remote-control men, living mechanisms, some sort of beam weapon, and you want to say nonsense?"

"Touché. Continue."

"It is evident, even with the worldwide technological stall, SYNRG is still working on grand things."

"It appears they were working on these things long ago. SYNRG would seem to have a huge technological edge now."

"They do. Through his own investigation, Adam concluded this anti-technology movement, unbeknownst to them, is actually doing SYNRG's dirty work to help prolong the stall."

"Of course they are," Jonathon said, with sarcasm.

"From what we have seen here, the technological gap is growing and so is the SYNRG army. The thing that really scares me..."

"...Is the stuff we can't see."

"Exactly. This may only be the tip of the iceberg."

Jonathon turned and slowly walked a few paces away from Jason. "What are they up to? It seems they have a firm grip over the world. I mean...what more does SYNRG want?"

Jason shrugged his shoulders. "I don't know."

"I'm surprised there isn't more of an uprising than just the Opposition."

"As far as I know, no one else knows the secrets of the Guardians. However, if they did, it probably wouldn't matter anyway. With the masses of people in their own little worlds... showing apathy in life itself....which could be SYNRG's ultimate goal." Jason picked up a tablet computer nearest to him, then hobbled toward Jonathon. Jason tapped on the screen and held it up for Jonathon to see. "You remember those medical implants I told you about earlier? The ones required by SYNRG for use of their services?"

"Yeah."

"I was able to examine someone recently who has one. It is attached to the brain stem here..." Jason pointed to a human figure on the screen with the implant, "...in the same manner as the master mechanism in Albert and Brent. It has nowhere near the operational power, but probably enough to subdue someone just enough to the point of being apathetic, maybe suggestive to someone else's whims. I mean, who can resist the allure of free medical care? Plus, there was the small ecological disaster of the lice infestation where people had to shave their heads as a means of control to mask the insidious nature of the required injection."

"Why do you think the infestation is connected to this?"

"The injections have to be precise and the insertion points are different for each individual, which would require a clear area to work with. Plus, I would not be surprised, if some of these people did not get these things voluntarily."

Jonathon shook his head. "I think I have heard enough good news for today. I need to let this absorb and sink in for a little bit."

"Sure. It is a lot to take in."

Jason reached into his pocket and pulled out what appeared to be an access card.

"Here, take my card. I'll use the one Adam was going to give you."

Jonathon taking it, slid the card into his pants pocket.

"Oh, if you could do me a favor and not tell Adam that last part about the medical implants. I haven't told him yet. I want to do a little more research."

"I understand."

Jonathon, with a slight sarcastic snicker said, "Good day, Jason."

"Good day, Jonny. Please, though, don't take long. Adam and I believe there is not much time left."

Jonathon turned and walked to and through the archway.

"Time…what an asshole," he mumbled.

CHAPTER FORTY-ONE
SYNRG'S HOME

Jonathon pulled into the driveway of his former residence and stared at the garage door.

"Do I knock or just go inside?" he said out loud.

Sitting with his hands still placed on the steering wheel, he reflected on the information, not just given to him today, but all of it since he came back. Jonathon gripped the wheel tightly.

"This is all too much."

Letting go of the wheel, he then thrust his head into the headrest and closed his eyes.

"I feel so alone, so out of place. This can't be real. This is all a ChronoSleep nightmare and I just can't wake up...but what if it is not? I wish I could just leave here...but then, where would I go? What would I do? Not that it would matter. I always seem to be running. It's all I seem to be good at now. I need to go think...and I have the perfect place."

A knock on the car window interrupted Jonathon's stupor. Startled and confused, he opened his eyes and saw a figure to his right. It was Angie peering into the front passenger window. She gave him a short wave and smiled. Fumbling around with his left hand, Jonathon frantically searched for the window button. He tapped on the corresponding switch, then the window groaned down into the door.

"I didn't mean to scare you while you were talking to yourself. Suzie and I saw the car and were concerned."

Jonathon smiled nervously and was somewhat mortified. "Oh yeah, everything is fine. I was just...uh..."

Angie still smiled. "Don't be embarrassed, It's not the first time I caught you." *That's supposed to make me feel better?* Jonathon thought.

"Besides, you talking to yourself is what got my attention…right?"

"Right, I guess?"

She nodded her head. "Yes."

"Listen, I was…well, convincing myself…I need to go somewhere to be by myself and think for a bit. Would you like to join me?"

Angie smiled bigger. "Wouldn't that defeat the purpose of being by yourself?"

"Uh…well…uh…I guess so."

She briefly chuckled. "You are too much but yes, I would like to go with you. Let me just go say bye to Suzie. Okay?"

"Of course."

Angie quickly stepped up the walkway and around the corner. Fumbling around again, Jonathon placed his finger underneath the overhang of the power window button, pulling it up to roll the window up.

"Jonny what are you doing? You don't even know her and you're bumbling around like an idiot…like Adam when he was courting Suzie. I can't have feelings for her. I met her just yesterday. It's insane. I still feel so much for Dana…and so lost…yet I feel like I've known her…" Jonathon placed his hands on the wheel. "I'm all out of sorts. My emotions are all out of whack. There is nothing. Hopefully, I will get a little clarity at the beach. A little sense of home…and direction."

Angie emerged from the corner, onto the walkway. She opened the front passenger door and maneuvered herself into the seat. "Other than last night, I don't remember the last time I was in a car."

He shifted the car into reverse and rolled down the driveway. Out on the street, Jonathon shifted the car into drive and proceeded to his destination.

"Where are we going?" she asked.

"There is this little place down by the beach my grandfather used to take me when I was a child. It is my special place where I go when I need to figure things out."

"I understand. I have a spot like that, too. It is under a big tree at home."

Arriving at the end of the neighborhood street, Jonathon paused. There was no traffic, but he just sat there.

"Is everything okay?" Angie asked.

"Yeah, this is so…hey, is it all right if we go downtown real quick?"

"I'm a guest on your little trek here."

He drove out onto the roadway toward Gulfside. "It is going to take me awhile to get used to no traffic and an immense…" Jonathon stopped himself short before he said too much. Glancing over to Angie, he saw that she was smiling and looking back at him. *Focus back to the road,* he thought. *Crap, there is no way she didn't catch my slipup.*

She did not say anything, which made him more nervous.

He attempted to change the subject. "This will be real quick, before we go to the beach."

"I have time. I'm not going anywhere. Besides, I have something to ask you."

Jonathon feared the worst. "Go ahead."

"Please don't be mad at me."

Jonathon still concentrated forward. "You know, that is never a good way to start a question. Go ahead and ask."

She knew the answer, but she wanted to hear it from him. "Are you Jonathon Scott?"

Crap. She knows, he thought.

"Yes," he responded. "Just out of curiosity, what gave me away?"

"I'm just real good."

Jonathon smirked then glanced over to her very briefly.

She was smiling again. "Well, I had help. There are some pictures of you, back from your day, in the room I slept in last night."

"Oh. I didn't count on that."

"Why the mystery? The need to hide?"

"A very good question to ask. I wish I had a good answer for you. This whole experience has left me…" he briefly glanced back at her, wondering what it was with her that made him feel safe to talk. Focusing back to the road he said, "I feel vulnerable. Out of place. Out of time…in more ways than one. The last few days have been overwhelming…I really don't know how to act or feel or what to do. I'm in a strange place I once called home, but has some very unusual quirks now. And the bitch of it is, this is what I wanted. I am home…but it isn't home. Moving to another city wasn't going to cut it. Just move to another time and not have all of the reminders, but here I am…full of regret. My family is still gone. My home is now gone. And I don't know what to do next."

Jonathon glanced over to a smiling Angie.

"Don't worry. Your secret is safe with me," she assured.

Jonathon put his eyes back on the road. "Thank you."

"Of course. I understand. I'm all alone, too. I'm scared and I don't know what to do next either."

"You know, Angie, I'm so focused on me, I really haven't

absorbed how hard it is for you, too. I'm sorry."

"It's okay, Jonathon."

"Well how about this: Let's be a support group for each other."

"I'd like that."

Jonathon looked up and around the sides of the roadway. "Wow these buildings are so tall."

"I guess there have been a few changes around here since your day."

"You have no idea. Castle walls, curfews, mysterious Guardians...well, like I said, it's a bit overwhelming. In fact, when I arrived here a couple of days ago, these sidewalks were packed with people. They're deserted now and I have no idea what's going on with that."

Angie looked at the car's clock in the middle and on top of the console in the dashboard. "Is this the right time...2 o'clock?"

"I think so."

"Well, let's see. Precisely at 5:12p.m., everyday, everyone will flood the sidewalks, going home I presume."

"Including weekends?"

"Weekends, holidays...it doesn't matter. In the morning, they will head to wherever it is they go, precisely at 8:17a.m."

"You might be onto something Jay," Jonathon said under his breath.

"What was that?"

"I'm sorry, thinking out loud. What about children and school?"

"All the schools are down here and they follow the same schedule. However, less and less children are being born in SYNRG cities."

"Weird. Does anyone know why?"

"The popular reasons are the economy and environment."

"You don't seem to buy those reasons."

"Nope."

"Do you have any theories?"

"Unfortunately, no."

"Okay. What about food shopping...regular shopping?"

"For those of us who are still coherent, there are stores, products, cashiers and such, but they don't open until after 9:30 a.m. and close at 4:30 p.m. Don't expect much of a selection. Just the bare essentials. Don't expect much chitchat from these shopkeepers and workers, either. They do only what is required of them to do, nothing more. Also, from what I can see, those on the schedule don't shop, which only adds to the mystery of what is going on here."

"Strange."

"Tell me, what was it like? Before you slept?"

"You ask as if you have never asked or heard about it before."

"I really haven't. I never went to school or interacted with many people outside my little farming community. I had some friends... that is...before the Outland came. They all subsequently moved to the city. Then when my parents died, I was so busy with the farm, I had no time to be social. Sure I kept in touch, but as time went on, my friends were in their own little worlds. They eventually stopped talking to me. Then there was James. He, of course helped, but I wanted him to have a life which didn't revolve around home. He was able to go out and make friends, have girlfriends, even study some schoolwork."

"That is a heavy burden for a young woman."

Angie turned her head and stared out the window, not responding. Jonathon sensed not to probe further and let the conversation be. Realizing this drive was taking a lot longer than it should have, Jonathon asked, "Are we going in circles?"

Angie now faced Jonathon and smiled. "I thought it odd, but I thought you had some 'super-long cut' you were taking."

"Gee, thanks. Is Ringling near here?"

Angie smiled. "You're asking?" she asked with sarcasm. "You seem to have it all under control here."

"Great. Sarcasm. That's terrific," said Jonathon.

Angie was still smiling. "At the roundabout coming up here..." She made a clockwise circling motion with her index finger. "...you are going to want to go around the big circle and go back to the one we just passed and make a left."

Jonathon now laughed and made a counterclockwise gesture with his finger. "Are you sure it is not this way, because if I go..." shifting to clockwise, "...this way, I might run into something and get into trouble."

She playfully slapped his shoulder. "You know what I mean."

"I don't know. You were so specific with the whole sarcastic circle thing...I don't know what to believe now."

Jonathon angled to go clockwise, with Angie quickly correcting him. "No, counterclockwise!"

"Okay, you're the expert here."

Jonathon adjusted to flow with the lawful direction.

Angie tried to keep a straight face and waggled her index finger at him. "The car is not a toy."

"Good for me there is nobody out here off schedule...we can't have that now."

Angie said with a chuckle, "You're terrible."

"All right, we're are about halfway through the circle. I should probably continue around, right?"

Angie grinned. "I don't want to be…what was it called?"

"A backseat driver?"

"Yes."

"How could you be? You're up front here with me."

"Okay, mister smart guy, I don't want to be front… passenger… seat driver then…whatever."

"Okay, if you're sure?"

Finishing the trek through the roundabout, Jonathon drove toward the next one. Angie pointed to the windshield. "Remember, left at this one here."

"What one…the windshield? Here you go again, confusing me."

Still pointing and now laughing Angie said, "No, no. The roundabout."

"Oh, because technically you were pointing at the windshield and did not specify…thank you for clarifying…wait a second…you didn't want to be a backseat…passenger seat driver. What happened?"

"You are driving me to crazy town."

"No, Gulfside City. Not crazy town…get it right."

She playfully slapped his arm again and he started to laugh. Entering the roundabout, Jonathon steered with the circle. The two calmed down and Angie looked over to Jonathon.

"Thank you. I'm having a wonderful time with you," she said.

"Me too. It is nice to laugh again."

Jonathon flowed out to the indicated direction. "Okay, wise one…where to now?"

"At the next intersection here, make a left. That will get you onto Ringling."

Approaching the cross-styled intersection, Jonathon slowed and then stopped, noticing the inactive traffic signals above. Attached to the cross-arms, were worn street sign housings with green glass faces and white lettering. They had a backlight to illuminate the street names at night, but probably didn't work now. The face of the one in front was still halfway intact.

"Ring?" asked Angie. "Oh, Ringling? I assume."

"It is," Jonathon said, now more stoic.

Angie looked up to the one on the right. "East Avenue? East what? That sign looks intact."

"It's correct. East Avenue."

"Wait, isn't the police station just to our left?"

"It is."

Jonathon stepped lightly on the gas petal and proceeded very slowly to the left onto Ringling. Even with driving slowly, the ride was very bumpy on the heavily potholed and uneven road.

"There is the department on the left."

"Yep," Angie acknowledged. "What are these other buildings?"

Jonathon pointed to the one directly across from it. "This was the Sheriff's department, along with the state attorney and public defender. The next building we're coming up to is the jail, which I'm told is not being used at the moment."

"Okay."

"Now this crosswalk we are approaching…" Jonathon pointed up to two inactive lights on their side, "…at one time was a full traffic signal. The city received numerous complaints from motorists, the light was unnecessarily delaying traffic. So, the city, replaced it with this thing. After watching in horror at the many cars disregarding the mandatory law directing drivers to yield to pedestrians, I assigned a couple of officers to stop these violators. They were busy for a month, until people got the hint."

Jonathon paused at the crosswalk, out of habit. Inching the auto forward, through the crosswalk, Jonathon paused again. Pointing to the right he said, "This was the old courthouse in my day. The complex, apparently, is one of the oldest still standing. The included tower was the tallest structure at the time. Built in the mid 1920s, the old courthouse was the government seat of its day. It housed the courthouse, of course…the sheriff's department, the jail…amongst other official offices."

"All in there?"

"Yep. In fact, it seems like this has come full circle over at the station. When I was around six, my grandfather took me up in the tower. Despite some of the modern buildings at the time, I still had an awesome view over Gulfside. I felt so alive overlooking the town. Now, the view is probably much different." Jonathon pointed to the left, across the street. "That ten-storied building there is, or was, the new courthouse. It doesn't look like it's in use anymore either.. And that stupid statue in front there…"

"Who is that of? I never got close to find out."

"Me."

"Oh."

"You asked what it was like back in my day. People lined these sidewalks all the time…cars jammed the roadway. Crowding was a real problem. After my family died, I would park my car over at what is now an alley and watch people go on about their lives while I stayed stuck in my abyss."

Rolling a little further toward another cross style intersection, Jonathon pointed to another wide ten-story dilapidated structure, next to the new courthouse. "The Veranda Building, as it was called, was also built in the mid 1920s."

"It has the same color scheme and basic design as your old courthouse," Angie said.

"That's right. Originally it was constructed as a hotel, and was used as such until the early 1970s. The expanding county purchased it to be used by some of its elected officials. It now appears to be abandoned as well. I just can't believe all of this is gone…now."

Angie briefly placed her hand on his arm. "I never knew any of this. Thank you for telling me."

"Thank you for listening. In a weird way, I feel a little better. Sharing this knowledge with you is almost like bringing a little of the past back to life."

Angie smiled. "I will always remember then."

"Come on. Let me show you my most favorite boyhood memory."

"Let's go. I can't wait."

Jonathon drove forward, then passed through the vacant intersection. Jonathon made a quick right, then a quick left, and followed the road down. There was no one on the road or on its sidewalks. Nonetheless, he was still careful despite being in awe of the surrounding sights.

"Is any of this familiar to you?" she asked.

"Nope. Not a thing. This all used to be small shops and stores. In fact, we probably just passed the ice cream shop…where…I used to take my kids for a little treat…without my wife knowing, of course. It was like a little secret the three of us had, but inevitably… Dana would get one of them to spill the beans. She would give me, 'The Look,' the kind a wife could give to a husband when she wanted him to know he was in trouble."

"What was she like, if I may ask?"

"You may. It's funny. When we first met, I wanted nothing to do with her. She was pushy, sarcastic, and had this weird sense of humor. She was also persistent. I mean, the more I tried to get away from her, the more she latched on, aggravating the crap out of me." Jonathon had a huge smile. "However, after getting to know her, she turned out to have the kindest soul I have ever known."

"How long did that take?"

Jonathon was still smiling. "The night I met her."

The two passed through another cross intersection and now approached a roundabout much smaller than the previous ones.

"Here is another roundabout for you."

"Actually, this one was here in my day. I might actually have this now." Jonathon followed the small curve and continued with the straight path ahead. "Yep. There is the roadway back." He paused for moment then turned to go back to the causeway bridge.

"What were your children like?" she asked.

"They were great kids. Full of life. They always kept Dana and I on our toes. Kim was a lot like her mother...stubborn, but very sweet. She always liked to be busy...like her mother. Of course, not a bad thing. She wanted to be a dancer. She just loved to move. Almost like she was flowing with the wind. JR was different. He had an analytical mind. He liked to put things together...to solve problems. He was going to be an excellent police officer. At least I always thought or maybe hoped he would choose that direction. Yet, he was still very young. The world was at his feet. He could have done whatever he put his mind to."

"Sounds like a nice family."

Jonathon was now curving up the bridge. "The best. What about you? What were your parents like?"

"I was very lucky to have them for as long as I did. They were the perfect model for opposites attracting though. My father was soft spoken...a man of few words. I think throughout my entire childhood he raised his voice to us four, maybe five times. My mother on the other hand was high strung. She was passionate for the things, which interested her, and she wanted everyone around her to be the same way. She would go off on tangents which could last for hours. Sometimes my father would have this look of...'Shut up!' But he never said it. They loved each other so much. They loved us so much. They were good role models for James and me."

"What is James like?"

"He's a mix between mom and dad. He talks a lot and definitely stands up for what he believes in. He is the spitting image of dad."

"Who are you most like?"

She turned her head toward her window, without answering. They approached what appeared to be Merchant's Circle, but the area was littered with tall buildings and structures. All of the strip shops and stores were gone. Following the curve out to the beach, he could see the open water ahead.

"Huh that's weird," he said.

She turned to him. "What is it?"

They neared the next intersection and passed by the last of the tall structures, revealing the full panorama ahead. The coast was all open except for a colossal monstrosity just to their left of their view ahead, standing in the middle of where his beach used to be. In fact, the beach was gone.

Jonathon stopped the car before the intersection. "What the hell is this?"

"What?"

Jonathon pulled the car to the side of the road and shifted it into park. He opened the door and exited the car. Standing behind the door and with his hands clasped on the top of it, Jonathon just glared at this massive edifice.

Angie exited as well, staying on her side. “What is it, Jonathon?”

“What is this?”

“It’s SYNRG.”

“That’s SYNRG!”

The sleek futuristic silver metallic, primarily rectangular, building was about two city blocks wide, one deep, and seemed to stretch endlessly to the sky. Four very large spire-like towers connected to and accentuated the corners of the structure, and were just as tall, if not taller. The tips appeared to be a lustrous black. There were no windows, anywhere, he could see. A large steel silver eight-foot solid wall surrounded the area around it, with a silver slide solid access gate on each visible side. The property itself was covered by concrete, extending to the road and well beyond the perimeter of the fence line. Examining the structure in more detail, he noticed something else, but not with the building itself. It was something behind it…out in the gulf itself. Jonathon walked out from behind his door. He marched, with a fast pace, closer to the coast. Angie, doing the same, hurried up to his side.

Jonathon angled to the right and pointed out to what caught his attention. “What is out there? It appears to be an identical building… on an island?”

“It is…and they are connected by that,” Angie said, pointing to the top. She directed his focus to a massive sky bridge connecting the two structures somewhere near the top floors. Angie glanced over to Jonathon. “You didn’t know this was here?”

“No.”

“I was wondering why you were bringing us down here.”

Jonathon was in complete shock. “They took my spot away, my connection to my grandfather. This was my only place of solace in this disaster of a world.”

Angie placed her hand on his shoulder. “I’m sorry.”

He let out a deep breath. “I guess I had this coming.”

“Why would you say that?”

He glanced over at her. “This is precisely what I asked for when I signed up with ChronoSleep. And now I got it.”

“This is not what you were asking for. Please forgive me, but you need to ease up on yourself, give yourself a break.”

Jonathon stared back to the SYNRG structures. “I can’t. All I see is a world I once knew vanish away. I was the stupid one who made this choice. I can’t go back. I can never go back.” Jonathon lowered his head. “I know you have your own things to work out. I don’t want to burden you with my baggage anymore. I think…"

Angie let go of Jonathon's shoulder and placed her index and middle fingers over his lips to stop him. "I think it's time to take me home. I think it's time for me to show you my tree…my favorite place. Maybe you can find comfort there as it has for me."

Jonathon nodded and responded with a muffled, "Okay."

CHAPTER FORTY-TWO

ANGIE'S HOME

The two arrived at Angie's farm. Angie leisurely made her way to Jonathon as he examined the house.

"This is my home," Angie said with pride.

"Very nice. Is this the house you grew up in?"

"Yes."

He twisted his head and pointed past her to a taller structure. "What is this building here?"

"It is were we keep all of our equipment. The doors are on the other side, more accessible to the land."

"Ah."

Jonathon stepped down the driveway, wanting to get a better view of the land behind the house. She, at his side, moved with him. Far enough down, he paused to see the apparently neglected fields. There was nothing but brown dead plants and dirt, except for what were obviously weeds sporadically thriving.

Jonathon turned to Angie. "What happened?"

"I gave up," she replied. "After James disappeared, I just could not move on. My will just eroded away. Everything around here is a reminder. He and I working together out here…the two of us growing up together, laughing…and then crying when our parents passed away. But we carried on. We were a support for each other. Then he joined that stupid Opposition. I felt it was going to get him into trouble someday, but he was his own person, capable of making his own decisions. I had no right to interfere. When he went missing, I just fell apart. I was alone. No support from anyone. Some days I just spent staring out into nothing. Others I went looking for him, hoping. I later joined the Opposition, even though I really did not like them. Initially, I think I just did it to just belong to something."

"Like a surrogate family."

"Yes. As it turns out, they are very loyal to those who have gone missing. They are very kind to me, but it just isn't the same. Their primary focus is their cause, no time for anything else. James was very passionate about the Opposition, but his passion for his Colleen was stronger.

"His fiancée?"

"Yes."

"What happened the night he disappeared?"

"It was sort of about her. She visited a SYNRG clinic earlier in the day, unbeknownst to him. She had been sick for awhile and had no choice. He found out through one of his friends in the Opposition. All he wanted to do was find her and did not care what he had to do. I was concerned, he might not make it back in time for curfew. One thing led to another and we were screaming at each other. Then he was gone. My brother…my friend…is gone. I hate SYNRG so much and I'm so ashamed of myself."

"Why would you say that?"

"My parents fought so hard to keep our home." Angie pointed to the field. "And this is how I show my appreciation. In the end, I feel I let SYNRG win."

Jonathon gingerly grabbed Angie's upper arms, turning her to face him. "Look…this is not the end. It is apparent; these bastards took…" Jonathon paused, knowing he had to be careful about what he said. "…many things away from many people it seems. You can't give up."

Jonathon let go of her and turned back to the field. "I'm probably the last person who should be offering any type of motivational advice. I gave up a long time ago."

"You are right though. I can't give up. Neither should you."

"I really hope you find James."

"I know you do."

"The truth is however…I don't know who I am anymore. I was hoping to go to my special place to think. Maybe to once again figure it out, but it's gone now."

"Let me show you where I go to think."

Angie reached out and clasped onto one of Jonathon's hands, pulling him forward. They stepped off of the concrete and onto the somewhat-grassy ground. As Angie and Jonathon rounded the side of the house, a large tree in the middle of the field was becoming more visible.

"That is a large tree," Jonathon commented.

"It has been here longer than the farm."

"This farm has been in your family for generations, hasn't it?"

"Yes, since my great grandparents. The house has been replaced a couple of times though. My parents had this one built a few years before I was born."

Jonathon, with a slight chuckle said, "Amazing."

Still clasping Jonathon's hand, Angie slowed down for a moment to have Jonathon come up to her side. "What's amazing?"

Jonathon, with his free hand pointed, slightly twisting to the street. "Your grandparents and even your parents had a stand and small shop near the road didn't they?"

"That's right."

"Leary farms…I should have realized it earlier. My grandfather, who loved fresh fruit and vegetables, brought me out here when I was a kid. He enjoyed talking to your family. They were so personable. He came here regularly, at least once or twice a week. Your father and I were the same age. We talked a lot, too, when we were children. We would also run and play, while the adults did their thing."

Angie began to tear up.

"I'm sorry, I shouldn't have said anything."

Wiping away her tears she said, "No, no…it's not you." Trying to hold back the tears now. "That is such a happy memory to share. You have know idea how much this means to me. My father talked a lot as a child…I've never known him to talk much. He was always so reserved with us. Mainly business…the farm, is what we talked about. I miss my parents so much and to hear you knew my father…is so surreal."

"I brought Kim and JR out here as well, not as much as my grandfather, but your parents made this apple butter…"

Angie, teary again, chuckled, too. Wiping the tears away she said, "Did you know your grandfather after your childhood?"

"Yes I did."

The two arrived at the tree and stood underneath, by the trunk. Angie let go of his hand. Jonathon continued with his story. He talked about his grandfather's deteriorating health…him moving away with his mother…his relationship with his mother…the lack of one with his father…his regret of not taking the time to go visit his grandfather…and he dying shortly after Dana and the children. He also shared with her his brief attempt at suicide…

He continued. "Then, I came up with this cockamamie idea of escaping to the future. And to add injury to insult, I couldn't even get that right."

"How can you get a long sleep…wrong? You are here, right?"

"Exactly. I was supposed to go a hundred years into the future. I fell seventy years too short. What does it matter, I probably wouldn't have liked it either."

"I'm glad you are here. I may not know a lot about the history of downtown, but I do remember reading about you. The hero who put himself on the line to defend others, strangers. People like you really don't exist anymore, but here you are standing under my tree."

"I was only…"

"Don't say you were only doing your job."

Jonathon, a little shocked, shook his head and did not respond.

"Yes, I remember reading an article Chief Stance wrote about a year after you left. He stated that was your usual response to this."

Jonathon nodded in agreement. "He's right."

"In the soulless world of today, it is a miracle to have a spirit like yours here. I can feel the love in your heart."

Jonathon looked directly into her eyes. *I can't believe I didn't notice before,* he thought.

Angie stared intently into his.

Her eyes…she has Dana's eyes. How could this be? Is that even possible?

"I feel safe with you Jonathon...and I haven't felt safe in a long time."

Angie and Jonathon both leaned into each other. Jonathon tilted his head slightly, and pressed his lips against Angie's with her reciprocating. Wrapping her arms around him, he returned the embrace.

CHAPTER FORTY-THREE

IT WORKS!

Angie and Jonathon were standing on the driveway, near the driver's door of the car, facing each other and clasping their hands into each other's in front of them. The afternoon sun had slipped away behind the house, giving way to the evening sky. The air cooled a little, with a light breeze brushing against them.

"I've got to go back into town and get Adam. Do you want to come back with me?" Jonathon asked.

"I should probably get things in order around here. Will you be able to find your way back?"

"I think I can figure it out."

"All right."

"I more than likely won't be able to come back until tomorrow. Are you sure?"

"Yeah. I want to show you my house. This way gives me a chance to tidy up a bit. Plus, I want to gather a few things up. I will probably stay at the Stance's for a while."

"Okay. I will see you tomorrow then."

Angie smiled. "I can look forward to tomorrow now."

Both leaned in to each other and embraced with a hug. Jonathon reached behind him and opened the door. Angie took a couple of steps back as he moved himself behind the door.

Jonathon smiled. "I will rush over here in the morning."

"You do that."

"Bye."

Angie smiled and waved. "Bye."

He closed the door and started the car. Glancing over to her, she waved again. He shifted the car into reverse, carefully driving down the driveway. Once he reached the end, he shifted the car into forward drive. Glancing out the window toward the house, Angie was still standing in the driveway. She waved once again, and he returned a short wave himself. Focusing back to the road, he began to slowly drive away. Feeling a little guilty he thought, *Was that all right? I don't know what happened. I'm more lost and confused now. What would Dana think of this?*

Jonathon arrived back to the station. After discreetly making his way back into the building and upstairs, he stepped off the elevator, heading toward Jason's lab. As he was about to access the door to the hallway, it swung open at him, almost striking him.

Adam emerged. "Jonny! I'm glad you are back. He got it to work."

"What to work?"

Adam held the door and waved him in. "Come on."

Jonathon squeezed past him, entering the hallway. Adam let go of the door and started to run for the lab. Jonathon hurried along with him. As they came within reach of the door, Adam already had his card out, quickly swiping it through the reader.

He opened the door. "Come on, slow poke."

Adam rushed in with Jonathon in tow. Jonathon passed Adam, as Adam let go of the door. They marched through the archway into the back lab room. Jason, standing with his back to the doorway and very close to the guardian, was tinkering with something.

"Jason, Jonny's here."

"Good."

Jason hopped around on his good leg to face the two men. Jason, with a big smile, was holding the Guardian weapon from underneath it with both hands. "All the lights are working."

"Jay, that's great! Did you fire it?"

Adam jumped in. "Oh goodness no. Not here."

Jonathon directed his next question to Adam. "How do you know it works then?"

"Uh, well…" Jason interjected. "With every indicator light on, I'm very sure it will. I'm modifying a mobile transmitter, so we can operate it independently from the guardian and take it to the range tomorrow."

Jonathon, with trepidation said, "Terrific, I guess?"

Adam faced Jonathon. "This is a good thing, Jonny. This will give us a little more insight to them. We can figure out what this thing does, maybe develop a good defense against it."

Jonathon glanced over to Jason, who was nodding.

Adam looked at his wristwatch. "Jonny, we need to get going."

"Right…curfew."

"Do what you can tonight and we'll see you in the morning."

"Sure thing, chief. Good day."

"Good day and great work."

Jason hopped to the counter and placed the rifle down. The indicator lights immediately shut off and Jason began to work on it.

"Good day, Jay."

Jason's attention was still on the rifle. "Good day, Jonny. See you tomorrow."

Both Adam and Jonathon directed themselves out of the back room, and went through the archway and into the front room. Adam raced ahead of the door and clutched the handle. Opening the door, he gestured for Jonathon to exit, who passed by, entering the hallway. Adam exited as well, and stood next to Jonathon.

"Oh, here are your keys," Jonathon positioning his hand to slide into his pocket.

Adam shook his head. "You keep them for now. It will be good for you to get used to driving around here. Besides, it will be nice to be chauffeured around for a while."

CHAPTER FORTY-FOUR

MISSING

"This is another big day for you sleepy head."

"What?"

Jonathon found Dana hovering over, leaning over him again.

"What big day?" he asked.

"All these people are to be saved."

"What are you talking about? The museum? They've been saved already."

"Think bigger."

Jonathon sat up in a panic to find no Dana again.

"My mind is just not going to let this go."

Whisking the covers off him, he swung his feet to the floor. Perusing around the room, he tried to find out what time it was.

"This room really needs a clock. Judging by the light in here, it must be early morning."

Inspecting himself he said, "Oh look. I fell asleep in my clothes again. Just dandy. Did I even eat last night? I don't remember. This is just getting annoying."

He shook his head and rose to his feet. "Let's see what happened."

He rushed to the doors, sliding them open. He moved through them and the hallway, emerging into the living area, and finding Adam and Suzie at the kitchen counter, in their respective uniforms, eating.

"There he is," Adam said.

Suzie peered around Adam. "Good morning."

"Did I get up too late?"

"Nope. You have time to shower and get ready," Adam replied.

Suzie added, "Plus I have breakfast for you here."

"Thank you. I don't remember eating last night."

Adam hopped off of his seat and stepped up to Jonathon. "You didn't pal. You passed out soon after we got home."

"Right."

"I called Amy again. She is really concerned this is not abating. So I cleared her to come into Gulfside…she should be here before tonight. Hopefully she can fix this for you."

"I hope so. I beginning to think Dana is haunting me. She is in my dreams every time before I wake up. Maybe Amy can help me sort this out as well."

Adam nodded. "Go ahead and get yourself ready, grab yourself some food, and I will make sure to keep you busy until tonight."

Jonathon smiled. "Sounds like a good plan."

During the car ride to the station, Suzie and Adam chitchatted with each other. Jonathon stayed quiet. It was obvious he was deep in thought, so they left him alone. He reflected on what happened yesterday. Arriving at the station, they waited for the security partition in the rear to open.

"If you excuse me gentlemen, I think I want to walk around the grounds for a few minutes before I go in," Suzie said.

"Sure thing, Suz. Jonny and I are going up to see Jason. He has another gadget or something or other he wanted to show me."

"Another dead end?"

"Probably."

"Well, you boys be careful. Oh Jonny…if you feel comfortable about it, I would like to hear how your time with Angie went."

"Oh Suz, don't pry," Adam said.

Jonathon responded. "No, it's fine. I don't mind. Maybe you can help me sort out some things."

Suzie nodded. "We're here for you."

Suzie leaned over to Adam and gave him a peck on his cheek. "I'll see you guys later."

Suzie opened the door and exited the car. Closing the door, she began her brisk walk. Adam slowly proceeded into the nearly vacant vehicle maintenance lot and angled the car to what was obviously a fuel station next to an open auto-repair garage attached to the rear of the building. Parked on the other side of the garage was a plain white van, a model known to have sliding doors on both sides with no rear windows. Inside the small repair facility was a propped-up motorcycle with no tires.

"So your cover story for Jay is, failed projects," Jonathon said. "Weak, very weak."

With obvious sarcasm Adam said, "I keep him around because of his medical expertise."

"You use that, too. It is a good thing for you nobody pushes the issue."

"Yeah, well, he is a good doctor and...mad scientist."

"Speaking of which, how crucial is it for me to be here this morning?" Adam smiled at Jonathon through the rearview mirror.

"Not very. In fact, this morning, I won't need the car either. So after we fuel up, you can go visit Angie."

Jonathon smiled back. "Thank you."

"I got you covered. She is a very nice girl. Is she coming back to the house?"

"It sounded like she was planning on it. Is that okay?"

"Absolutely. It is probably going to take all morning for Jason and I to discreetly load the van here, then we are going to go out to the range. I would like you there."

"Sure. I'll drop Angie off at the house and then go out there. Oh crap, I don't know how to get there."

"I have it programmed in the navigational system here."

"Perfect."

Jonathon arrived at Angie's house. He walked toward the front door, wondering if she would still be happy to see him.

"Many emotions were flying around yesterday," he muttered. "A lot was brought up. Maybe I said too much. Maybe I pushed too much. The past is...just painful. Maybe she was not ready. Maybe I'm not ready. She seemed fine. She was fine. However, I'm still not sure about myself."

Standing in front of the front door, he lightly tapped on it a few times, but forceful enough to hear inside. Jonathon patiently waited for her to answer. While waiting, he observed the stoop around him. Above was a plain rounded oval-shaped clouded glass dome over an illuminated light bulb. *I wonder if she leaves this light on all the time?* The rest of the porch area did not have any other distinctive characteristics.

"I don't think she heard my knock."

Jonathon knocked on the door again, but with more vigor. He continued to observe everything around him, including briefly turning around to see what else was around.

After a few more moments of waiting, he was now becoming concerned. "Maybe she just can't get to the door just yet or didn't hear the knocks. Maybe she had to go somewhere…but she knew I was coming over. Maybe she is out by her tree. Or maybe something is wrong."

He noticed a side pane of clear glass embedded in the frame, next to the door. The window was as tall as the door itself, and was a few inches wide. A very thin curtain covered the window from the inside. He leaned in toward the side window and peeked inside. Between the ambient light within and the semi-transparent fabric, he was able to see a wall on one side and part of what may have been a living room, which went to the other side of the house. It appeared the other end may have been a small dining nook off of the kitchen. He could make out a table with four chairs, but one was lying on its back. The portion of the back wall, he could see, was more like a double sliding glass door. One side seemed to have a fractured border around it.

"Shit!"

Quickly turning, he ran as fast as he could with all his might. Pushing his legs down the driveway around the front corner and onto the grassy dirt, he rounded the side of the house, and into the back yard. Reaching the rear of the house, he slowed, and stepped up onto a concrete slab in front the sliders. It was clear, one side was shattered. Crouching down and pulling up his pant leg, Jonathon retrieved his revolver from his ankle holster. Standing straight again, he held his gun in a readied stance, and cautiously and carefully stepped up and in through the broken door.

One chair was on its back on the floor in front of him. An upside-down plate was also on the floor, with some rice strewn about. A clear plastic tumbler was on its side with a dry purple liquid leading away from its top. There were visible dirt tracks on the floor, but they ended in the dining nook.

"She was taken…here."

Walking around the chair and table to the plate, he knelt down, flipped the plate over, and then picked it up. Other than the dried rice on the floor and a caked-on dark reddish substance on the plate, there was no food.

"Okay…so she was finishing up her meal. Everything is dry, so this happened a while ago."

He was about to place the plate back on the floor when he noticed a pattern etched in the reddish remains on it.

"What is this...are you trying to tell me something? Are these letters? Okay...you have a lower-case S and a Y together, then spaced away...is this a lower N overwritten with an upper R?"

Jonathon shook his head. "I don't...Oh, you fucking bastards."

Tossing the plate down, he stood up. Hurrying past the chair and table, he carefully exited back through the shattered door and down onto the concrete slab. Putting force into his legs, he ran off the concrete, back into the grass, rounded the corner and then passed by the side. Maintaining his balance, he dashed up to the side of the car. With his free hand, he anxiously opened the door and thrust himself in. Setting his gun on the front seat, he pushed the barrel into the fold between the seat itself and the backrest to secure it, then closed the door. Turning the car on, he shifted into reverse, and then drove down the driveway.

CHAPTER FORTY-FIVE

TIME TO FIGHT BACK

Running out of the elevator, Jonathon nervously swiped his card through the reader, then opened the door and rushed down the hallway to the end. He put his card through the next reader and then went through the door. Hurrying to the archway, he entered the back room to find Adam and Jason fidgeting with the Guardian weapon. However, the guardian, the prowler, and their beds were gone.

"They took her!"

Both of them turned to face Jonathon.

"Who took who?" Jason asked with confusion.

Adam, chiming in, placed his hand on his forehead. "Angie?"

"Yes!"

Jason, still trying to get a grasp on the situation asked, "Angie, the resistance girl?"

"Yes," Adam responded.

"How?" Adam asked Jonathon.

"They snatched her out of her house."

Jason shook his head. "We are out of time. Curfew or not, we are all in danger now."

"We have to go get her!" said Jonathon, adamant.

Adam marched up to Jonathon. "Wait a second there. Let's be rational about this…I'll contact the facilitators with a forceful request."

"What! Why?" Jonathon asked, annoyed. "So you can get the same bullshit you've been fed all these years? I don't think so."

"What do you suggest we do?" Adam asked, raising his voice. "Storm the castle?"

"Yes!" Jonathon said, equally as loud. "You just heard Jay, we are out of time!"

"We don't know that! That is just his opinion!"

Adam shook his head and walked away toward the other side of the room. He moved to the opposite counter, hunched over and slammed the palms of his hands on the surface. "We can't anger them…we don't want to trigger an assault."

Jonathon inched closer to Adam. "Anger them? Assault? They are already assaulting you, abducting you, one by one…and now directly from your homes. We are not safe!"

Adam slid his hands across the counter as he stood up straight. "We are not going to do anything rash. We are going to play it calm. I will send an investigator to her house, collect our evidence. I then can go to the military and see if I can get help from them. We don't have many options."

"From what I understand, that is a fucking waste of time," Jonathon said, turning away.

"Well, I'm the chief of police. I'm not going to needlessly endanger the lives of everyone in town here."

Jason set the weapon down and limped in closer to the men, still keeping his distance.

Jonathon turned back to Adam. "Chief of police. That's a joke. You have no police left. SYNRG has insidiously whittled you down, over time, too. You idiot!"

"What did you call me?"

"Turn your hearing aid up, grandpa. You…are…a…fucking… IDIOT!"

Adam lunged at Jonathon but was stopped by Jason who rushed in between the two, placing his hands on both of their chests. Adam and Jonathon continued to stare each other down.

Jason calmly tried to defuse the situation. "All right you two, we are not going to do this. Chief…sir, go start your process. I'll keep Jonny here. This will give both of you time to cool down."

Jason turned his head to Jonathon. "Okay, Jonny?"

"Sure."

Jason to Adam now, "Okay, sir?"

"Fine."

"I'm going to let go." Jason cautiously said.

Jason removed his hands from the two men who were still staring each other down. "Let's play it cool, gentlemen."

Adam, who broke the eye contact, turned to Jason. "I'll go get everything going."

Adam rushed by Jonathon, who was standing still in a trance, and passed through the archway. Jason turned and walked back to the counter, near the SYNRG weapon. He hunched over and placed the palms of his hands on the surface. With the exception of the door closing in the other room and footsteps in the hallway outside becoming more faint, the room fell silent.

Jonathon, unsettled by the quiet, shifted to Jason. "Jay, I'm sorry about that."

Jason stood straight. "Don't worry about it. This is an impossible situation here."

"Yeah, and our leader is being a moron about it."

Jason facing Jonathon. "You may be right, but you need to cut him some slack. He does have everyone's best interest at heart. He is walking a very tight rope...and yes...I do believe he is about to lose his balance. His entire stretch as chief has been marred by this mess, which is a damn shame. During normal times, he really could of done some good for Gulfside."

"I guess you're right."

"However, we should of taken action long ago."

"Did you express that to him?" "Numerous times. But he is the chief. He calls the shots."

"I'd love to do something myself, but I wouldn't get far."

"Yeah, well, I think it is time I become a nuisance to this SYNRG."

Jason hobbled up to Jonathon. "Why? Why get involved here? Walk away. Leave this place. There are still many places you can go... at least for now."

"Then what kind of person would I be?" Jonathon nodded his head. "I'd be running away...again. A coward. I am not a coward."

"No one said you were."

"But it is precisely what I am. I have become so good at running away. And for what...I'm still distraught over my family. I've just let my emotions ruin me."

Jason did not respond.

Jonathon continuing. "To add injury to insult...I see Dana in her."

"In who?"

"Angie. I don't know. I could be just projecting my feelings for Dana onto her...wanting to see only what I want to see. My emotions are so screwed up right now...but I feel it in my heart...my soul... SYNRG is not going to get away for the death of my family...and I'll be damned if they are going to take someone else from me."

Jason patted Jonathon on his shoulder and smiled. "Welcome home, Jonny." Jason, turning a way, hobbled to the SYNRG weapon. Hopping on his good leg, he faced Jonathon again. "Like I said, I would like to do something myself, but other than lab work...out of morbid curiosity, what is your plan?"

"Well, they more than likely took her to that monstrosity down at the beach. Like any superior force, they probably feel sure enough of themselves… if I could somehow infiltrate the building and find her."

"So just go in like some sort of specially trained soldier and…"

"I don't know."

"I agree with your logic. They feel like nobody can stop them. The smaller the detail is also a good idea. It will require a great deal of stealth to do this, but it is going to take more than what you have. But you is what we have and you're motivated enough to do it."

"What are you saying, Jay?"

"The men who I saved…the night we got the guardian and his weapon…were very grateful. Adam knows they helped me, but for small things."

"They do more than you let on, don't they?"

"You bet. I had been living a bad dream until the guardian showed up. Now it is a nightmare. I'm here at night by myself with all the time in the world. Needless to say, I don't get a lot of sleep. The things I'm about to tell you, no one knows."

"I may be pissed off at Adam, but he is like my brother. What makes you think I won't go to him."

"I lost a family because of this situation too. Maybe not in the same manner as you, but gone nonetheless. For sometime I have been waiting for the right person…someone I can fully trust…someone who can pull this off…not worried about the consequences. I never thought it would be you, Jonny."

Jonathon nodded. "Okay. Let's get started. What do you have?"

"The Guardian uniform. This will be a valuable tool. It generates a protective field around it to shield the user by repelling small projectile-style objects. However, that will probably be of little use to you as the SYNRG weapon seems to be energy based. You will also not be protected from objects, such as larger stabbing weapons, like a big knife or sword. I don't think those are in the SYNRG arsenal, but you should be aware of this anyway."

"Got it."

"Fists on the other hand, forgive the pun, are. Guardians favor hand-to-hand combat and the field is useless against this as well. As we know, the Guardians are far stronger than the average human. So, I have modified a hand-held stun gun to use as a weapon against them."

"Modified?"

"Yes, to operate within the distorted field around the suit. Plus, I attached a SYNRG power cell to it."

"Power cell?"

"The rounded protrusion on top of the rifle. The uniforms have the same thing on them, so I deduced these are the power sources and they are interchangeable."

"How long do they last?"

"I don't know. Given their level of technology, probably far longer than anything we have."

"Good point. Now why a stun gun?"

"We've proven, at least twice now, the electric shock from the gun disrupts the connection to whatever is controlling the Guardians."

"Right!"

"Simple and effective."

Jason reached down, opening the top drawer in front of him and began to retrieve multiple objects. He placed the items one by one on the surface next to the rifle. The last piece he took out was large and seemed to be an article of black clothing. Setting it down over the rifle, he closed the drawer.

Jason picked up one of the items, which was similar to the bulge on top of the gun. "This is a SYNRG power cell. About the size of a D battery, half as tall, but much lighter. Placing it back on the counter, he selected another item. A black hair-brush shaped device. "This is the modified stun gun." Jason angled it so he could view the top portion. Directly in the middle of it, was the imbedded power cell.

"Is this the one you found?"

"Yep. I find it fitting. This saved my life and now it will be instrumental in saving others."

Setting it back down, Jason then swept the huge garment off the rifle, on to the bare section of the counter next to it. "Can you help me spread this out?"

"Sure."

Jonathon stepped up to the counter, unfolded the lump along its surface, and revealed a guardian uniform. Still somewhat scrunched up, it was evident this was one piece. The material had a texture and luster similar to leather. The suit was relatively smooth, except for small penny-sized-and-shaped welts consistently spread apart all over it.

"Is this leather?" Jonathon asked.

"I believe it is a synthetic composite mix resembling leather."

"The sleeve ends at the wrist. Are there gloves for this?"

"Yes."

"A turtle neck. Okay. Shoes?"

"The suit has the matching boots as well. And there is a beret to reinforce the field around the head."

"What are these bumps?"

"These are the emitters that manipulate the field. Turn the sleeve you are holding over."

Jonathon turned it over and noticed a small display screen with a thin, somewhat translucent piece of the material covering it. Attached to the side of it was a thicker piece, like a flap, appearing to be large enough to fold over the screen.

Jason continued. "That is a control panel and a radio transceiver."

"Why is it covered?"

"I guess we will discuss this next. The SYNRG weapon is energy based."

"You sound more certain now."

"I couldn't wait till today. I noticed it has a level of intensity indicator, so I set it to the lowest one. I fired it against the wall and it did nothing. I think this level is used to just stun someone."

"Does Adam know?"

"No. He still thinks we were going to test it for the first time today."

"He is going to be so pissed, if he ever finds out."

"At this point, it is moot. Besides, I got so much valuable information. I went to work right away."

"Okay. Again, is it a laser?"

"I still don't know for sure. But laser or not, it uses light as the method of delivery. So using the frequency code I found to activate it, I programmed the emitters to bend the light away and to screen out the frequency."

"Huh?"

"The beam should bounce off of you at the same time absorbing the destructive force behind it."

"Wait a second. Let me see if I follow. You just found the code out yesterday."

"Yep."

"And you modified the suit last night?"

"Yep."

"And you can block the laser or whatever from the SYNRG weapon?"

"Yep."

"Unbelievable. How in the world…"

"It really is simple when you think about it."

Jonathon with a chuckle said, "Right." He shook his head. "You haven't had time to test this. How do you know it will work?"

"I was afraid you would ask. I don't. I would not try or count on it unless you had no other alternative or were in a tight spot. But the logic and math are sound."

"Terrific," Jonathon said with sarcasm.

"I wish we had more time."

"It's fine. No time like the present I guess."

"The uniform does have one other ability I know does work."

"What? Does it fly?"

"No. This is something I also devised. Actually, it is what helped with the programming of the emitters last night, early this morning."

Jonathon shook his head. "What do you have Jay?"

"There is absolutely no way we can fight the Guardians straight on. Plus, they also have aerial drones."

"Yeah, we encountered those the other night."

"The Opposition also has reported SYNRG has some sort of tank."

"Tank?"

"I'm sure there is more than one, but on occasion, especially lately, one has been seen roving around the city. They have too many numbers. And once they find out we can filter out their weapons, it might not take them long to develop a fix. So, we need to get inside the SYNRG building and search out what is controlling the Guardians."

"What makes you think it is here?"

"This is SYNRG's main hub…it has to be here. At least I hope it is here. I know your goal is to find Angie, but if we don't stop SYNRG, it will be only a matter of time before they get all of us anyway."

"What do you have?"

"You need a way to sneak into SYNRG undetected. We don't know what is inside. So you are still going to have to be undetectable for a good amount of time. Again, using the emitters in the suit, I found a way to bend the light around you to the point of making you invisible."

"You're kidding me right?"

"No."

"You developed some sort of invisibility cloak?"

"Yep. This I did test, but it is not perfect."

"What do you mean?"

"It will shield you from cameras, motion detectors, and any other mechanical devices. No problem. The human eye, however, is far more sophisticated. To a guardian, you will be a distorted blob. That may not get their attention, but then again it may."

"Oh, this is way too much to grasp. Let me recap here." Jonathon moved away from Jason and paced about the room. "Okay.

You cracked the code to allow us to use the Guardians' weapon. Using the same code, you modified a uniform to basically make me impervious to the same weapon, in addition to, the original programming to block conventional guns. Then you developed an invisible screen."

"Well, not in that order, but yes."

Jonathon paused, staring back to Jason. "What can I say, but... wow!"

"Welcome to the future, Jonathon Scott. Now, it's time to introduce you to the future. I'm going to go see where the chief is at and delay him from coming back up here for a while longer. Go ahead and change into the uniform. It is a one-size-fits-all deal, so it will form to your body. We have more to go over...so don't worry if something else on the counter here doesn't make sense."

"I've got a quick question. Why have you kept this from Adam?"

"I guess, because of his apprehension all of this time...he might have told me to stop."

"Which is something you won't do."

"Absolutely not."

"Then on that note, thank you, Jay...for all of this."

"Hey...we haven't done anything yet. However, the future from here has the potential to be a good one. Let's give it our best shot."

Jonathon finished dressing in the uniform. The suit itself, the gloves, and the boots were all a perfect fit. The gloves, which formed an airtight seal around the sleeve cuffs, especially fit well. Jonathon had full range of motion with his fingers. No pull or hesitation whatsoever. A zipper, with a self-closing mechanism, ran down the middle of his back and formed an airtight seal. The cuffs of the pant legs also formed a seal around the tops of the boots. The beret was snug on his head and clung on to it for most of his forehead and the corresponding area around the top. Even as he wiggled to try and fling it off, it stayed on securely. Every part of him was covered, except for most of his head not covered by the turtleneck and beret.

"This is surprisingly comfortable and nimble," said Jonathon.

"For all the enhanced abilities the Guardians have, that stands to reason," Jason responded.

On the upper sides of Jonathon's arms were some sort of self-sealing pockets. The same types of pockets were near his outer thighs as well. He placed the stun gun in one of the arms and his regular gun in one of the thighs along with a good luck charm...JR's gift. Even with the emitter components on the pockets, the folds themselves sealed very tightly.

"Now, I could not help notice one little detail. My face is exposed."

"Let's go ahead and go over a few more things. As far as the shield is concerned, there is sufficient coverage. No need to worry. The cloak is a different story. Right now if you were to turn it on, you would be a floating head, which defeats the purpose here. Fortunately, the uniform comes with a matching folding helmet of sorts."

Jason reached over to the counter and picked one up. Holding it out and looking down at it, he twisted the welted headpiece around his hand, trying to locate something.

"Ah, here it is. This is the front."

"Okay."

Jason handed the headpiece to Jonathon. "These two shiny raised protrusions are the eyes?"

"Yes."

"Oh, this larger bump here is for the nose and this protruding slit is for the mouth."

"Yes."

"The mouth seems to be closed."

"Don't worry, there is enough of a gap to breathe normally. If you have to breathe heavier, you may have in issue, so just pace yourself."

"How do I put it on?"

"It is designed to slip over your head and will go over the hat."

Jonathon flipped it over, slid it with ease over his head, and sealed it onto the suit neck. "Wait I can't see."

"Grab the eyes of the mask and fit them comfortably over your eyes."

Jonathon gripped the eyepieces and adjusted them. "What are these?"

"Tiny monitors inside, attached to outside camera lenses."

"This is going to take some getting used to."

"You will."

Jonathon reached to behind his head and felt a bulge. "What is this?"

"That is the embedded power cell for the headpiece."

"Oh."

"These eyes, are they something you made or of SYNRG design?"

"SYNRG design. They have night vision capabilities, which I suspect is the original purpose for the headpiece."

"Now why can't we have just eye slits?"

"You could, but the cloak won't cover your eyes then. The outside lenses are reactive to the emitters and no, you just can't have the lenses. There needs to be an electrical current running through."

"Well I wasn't going to ask," Jonathon said, chuckling.

"Yeah, right."

"This is really a weird sensation."

"Before we leave, we will have you practice walking. I promise, you will get used to it."

"If you say so."

"Now, just be aware, after awhile you will have eyestrain and headaches. The severity will depend on how long you stay invisible. So again, pace yourself."

"Got it."

"Another tip: Don't expect to use the cloak in a hurry. You saw how long it took to adjust the mask and then you have to allow time for your eyes to adjust."

"This is all good stuff. Keep it coming."

"Go ahead and take the mask off."

Jonathon reached over his head and gripped the top sides, trying to gently remove it. "It's stuck."

"Give it a quick jerk."

Following the instruction, he successfully removed it. "Ah, there we go."

"The seals are tight but can be broken with a quick motion. This goes for the gloves, boots, and beret as well. All right, now the console screen on your arm."

Jonathon set the headpiece on the counter, then flipped his arm over.

"You see the flap next to the screen," Jason said.

"Yes."

"This is my own addition. You will need to cover the console when you go invisible."

"I guess if I don't, I'll be a walking screen."

"Exactly. You're catching on. Now go ahead and tap anywhere on the face of it."

He did so. The display illuminated.

Jason continued. "I reprogrammed this touch pad for our purposes and kept it simple. Plus, it will react with the gloves on. The upper portion is marked shield and the lower portion is marked cloak. When the screen is illuminated, just tap on what you want. Once, to activate and again, to deactivate."

"Can I go from one to the other?"

"No. You must deactivate one before the other."

"Can they be on at the same time?"

"You could, but I would not recommend it. You see the blue meter between the two sections?"

"Yes."

"That is a health meter."

"Why do I need a health meter?"

"Examining the guardian, I have discovered a history of neurological and cellular damage. Now fortunately for them, their implants assist in slowing down the damage."

"The protective field I'm about to use causes this damage. Doesn't it?"

"Yes. Every night the Guardians accrue damage, but have a way to repair it quickly. You don't have the benefit of the implants, so you have a much shorter time limit."

"How long?" Jonathon asked.

"If you use it in a straight shot...two hours. If you use it intermittently, you could probably stretch it out to by another half hour. The bar will calculate this for you. What ever damage you sustain will be reversible and can be repaired over time."

"If I go beyond the time?"

"The effects will become permanent. A portion or all of your body will lose its motor control and you will become paralyzed or even worse. If your involuntary functions like those controlling your breathing or heart are damaged, you could die without immediate treatment."

"Okay. Two hours it is."

"Going back to the simultaneous operation of both functions. The load on the emitters will be far greater and will reduce your time to a mere half hour or so."

"So use them separately and sparingly."

"Remember, it is vital to turn one off before using the other. And when the bar expires and if you are still using the field, you will be in serious trouble."

"I'll remember."

"Now, I guess you are wanting to do this today?"

"The sooner, the better."

"Okay. Then we need to get you in there before nightfall."

"Why nightfall?"

"So far, the Guardians do not come into the city during the day...and I suspect this is their repair time. They can repair the body fast, but I believe they can't do it while the field is active. Studying the interaction of the body with the implants, I believe they are put into a dormant state during this time as well."

"This should make it easier to move around then."

"They do have dedicated guards for inside. The Opposition

screws with them all of the time."

"How?"

"Some one will run in close to the wall and trip one of the motion sensors. That person will run and hide before the Guardians come out an access gate. It is always the same six Guardians who respond to search the perimeter and they do not travel much beyond it."

"What would happen if someone were to just stand beyond their search path?"

"The Guardians will act accordingly, but will not deviate from their routine unless it is necessary."

"Six huh? It does not seem like a lot."

"There may be more active inside. In addition, I have no idea what other security measures they may have like secured doors, motion sensors, and what not. I wish I had more answers."

"We'll work with what we have. I do have a weird, possibly related, question."

"Sure."

"What about all of the guards at the various checkpoints around he city? Are they Guardians?"

"Those are regular security folks. They, are more than likely, under the SYNRG influence with those medical implants I was telling you about. However, they are definitely not Guardians. SYNRG may have mastered control over the body and mind...except for one part...speech. None of the Guardian implants access the vocal cords, which tells me they don't know how."

"Interesting."

"You know, with all this guessing, I almost forgot." Jason twisted to the counter, and picked up a tablet computer and a small object. Tapping around on the screen while still holding onto the other item, he apparently was searching for something. "Ah, here it is."

Jason, hopped to Jonathon's side, holding out the object for Jonathon to take. "Here, take this. It is an earpiece."

Jonathon accepted it and inserted it into his ear. "What is this for?"

"The pad on your arm has a two-way radio and this is the corresponding earpiece."

"Ah, so no one can hear...when you respond?"

"Yes, I will stay in contact with you. Oh, I forgot...I sort of, have a map for inside the building."

"Map?"

Jason held the computer up for him to see. "Well, it is more like a preprogrammed Guardian flight plan if you will. I've actually been able to access certain memory data files from our guardian's implants.

The information is fragmented, but I was able to put this together. It seems, while inside the SYNRG building, the Guardians are programmed to operate independently from the master system."

"The master system controlling the master signal?"

"That's right. I could not say anything with the chief around. The Guardians, according to the files in the implants, receive their instructions from a massive computer which coordinates all of them and their activities. It must have a tremendous amount of computing power to do all of this, but if I had to guess, even this thing can get overloaded at times. Hence, the need to have the Guardians off the network for a bit, probably to ease the burden on the master system itself."

"You would think a sophisticated computer like that wouldn't have issues."

"Like all machines, they are at the mercy of human error and hindsight. Nonetheless, it definitely seems to be the most advanced thing ever built. Anyway, I determined, the Guardians are programmed with the precise dimensions of the SYNRG building. So, out of boredom one night, I was able to convert the data into the map here. We can use this as a guide."

"This will be a big help. I'm glad you were bored and remembered."

"Me, too. Plus, it is also interesting to note, all of the SYNRG buildings around the world have the exact precise dimensions."

"They're all the same?"

"With the exception of one, yes."

"Let me guess. The oddball is the one on the island, here?"

"You got it."

"As far as the other alike structures are concerned, this would make it very easy and quick to transfer a guardian from one city to another."

"Yes. In fact, Brent was in two other cities before coming back to Gulfside."

"Let's take a look at what you have."

"It seems to be a very simple layout. Ten floors, with a huge service elevator in the middle."

"Ten floors? But the buildings are so tall."

"Yeah, about eighty conventional stories, but the floors are enormous and widely spaced. Now the spires have a winding pattern which I think are stairs. Even though Brent has the programming for them, according to his log, he has never used the stairs here or in the other two cities."

"This could suggest the stairs aren't used much."

Jason tapped on the screen and switched to a different map.

"This is of the one on the island. The outside is the same, and the same stairs are in the spires, but this dark area in the middle has me thinking this is where the master computer is."

"How do we get to the island building?"

"There is only one way…the massive sky bridge, connecting the two structures, on the tenth floor."

"What about the water?"

"Heavily mined."

"By air?"

"The drones will shoot you down, before you even get close… and then your back to dealing with the mines."

"Okay…sky bridge it is. I can make my way to one of the spires, hope there is no detection equipment, and make my way to the tenth floor. Of course, none of this matters if I can't get in the front door."

"Like I said earlier, stealth is going to be the key."

"What if I just storm the front door? I'm supposed to be impervious to their weaponry."

"Yes you are, in theory. Nonetheless, if all of the Guardians were to swarm around you…you can't fight them forever."

"It was a thought."

"There is also a possibility the six guards are the only defenders. The other guardians may not be programmed to defend the castle."

"Yeah, that would be too easy."

"When it comes to whatever is going on inside the buildings, I have no concrete answers for you, just theory and some data. Anything can happen."

"Well, as far as I'm concerned, I have a better chance now than I did earlier this morning."

"I don't know how much longer the chief will be. So I would like to get out of here."

"Let's do it then."

"When we get over there, I'll find us a nice alley for you to practice walking with the head mask."

"Sounds like a plan."

CHAPTER FORTY-SIX

WRAP UP

"All right Jay, I think I got the hang of this."

Jonathon was walking around an alley space between the two structures, near the SYNRG building on the coast.

Jason limped up to him. "Good. Let's review how you are going to do this."

Jonathon stopped and removed his headpiece. "I'm going to go up to one of the side access gates while invisible. I will deactivate for a moment, trip the alarm, then reactivate. I will line my self up to the wall, next to the gate. They will come running out and hopefully will not notice me. Once they pass, I will slip in making my way to the front entrance by skimming along the perimeter wall, then the front of the building, just in case there are more. I'll scoot inside the front door before the Guardians return."

"You will only have a few minutes."

"Once inside, I still need to be careful. I'll make my way to a spire and up I go to the top."

"I'll guide you as best I can. Remember to watch your meter and use the field as sparingly as you can."

"Hopefully, there are no cameras or detection equipment in the spires."

"Hopefully."

"How large is the sky bridge?"

"I'm not sure. However, judging by the proportion, probably the same width as a four to six lane highway and roughly a half a mile to the other side. I have no idea what to expect…no one has ever been inside."

"What about a construction crew?"

"Construction crew? No. The SYNRG buildings were built by the Guardians...and only at night."

"It was worth a shot."

"Let me think if there are any other details. Ah...the eyes in the headpiece. They will automatically adjust to different levels of lighting."

"That's a nice feature."

"Let's get the rest of your gear."

The two men moved to the opened sliding van door. Jason leaned in the van and retrieved a long black bag, picking it up by the attached black shoulder strap. Jason faced Jonathon again, giving him the bag.

"The rifle is inside the bag."

Jonathon slung the strap over his shoulder, then over his head. "Where did you get the material for the rifle bag?"

"You know...when I ask for the things I need...I stopped asking where it was coming from."

"How does the bag work?"

"I installed a transmitter inside the bag to correspond with the control panel. The shield from the uniform will protect it, as long as you keep the rifle near you. The rifle will cloak along with you, as long as you keep it in the bag."

"Just out of curiosity, how far away from me does the emitter field extend?"

"Not far. About six inches maybe?"

"Oh. So if I use the rifle, holding it out in front of me, is it protected?"

"Actually, yes. The gun must have its own set of emitters. I can't tell, but it is capable of generating it's own field. It will operate in sync with the uniform."

"You are just making this way too easy."

"Well, one point of caution. There is no field around the tips of the gun. I suspect, not to interfere with its operation. So make sure to guard them."

"Got it."

"Well, I guess no point in delaying any further."

"Jay. I don't know what to say, except, thank you."

"When this is over and we are successful, it will be me saying thank you...to you."

"I wish Adam would come to senses on this...I would feel better if..."

"Well, he is going to have no choice after this. After you go, I'm going to call him and let him know what we are doing."

"That's actually a good idea. If for some reason something goes wrong…"

"We can get as many people out of harm's way for now."

Jonathon offered his hand. "Well then, let's not let it get to that point."

Jason clasped Jonathon's hand. "Right."

Jason, inching closer, leaned in and wrapped his other arm around Jonathon, patting him on the back. "Good luck, Jonny."

"Jonathon returned the embrace while still holding onto Jason's hand. "To you, too…to everybody."

Both releasing, they stood up straight.

Jonathon smiled. "Here I go." He flipped the headpiece open, sliding it over his head. Quickly adjusting it, he then, pushed onto the control panel.

Jason stepped back and watched him slowly vanish away.

"How do I look?" Jonathon asked.

Jason examined the warped translucent field in front of him. "You look like a distorted blob…with a computer screen."

"Oh yeah, right."

Jason could hear, and somewhat see, Jonathon fumbling around. The panel now disappeared. Jason conducted a another quick inspection.

Jonathon seemed to spin around once. "Is that all?"

"Sure looks like it. When you leave the alley here and go around the corner, we'll test the radio. If anything is wrong, come back and we will correct it quickly."

"All right, off I go."

Jason listened to faint footsteps rapidly striking the pavement, and watched the distortion move away from him. Jason limped to the van and pulled himself in. He hobbled to the rear of it. Jason sat down on a nearby secured stool next to another passenger; the Guardian. He was lying in his secure bed, next to a small computer console built into the opposite side. The machine was on and monitoring the dormant man.

Jason grabbed a marked tablet computer from the console, tapping on it briefly. "Establish connection!"

"Connection established," replied a dulcet digital female voice.

"Jonny, can you hear me?"

"Perfectly." he replied, faintly.

"When you need to respond, speak into your panel."

"Oh, sorry."

"Better. Just remember, you can still be heard, so use discretion when doing any movements or speaking."

"Got it."

"The panel is sensitive, so you will be able to whisper, which I recommend when you get there."

"I'm running to the south gate now."

"Why the south gate?"

"It is where my grandfather's beach spot was…for good luck!"

"I understand. I'll be in touch in a little bit. I've got to make… the call."

"Good luck."

Jason tapped on the screen, severing his connection with Jonathon.

"Call chief!" Jason directed.

"Calling chief."

As the phone rang, Jason became queasy.

"Jason where are you?" Adam demanded. "I can't find you anywhere around here."

Jason said with a confident tone, "I'm not there."

"Why not? Where are you?"

"Sir. You know I have the utmost respect for you and I'm very thankful for everything you've done for me, but I have been telling you all these years we've needed to do something about this SYNRG problem."

"Jason, you know there is no easy fix to this."

"You have waffled far too long on this and we are out of time. SYNRG snatching that girl out of her house is a clear indicator of this."

"I've got a guy there now, we don't know for sure it was a guardian."

"Come on, boss, we haven't had a crime like this in a while. Who else would have done this? There's nobody left."

"There are still enough coherent people who are duly capable."

"Jonny says it was a guardian…so I'm inclined to believe him."

"Jonny doesn't know what he is talking about. He doesn't know what you and I know."

"Don't be so sure about that, sir."

"Enough! Where are you?"

"I don't think I'll divulge that at the moment."

"Fine. I'll get someone to find you."

"I've already disabled the tracker in the van. By the time you locate me, it will be too late."

"Too late for what? What are you doing?"

"Jonny is heading into the SYNRG building as we speak."

"WHAT!"

"You left us with no choice at this point."

"It wasn't your call!"

"Perhaps. But what is done...is done. When you calm down, we can discuss this further, however, you should start planning for the worst."

"Damn the both of you..."

The audible female voice said, "Connection lost...would you like to reestablish?"

Jason lowered his head and did not respond.

CHAPTER FORTY-SEVEN

SNEAKING IN

Jonathon quietly talked to himself. "Okay. You're staring at the wall, but not moving. All you have to do is ring the bell."

Looking down he said, "It is so weird, not being able to see myself. Focus Jonny, focus."

Facing the wall again he said, "All right…let's wake the kiddies."

Fumbling and feeling around his arm, he located the panel. Carefully peeling a part of the flap away, he gingerly curled his finger under, hoping it was where he thought it was. Pushing down, he felt the screen against his fingertip. The cloak portion indicated the deactivation and he noticed himself becoming visible. Keeping his hand steady and in place, a repeating audible alarm started to sound. Touching the button again, he began to slip back into disguise. Once he could no longer see himself, he trotted up to the wall next to the gate, waiting for it to open. He slammed his back against the surface. "Ouch. Hopefully I'll guesstimate better once inside."

All of a sudden, a massive metallic rumbling and reverberating noise overtook the alarm. Looking to his side he could see the gate sliding toward him, into the wall behind. Halfway open, guardians streamed through the gap one by one, fanning out as soon as they were beyond the wall to begin their search of the perimeter. The sixth and last guardian emerged. Jonathon waited for the gate to hopefully open all the way. This would make it far easier to just slip in without much of his distortion becoming noticeable.

The guardians walked farther away from him, and he was more relieved. The ominous gate clatter ceased. He slowly peeked to his side and sure enough, it was completely open. He began to move to his side and around, being mindful not to make too much noise, especially if there were more guards nearby. Once inside the perimeter, he gave himself a quick and quiet deep breath. Continuing to step to his side along the wall, he observed the giant open concrete field in front of him. A concrete ground. No grass. No shrubbery. No trees and more importantly, no human figures.

Angling his head toward the building in the distance, he noticed an immense open ground base door in the middle. "This is going to take forever going at this pace. They'll be back before I get up there. I have got to risk, at least, jogging up there."

Jonathon turned to the building and performed one final visual sweep to make sure there were no other guardians around. Satisfied he was in the clear, he accelerated his pace. Staying beside the wall, he was now advancing up much quicker. Closer to the spire he said, "Yeah that looks big enough to house a stairwell."

Still not satisfied with his progress, he pushed himself into a full run, being careful not to lose his balance. Approaching the gap between the wall and the spire, he angled to run along the front of the building. With the sun behind the building, once he entered the shade, his camera eyes adjusted to the reduced light accordingly. Pushing himself to his limit, he started to have trouble breathing. Reducing his speed down to a jog helped, but he still found it difficult to get sufficient air. He tried to take in multiple deep breaths, but without success. Now, with the massive hatch within a short distance and the fear of passing out, he reduced his speed to a fast walk, allowing his breathing a chance to return to normal before entering. Aside from the fact he was almost out of breath, he was quite loud, trying to get it back. Jonathon looked up at the opening and thought, *That has got to be at least three stories and what forty… fifty…feet wide?*

Almost to the door he stopped, kneeling down to rest for a moment. *That was stupid, but…* The alarm ceased and he twisted back to the open gate. The guardians started to shuffle in slowly and lined up, appearing to wait for the rest of the group. With his window of opportunity fading, he got back up and proceeded to the colossal opening. His breathing was much better, but he still needed a bit more time for it to become regular and, more importantly, quiet.

Passing through, he guessed the outer wall here was about ten-feet thick with a two-foot wide vertical groove in the middle, possibly for the door, but with no apparent mechanism. Even though he was curious, he did not have time to investigate. Turning the corner and fully inside now, his camera eyes adjusted again. Already knowing what way not to go, he turned to go for the nearest spire. Still in line with and against the wall, he scurried toward the corner, ascertaining there were no obstructions in his immediate path.

Perusing around, this seemed to be one huge open room, similar to an airplane hanger. Steel girders consistently spread about, concrete floors, and the boundary walls as sleek in here as they were out there. The ambient light appeared to be from above, but he could not make out the actual light source. Just as Jason conveyed, there was an enormous maintenance elevator, more like a platform, in the exact middle. In addition, there were two smaller ones on each end. The one in the middle was by far the largest. All were of an open design with no walls or borders.

Balancing speed with the striking of his boots on the ground, Jonathon was aware of the slight echo he was producing. Even though he was being relatively quiet, the guardians would enter at any moment and might possibly hear the footsteps. Closing in on a curved wall ahead, presumably the base of the spire, he muttered to himself, "An open door way. I couldn't be that lucky."

Hearing commotion by the main door, he picked up his pace, hoping his steps were being drowned out by whatever was going on back there. An ominous mechanical sound now filled the room, definitely masking him now. Running the rest of the distance, he arrived at the oversized rectangular doorway. Pausing in the threshold, he noticed grooves, similar to those at the main entrance, indented in the two-foot thick curved wall. Looking straight up, there were seams consistent with a retractable vertical sliding door. Muttering again he said, "Boy, I'm glad this is open."

Peeking behind him, the outside light was almost gone as six human figures marched in unison toward the elevators. Still muttering he said, "They don't know I'm here."

The natural light was gone and with a loud thud reverberating about, the main door compressed. Jonathon turned around and quietly proceeded in, finding himself at the base of a large concrete winding stairway connected to one side of the wall. A metal hand rail wound with the staircase, which consistently ascended. Jonathon walked to the first stair and began to climb the first several steps.

Pausing, he leaned over the railing, trying to determine if he could look up and through. "That is a lot of stairs."

Another mechanically produced noise bounced around the walls.

He muttered to himself, "Sounds like an elevator lifting."

He continued to peek around. "This tower has to be at least thirty feet in circumference. This is going to take me forever."

Resuming his ascent, he felt the stairs were sturdy enough and he did not make too much noise. The elevator sound now ceased. *That did not last long, I wonder what floor they went to.*

After some more steps, he paused again. "Crap, where am I at on my meter?"

Patting his arm for moment, he felt the panel. Searching for the flap, he found the bottom corner and peeled enough of it away to see the meter. All the bars were still there, but he knew this climb was going to use a good portion of them. *Jay said the guardian we have never used the stairs…that could go for all the Guardians. What about detection devices or non-guardians?*

Glancing around quickly again he mumbled to himself, "I don't see anything that could get me into trouble. As far as people…these are a lot of stairs. I'm going to turn this thing off and see what happens. I'm not far enough in…"

Jonathon tapped on the screen and slowly watched his arms and other parts of him within his view become visible.

He advanced up one more step, then another, then another, and one more. "I think I'm okay. It's a good thing too, my eyes are starting to hurt."

He clasped the top of the headpiece and with a quick tug, he slid it off. "It's cool in here."

Jonathon took a few more steps. "Let me put the mask away for now," he said quietly. "Hopefully I wont need it."

He reached down to his empty side pant pocket, opened the fold, and slipped the headpiece securely into it. Pressing down on the fold, the pocket resealed.

"Should I take the rifle out? Do you feel like carrying it up all the way? Do you think it is healthy for someone to continuously talk to himself? Why no, Jonny. I don't think it is, but thanks for asking."

Gripping the handrail, Jonathon continued with his long ascent. Altering his speed, he tried to figure out what was the fastest he could go, without too much of a ruckus.

"Jonny, are you there?" Jason asked through the earpiece.

Still at a near whisper he answered, "Yeah."

Realizing Jason probably did not hear him, he fully peeled back the flap, sealing it on the sleeve. Raising the panel close to his mouth he said, "I'm here…I made it in."

"Great! It worked!"

"You were right, the spires have stairwells."

"Good."

"Also, it appears there is no monitoring equipment in here, so I turned the field off to limit my exposure."

"Hey, you're the one inside. You're the only one who can weigh those risks. But I am glad to hear you are using the emitters sparingly."

"It's just going to take me forever to get up these stairs."

"Are you able to converse for a little while longer?"

"As long as I keep my voice to a whisper, I've got plenty of time."

"Good. Well, the computer I've been using to control my guardian is picking up these weird signals coming from the SYNRG building."

"Have you ever seen them before?"

"No. I think it has something to do with me being so close to the building itself, my access to the guardian code, and the guardian being here, too. Of course this is all just a guess. Yet, just off of a hunch, I shot the code I found for the guardian through his transceiver, and what do you know? I have a limited access into SYNRG's master signal."

"Do you think you'll be able to use it to shut down the master computer?"

"Unfortunately, no. I won't be able to do anything grandiose, but I do know where all the Guardians are positioned inside the building."

"Hey, great. That will be a big help."

"Where are you at the moment? I want to manually track you."

"I'm in the southeast spire."

"Okay. I have you plotted. It's strange, though. The six guards you encountered at the door are on the second floor."

"What's strange about that?"

"All of the other guardian signatures are all on the top three floors."

"Should I be concerned?"

"I don't know, but I will keep a close eye on them."

"If there is nothing else pressing at the moment, how did it go with Adam?"

"He was pissed. He hung up on me. When he cooled down, he called back. I leveled with him and he seems to be okay. I told him where I am and he is on his way down here now to discuss things further."

"Sounds promising."

"He is recalling the rest of the force back to inner Gulfside and enlisting Opposition members to assist. They are all on their way down here."

"Hopefully he has a plan."

"We are going to work on one when he gets here…scratch that…he's here. I'm going to have to disconnect for a while…but just speak into your arm if you need me."

"Sure, do what you have to do."

CHAPTER FORTY-EIGHT

HELP IS ON ITS WAY

"Jay, are you there? Hello?" Jonathon waited for a response, concerned something had happened. "Jay?"

"You okay?" Jason replied.

"Yeah, I haven't heard from you in a while...I was starting to feel lonely here."

"I lost track of time...wait...two hours?"

"Yep."

"There has been a lot going on down here. Have you reached the top floor yet?"

"I've passed eight landings, so I'm almost there."

"Good. I've been working on this SYNRG signal...hoping to have something else for you soon. Hey, you've been amazing so far."

"Well, the more of an advantage we can have the better...and speaking of advantage, Adam is on his way up to meet you."

"What! How? Why?"

"He sees no real way to combat this, except to shut this thing down at the source."

"We aren't a hundred percent sure it is here or if, for that matter, that will end it."

"After I showed him what I know he thought it was more than worth the risk...in fact, I think he was actually relieved to have a possible solution."

"How is he going to get to me?"

"I had a second uniform."

"A second, huh."

"Well, with everything going on, you can't expect me to recall everything."

"Right. How far behind is he?"

The alarm sounded again. "Is that him?" Jonathon asked.

"I think so."

"Am I in danger? Should I go invisible?"

"You're fine. It's the same six responding and going to the main entrance as they should. At this time, there appears to be no movement on the top floors near you."

"Well, if you can watch over me, I think I'm actually at a good spot…I'm just going to wait for him then."

"He was hoping you would. The two of you together will greatly accelerate your chances."

"Although, I don't want to wait too long..."

"She's probably still all right, Jonny. If they are planning on changing her, I don't see how they could do it quickly."

"What if they are going to move her to another city?"

"If they didn't do it last night, then they may do it tonight. SYNRG does all of their intercity transporting at night, but I don't think she is going anywhere anytime soon though."

"Okay, Jay, I trust your judgment."

"I will let him know once I get back into contact with him."

"What do you mean back into contact?"

"I'm trying to program this thing, so the two of you can communicate with each other without me brokering. Just so you know, I may lose you for a few minutes as well."

"That's fine. I'm in a spot were I'll know if there are any dangers coming my way."

"Good, because I have to cut my link with you now. I'll be back in a few."

Jonathon muttered to himself, "I guess I can sit down for a little while. However, I think I should put my mask on, just in case I need to disappear in a hurry."

CHAPTER FORTY-NINE

LOOK-A-LIKE

"Jonny!"

Jonathon opened his eyes and stared through his computer-generated images. "Dana? Are you there? What happened? Crap, did I doze off?"

He leaned against the barrier wall of the stairwell and balanced himself, trying to get up. The strap of the bag was still secured to him. He stood up straight and once he was satisfied he was not going to go tumbling down the stairs, he adjusted the bag back to his side.

"Jonny, if you can talk, please respond," Jason said through the earpiece."

Jonathon quietly responded. "Sorry, Jay, I think I fell asleep."

"Oh, thank goodness nothing happened."

"Yeah, me too. After the alarm stopped, I got comfortable and... that was it. How long has it been?"

"A little over an hour. Sorry it took that long to get this thing straightened out."

"Where's Adam?"

"I'm about halfway up this ridiculously long stairway," Adam responded softly.

"It's good to hear your voice."

"Hold on a second, I need to turn up my hearing aid."

Jonathon felt a little ashamed. "Adam about..."

"Don't worry about it," Adam said, chuckling. "In another time or place, that would've been funny. Forget about it. Besides, I'm the elder one now and you're the one napping?"

Jonathon was very relieved. "I can't wait for you to get up here."

"Me too, pal. I'm ready to kick some SYNRG keister, especially for making me drag my ass up these stairs."

"Okay, good. You two are linked," Jason said.

"Yeah, I hear him perfectly," Jonathon assured.

"Good on my end, too Jason."

"All right guys, I'm almost done working on getting further into the SYNRG system. In fact, I'm there…Shit!"

The alarm blared again. "What happened Jay?"

"They discovered me hacking in. Fortunately, I broke the connection before any permanent damage, but I suspect they know you two are in there and I'm going to have to move."

"Adam, did you get that?"

"Yeah, I just put my helmet on."

Jonathon tapped on his cloak button and covered the console, which began to fade out of his sight.

"Do you know what's behind any of the doors on the landings?" asked Adam.

"No. I stayed away from them, in case they open by themselves and/or trigger an alarm." Jonathon replied.

"That really doesn't matter now, I guess. Don't wait for me to get up there. When I get to the next landing, I'm going through the door, take my chances, and find a faster way to get up there."

"All right, be careful."

"You too."

Jonathon began jogging up the stairs, holding onto the railing. "I have got to be close to this thing."

Sure enough, coming over the last curve he came upon the top floor door. "I hope this thing will open."

Stepping off the final stair onto the landing, he marched for the door. The door opened. A guardian came out. Seeing Jonathon, he lunged at him. Reacting quickly, Jonathon swung out of the way. Adjusting his footing, Jonathon ran behind his opponent and thrust into his back with a tremendous amount of force, pushing the man to and off the stair ledge. The man, striking his head on the adjacent wall, tumbled lifelessly down the stairwell.

"Okay…enough of this stealth nonsense…let's get real!"

Jonathon felt for his forearm, swiftly peeled back the flap and tapped on the cloak button. He slowly became visible. He hastily tapped the shield portion. He tugged the top of his hood off of his head. Opening his free pocket, he jammed the headpiece inside of it and then closed it. He clasped onto the bag, jerked the fold open, and pulled the rifle out. He knelt down, setting the gun on the ground for a moment. He quickly maneuvered the bag against his back, then tightened the tension on the strap to where it was secure and would not cause him any issues. Picking up the gun, he stood up and examined the weapon.

"Oh, where is the indicator?"

He flipped the gun over and spotted the narrow electronic slider on the underside of the stock, near the side of the trigger guard. "It's on 2 and this thing goes up to 10. Let's leave it on 2 and see what happens."

Flipping it topside he said, "I hope this thing works."

He clutched onto the trigger grip and threaded his finger through the trigger guard. "This thing is so light, I probably can carry it with one hand."

Not sure how the weapon fired, he grasped the front grip with his other hand to be safe, pointing it in firing readiness. Moving forward, he proceeded to the door. The door automatically slid open and Jonathon stepped through.

The alarm ceased again and Jonathon paused, probing around the long hallway ahead in complete astonishment.

"What's going on here? This looks exactly like the hallways in ChronoSleep."

The path in front of him was straight, with only one door lining the immediate walls near a steep rightward curve ahead. Continuing forward cautiously, he moved at a quick step. Somewhat down the corridor, another guardian came running around the corner, holding a rifle. Jonathon aimed and pulled his trigger before the guardian had a chance to react. There was a distorted hum and flash of light, then the man was pushed back to his nearby wall and slid down to the floor.

"It works, just like Jason said."

Jonathon lowered the gun and ran up to the sagging man.

"It's a woman," he said.

Still staying alert, Jonathon knelt down on one knee, picked up the other rifle and tossed it away. Studying her further, she appeared to be more or less Angie's age. He placed his fingers on her neck to check for a pulse. She was very much alive. Removing his hand, she started to lightly moan and slowly move her head about, as if she were in pain. Her eyes were still closed.

"Miss, are you okay?" he asked.

"Where…"

Her head leaned lifelessly against the wall and she stopped moving all together.

Jonathon again placed his fingers on her neck. "Her pulse is very strong and she seems to be breathing normally."

Standing up straight and stepping back, he maintained his sight on her. "She can't be a guardian…otherwise she would not be able to speak. Unless they've solved that."

Staring at his weapon he said, "Let's slide this sucker down to one and see what happens."

He slid the indicator to 1. "Maybe this will keep the next one conscious."

Close to the nearby door, he marched right up to it. Nothing happened.

"There seems to be no handle or mechanism of any kind," he said. "Jay? Are you there? I need help with a door…Jay? Adam?"

He clasped the underside grip and pointed his rifle forward. "Crap. I hope everything is all right."

Now running, Jonathon followed the curve around and up an incline. The pathway was straightening out, but he was still inclining. The path curved to the left, and the incline became more steep. Rounding this corner, the corridor again became linear and the ground leveled off after a short jaunt.

"I think I'm going back, but a floor or level higher," he said.

The only visible exit was a door directly down the long passageway in front of him. He pushed forward but before he could get to the door, it slid open and another uniformed person rushed in. He pulled the trigger and the person fell to the ground.

"Got him," Jonathon said.

Jonathon hurried up to him, to see if he was conscious.

"Damn it. He's out. This is the lowest…"

All of sudden the man tried to get up. Jonathon set his weapon down, knelt down and secured the other weapon, tossing it away.

"Where is she?" Jonathon shouted.

Crouching down, Jonathon grabbed the guy as he sat up. With a firm grip on the man's chest balling up the section of the stretchable uniform in his hand, Jonathon slammed him against the wall. The guard became more conscious.

Jonathon shouted again, "Where is she!"

The man looked up at him with a glazed expression. "Where is who?"

"The woman your gang brought in from the Outland last night."

The man shook his head. "Where am I?"

Jonathon pulled him away from the wall and then thrust back into it. "I don't have time for your nonsense."

Still seemingly confused and looking back up to Jonathon the man said, "I don't know where I am."

"This is SYNRG."

The man, now very lucid, was suddenly much more brazen. "She's across the bridge on the island. You'll never get to her."

With more strength and both hands he clasped onto Jonathon's arm. Jonathon reared his free fist and punched the man in the face with all of his might. The man went limp from the force of the blow, and was unresponsive. Jonathon released him and the guard fell lifelessly to the ground. With haste, Jonathon hopped over to his gun, scooped it up and readied himself into a firing stance. He turned to the door.

"Jonny, can you talk?"

"Adam, I was concerned."

"Sorry, I had to be quiet. There are some guardians scouring the place for us."

"I don't think they are guardians."

"Oh?"

"According to Jason, they can't speak…and I just had a brief conversation with one."

"What did he say?"

"Well, it was weird. He was out of it briefly, seemingly scared. Then, without pause, he was almost…brash. Anyway…Angie is on the island. Adam, I'm going in."

"Where are you?"

"To be honest, I haven't a clue. There is a door ahead of me…I'll figure it out. How about you?"

"I'm trying to get the elevators, but every internal door I come to is locked. Don't worry, I'll make my way to you. Ooh, got to go."

Jonathon stared ahead. "All right door…lead me where I need to go."

He stepped past the guard and hurried to the door, which swooshed open. He went through it to…

"Outside?"

He realized he was out in some sort of circular covered veranda. "This must be the top of the spire."

The day was giving way to night. The area was bare. There was nothing but the concrete ground beneath him, the black ceiling above, no lighting, and a fantastic haze free view of Gulfside City in front of him. Moving up to a metallic barrier, Jonathon surveyed over the city from this…the highest point.

"My God, it's so beautiful. I've never seen the city from so high."

Scanning across the cityscape, the wind blew over his face. This was the first time, since awaking, he felt like he was home.

"I feel so alive!"

In his moment of bliss, the reality of the situation began to set in. The buildings were dark, there was no traffic, and no signs of life he could see. Except, glaring down, toward the base of this structure itself, a black cloud was slowing spewing out from the main entrance.

"Jonny, I had to step away. What's going on? There are

guardians pouring out in droves from the SYNRG building, lining up in their courtyard inside the front wall."

"I don't know, Jay. I think we may have upset the balance Adam was concerned about."

"I just tried to call him."

"He was in an area with a lot of activity I guess…he had to go dark."

"I think we're about to feel SYNRG's wrath. I'm being told this is also happening in the other SYNRG cities."

"This could be the beginning of the end."

"Unless…"

"Yes. Unless I do my job."

Jonathon overlooked the city again and observed a dying Gulfside in desperate trouble.

Gazing up above the city, a lone bright star shone at him. "Jay. Can you see the eastern sky from where you are at?"

"Some of it. Why?"

"Do you see the one star?"

"Yeah…it's interesting…that is a new star which showed up days ago. It comes out much earlier and much brighter than any other star, from what I understand. Hey, I don't mean to…"

"I know, I need to get moving, but I feel…something up here, something so euphoric…I just can't describe…don't worry…I'm going to kick SYNRG's ass. Gulfside's hero has returned. I'll call you when I get over to the island."

"I'm trying to get back into the SYNRG system. I hope to have something for you by then."

Jonathon perused to his side and noticed a small descending stairway. Walking over to it, he leaned out over the side. There was some sort of metal scaffolding, attached to a curved platform below the steps and to the side of the building, stretching out to and up to the top of the spire at the rear end. The other side of this narrow viaduct was lined with a waist-high metal wall. Extending out from behind the main structure was the massive sky bridge to the island building.

"Well, unless I go back and blast the door inside open, this appears to be my only option. And I don't even know if the door will lead anywhere and assuming the gun can blow things up," he said to himself.

With a big sigh, Jonathon forged forward down the stairs and onto the platform curving into the suspended walkway. "Helicopters, sky high walkways…sky bridges...why me?"

Jonathon made sure he had a good grip on the rifle. Readying it into a firing stance, he began to run. The sound of his boots clanged against the metal as he pushed through with the wind blowing into his side. Maintaining his balance, he continued down the pathway, making sure he did not slam into any obstacles as the dusk light faded away. He could see some sort of light emanating from ahead, but he wasn't not sure from what.

"Jonny, can you talk?" Adam asked. "I just used my gun to blow open a door."

"So it does blast things open."

"There is no recoil and yes, it most definitely blasts things. The department could use a few of these things. How are you progressing?"

"I wasn't sure if these would…you know…open a door…I'm outside running on some sort of scaffolding, on my way to the rear of the building."

"Ooh, you must hate that."

"I really don't have a choice at this point. Are you encountering much resistance?"

"Surprisingly no."

"Just a moment ago, the guardians started coming out the front door."

"Yeah, I heard Jason. It would seem we are almost out of time."

"I'm afraid so."

"I think I found an internal elevator, not on Jason's map. I'm going to see if it will get me to the top floor. Hey, this isn't over."

"I know. I'll feel a lot better, though, when we meet up."

"Me too. The doors are closing. We may…"

"Adam?"

Jonathon, close to the rear spire, began to slow as he approached the small stairway. Climbing up the stairs, he stepped up onto the tower veranda. Similar to the one he came from and ran through it.

Emerging out onto a platform, he overlooked the sky bridge. "Hmm, it has a rounded roof, with the exception of…what is that…a retractable covering on a small portion and the source of the light. And look at that, a winding ramp circling down and connected to the opening."

About to run down, he noticed several objects flying out from the hatch.

"Drones."

The machines, moving fast with the familiar turbine noise and roving lights, ascended on him rapidly. Three of them stopped several feet away from him, hovering motionless in front of him, illuminating the area around. The drones were black and the size of a compact car. All were triangular shaped with a small oval bubble in the middle on the top of the housing. All had one end pointed at him. The sound of the engines were loud, but surprisingly not deafening. With other drones buzzing out and away, these three rose a few feet above him, and Jonathon could now see their undercarriages. Hanging down from the midpoints of the housings was some sort of weapons' array, with the same tips as the rifles and they were all aimed at him.

"Oh…shit!" he exclaimed.

Before he could take evasive action, he was quickly enveloped by a flash of light, which instantly dissipated. There were two more bursts of light and nothing else.

While holding the gun, he threw his arms into the air. "IT WORKS!"

More flashes of light blasted at him, then ceased. Jonathon lowered his arms and felt underneath the gun for the intensity setting.

Sliding it up to as far as it would go, he gripped the gun on its underside and pointed it at the lead drone. "Let's see what 10 does you assholes."

Pulling the trigger, the machine scattered into bits, and fell down below. Taking aim at the second one, he pulled the trigger, and instantly destroyed it. The third one increased the frequency of its firings but all had negative results on Jonathon. Jonathon trained the weapon at the remaining drone and fired. The apparatus fell lifelessly out of his sight.

Jonathon quickly vacillated around, searching for others which might have been around him. "Huh, I would of thought I would have had more surrounding me after my own light display."

Jonathon spoke into the control pad. "Jay! Everything works!"

"That's great, Jonny! Just be careful though. I don't know how reliable the field is and how long it will take them to filter out their own guns."

"All right, I'll be careful. Adam, if you can hear me, I think I found a way in."

Setting his sights on the opening, he proceeded carefully down the ramp.

"Jonny, you don't have to respond…I'm getting far in the SYNRG system again…I'm hoping to give you some help on this end." Jason said.

Jonathon yelled out. "Thanks! I do have a question however!"

"Go ahead."

"I just shot down three drones, which were probably programmed to be defenders…but why are there no others coming after me?"

"It could be as simple as the three you destroyed were the only ones programmed to defend. Why they are not assigning more to you…I haven't a clue. It may have something to do with what's going on down here. There are multiple drones just hovering over their courtyard. Whatever is going on, again be careful."

"I will. I'm almost at an opening on top of the sky bridge."

Jonathon approached the edge of the massive hatch, kneeled down, and peeked in, trying to investigate the situation below. Attached to the wall just below him and leading to the ground inside were rungs of a ladder. The ground was a smooth concrete and was as wide as six lanes of traffic.

"Here goes," Jonathon said.

He hooked the rifle on to his shoulder which sealed to the uniform. Jonathon swung around and placed his feet on the first rung, descending as quickly as he could into the unknown.

"Jonny, are you there?" Adam asked.

"I'm here."

"I can barely hear you, but I think I'm almost to the bridge."

"Sorry, I'm actually in the bridge going down a ladder. I can't hold up the receiver to my mouth."

"I still can hear you though. Great! I think I'll be to you very soon."

"Did you hear my last conversation with Jay? About the drones and shields?"

"No."

"The SYNRG bastards sent some of their flying drones after me, firing at me, but the shield held up."

"That's good news."

"I blasted those things to bits."

"Awesome!"

"However, Jay warned me that the shield isn't perfect and they may figure out a way through, so be careful."

"I'll be careful. We can talk more about this when I get to you."

"See you in a few."

Stepping off the last rung onto the ground, Jonathon tugged the rifle from his shoulder, readied himself into a firing posture, and perused the situation all around. Looking behind him he could see a set of closed massive slide type doors to the entrance of the building he just came from. Overhead, embedded in the ceiling were six rows of white lights appearing to run the whole length of the sky bridge.

Other than this, there was not much else. Facing forward to the long expanse ahead, he could see the figures of about six persons running toward him. Reaching to the underside of the gun, he slid the indicator back down to 2. Jonathon began to start running toward them, ready to fight. Flashes of light came from his opponents ahead, but just bounced off of him. Jonathon paused and took aim, firing at the approaching guards. He quickly neutralized three of them, while the other three scattered and jumped high and erratically about.

"Shit these are guardians!" Jonathon exclaimed.

Looking up he found one had tumbled over him. He quickly pointed at, and shot the man, who fell behind him. The other two rapidly approached from opposite sides. Jonathon picked one and gunned him down, but the remaining one pounced on him, knocking Jonathon to the ground and the rifle out of his hands. The guardian struggled to subdue him but Jonathon managed to get into his arm pocket and retrieve his stun gun. Once the moment presented itself, Jonathon jammed the device in the man's neck. The guardian fell lifelessly on top of him. Pushing the inert hulk off of him, Jonathon sprang to his feet, ready for anymore guardians who might be coming. Determining he was safe for the moment, he returned the stun gun back to his pocket, bent down, and retrieved his rifle. Shaking his head, he sprinted forward, continuing without delay.

"Adam, I'm encountering heavy resistance," Jonathon yelled.

"I'm on the bridge. I'm right behind you."

Jonathon, not slowing down said, "I think I see more ahead."

He was preparing himself for this next encounter when his legs began to give out. "No, not now, I can't go now…"

CHAPTER FIFTY

SYNRG'S WORLD

"Jonny, it's no time to sleep now!"

Jonathon sat up and found himself on the ground, but not in the SYNRG complex. In fact, he was not sure where he was. It was just white, all around him, very peaceful and serene. No sound or commotion whatsoever.

"Hello?"

"Jonny, you are so close my love. Just stay focused. It was wonderful advice you gave me once, now I'm returning it to you."

"Dana?"

"She is very lovely, Jonny…I like her a lot. But she is in terrible danger. The future of our family is in danger. You can't let anything happen to her…to me…and our wonderful children."

"What do you mean, Dana? Our family is gone."

"I am of her and she is of me."

"What?"

"Humanity is on the brink of a major discovery, but humanity is not ready."

"Not ready for what? What discovery?"

"A person's soul. The soul is very complex, Jonny. When you feel your heart beating in your chest, when you love, when you dream; you are accessing your soul. However, this is only scratching the surface of and to what lies beyond. And it is being robbed by those you fight. You cannot let this continue. Humanity must progress naturally to reach the soul's true potential. The world needs you back, so it's time to get moving, mister."

"How can I fight what I don't understand?"

"It does not matter now...only know, it needs to stop. Come on now, let's get moving sleepy head."

Jonathon, in a daze, found his face against the ground. With his hands, he pushed himself up, trying to get up and gain his bearings. Sitting up on his backside, he could once again see figures closing in-six of them in all.

"Damn it, I can't move."

The lead guardian approached and aimed his weapon at him. Jonathon looked down at his control panel and could see his shield was deactivated.

"This is it," he said.

Without warning, a disincentive hum and a flash of light enveloped the guardian, who then collapsed. Just then, from behind, someone in a guardian uniform ran in front of Jonathon. This individual repeatedly fired, preventing the remaining five from reaching him. The individual turned and then looked down at Jonathon with his beret-covered head.

Jonathon returned the gaze. "Adam?"

Adam held his hand out and smiled. "I don't think it's a good time to take a siesta. Let's get moving here, lieutenant."

Jonathon smiled. "Yes sir."

Now able to move, he reached up and clasped onto Adam's hand. Adam pulled him up.

Adam smiled again. "It's good to see you, Jonny."

"It's great to see you. You saved my life."

"I was only doing my job," Adam said with a smirk.

"I guess I had it coming to me."

Adam bent down and retrieved Jonathon's gun.

Jonathon glanced around and could not see any other dangers at the moment. Examining his pad, he tapped the shield portion to reactivate it.

Adam stood up straight. "Something wrong?"

"My shield was off. I don't know what happened, but it seems to be fine now. Oh, my health meter has lost some bars."

Adam peered at his. "I'm already almost at the halfway point."

"We're running out of time."

Adam held out Jonathon's gun to him. "Let's get going then."

Jonathon clasped onto it. "Thank you for coming up here."

"No need to thank me. This is something that should have been done long ago. But, I must say, this is going to be far easier with the two of us."

"I have a feeling something big, something life altering, is going on up ahead."

"Of course. That's why were are here."

"No. There is something much more going on…I don't know."

"It doesn't matter. Let's go kick some SYNRG ass."

Both men held their respective guns into a firing pose and started marching forward.

Adam looked over to Jonathon and asked, "Can you run?"

"Try and stop me."

Both men began to run.

"Adam? Jonny?" Jason called.

Jonathon responded. "Yeah, were both here."

"Great to know you two are together. Listen I have a major update here. The townspeople are…I don't know how to describe it, but they are walking to and into the SYNRG building en masse."

"What!" Adam blurted out.

"It may be more like drawn in…I think it has to something to do with the medical implants." Jason said.

"What makes you think that?"

"All the guardian signals I was able to track earlier, I'm now seeing them outside here corresponding to all these people."

Jonathon spoke loudly to his receiver. "You maybe on to something, pal. They're calling them in."

"Yeah, but for what purpose. Damn it. Too many questions., not enough answers." Jason retorted.

"What about the Opposition? Are they being drawn in?"

"No, which reaffirms the implants. In addition, the Guardians are streaming out of the access gates and onto the streets, forming some sort of skirmishing line."

"This is not good." Adam said to Jonathon.

"Adam and I are hurrying as fast as we can. We will be in touch."

"Jonny!" shouted Adam.

"I see them. Another six."

Adam and Jonathon paused, readied for their next bout.

Adam examined his weapon. "What setting do you have yours on?"

"Two."

"That makes me feel better. I've been using two on these people as well. What do you say, I'll take the three on the left, you the three on the right?"

"Sounds like a plan."

There were six flashes of light from ahead, and all enveloped and reflected off of Adam and Jonathon.

Adam took a step forward. "Light them up."

They both aimed at the first of their respective marks, repeatedly pulling their triggers as they switched targets. One by one the guardians fell.

Jonathon stepped up to Adam's side. "I think I see the end of the bridge."

"It's about time."

The men ran again, hurling toward what appeared to be the way into the island structure.

Jason chimed in again. "Another update: The same thing is happening with the townspeople in the other SYNRG cities. All are marching into their respective SYNRG structures."

"What is all of this about?" Adam asked Jonathon.

"I don't know. But I have a feeling, once all of these people are inside, those of us remaining are going to be in big trouble. Possibly, the end of humanity as we know it."

"Grim, but agreed. We need to find what makes all of this tick."

"Oh great, what is this now? It looks like it forks out into two different directions."

"Let's go to the right," Adam suggested.

"Any particular reason?"

"No."

"I like it."

Adam and Jonathon veered to the right and followed the curved path outward. They went inward and eventually straightened out and were led up to an enormous door As they approached, a loud clang emanated from the door, which started sliding open. Not waiting, the two scooted in with the door not even a quarter of the way open. Other than being massive, the hallway inside was the same basic design as ChronoSleep. There are no doors and this hallway did not curve.

"Hey guys, it's confirmed, they just brought out some sort of tank. It's huge. The turret end is a larger version of the one on the rifle…wait a second…It has no tracks."

"No tracks," replied Jonathon. "What's it on?"

"Air. It is hovering about a foot off of the ground."

"Get everyone not affected out of harms way," Adam directed. "Let's hope Jonny and I find the heart of this before anything happens."

Adam and Jonathon approached what appeared to be a large room ahead.

"What do we have up here?" Jonathon asked Adam.

"Looks almost like an empty warehouse or aircraft hanger."

The two left the access hall and entered into a massive open room. The two men paused and perused around them. The room was similar to the hanger on the first floor of the mainland building and had light emanating from above, but they could not determine the precise source.

"I wonder if the contents of this room are now outside," Adam commented.

"If they are, at least there are three fewer of them now."

Jonathon pointed to a nearby small platform. "That could be an elevator or lift of sorts. It appears to have the same design as the ones on the first floor of the other building."

Adam nodded. "Jason mentioned to me that the layout of this particular structure would be different."

"Yeah, he said the same thing to me. The elevator seems to be avoiding the middle and staying close to our side for a reason."

"Only one way to find out."

Both quickly hiked over to the mechanism.

"I expected far more resistance than what we have encountered," Adam continued.

"Maybe they couldn't spare any more guardians or whatever. You know, preparing for…whatever is going on outside…or maybe they're waiting for us somewhere else."

Adam and Jonathon ran up to the contraption.

Adam examined the flat raised surface. "Its not big. If it is an elevator, how does this thing work?"

"Shouldn't you know? You said you took one."

"It was a regular elevator."

"Okay. Maybe this is not one. I mean, it does not have any walls or any guide paths."

"According to Jason's map, they were being utilized like elevators."

"Then…we'll be able to see ourselves go through the floors. Terrific," Jonathon added with sarcasm.

"Youth before beauty." Adam motioned.

Jonathon smirked, stepping carefully onto the platform. Adam followed. The two studied about.

Adam leaned somewhat to Jonathon. "Where is the control pad?"

A virtual image of a number pad appeared in front of them.

"Where did that come from?" Jonathon asked with confusion.

"I don't know, but it goes 10, 9, and 8, then 3, 2, and 1. Weird."

"Let's see what's on nine."

Jonathon pressed near the 9. It illuminated, then the whole panel disappeared. The sound of gears and cogs engaged, echoing throughout the room. The lift surprisingly moved into its descent without any bumps or jolts.

"We better not lose our balance or we will fall off." Jonathon added.

"I wonder..." Adam reached out in front of him toward the edge of the platform. His hand met resistance at the rim. "It is like I am touching a wall, but nothing is there."

The plane in front rose above them and their view was momentary blocked with the thickness of the concrete slab floor. After a few seconds of watching the ground rise above them, they passed into the next level. Both of them curious, they turned around to see what was waiting for them on the next floor.

Jonathon covered his mouth. "Oh my God! It can't be."

"What is it, Jonny? What is all of that down there?"

"This is very similar to a ChronoSleep...sleep room."

"What!"

The lift neared its landing and slowed down. Still smooth and effortless, the platform settled into place and the noise of the machinery ceased.

"What do we do now? Just Walk off?" Jonathon asked.

Adam stepped forward and off the platform without any resistance. He shook his head. "Come on, Jonny, let's see what this is all about."

Jonathon followed Adam off of the platform. Both paused near its side and scanned down the massive room. Adam, in complete awe asked, "What are these things?"

"They're sleep chambers."

"There must be thousands of them."

"Tens of thousands maybe."

Adam and Jonathon stood there, skimming over the rows upon rows of horizontal cylindrical housings. These were stacked into ten translucent inter floor echelons with access ramps running up to each tier. The ten levels seemed to be equal to ten standard building stories.

Jonathon stepped closer to the capsules. "These look slightly different." He then ran toward the closest one.

Adam followed closely behind. "Jonny, be careful. We don't know what is in these things and what possibly could be protecting them."

"Like you said, you were expecting more resistance from them. I doubt there are any security problems."

Jonathon ran up to a random cylinder. There was only about two feet of space between them, side to side and end to end. Jonathon hooked his rifle to his shoulder and Adam did the same. Jonathon glided his hand over the seamless surface.

"These may be similar, but they have a very noticeable difference...I don't see any creases or openings...are there any hinges or anything on the other side?"

Adam carefully inched around the chamber, peering around the side. "No. I don't see any hinges, creases, latches...nothing. It is completely smooth."

Taking a step back, Adam examined his nearby end. "There are no notches or any thing here, either." Glancing at the end of the neighboring tube he said, "The opposite side on this one is solid too."

"How in the world do we open these things? The ones at ChronoSleep opened like a coffin, hinged on one side."

"These may not be sleep chambers." Adam looked up to the ceiling of this tier and noticed some sort triangular-shaped tip on the edge of a foot-long rounded protrusion. Encircling the base was a soft white circular light. Pointing to it he asked, "What is that?"

Jonathon faced upward. "I don't know. We didn't have those at ChronoSleep."

Jonathon scanned around to the neighbors. "They all have one of these hanging over them."

Both looked down at the cylinder.

Jonathon put his hand on the top again. "I wonder if that is the opening mechanism."

"Open what though?"

Adam stepped back, accidentally bumping the bottom end of the chamber behind him.

"Adam what did you do? There is an image hovering over that one."

"I don't know."

Jonathon hurried over to the side, but the image disappeared. "What did you do?"

"I just bumped in the end here."

"Try giving it a forceful tap with your hands."

Adam lightly slammed the palms of his hands against the end and the image reappeared.

"This is pretty cool," Jonathon said with a smile.

Adam rushed to his side. "What is it?"

"It almost looks like a human status monitor. The image is so crystal clear."

The screen disappeared again.

"I got it," Adam said, and tapped the casing again. The picture resumed.

Jonathon shook his head. "What is this, a hologram of sorts?"

Adam looked up again. "That diamond end is glowing."

Jonathon gazed up. "Oh, this must be some sort of super-concentrated light…arranging into this."

Both stared back at the image.

Jonathon reached up to it. "There appears to be an access menu on the right here."

Extending his index finger, Jonathon moved it toward the square marked "menu" on the bottom right corner, the selection illuminated and the screen changed to a different background. There were now multiple selections available.

Adam was in awe. "A tactile response? Did you feel anything?"

Jonathon shook his head. "No. It was the same as the elevator."

Reading through the choices, Adam found, "open unit." "Try that one."

Jonathon moved his finger to it. The selection highlighted, then the screen disappeared. Jonathon waved his hand in front of where the screen was. "What happened?"

"Did you break it?"

"I don't know."

Jonathon stepped back. The diamond above now began to rapidly flicker.

Adam pushed Jonathon farther back as he moved back. The top surface of the cylinder was now glowing. The top was now completely enveloped by the light and cascaded exactly halfway down. Then, in an instant, the top half disappeared.

Adam shook his head. "This is a joke, right?"

The two inched back up and now could see inside the unit.

"Yeah, we did not have that at ChronoSleep. I have no idea what that was."

"Well, whatever it was, it opened the unit for us."

"Just as the selection indicated, but how?"

"This is some weird stuff."

They examined the open canister and it was clear there was no one in it. In fact, other than some cushioning, it was rather sparse inside.

"Is this how a sleep chamber is?" Adam asked. "These seem to have nothing to it."

"No. There was much more in mine. Wait, what is that?"

Jonathon reached inside and pointed to a small square-shaped protrusion sticking out. He pushed on it. It retracted as he applied pressure. He then lifted his finger and the device seated back to its original position.

"Okay, where does that go?" Adam asked.

"I don't know. But it seems to be adjustable."

"You know if someone were to lie in here face up, with their head up at this end opposite…" Adam tapped the mechanism. "…it would line up, probably flush, with the main implant on the back of the neck of a guardian."

"Or anyone else who got implants to get SYNRG medical services or employment."

"You may be right."

"But for what purpose? Extended sleep?"

"This just does not add up."

"Jay would have a ball with this stuff."

"Speaking of him, things are more than likely getting dicey outside. We really need to get moving."

"Yeah."

Adam and Jonathon turned and dashed for the elevator.

Jonathon spoke into his arm. "Jay, are you there? Jay!"

"Either he can't hear us or…"

"He can't hear us…let's leave it there."

They stepped up onto the platform.

Jonathon looked around. "How did you get the control panel to appear?"

The panel then appeared.

"Apparently that's how," Adam replied.

"Where to next, boss?"

"Let's try three. It's after the big gap."

"I see your logic."

"Which happens to be just winging it."

Jonathon pushed the air near the 3. The platform descended again.

"Let's see what we have on eight," Adam commented.

The floor divider passed by them.

Adam continued. "This seems to be the same as nine."

"This is scary. What are they planning?"

"Or doing."

As they rode down they heard, "Jonny, chief, are you there?"

Adam responded. "We're here, Jason."

"SYNRG is on the move. They've opened fire, but are only targeting buildings and structures at the moment."

"What about the people?"

"They are still bringing the people in. It's strange, though. Some of us tried to stop or even block random individuals. They just walked around us without a word…like we didn't matter."

"Are you guys in danger at all?"

"Not at the moment. SYNRG is being methodical to avoid the areas where these folks are, so we are staying near them for the moment. Other SYNRG cities are reporting the same thing."

"This seems to be coordinated and synchronized," Jonathon said to Adam.

Adam nodded. "I called the military. I hope they get here soon. They were not very receptive at first, but indicated they would send a small company."

"Of course, with SYNRG's advanced technology, they may not stand a chance. This could be the beginning of the end for us."

"Then, let's hope we are headed in the right direction."

"They've already destroyed one building." Jason added.

"Why are they attacking the city, or cities, but not the people?" Adam asked Jonathon.

"It doesn't make sense."

"Wow, it is really getting dark in here."

"I wonder how close to the next level we are?"

Just then a bright light surrounded them as the elevator slowed into position.

"Oh, that close." Jonathon said.

"It's a small hallway…to where?"

"Come on, let's find out."

The two men walked off the lift the moment it stopped and headed into the hallway. The pathway, still of ChronoSleep design, was barley wide enough for them to walk side by side.

Jonathon maintained a step behind. "This is not long at all. I see a door ahead."

Adam kept his pace. "I guess it will be door No. 1."

Both jogged to the door, but it was not a sliding or hinged-type door. Before either could try to find an opening mechanism, the door glowed, then disappeared.

Adam stepped through without hesitation. "Just like the top on the cylinder."

Jonathon followed Adam, as Adam advanced farther in. The area itself was dark, with the only light present coming from the hallway. Jonathon was now far enough in the door reappeared, trapping them in complete darkness for a brief moment. A square shaped glow illuminated to right of Adam, as it was another door…opening. The glow disappeared, revealing a white glow beyond and a gusting wind sound with no airflow. Adam turned and stepped through with Jonathon close behind. Jonathon looked up at this immense, oblong, DNA-outlined something hovering above the floor, with it shape shifting at multiple intersecting points.

"It looks like several mutated stands intertwining and interweaving with each other," Jonathon said, with astonishment.

"I wish Jason was up here. He…"

A calm white pulsating glow corresponded with each shift. They were still a bit of a distance away from it.

"This thing is huge. What in the world is it?"

A dulcet male voice echoed in the darkness. "It's SYNRG! Isn't it marvelous?"

Adam and Jonathon retrieved their rifles from their shoulders and stood in firing stances waiting for someone or something to come at them.

"Who are you?" Adam responded.

"You're the intruders here…who are you?"

"I'm chief Adam Stance of the Gulfside City Police Department."

"Ah chief…very good. Well then, I'm going to please ask you to stand down before someone gets hurt."

"You know I can't do that. I'm investigating multiple missing persons and you are in the process of destroying our city."

"Correction, my city. As far as the people...no need to concern yourself. They are and will be taken care of. I assure you."

"I'm not buying that tripe. And we're not going anywhere."

"I see. It's absolutely aggravating, to say the least. I guess I'm going to have to have a talk with your tailor. I never expected anyone to get in here. You caught me off guard. Nonetheless, you are here now…as I now want. As we speak, SYNRG is analyzing you. A solution will be found."

"You say this is SYNRG. What is it?"

"Okay, chief. I will entertain your question. SYNRG is a living, breathing, thinking…human computer. Possibly the next stage for humanity."

"What?"

"I've been growing and developing him, ever since I was a child. And my son has almost reached maturity."

"She said this must be stopped," Jonathon said under his breath.

"Who is your companion chief?"

"I'm Jonathon Scott!"

"Jonathon Scott?"

The sound of a single set of footsteps calmly struck the ground, and a human figure emerged, but not clearly visible.

"It is you."

The man inched closer. Now more in view he was roughly Jonathon's age. He had very noticeable scars on his chin, nose, and left cheek,.

"And you have not aged a day, Jonathon. It seems you and I have something in common."

"ChronoSleep." Jonathon softly responded.

"Yes. Thanks to my commitment and access to their research,

and a little tweaking from me, the world is ready for its rebirth."

"Rebirth!" Jonathon exclaimed.

"Yes."

"You call kidnapping innocent individuals and now destroying cities a rebirth?"

"Yes, Jonathon. I can see this is all a bit confusing to you, but in the end…this is better for the human race."

"Better? By taking a person's God given free will and turning them into mindless zombies?"

"And what of free will, Jonathon? How does the human race choose to exercise this privilege? War. Weapons of mass destruction. Look what happened to the Koreas. Awful. Absolutely awful. But then…necessary."

"Necessary!" Jonathon snapped back.

"I used the world's arrogance and disregard for life to create several opportunities to my advantage. I constructed nuclear weapons of my own and used them…for the greater good of humanity. I polluted the atmosphere…again, for the greater good of humanity. I then…"

"…Who do you think you are? Greater good? By murdering whole cities? By choking off the food supply?"

"Don't you dare look your nose down on me. You honestly think you're better than me. Let's get back to some of your humanity's traits. Greed. Look where that got everybody. Backstabbing. Bullying a young man because all he wants to do is learn. Murder you say? How about a young boy's family, all because his father took pity. Just a disgusting waste of life. All of these traits, and more, have plagued mankind for thousands of years. Now the world will have a new order. A new direction."

"Who's order…yours?"

"Of course. This is why all of this is necessary. I'm wiping the palette clean as we speak. The facilities here within and in our structures around the world will help prolong and extend the life of our brethren. I have found a way to bring humanity to its next level. Our new renaissance is nearly at hand, a reality where emotion is removed and genuine scientific logic is employed."

"There are good aspects to life, too…love…compassion…kindness. You will wipe out these best parts of humanity."

"Those things don't exist in my world, Jonathon. I watched a man strip those, and more, away from me…one by one. Again, because my father took mercy on this poor soul. So, I found this thing…this animal, and gave him a fitting sentence. A life with no soul."

Adam chimed in. "You found your family's killer?"

"Yes. I did your job chief…you're welcome. He now serves in my army…to rid the world of all of the other thoughtless malcontents. The boy is no longer scared. No longer seeking the false emotion of love. Seeking false comfort in someone who he thought would protect and shield him in his greatest time of need. To keep the rest of the monsters away, only to be shipped hundreds of miles away…isolated and alone. And for what…Possessions! Money! Huh, there's your greed again. No more. Once SYNRG, my son, is fully grown, which is anytime now, we will rebuild. The human race will be transformed to live life to its fullest potential…in the mind, body, and a new soul…given by its new god here…devoted to scientific research…the exploration of our oceans…the mysteries of the universe…even the spark of life itself. By eliminating the wasteful actions of people, I can fine tune attitudes to what is truly important. This is my gift to humanity."

"You know I can't allow you to continue with this."

"Why Jonathon? Why must one more human being suffer… from hunger…disease…pain…and yes, loss. I would think, you of all people, would be receptive to this."

"Why me?"

"The loss of Dana, Kim, and JR must have been…unbearable."

"Stop it."

"The agony of waking every day, knowing the ones you care for the most, will never return."

"I said, stop it!"

"Angry at the ones who cause this distress in your so called life."

"Yeah. And you were the one who caused it!" Jonathon lunged forward and was shocked and thrown onto the floor by some sort of electrical field. He landed on his back, with the rifle sliding somewhat away. Adam pulled the trigger on his rifle, but it failed to fire.

"Regrettable, of course. But necessary. You should not have stuck your nose where it did not belong. Foiling my initial plans for Gulfside City in the past. Twice. You are responsible for your actions."

Jonathon sat up, somewhat dazed. "It was my job. And now I will do it again."

"There won't be a third. I've come too far."

Two more sets of footsteps approached in the darkness, with one speaking.

"Sydney, the military is here. They are advancing here."

"Redirect the guardians and drones to repel the invaders. Eliminate them all."

"Yes sir."

The footsteps moved away and Sydney moved a step closer to

Jonathon.

"This is where we part ways. Your salvation is on its way. Don't worry, you won't…feel…a thing."

Turning to Adam Sydney said, "Good day chief."

Turning around, he walked into the darkness around SYNRG.

Adam shouted, "Sydney!"

The footsteps continued to move away, becoming less audible. Adam turned, rushed to Jonathon and offered his hand. Jonathon accepted and clasped his hand into Adam's. Adam pulled him up to his feet.

"Thank you," Jonathon said.

"You're welcome."

Jonathon released his hand and stumbled over to his rifle.

Adam followed. "After you were thrown back, I tried to fire my gun. Plus, the little lights are not on."

Jonathon knelt down, picked up his inert rifle and then stood upright again. "I take it our salvation is a swam of guardians headed our way."

"If our guns don't work, we are definitely in trouble."

"Guys, the military is here. The guardians diverted their attention to them. It is a real mess out here," Jason said.

Adam responded. "We know…we just met Sydney. This whole thing is really twisted."

Jonathon chimed in. "Jay, do you still have access into SYNRG?"

"Yes."

"Could you try and see if there are any active guardians inside the building?"

"Yes, I can, but every time I poke around, I risk getting discovered."

"At this point, it may not matter. It seems the bulk of their… army…is currently occupied, but we might have a small one on the way to us."

"I'm on it."

Adam and Jonathon turned their attention to the pulsing glow.

Jonathon shook his head. "A living…growing computer. You know…when I went into sleep, all my thoughts about what the future would be like did not come up with anything like this."

"If it helps, I never saw this coming either. And I've been awake."

"It doesn't. I'm going to tell you something and you are probably going to think I'm crazy."

Nodding toward SYNRG, Adam said, "Crazy? Try me."

"All of those times I passed out, I saw Dana. The last one…the one here, I did not see her, but…she told me we had to stop this.

And now I see why."

Adam did not respond.

"Jonny…chief…there are a dozen guardians traveling up an elevator in the mainland structure. They may be on their way to the island, but should be no problem for you."

Adam replied, "It is a problem. Our rifles are not working. Sydney must have found a way to shut them off."

"Then I guess I need to turn them back on for you…hold on."

Within a few moments, the lights illuminated on the guns.

Jason continued. "Like I said, no problem. Jonny, I found Angie. She is in a location near the area of darkness."

"Jay that's great."

"Where exactly are you guys?"

Jonathon answered. "The area of darkness. This is the heart of it all. Sydney referred to it as SYNRG."

"Then you guys are definitely where you need to be."

"What do we do? Other than SYNRG, there is nothing else in the room."

"Hold on a second, I might be able to help with that. There has to be a control console of some sorts around there. Ah, there we go."

To the far left of Adam and Jonathon, in the nearest corner of the room, a rectangular image of a computer screen appeared, floating and suspended in the air. Also, to the right and behind it, a glowing doorway opened to a hallway.

"I found you a console, along with the doorway to get Angie. Hurry guys, after a second thought, Sydney may have found a way against the suits. You might be in trouble after all if we can't get that thing shut down. You have a few minutes before the guardians get to you."

"Jonny, go get her. I've got this. I'll tinker with the computer and greet our…salvation…if necessary."

Jonathon hooked the rifle on his shoulder. "I'm on my way."

Adam made his way over to the screen as Jonathon darted for and through the door. The hallway, similar to the others, was straight with no seeable doors. Pushing himself as fast as he could, he ran down the narrow corridor and arrived at a slight curve to the left. Rounding the bend, he came upon a single door at the end of a very short jaunt. Marching right up to it, the door did not open. Looking to his sides, he examined the area for a button, lever…something to open it.

"For crying out loud…I don't have time for this."

Stepping far enough back, he retrieved the rifle from his shoulder. Placing his hand underneath the frame, he felt for the level indicator, sliding it up to 10. Supporting the front, he pointed it up to the door. Squeezing the trigger, the door shattered into pieces, along with some of the wall.

He slid the indicator back to 2. "That's right!"

Rushing up to the now open access, he carefully proceeded inside. Turning to the right, he could see this was some sort of examination room, or more specifically, a surgical prep room. Sterile walls, counters and drawers lined the side walls, and a lone rolling table was in the middle. It was open on the opposite side, so Jonathon quickly passed through the area. He entered into what may have been a patient room, with many rows of beds. They were all empty except for one.

"Angie!" he cried out.

Fastening the weapon onto his shoulder, he hurried up to her. "Angie?"

She was attached to a whole bunch of wires and monitors. Some sort of liquid was being put into her veins. The wires were concentrated around her forehead and face, and some were on her wrists and hands. Angie's eyes were closed and she was unresponsive. She appeared to still be in her own clothes.

"They must have not gotten far," he surmised. "I'm going to get all of this shit off of you, sweetheart."

He raised his arm to his mouth. "Jay! I found her, but she is hooked up to all of this medical type stuff, with something being pumped into her vein. Is it safe to remove this stuff from her?"

"I'm not there. The best thing I can suggest...wait a sec...I can tell from here. Sort of. I can see...yes, you're fine, they did not get too far. Just be warned though, she will be very disorientated when she wakes. Plus, make sure you have something to stop the bleeding when you remove the needle from her vein. It's like when you go and get blood work done."

"Got it. Thank you."

"Jonny, the guardians have reached me. This group must be able to shield the weapon, partially. They only get stunned for a moment before continuing to move again. I will try and keep them from reaching you...but hurry. I don't know how long I can hold them off."

Jonathon lowered his arm.

"Damn it!"

Running back to the prep area, he frantically opened the drawers one by one searching for what he needed. After opening a few of them, he found his bandages and cotton balls. Retrieving a couple of self-adhesive bandages and a couple of white cotton balls, he ran back over to Angie. Setting the cotton down, he ripped the wrapper off of the bandage.

"Okay here goes."

Removing the adhesive tape from the base of the inserted needle, he then gripped it and pulled it out of Angie's arm. Quickly snapping up a cotton ball, he pressed it down on her wound, applying a good amount of pressure. Still with the bandage in his hand, he managed to pry the protective covers off, and then stuck it on her arm and over the cotton, securing it nice and snug.

"Thank goodness that's done. Now to get all this other nonsense off you. It looks like just suction cups. Maybe."

Jonathon grabbed the wires individually, removing them one by on from her body.

"Ouch, that one hurt," Angie said with a weak voice.

"Sorry. Are you okay?"

She opening her eyes, squinting. "Jonathon? Is that you?"

"Yes. Listen, I know you are disorientated, sweetheart, but the place is crawling with guardians. We've got to go."

"I understand."

Angie slowly sat up and swung her legs toward Jonathon. Jonathon caught her as she slid herself off of the bed.

Wrapping her arms around him she said, "Thank you for coming for me."

"Of course. We can talk about this later…can you walk?"

"I don't think so. Not at the moment. But I think I might be able to hobble alongside you."

"Good enough."

Grabbing her waist, he gently swung her to his side as she reached around his back and neck with her arm.

With his arm and hand secure around her waist he asked, "Are you ready?"

"Yes."

Jonathon moved forward, with her hobbling at his side. Around the bed and through the prep room, they reached the doorway.

"Be careful stepping through here…I had to make a mess of things," he said.

Through the doorway, Angie and Jonathon emerged into the hallway. Continuing forward, they began to round the corner when the building violently started shaking, triggering the alarm.

"What was that?" Angie asked, somewhat more coherent.

"I don't know…but we need to move faster if you can."

"I'll try."

Angie, with more force was now slightly walking.

"If one of you can please respond…a military jet was just shot down and crashed into the rear of your building," Jason said. "Wait…what is going on…I don't know if you guys did something, but the guardians just stopped moving."

"They stopped moving in here, too. Jonny, are you all right?"

"I'm fine. And I have Angie with me. We're almost to you."

"That's great news."

"Who are you talking to?" Angie asked.

"Adam and another friend of mine. I have an open radio line with them."

"I can't wait to hear all about this."

"Soon. We are not out of this yet."

"Chief, Jonny, what did you do?" Jason asked.

"Nothing. I don't understand. They were all attacking. Fortunately my suit is still protecting me, then once the building shook, they stopped," Adam said.

"Jay, could the building have something to do with it?"

"I don't know. I'm going to probe further into my connection with SYNRG and see what's up."

Angie and Jonathon approached the doorway to the SYNRG room and passed through.

Angie was more awake. "What is that thing?"

The two walked up to Adam, who was tapping around on the floating access screen.

Jonathon responded to Angie. "It's a massive computer... controlling everyone and everything."

"What?"

"I want to explain..."

Angie smiled. "I know. Later. Just set me down next to you guys. Do your thing."

"Are you sure?"

"Yes."

Jonathon knelt down with her. She put a hand on the floor, balancing herself as Jonathon let go of her. Angie curled up with her arm under her head. "I'm okay."

Jonathon looked around him and noticed the guardians, in various positions around, just standing still, suspended in time.

Reaching back, he retrieved his rifle. "Do you know how to fire a gun?"

"Are you kidding? It's one of the requirements to working the land," she said.

Jonathon carefully set the gun next to her. "If you can, if any one of these bastards start moving..."

Winking at him she said, "Got it."

Standing up, he inched over to Adam who as tapping away on the screen. "What do we have here sir?"

"It is an access panel for this thing, but I don't understand what

I'm looking at."

Jonathon raised his arm to speak. "Jay, I'm with Adam. We can't make heads or tails of this console."

"I see it. It does not make sense to me either. Hold on..."

All of a sudden, the guardians jolted around for a moment.

Angie reached for the gun. "What was that all about?"

Jonathon was still staring at the screen with Adam. "I don't know. Adam, the system is going haywire. I'm no computer expert, but it seems everything here is being overwritten."

"Jason, you have to have an idea what is going on."

"I'm sorry, I'm still trying to figure this out."

Adam looked over to Jonathon. "I wonder if the jet crashing into us screwed something up."

"Is SYNRG resetting itself? Jay!"

"I think you're...partially...right. It looks like the code is being overwritten with more advanced algorithms," Jason responded.

Jonathon peered over to SYNRG. "Could it be...SYNRG just grew up?"

"What was that?" asked Jason.

"Sydney said SYNRG was alive and was about to mature."

"Uh, okay. Maybe? However, once it is done with whatever it is doing, we will be back to square one again. Possibly worse, if what you say is true."

"Can you do anything on your end?"

"I don't think so...not while it is in this mode. None of the information on my screen makes sense."

Adam looked back to Jonathon. "We need to do something ourselves. Quickly."

"Wait, a new menu appeared...what does that mean?"

The guardians, once again in motion, pointed their weapons at the trio and started to fire at them. Jonathon, without thinking, jumped in front of Angie to protect her against the onslaught. Adam raised his gun and started to fire around, but the impacted guardians remained stunned for only a few seconds before resuming.

Angie rolled onto her stomach, took aim as well, and shot at what she could see. "Chief, take the ones flanking us to the sides, I'll concentrate on the ones ahead."

"Got it."

Jonathon anticipated angles and kept shifting around to protect Angie. "I don't know how long we can keep this up, Adam."

"You are the only one who is free. I'll step back to you to shield her. Get on the console. It is our only hope."

Two guardians jumped in the air. Adam stunned one on the ascent up. Angie missed the other one, who jumped down next to

Jonathon. Quickly retrieving his stun gun, Jonathon jammed it into the man as he moved into to attack. The lifeless hulk fell to the ground, with no signs of getting up.

"The stunners still remove them from SYNRG!" Jonathon shouted.

"That's great, but I still wouldn't let them get close."

Jonathon moved up to the screen. "It's encrypted. I can't read a thing."

"Now what?"

Jonathon turned to the immense object and reached down to his side pocket on his pant leg. Sliding his hand through the fold, he gripped and retrieved his revolver. Pulling it out, he raised it up, aiming it at SYNRG.

"Jay! What would happen if I shot the core itself?"

"It probably won't react very well. Depending on its power source and how far it goes, it could cause a very large explosion."

"But it may be our only chance to save most everyone else."

"Yes." Jason reluctantly acknowledged.

Jonathon squeezed the trigger and the streak of the bullet could be seen flying off to the right.

"What happened?" Jason asked.

"The slug just flew off to the side."

"The field from your suits is going to throw the trajectory off. You are going to have to compensate."

Jonathon aimed far to the left and squeezed again. This time it went left.

"Damn it!"

Another guardian, dodging Angie and Adam, leapt behind Adam to advance on Angie. Jonathon, with his stun gun still in his other hand, lunged at him, pushing him away from her. Before the guardian could react, Jonathon plunged the stun gun into the man's neck, shocking him to the floor. With the force of his action, Jonathon lost his hold on the stunner. It fell to the floor along with his lifeless victim. Jonathon, facing SYNRG again, ran toward it. Aiming up, he shot off two more rounds with both of them narrowly missing.

"Damn it. One more shot left."

Pointing the gun slightly to the side of SYNRG, he noticed in his peripheral vision two more guardians evading Angie and Adam, advancing to him. Firing his last round, the slug curved directly into SYNRG. An ominous eerie screech reverberated through out the room. The strands of the core stopped motion and began to flash intermittently and out of synch. The guardians froze in their positions and intermittently jolted around.

Jonathon yelled back to Angie and Adam, "Shoot at SYNRG!"

The two quickly aimed at the core and fired, and the flickering glow became more stabilized.

"Shit! I think that actually helped it," Adam said with frustration.

"Adam, do you have any bullets on you?"

"No."

"I just need one more shot…wait a second." Jonathon reached into his pocket and pulled out JR's gift. The remaining guardians were more lucid and resumed their fight. They all moved toward Jonathon to intercept him. Angie and Adam, resumed their barrage to protect him as long as they could. Shaking the housing loose from the bullet, Jonathon opened the cylinder wheel on his handgun. Emptying the spent shell casings, he slid his long shot into the next chamber.

Closing the cylinder, Jonathon aimed again in the same fashion as before. "Okay, Dana, this cannot be a coincidence."

Squeezing the trigger, JR's gift launched without hesitation and curved directly into SYNRG. With another loud screech the glow extinguished. The only light was provided by the screen and the doorway behind. The guardians, once again, froze in place.

"Are either of you there?" Jason frantically inquired.

Adam responded. "Yeah, we're here."

"They all stopped out here, again." Jason conveyed.

Jonathon added. "I think this may be permanent. I hope. SYNRG appears to be offline. Can you confirm that?"

"Hold on. Let me check."

Jonathon turned around and walked back to Angie and Adam. "Nice work, buddy."

Adam, with a smile said, "You, too."

Angie, who was now sitting up with the rifle in her lap said, "Hey what about me? I put on a nice show, too."

Jonathon smiled. "Of course. You, too. Are you okay?"

"I think so. All things considered."

Jonathon examined his now useless revolver, and slid it back into his pants pocket. Angie clutched the rifle and held it up to Jonathon. Taking possession, he slung it back, clipping it onto his shoulder.

Offering his hand to her he said, "Let me help you up if you think you can stand."

Clasping his hand she said, "I feel a little better now."

Jonathon pulled her up to her feet as she balanced herself.

Adam, with his rifle attached to his shoulder, turned to the two. "What do we do now…with this?"

Jonathon turned to face SYNRG. "I don't know."

Angie walked to Jonathon's side, staring at the dormant device. "Does this mean I can find James?"

Jonathon turned his head. "I think so. Amongst others. Our friend on the outside is trying to determine what is going on with this thing."

"What is going on here? Angie asked.

"Jonny, Chief. You need to get out of there now! I am reading a pressure overload, underneath the island. It is the power source for SYNRG and it is no longer being regulated." Jason advised.

Jonathon responded. "How do we get out quickly? It's going to take us forever to get back to the mainland if we go back the way we came in."

"I have located an external elevator on the back of the building. Take the hallway you used to get Angie. I will relay as you go."

Jonathon looked over to Angie. "We have to go."

Angie looked to Jonathon. "What's wrong?"

Jonathon clasped Angie's hand. "I think the building is about to explode."

Adam motioned to the two. "After you."

Jonathon turned to the door and hastily pulled her with him as he rushed to the exit.

"What about James?" she asked.

Jonathon spoke to his receiver. "Is Angie's brother James in this building?"

"I don't know. I can see if SYNRG has a listing." Jason said.

The trio entered the corridor, heading to the prep room.

"How about this, do we have time to get the people in this building out?" Jonathon asked.

"I don't think so. I'll try to see if I can find some sort of override and call them here…I will do what I can. However, the bulk of SYNRG is out here and in the building over here."

"All right."

Jason continued. "The elevator will take you up to the roof. The colonel in charge has dispatched a helicopter to pick you up."

Jonathon briefly glanced to Angie. "Our friend is going to look for him. There is a good chance he is outside."

"Jason, how do you know the elevator is there?" Adam inquired.

"The military jets flying by, well, before they were shot down, spotted it. I confirmed this with the information I accessed."

The three reached the blown entrance and stepped carefully, one by one, through.

Jason continued to advise. "If I'm reading this correctly, you will go past the two main rooms ahead, to a small narrow hallway. This will take you to the elevator. I've already called for it and opened the doorway to the hall."

Adam responded. "Thank you."

Making their way into where Jonathon found Angie, they ran through the rows of beds, noticing an opening in the rear wall to their right, and veered toward it.

"The helicopter is on the roof and waiting for you guys."

"How much time do we have?" Jonathon asked.

"I don't know. But hurry! The pressure is continuing to build."

The trio reached the very narrow dark corridor, which was wide enough for one person at a time. There was no way to see if there was any danger ahead.

Jonathon was insistent. "I will go first."

Adam added, "I got the rear."

Jonathon slipped in and maintained his hold on Angie's hand as she followed behind. Adam marched in behind her as Jonathon reached the end of the path.

Talking into his arm he said, "The door is not opening and I can't see anything that indicates any opening mechanism."

"Oops, sorry."

The door dematerialized open, exposing an open-glass elevator car with a single dim light emanating from its ceiling. Jonathon hurried inside with Angie and Adam filing in one by one. Jonathon scanned the darkness of the outside world and took note of a fire burning below, near the base of the building. The car was just wide enough for the three of them to fit.

The lift door slid close and Jonathon peered around looking for a call panel. "Where is it?"

Then he recalled the elevators at ChronoSleep. "Roof access!"

The car began to travel upward.

Adam glanced over to him. "How did you know?"

Jonathon, still facing forward said, "Does it matter?"

Adam did not see the need to reply. The elevator slowed down and seated into position. The door vanished and the commotion of a helicopter rushed in. Jonathon rushed out into the darkness, followed by Angie, then Adam. It was evident they were running up an incline. As he was reaching the top of this pathway, the side walls recessed, revealing the landed chopper to his right. Once the ground leveled off and once he was able, Jonathon turned toward the flying craft, which was still a good distance away. Peering back, he made sure his pack was still keeping up with him. As the trio approached the landing pad, the helicopter became more visible than just by its lights and noise.

It was a very large aircraft. The interior was illuminated from within, by several red lights.

A single man, emerged from the mid section of the craft and approached Jonathon with a military rifle pointed at him. "Who are you?"

Adam hurried up to the front. "I'm Chief Adam Stance."

The man, dressed in camouflage-patterned fatigues, lowered his weapon. "I am Captain Stanley Roberts. I have been ordered to get you three to safety right now! Please come with me."

Roberts, turning away, hurried back to the aircraft. Adam and Jonathon, motioning to Angie to follow him, proceeded to do so. As she passed by the two, Adam indicated for Jonathon to go next.

Jonathon smiled. "Okay."

Tagging behind Angie, he made sure Adam was close behind him. Once he reached the helicopter, Captain Roberts turned to assist Angie inside.

Gently placing his hand on her back he said, "Watch your step ma'am, and please take a seat on the other side."

Jonathon marched up and noticed the seating ran down the middle facing the open sides. *Oh that's just great,* he thought.

"Sir if you could please sit with the lady on the other side."

Jonathon nodded in agreement, and climbed up onto a step rail and into the helicopter. Captain Roberts gave him a boost on his back. The floor extended out far enough from the seats for anyone to walk in front of them with plenty of space. Jonathon, crouching down a bit, even though he had more than enough room to stand fully erect, maneuvered around to the other side. Angie was already seated and appeared petrified. She stared straight ahead. Jonathon removed his weapon from his shoulder and sat down next to her.

Setting the gun on his lap, he asked, "Are you okay?"

She did not move. "I guess there is nothing I can do, but...I have never flown before and I'm scared."

"I know this probably won't help, but I hate flying...so, right now...I'm scared out of my wits."

Turning to him and smiling she said, "No it doesn't help."

She reached over and clasped onto his hand.

Adam, seated behind with his back to Jonathon asked, "How are you doing, Jonny? You must be hating this right about now."

"Well, I'm not liking it."

"It's just to get to the other side, you'll survive."

Captain Roberts stood in a small gap between the seats and cockpit.

"There should be restraints for every one of you, please secure them at this time. Give a thumbs-up when you are done. Jonathon reached behind and quickly found the strap. He grasped on the latch and pulled it around him, fastening it into the socket. Looking at

Angie, she already had her thumb up. The captain nodded and turned to face the open cockpit and the two men settled within.

"Colin, we're all clear! Begin your ascent."

"Yes, sir!" the man shouted.

The sound from the rotors intensified as Captain Roberts sat himself down next to Adam. The interior light shut off, exposing them to the night sky. Jonathon turned his focus to Angie as she squeezed his hand tighter.

Twisting her neck to him she said, "I don't see how these people do this all of the time."

She closed her eyes, squeezing his hand even tighter. Jonathon's stomach sank as the aircraft lifted off of the roof. His side faced the gulf so he just focused on the view. There as not much to see in the dark, but he did not care. Whatever he needed to do to get his mind off of this experience, the better. The craft banked to the side as it maneuvered to the mainland, and Jonathon now could see the island below. As the helicopter continued to tilt, he noticed something strange in the distance. Lighting and what seemed to be a much larger version of a SYNRG drone was parked on some sort of landing pad. The helicopter was in a pattern, almost encircling it.

"Angie, open your eyes." Jonathon said.

She complied, but was still facing him.

"What do you make of that out there?" he asked.

She turned her head. "I don't know. But, it looks like they're getting ready to take off."

"Exactly."

Jonathon turned his head to Adam as best as he could. "Adam! If you can, take a look out here." Adam turned his head in a vain attempt. "I can't see…hold on."

Adam unlatched his restraint, stood up and grasped onto an overhead handrail, "What in the world?"

"Chief! Please sit down!" shouted Captain Roberts.

"Captain, what is that over there?"

Roberts stood up and holding onto the rail, peered out the other side. "I don't know…wait…"

The captain paused for a moment, placing his finger on what seemed to be an earpiece.

Adam turned his attention to Jonathon. "Could that be Grant, Jonny?"

"I was thinking the same thing! The bastard may be trying to escape."

Captain Roberts inched toward Adam. "Chief! The colonel wants me to take a quick and closer pass over the object down there. Whatever it is, was not there a few minutes ago."

"My lieutenant and I believe that is Sydney Grant…the one responsible for all of this. He should be considered a priority target."

"I'll call for reinforcements right now. Excuse me. I need to relay our new orders to the pilot."

Adam spoke into his receiver. "Jason any updates?"

After a brief moment, he tried again. "Jason? Are you there?"

Still no response.

"Jonny, can you try?" Adam asked.

"Angie, may I have my hand back?"

With reluctance she said, "Okay."

She released his hand.

Jonathon spoke into his arm. "Jay, what's going on? Please reply."

A voice responded, but it was not Jason. "So you killed my son. That was not wise Jonathon."

"Sydney?"

Adam, keeping hold of the railing, carefully walked over to Jonathon's side.

Sydney continued. "You may have stopped me here, but only delayed the inevitable."

"Sydney, you just can't impose your will over everyone. I agree, we are not perfect, but…"

"But what…it's our way? How small of you. Some disease of a life killed my family. I in turn killed your family. You killed my son. Where will it end. No matter…you've interfered with me for the last time. If you want to act like a barbarian, I will treat you like one."

"What is that supposed to mean?"

Just then the larger drone began ascending into the air.

"I see you. And I know you can see me. And that, you parasite, will be the last thing you see."

"Adam!"

"I heard him."

Adam rushed forward. "Captain, we need to get out of here! That drone is about to attack us!"

Captain Roberts glared at his pilot. "Evasive actions, Sergeant!"

The helicopter instantly banking away, started to move faster.

Jonathon handed the rifle to Angie. "Can you hold onto this for me?"

She accepting it as he released himself, stood up, and then grabbed the rail as a flash of light narrowly missed them.

"Jonathon what was that?" Angie asked.

"We're under attack."

Jonathon rushed behind Adam, but glanced over to Roberts. "How can we help?"

"There is not much for you to do. This is an unarmed transport. However, help is on the way..."

Orange streaking flashes, sounded with impacts on the hull of something in the air near them.

"Never mind. They're here," stated Roberts.

The orange flashes continued and became less intense.

Captain Roberts listened to his radio. "Our attack choppers are reporting they are not able to bring the object down with standard rounds. They are armed with rockets and are going to use them as we are now safely out of range."

The helicopter turned again, heading to the mainland. The fight in the air intensified, as larger explosions impacted the SYNRG aircraft. The larger drone, appearing to be unaffected, just hovered in place.

"Watch this, Jonathon. This is your future," Sydney said with an eerie tone.

"Captain! Get your men..." Jonathon shouted.

Before he could finish, flashes from the drone impacted both of the helicopters in the distance. Both instantaneously exploded and fell to the ground.

Sydney continued. "There is no need for all of this violence, Jonathon. But here you are escalating the circumstances. Those men did not have to die. Nobody else has to die. Their lives could have been put to better use. No matter. You...your friend...and your girlfriend there, don't have to join my new world. I'll make sure of that."

The drone turned and rapidly accelerated toward them. "I want you to see my face before I end you."

Adam looked back to Jonathon. "He is on the drone."

"I don't think that's a drone." Jonathon replied.

The SYNRG vehicle closed in and Jonathon shouted to Adam. "Our rifles! They may still work."

Angie now standing, with the rifle pointed out. "Way ahead of you boys."

Holding secure to the railing above her, she squeezed the trigger, firing at multiple points. Quickly shifting to the front turbine, it caught fire. A flash of light enveloped the helicopter as their opponent fell, spiraling out of control toward the gulf.

"WE'RE HIT!" the pilot shouted from the front.

"Lady and gentleman, I urge you to strap in, this is going to get bumpy." Captain Roberts said.

The helicopter shuddered and slowly began to sink.

"Chief, come to my side to balance the weigh," Captain Roberts directed.

Adam complied and followed Captain Roberts around. Jonathon rushed to the seat next to Angie. Angie quickly belted herself in.

Strapping himself in, he glanced over to Angie. "Are you okay?"

"I think so. That was probably stupid on my part."

"Stupid? You just saved our lives."

Looking up, he could see smoke billowing out from the top. *I wonder how long we've got before the engine conks out on us.* he thought.

The craft banked again and he could see they were hovering over the mainland. The helicopter descended down to what he assumed was the road below. The island building lit up, now completely engulfed with fire. Panels of molten metal were falling into the water below and the island behind.

Strange, there was no audible explosive noise. Jonathon thought.

Still heading downward, the rotor blade sounded like it was struggling. The ride jolted a bit more. Beams of artificial lighting were becoming bright and apparent as they drew closer to the surface. The now visible shoreline was illuminated as the helicopter settled on the ground.

Secure and in place, the sound of the motor ceased. The blades above slowed and Captain Roberts could be heard shuffling out of his seat.

"That was close," Jonathon shouted.

"It could have been closer," Roberts responded. "At least my pilot was able to voluntarily shut this thing off once we touched down."

Jonathon turned to Angie. "We made it…thanks to you."

Still facing straight she said, "No, thanks to you…for saving me."

"Come on, let's get out of here."

She turned to him and smiled with relief. "Gladly."

The two cast off their restrains and stood up.

Adam walked to their side, with his rifle attached to his shoulder. "Great work you two. Let's get out there and see what were are dealing with."

"Yes sir," Jonathon responded.

Adam stepped down the side and exited the craft.

Jonathon turned to Angie. "You ready?"

She handed his gun to him. "Here…I have had enough fun for one day."

Jonathon took it and attached it to his shoulder. Holding his hand out to her he said, "After you."

She marched out and down the step, and stood confidently on the ground. Jonathon followed, planting his feet firmly on the earth.

The two stood and watched the fire consume the island building. The fire also ran part way down the sky bridge, but seemed to not be advancing much to the mainland building.

Angie clasped Jonathon's hand. "What now?"

Jonathon shook his head. "I don't know. But I have a feeling we were all given a second chance here."

Holding his hand tighter she said, "I think you're right. And, I will be here as much as you want me."

Jonathon turned his head to her. "I know you will. I think I need time to sort out my feelings, though. With all of this nonsense going on, I really haven't had time to absorb all of this."

"I know. Take your time."

"However, I'm glad you are here to help me."

Angie looked around. "Jonathon what is going on here?"

"Well the meat of it is, the Guardians were being controlled and used by that thing inside the other building. In fact, you were being prepped to be a guardian as well."

"Oh. Then, I'm glad you showed up when you did."

"Me, too. The others, like your friends…the general non-interactive townspeople, were also being controlled on a somewhat limited basis."

"Will everyone be okay now?"

"I'm not really sure. My friend, the one I was talking to earlier, is the one who uncovered all of this. I haven't found out the details yet. However, from what I do understand, the Guardians may never be able to rejoin us. Their essence of who they were may have been wiped out. But there is always hope. We may find a way for them to come back."

"It sounds like there is a lot to sort out, but do you think this is what happened to James?"

He hesitantly answered. "I believe so. If he hasn't made contact or even surfaced after all of this time…"

She quietly nodded her head, then nervously smiled. "Thank you for being honest with me. You're right though…there is always hope. Come on hero, let's go get our answers."

Angie, still with a firm grip on him, pulled him with her, rounding the tail of the helicopter.

Captain Roberts approached from the other side. "Lieutenant Scott is it?"

"Yes sir."

"I just wanted to inform you, and if you could pass this on to your chief, we will be searching for the wreckage of our attackers shortly. As soon as we find something or someone, I will let you know."

"Thank you, Captain."

Roberts, turning his attention to Angie, snapped her a big salute. "Nice shooting, ma'am. You saved us. Thank you."

Lowering his arm, he about faced, and marched away toward a group of soldiers.

"You see, you're the hero this time," Jonathon said.

Angie shook her head and did not reply. Adam ran up to them as they walked to all the commotion ahead. They had landed, just off to the side of the main intersection in front of the SYNRG mainland building. The other nearby structures laid in ruin from the guardian onslaught. On the actual road itself, not covered with debris, were multiple sets of artificial lights, connected to generators, sufficiently lighting the street and the surrounding areas. Scores of people, dazed and confused, also lined the pavement. They were being directed by the military and Gulfside's limited police force away from the SYNRG building. Those in guardian uniforms stood frozen, not moving at all.

"Jonny, this is a complete mess." Adam stated.

"What is going on with the people?"

"The Guardians are all stopped…like Albert and Brent. The others who simply had the neck implants…I don't know. They appear to be free and interacting, but are confused. I'm trying to find Jason. I hoping he has some answers. The communications in our controllers aren't working."

Jonathon raised his arm. "Speaking of which, we need to shut our fields off. My indicator bar is completely gone."

Jonathon with his captive hand, deactivated his field.

Adam reached to his panel as well. "Yeah, mine was out too. Hopefully, not for too long."

"We should have the good doctor examine us thoroughly as soon as possible."

"Sounds like a good idea…if we can find him in this…"

Jonathon and Angie continued their pace, with Adam matching at their side.

"Jonny…Chief…there you are!" shouted a man running through the crowded street.

"Jay!" Jonathon shouted.

The trio stopped as he wildly neared. Angie let go of Jonathon as Jason ran up, wrapping his arms around him, giving him a big bear hug.

"It's good to see you, Jay."

Jason patted him on the back. He then let go and with a smile said, "You, too."

He turned his attention to Adam, who was holding his hand out to shake. Jason, ignoring it, wrapped his arms around the chief, who was a little taken off guard.

"It's good to see you, too, doc. Now please tell me you have some answers."

Jason let go and looked over at Angie. "Oh, what the heck. I don't want to leave you out."

He sidestepped over to her, and gave her a big hug.

Jonathon glanced over. "Angie. This is our friend, Dr. Jason Mayers."

She was somewhat stunned. "How do you do?"

Adam, now impatient, "Jason…answers?"

He let go of her. "Right. The people with the single implants are going to be fine. For them, they knew what they were doing, but had no control over it. SYNRG did not have as evasive control like they did with the guardians. These folks will probably need a lot of counseling, but there won't be any permanent physical or neurological damage. The Guardians, however."

Jonathon nodded his head. "Right."

"I'm going to work on it. There has to be a way to snap them out of it."

"How far did they get destroying the city?" Adam inquired.

"It appears they were stopped before leaving Merchant's Circle."

"That's still a pretty good chunk." Adam retorted.

Angie raised her hand. "Dr. Mayers?"

"Jason. And Yes?"

"Jason, do you know what happened to…well…do you know were my brother is?"

Jason reached back behind him and retrieved a tablet computer. Holding it in front of him, he tapped on the screen with the other. "Let's see. It appears SYNRG kept accurate records with their victims and with the encryption removed…James Leary right?"

Jonathon nodded. "Yes."

"Okay. It looks like he is still here in Gulfside…inside the mainland building, level 8. He is currently in extended sleep."

"What does that mean?" Angie asked with confusion.

Jonathon responded. "It means he's safe. You may have to wait awhile before you can talk to him, but he's here and safe."

Angie began to tear up. "I understand. At least he is alive."

Jason chimed in. "I will watch over him…I promise."

"Thank you doctor…err, Jason."

"You're welcome."

A female voice spoke from the darkness. "Jonathon Scott…it is good to see you again."

Jonathon watched the advancing female figure come into view.

"Amy?"

"Hi. You guys sure know how to make a gal feel useful again."

Jonathon was very perplexed. "How in the…"

Adam chimed in. "I'll field this one. Jonny, it was because of you constantly passing out. Remember, I called her for help and she arrived…"

"I arrived just before all of this. I'm going to be busy for a very long time."

Jonathon extended his hand. "Welcome to Gulfside City… what's left of it."

Amy clasped on to his hand. "Thank you. I want to talk to you about your issue, but…"

"I know. They need your help more."

"Don't worry, I will not forget about you."

Amy turned her attention to Jason. "Doctor Mayers, may I have a word with you? I have some more questions."

"Sure thing, Doctor Weiss."

Amy turned and headed away toward another group of people.

Jason faced Jonathon. "Where have you been hiding her? She is incredible. Smart…funny…hot!"

Jonathon shook his head and smiled. "Go help her."

With a bigger smile he said, "Yes, sir."

Angie at this point had moved back down the road a little bit, just out of earshot.

Adam turned to Jonathon. "What are you going to do, Jonny?"

"Do with what?"

"With her. Is there something there?"

"It's going to take me awhile to get my head on straight…but I definitely think there is something there. Besides, it seems, I'm meant to get my family back."

Adam, with a confused but happy expression said, "Good to hear it. Plus, I need you bright eyed soon as possible. The city is going to need a good man."

"Listen, Adam. I think I'm done with police work. I kind of was. Even when I left."

"That is good to know. It will be hard for you to be mayor otherwise."

"Um, what?"

"I just sent Buchman to arrest the mayor for his involvement in this mess. We are going to hold a recall vote as soon as possible and I'm going to endorse you as his replacement."

Jonathon shook his head. "No. No, I don't think so."

"Yeah, I think so. This town is going to need a trustworthy face to get it on the mend. Whether you like it or not…that is you. And with your history…it will be a landslide."

"Yeah, we'll see about that."

"Yes, we will."

"I think I'm going to walk for a while…gather my thoughts. Can you take Angie over to see Amy? I think it will be a good idea for the two to meet."

"Will do. Don't wander too far. I don't want to lose you again."

Jonathon smiled. "I won't."

Adam veered away from Jonathon and headed over to Angie. Jonathon turned to face the road ahead and could see thousands of people lined up on both sides of the road…scared…displaced. All sought the comfort of strangers, their neighbors. They all talked about their experiences. The ruins of Gulfside were just to the side of them. Debris spilled out onto adjacent streets as some men in uniform worked to clear this particular street. Guardians were poised like statues, as they had no one or nothing to guide them.

"What is to become of them?" Jonathon asked himself as he warily stepped forward. "Okay, Dana. Looks like our world is safe. We were able to stop them. But at what price?"

Jonathon glanced up to the sky and took in a deep breath of air. Due to the surrounding lights, the stars were not visible to him, except for one.

"That new star really is intense. Shining past all of this. Hopefully our future will be as bright."

Facing forward again he stepped up his pace and was approached by a woman holding some sort of electronic device. He kept walking.

However, it did not stop her from talking to him. "Hi…hello there, sir."

He continued along. "May I help you?"

She matched him at his side. "You don't seem to be part of the regular crowd."

He smiled. "No. I'm not."

"Then do you have any idea what is going on here?"

"If you want to know everything there is to know, find Chief Adam Stance. Who are you?"

"I'm sorry. My name is Roxanne. I was a reporter…well I still am of sorts…going behind SYNRG's watchful eye."

"Nice to meet you, but I'm not interested in talking with anyone right now."

"But you're obviously someone who is involved…uniform…gun over your shoulder…what gives."

"I was a police officer, but I just retired. Right now, I'm someone out for a walk. Again, go pester Stance."

"Okay, I can appreciate wanting quiet, but our world here has been turned upside down and then twisted around. Any insights?"

"Let me ask you a question, Roxanne. Are you from Gulfside… originally?"

"Yes, born and raised."

"Very good. This is a great city…a nice place to raise a family."

"Are you from around here…uh…"

"Jonathon. And yes…I was born here. And I plan on staying here. Our city has been plagued by a cancer, but that cancer is now in remission."

"Interesting statement. Wait. You said…Jonathon. A police officer?"

She raised her device, which appeared to be some sort of portable computer. Tapping away on the screen, she fervently searched for something…or someone.

"Let me save you the trouble. My last name is Scott."

"So you are Jonathon Scott?"

"Yes. And yes, the same one who saved all of those children years ago."

"I was one of those children."

"You don't say. Well, Roxanne, nice to meet you…or see you again. I'm very glad to see you are okay."

"Thank you. I really would like to get a statement from you…my personal hero."

"You know how to lay it on thick."

"Please…I don't mean anything bad…especially toward you. Besides, I'm a little confused. You look younger than me."

"Younger…older…does it make a difference? I'm here now."

"And what do you think of now?"

"That is going to be the defining question moving forward, isn't it? Are we better off now than when you were a child, or when I was? And if you are looking for a positive response, you probably shouldn't ask me."

"If you are referring to your…"

"Please, I don't want to go there. Not right now at least. Look around. There are more pressing issues we need to face. Everyone's lives are kind of on hold until we figure out how to forge ahead. I don't know how, but we will."

"That sounded positive."

"I guess it did."

"May I have at least one statement from you…please."

"Sure, why not. I get the feeling I'm not going to be able to just quietly slip away this time."

"Thank you, Jonathon. This means a lot to me."

She held up her little computer, turning the back of it to her.

"This is Roxanne Tanner, reporting to you live from the Underground. I have with me former police officer and Gulfside hero, Jonathon Scott. Jonathon what would you like to say to all of those who are uncertain about their futures?"

Stopping his pace as she turned the camera piece to him he said, "Don't be afraid. I'm just like you. I have no idea what to do. But this city thrived once with everyone working and sticking together. If we do that now, we will prevail. No one will interfere with us here again."

Jonathon felt more confident and bold, almost like a leader. "If someone does come to Gulfside looking for trouble…"

Jonathon struggled to find something clever to say, and chose the first thing he could think of. "…Then come see me. I'm the Ice Man, and I am waiting!"

The City, long blinded by sadness and sorrow, has the light of a new star to guide her along. A new leader is to emerge and direct her people, her community, to a happier and prosperous life, full of love, compassion, and devotion. Her soul, stifled and subdued, is about to erupt with laughter, cheer, and hope, embracing the path ahead. Your long sleep is over Gulfside. Welcome to the future and good day!

ABOUT THE AUTHOR

Eric Gaeta was born in the southern gulf coast of Florida, where he currently resides with his family. He earned a Bachelor of Arts in Criminology from the University of South Florida. He has worked in the criminal justice system for ten years.

Eric combined his experience and love of imagination by completing his first novel, The Ice Man, in 2013. He is eagerly working on his second book which is based on the current political climate and economy.

Printed in Great Britain
by Amazon

85300317R00221